The Lyons Garden Trilogy

SPECIAL EDITION

FAMILY TIES

ERASING SECRETS

PAWNS

D.M. FOLEY

REMEMBER MY ROOTS PRESS

Copyright @ 2024 by D.M. Foley

All rights reserved.

The characters in this book are fictitious. Any similarity to real persons, living or dead, is coincidental and not intended by the author. While some places mentioned are real, they are to add to the storyline and setting. Other places are just fictitious.

No portion of this book may be reproduced in any form without written permission from the publisher or author, except as permitted by U.S. copyright law.

ISBN-13: 979-8-9891130-6-4 (Paperback)

ISBN-13: 979-8-9891130-7-1 (Hardcover)

ISBN-13: 979-8-9891130-8-8 (eBook)

Cover Design by Dawn's Designs

Printed in the United States of America

Contents

Family Ties

Prologue — #

1. Who am I? — #
2. The affair — #
3. The assignment — #
4. The secret — #
5. The manor house — #
6. The agreement — #
7. The meeting — #
8. Status quo — #
9. The revelation — #
10. The fire — #
11. The visit — #
12. Charades — #

13.	Family	#
14.	Memorial service	#
15.	Home	#
16.	The move	#
17.	Bad news	#
18.	Lena's wedding	#
19.	Reunited	#
20.	Going home	#
21.	Alexandria's funeral	#
22.	His story	#
23.	Confessions	#
24.	The will	#
25.	Family Thanksgiving	#
26.	In the shadows	#

Erasing Secrets

	Prologue Two	#
1.	Winter Chill	#
2.	Secrets	#
3.	Family Tensions	#
4.	Siblings	#
5.	New & Old Love	#
6.	Sisters	#
7.	Connections	#

8. Meetings #

9. Darkness #

10. The Move #

11. Home Creepy Home #

12. Good Morning, Surprise! #

13. The Date #

14. Change of Plans #

15. Empty Nest #

16. Preparations #

17. The Party #

18. Christmas Morning #

19. The Fury #

20. Family Matters #

21. The Late Gift #

22. Ireland Escape #

23. Happy and Sad News #

24. Notifications #

25. Re-evaluating plans #

26. Preparing to Say Goodbye #

27. The Funeral #

28. Unexpected Opportunity #

29. Love and Loss #

Pawns

Prologue Three #

1. Surprises #

2. Truths #

3. Connecting Dots #

4. Weekend Plans #

5. More Tragedy #

6. More Bad News #

7. Last Plans #

8. Realizations #

9. Going Back Again #

10. Goodbye Again #

11. Preparations #

12. Boats and Bad Luck #

13. Judgement Day #

14. Sharing Secrets #

15. The Wedding #

16. Chaos #

17. Perfect Timing #

18. Big Revelations #

19. Disappearing #

20. Lady Beatrice #

21. Visitors #

22. New Boss #

23.	Starting Over	#
24.	The Big Soiree	#
25.	Sweet Freedom	#
26.	New Friendship	#
27.	Goodbye Betty	#
28.	New Beginnings	#
29.	The End	#
Acknowledgements		#
About Author		#
Books By This Author		#

Family Ties

The Lyons Garden Book One

D.M. Foley

Remember My Roots Press

Prologue

"A family is a risky venture, because the greater the love, the greater the loss... That's the trade-off. But I'll take it all."
BRAD PITT

Chapter One

Who am I?

Walking to the mailbox, Jessica noticed the crispness of the air as the wind swirled leaves across the driveway. It always filled fall in New England with beautiful colors and scents. However, Winter, Spring, and Summer brought their own delightful bombardments to her senses, which is why she lived here in the small town of Preston, Connecticut. Nestled on fifty acres of land, the small log cabin she owned is where she lived. In the Fall, she especially enjoyed the long walk down her driveway over the little wooden bridge that spanned the babbling brook running through her property.

Grabbing her mail out of the mailbox, one piece of mail caught her attention, and she felt a tinge of excitement bubbling inside her. It was the DNA kit she had ordered off the internet through a genealogy website. *Will she finally find out who she is and where she comes from?* Her parents were very loving people whom she loved very much, and a small feeling of guilt crept into her gut. *They would understand,* she told herself.

Noreen and Glen Greenhall could not have children of their own and after years of unsuccessful fertility treatments, had adopted Jessica. The diagnosis of breast cancer in Noreen in 2008 compelled them to tell Jessica about the adoption. It had been a closed one that an attorney friend of theirs had orchestrated. All she knew of her biological mother was that she was an unwed teenage mother who gave birth to her when she was sixteen in 1992.

Being adopted wasn't much of a shock to Jessica. She had long suspected it. She looked nothing like either of her parents. Her green eyes and dazzling red hair with its long curls were such a stark contrast to her mom's blonde hair and brown eyes and her dad's brown hair and blue eyes. There was no way they were her biological parents. Her parents were also much older than her peers' parents. They had adopted her when they were in their early forties. What was shocking was how quickly Noreen's cancer had spread and how none of the treatments worked. The disease abruptly took the woman she called mom all her life from her within a year of her diagnosis.

Losing her mother left such an emptiness inside her, she couldn't even describe it. That was when she asked herself *who am I?* At first, it was a little nagging in her gut; she tried to quiet by taking nature hikes at Bluff Point, Hopeville Pond State Park, or Pachaug State Forest. Although, as her eighteenth birthday approached, she felt more and more compelled to find out the truth about her biological parents. Glen understood, and after losing his wife, Jessica was his world, his everything, and he would stop at nothing to make her happy. He reached out to his attorney friend, who handled the adoption. However, his friend's office had burnt to the ground and, along with it, the records of Jessica's adoption.

When Jessica turned eighteen, she tried using social media to find out who her biological mother was by posting her birth date and the hospital she was born in. Even though the posts went viral, shared thousands of times, she received no leads about who her parents were. It seemed as if there would never be a way for her to know who she was and where she came from. Her first semester at college kept her so busy she put her quest on the back burner.

Then, the unthinkable happened during her senior year of college. The only father she had ever known, the man who tried to give her everything she ever wanted, died in a tragic car accident. Her world came crashing down around her and as she struggled to finish college, the nagging question rose back into her gut: *who am I?*

She had inherited the log home and the acreage when her father passed away. Tucked away in her little serene part of Southeastern New England, she had thrown herself into her passion for nature photography and had made a name for herself, taking pictures for publications like National Geographic and even Time Magazine. In the three years since her father's passing, she had been to so many beautiful places in the world she had almost forgotten that she was alone. She had plenty of friends, however; she had no family ties.

Both her parents had been only children and their parents, her grandparents, had all died when she was very young from varying circumstances. This left her with no aunts or uncles, no cousins, and being adopted, no siblings. When a friend of hers mentioned the genealogy website and DNA kit and how it had helped her track down her family history, she figured it was worth the shot.

Now it was here, and she was holding it in her hands as she hastened back to her log cabin. When she got closer to the cabin, the knots in her stomach built. Her hands shook, and the questions flew through her mind. *What if I find my biological parents and what if they don't want to be found? Could I have brothers and sisters? What if I don't find my parents? Can I live with not knowing?*

As she climbed the steps to the cabin, she heard her house phone ringing. *Ugh, why now?* She only used her house phone for her photography business assignments, which meant her agent was calling her with a new assignment. She rushed through the doorway and hurried into her office, which was to the right of the foyer. Slightly out of breath, she answered the phone.

"Hello Ann, how are you?"

"Jessica, how long would it take you to get to East Hampton, New York?"

"Let's see, a half hour from here to the Long Island Ferry, then it's about a two-hour ride across, and then maybe one and a half hours to East Hampton from Orient Point."

"Can you be there by tomorrow afternoon? National Geographic is doing an article on Gardiners Island off the coast of East Hampton and they want you to take pictures for their article."

"Sure, send me the address and who I need to meet and I will be there. It isn't often I get to work so close to home. You are usually sending me halfway across the world."

"Jessica, very few people get to set foot on Gardiners Island. You should feel very privileged. It is one of the largest privately owned islands in our country and it has been in the same family for hundreds of years."

"Sounds intriguing. I can't wait to see it."

"I will send you the address and all the information via email as soon as we are off the phone. I trust you can make your travel arrangements?"

"Sounds like a plan. Of course, I can make my arrangements. Talk to you later, Ann."

"Good. Have a pleasant trip and call me when you get back."

Wow, a private island. I may have to do some research about this place. Jessica thought to herself as she fired up her laptop to retrieve the email Ann was sending her. As she typed Gardiners Island into her Google search bar, she remembered her DNA kit sitting on the little table in the foyer. Jessica quickly got up and got the kit. As she opened it, the knots started in the pit of her stomach again.

Following the directions in the kit, she opened up a new tab on her laptop and logged into the genealogy website, activating her kit by entering the kit number. She then opened the vial in the kit and filled the vial with spit. As she did so, she wondered how the paltry amount of saliva she was providing may help her find out who her biological parents were. Science truly was amazing sometimes. She added the blue solution provided, sealed the vial, shook the vial, and put it in the envelope to send back. She would place the kit in the mailbox on her way to Gardiners Island in the morning. Then she logged out of the genealogy website and closed the tab, returning to her search on the island.

In her quick search, Jessica learned Gardiners Island was the first English settlement in New York. Lion Gardiner settled it in 1638. He had bought the island from the Montauket Indians in a trade because of his support of them during the Pequot War. She also learned that Captain Kidd had buried treasure on the island in 1699, all of which the Gardiner family had to turn over during Captain Kidd's trial for charges of piracy. It was even the birthplace of Julia Gardiner who married President John Tyler and became First Lady in 1844. *Intriguing,* she thought to herself as she concluded her research and made reservations to take the 7:00 am ferry across the Long Island Sound.

Her schedule was to meet Arthur Brockton, the lawyer for the island's current owner, a descendant of Lion Gardiner, at 3 pm at a café in East Hampton. As Ann had told her, the island indeed had stayed in the family for hundreds of years. The current owner was a millionaire who owned a real estate development company in Manhattan. National Geographic had contacted the owner to do an article on the largest colony of osprey that lives on the island since it is one of the few locations in the world where the osprey build their nests on the ground because of the lack of natural predators. The owner was more than happy to oblige.

Jessica fell asleep that night thinking about all the intriguing history Gardiners Island held. She dreamt about pirates and buried treasure, Indians, and even about the President of the United States possibly being on the island. She never dreamed the course of her life was about to take an unsuspecting turn.

CHAPTER TWO

The affair

East Hampton, New York, is known for its old family wealth. Where many rich and famous people go on vacation during the summer. It was the summer of 1991 and Mira was spending the summer with her best friend Lena at her beach house in the Hamptons. The girls had met in the fall when they both started school at the prestigious all-girls. St. Catherine's Preparatory School in Thompson, CT.

Lena's family was from East Hampton and was part of the old wealth. Mira had gotten into St. Catherine's on a full academic scholarship. Her family was what they referred to as middle class, however, the girls hit it off the very first day they met in their dorm room and quickly became best friends. When Lena had asked her parents if Mira could stay with them for the summer, they were skeptical at first about whether Mira would feel comfortable and fit in with the Hampton social scene. Lena convinced them she would help Mira. It elated Mira's parents that Lena gave their daughter the opportunity to spend the summer with such successful people. Their motto was, "*Your success depends on who you know.*"

Mira's father was an insurance salesman, and her mother was an aspiring artist. They weren't what you would call successful in terms of wealth, however with Mira being accepted into the prestigious St. Catherine's, they hoped that would change. Mira's father, Brad Kennedy, was already peddling life insurance to some of the more affluent parents at Mira's school, and some parents had already commissioned Kathleen Kennedy to paint their portraits. They knew their daughter aspired to go to Harvard Law School, so they hoped some connections they were making would help make that dream come true.

As the car pulled into the circular driveway of the beach house, the view took Mira's breath away. She never imagined the beach house would be so magnificent and large. The stone façade gave it an aged look with stone pillars accenting the wrap-around veranda. The car came to a stop, and the driver got out and opened the car door for the girls. Lena jumped out, pulling Mira out of the car with her.

"Thank you, James. Could you see to it our bags get brought up to our room?"

Lena called over her shoulder to the driver as she continued to pull Mira along toward the house.

"Yes, ma'am."

James replied as he gathered the girl's bags to bring into the beach house.

Lena brought Mira around to the back of the house where Mira caught the smell of the salt water blowing along the breeze. The view of the Atlantic ocean was spectacular as the house was right on the southern fork of Long Island. Lena's parents were sitting on the veranda drinking lemonade as the girls came over.

"Lena, Mira, we are so happy you are finally home!"

Rita, Lena's Mother stood up and embraced both girls.

"I hope you two girls are up to a party tonight. The Gardiners are having their annual start to the summer party on the island and they have invited us. Lena, you know how anyone who is anyone will be there. I am sure Mira would love it!"

"Yes, mother, we will be up to the party and I am sure Mira will love it!"

The girls went into the beach house and Lena showed Mira the room they would share for the summer. As they unpacked, Mira couldn't believe the absolute luck she had in meeting Lena and befriending her. The bedroom had two double beds with lilac bed shams and what seemed to be a dozen throw pillows on each. The walls were a very pale purple, and the trim was a brilliant white. It looked like the furniture was old pine. There was a bathroom connected to their room with a claw-footed bathtub that Mira couldn't wait to take a nice soaking bath in.

"Mira, you can borrow any of my clothes in the closet over there. I have dozens of sundresses. I am sure you will find one that will be perfect for the party tonight."

Lena pointed to the walk-in closet.

"Oh my gosh, Lena! This closet is the size of my bedroom back home!"

Mira looked through Lena's extensive wardrobe.

Lena chose a pale yellow strapless sundress and paired it with white sandals. Mira chose an emerald green strapless sundress and paired it with a pair of tan sandals. The girls did their hair and makeup, copying the latest *Teen Beat* magazine styles. They painted their fingernails and toenails. Mira's heart pounded, and her stomach swirled with mixed emotions. As much as Lena treated her as her equal, she knew others in the Hampton social scene might not be as accepting. Lena looked at her friend and saw the worry on her face, the way she always furrowed her brows when she was deep in thought.

"Hey, what's got you worried?"

"This is all surreal. It's amazing, but I am concerned that people will find out I am not one of you."

"I already told you. Be mysterious. Your last name will be enough for people to accept you. They will assume you are one of us. Trust me, once they hear you're a Kennedy, they will fall all over you!"

"I am a Kennedy, but I am not one of those Kennedys."

"I know that and you know that. They don't have to know that."

"Girls! It's time to go!"

Rita called up the stairs.

They piled into the car and headed to the private ferry that would take them all over to Gardiners Island. Lena had given Mira the rundown on the Gardiners and their famous island while they were unpacking and getting ready for the party. Richard Gardiner shared ownership of the island with a cousin. Richard, twenty-four, just married another East Hampton socialite, Mary Klein.

As they pulled up to the manor house on the island, Mira saw the throngs of people milling around the outside of the house laughing and socializing. She noticed how sophisticated and glamorous they all looked. That feeling of dread crept through her. Lena squeezed her friend's hand to reassure her and as the door to the car opened for them, the feeling subsided and pure excitement took over. There was a couple welcoming everyone, and Mira automatically recognized they must be Richard and Mary. Soon it was their turn to be welcomed and as they introduced Mira to Richard, she felt like she was in a dream.

She couldn't remember what she had said when he had reacted to hearing she was a Kennedy. All she could remember was how he took her hand and ever so gently brought it to his lips while his deep, icy blue eyes pierced through her soul and lit her on fire. Mira had never felt like this before. As she walked away with Lena, she felt the yearning to turn around and gaze into those eyes again. She resisted well, though, telling herself, *He's married, and he is nine years older than you!*

"Oh my God, Mira! Did you see how he was looking at you?"

Lena swooned as soon as they were out of earshot of her parents.

"See it? Lena. I felt his gaze piercing through me! He is the most gorgeous man I have ever seen!"

"He is married!"

"I know. Tell him that, though!"

"He is nine years older than you, too!"

"I know! I know! God, I wish it wasn't so. He is so dreamy!"

"Mira, please don't even entertain the thought of being attracted to him."

"Lena, I can't help who I am attracted to or who I fall in love with!"

"In love? You just met him!"

"I know it sounds crazy. I never believed in love at first sight, but oh wow, I do now!"

"Let's go mingle with the other teenagers. You are not in love, you're just awe-struck with your surroundings!"

"No, I am definitely in love with him!"

Mira looked back at Richard and felt that rush of fire burn through her again.

The girls joined some teenage boys and girls that Lena knew from previous years. Lena introduced Mira to them all, although Mira barely paid any attention. All she could focus on was Richard. His tall, lean body with his well-defined muscles. His curly strawberry blonde hair and those icy blue eyes. Was she imagining him glancing back at her? One boy snapped her out of her gaze.

"Do you want to go down to the beach with us?"

"Um, yeah, sure."

They all went down to the beach, and some boys made a fire to sit around. Mira tried to follow the conversations happening around her however, most revolved around the group's memories from previous summers. She heard about the time they took one of the boy's parent's sailboats for a joy ride.

Then one boy lit a joint and started passing it around. Mira, panicking, shot a look at Lena. She wasn't into drugs or drinking. She knew Lena had tried some last summer, and she had promised Mira she wouldn't make her do anything she didn't want to do. Lena took a hit and shrugged her shoulders, passing it to Mira.

Mira felt every eye on her. She didn't want to take a hit off the joint, but she knew if she didn't, it would give these kids reason to question her. She put the joint up to her mouth and drew in a breath. Coughing as she exhaled and passed the joint to the boy sitting beside her. The joint continued being passed around until it was completely gone and they were all stoned. Some boys and girls paired off and went in various directions. Mira's stomach growled and her mouth was dry, so she made her way back to the manor house while Lena went off with some dark-haired boy.

The crowd had dwindled considerably, and there were small groups of guests here and there throughout the house. Mira found the buffet table and filled a plate. Then found some lemonade to quench her thirst. Wandering out into the garden area where there was a gazebo with climbing vines of roses and other flowers, she couldn't identify. She sat down on the floor of the gazebo and ate her plateful of food. She was hoping nobody had noticed she was high as a kite. A man's voice startled her.

"Is this a private party?"

"No, it's the Gardiner's party..."

As she looked up and stared into those icy blue eyes again.

"Why indeed it is my party. May I join you in here, though?"

"Uh, yes, of course."

She stammered. *What is she doing? She shouldn't be alone with this man,* she was telling herself. However, she felt compelled to stay.

"Do I make you nervous, Mira?"

He knows my name! Her heart felt like it was going to beat right out of her chest as he sat down right next to her.

"Yes, I mean no. I mean, you are married."

"You are mesmerizingly beautiful. Did you know that, Mira?"

She couldn't tell whether she was dizzy from being high or dizzy from his flattering words. She couldn't answer him. Her instincts were telling her to run, but the fire in her was spreading like a wildfire all over her body, making her stay. His scent was intoxicating to her, and she leaned closer to breathe in his heavenly scent. He reached for her face and cupped her chin in his hand, leaned in, and kissed her. Fireworks exploded in her mind and she gave in to the taste of his lips on hers. She knew this was wrong, oh so wrong, but it felt so right. His hands explored every curve of her body as hers explored every muscle of his. He brought emotions to the surface she had never felt before, pure burning desire.

Mira did not know how long she had been with Richard and it startled her when she heard Lena calling for her. Richard was fast at gathering himself together, and before slinking off so that Lena wouldn't see him, he kissed Mira gently on the forehead and mouthed, "*I love you, Mira. I will see you again.*" She quickly gathered herself and tidied herself up and met Lena on the garden path.

"Where were you?"

Lena was looking her friend up and down.

"I got hungry and thirsty. I came out to the gazebo to eat and I must have passed out."

Mira lied, hoping her friend would believe her because of her disheveled look.

"Oh, okay, my parents are looking for us. Let me help fix your hair, so they suspect nothing."

"Thanks."

The summer flew by and, as promised, Richard saw Mira again. They snuck around all summer, seeing each other any chance they got. As the end of August drew nearer, Mira knew her time with Richard would be ending. She also knew she didn't have a future with him, although he set up a post office box for her to write to him when she left.

Chapter Three

The assignment

Jessica awoke early so she could get down to the ferry docks. She preferred to be one of the first ones on the boat so she could be one of the first to disembark. She made sure she had all of her camera equipment and a small overnight bag with a couple of changes of clothes, in case she wound up having to extend her stay a day or two.

One thing she had learned about photographing nature was that to get the right shots, you could not rush the process. She had once camped out in the Amazon rainforest for an entire week just to capture some rare photos of the wildlife. It was worth it to capture the magnificent colors and views. Those photos had earned her some prestigious awards, too.

This assignment sounded pretty tame compared to that one, and she was looking forward to doing a shoot in her backyard, so to speak. She finished packing her car, grabbed her DNA sample to drop off in the post office box, and headed on her way.

The sunrise was bright, so she put her sunglasses on as she pulled out of her driveway. Jessica enjoyed driving, especially when it wasn't in a city. Passing hay fields and cow pastures made her smile. The laid-back atmosphere of the small town in the country that she grew up in and called home always brought her balance. As she drove past Lopresti's farm stand, she noticed their selection of mums and pumpkins and told herself on the way home she would stop to pick some out. She made a quick stop at

LuMac's Plaza to drop off her DNA sample into the postal box out front, and as she did, her stomach flipped. There was no turning back now.

By the time she checked in to the ferry and got in line, her nerves had settled a bit. However, she still questioned if she was doing the right thing trying to track down her birth parents. It was more than just wanting to know who she was and where she came from. The knowledge of her being adopted had deterred her from really getting involved in any romantic relationships because she always had this nagging thought in the back of her mind, *what if this guy is your brother?* Not that she didn't have her fair share of dates over the years, but it was hard to settle down in a relationship not knowing her biological family. Also, traveling constantly for work truly hampered any long-term relationships. Her successful career utterly intimidated many men as well. They didn't appreciate a self-sufficient twenty-five-year-old woman. Someday she would find Mr. Right, but right now, that wasn't her priority.

Soon she was driving onto the ferryboat, parking her car, and climbing the stairs to the cabin. She walked up to the snack counter and checked over the menu. A voice interrupted her thoughts.

"What can I get you? Beautiful."

Startled, she looked up and saw a tall, tanned, blonde-headed, green-eyed, smiling young man leaning on the counter waiting for her reply.

"A large hot tea and a blueberry muffin, please."

As she fumbled through her wallet for the money to pay him, she knew she should thank him for the flirtatious compliment. However, she always felt so awkward in these types of situations.

The young man handed her the tea and blueberry muffin.

"Where is a beauty like you going so early in the morning?"

"I am a photographer and I have an assignment out on Gardiners Island."

"Wow, nobody goes out there. It's pretty secluded. You are not only beautiful, but you are lucky also!"

"That's what I hear."

She walked away from the counter and found a window seat with a table.

Jessica loved to watch the shoreline as the ferry left the New London terminal, heading out of the mouth of the Thames river into the Long Island Sound. On the one side was New London, with its mixture of housing and commercial buildings, a once bustling whaling city, now a struggling municipality trying to reinvent itself by attracting tourists. And on the other side was Groton, with houses and businesses, along with historical Fort Griswold, Electric Boat, Pfizer, and Eastern Point Beach. Both towns were much more city than her hometown was and she just couldn't imagine living so close to her neighbors.

As the ferry passed the New London Ledge Light Lighthouse, she recalled hearing the stories of it being haunted. She was more interested in its red and white square architecture and how it was such a picturesque contrast against the blue ocean waves crashing against the rocks at its base with the blue sky that was its backdrop. She took out one of her small cameras that she always carried with her and went outside to take a few pictures.

Seagulls swooped down to the water to get some fish, and Jessica started snapping pictures of their efforts. There were some teenagers out on the deck eating French fries and as Jessica got one seagull in focus, she followed it as it dove down and stole a fry right out of an unsuspecting teenager's hand. She got the shot and then burst into laughter.

The wind was picking up, which gave Jessica a chill, so she went back inside to finish the rest of the journey across the sound. They were passing Plum Island and entering Plum Gut. As the ferry prepared to dock at Orient Point, Jessica got her first glimpse at Gardiners Island in the distance. She had taken trips out this way in the past, but she never really paid attention to the island in the distance. This time, her research piqued her interest even more. While the island had remained in the family for hundreds of years, it seemed to be shrouded in various tragedies, and even one of Lion Gardiner's daughters, who died shortly after giving birth herself had accused one of his trusted employee's wives of being a witch.

Richard Gardiner, who had owned the island with his cousin Alexandria Cromwell, had died at 27 in a sailing accident. It dismayed his wife Mary to find that she had not inherited his portion of the island at the reading of his will and the sole heir had become Richard's cousin Alexandria, who currently owned it. There had been a long drawn out court battle contesting Richard's will, however in the end the will remained in effect. Alexandria had conceded to allow Mary to continue to live in the manor house where she and Richard had lived until she died or remarried. As far as Jessica could tell, she still lived on the island.

Alexandria Cromwell was the last known heir of Gardiners Island. She had married David Cromwell and built a successful real estate company in Manhattan alongside her husband. They had raised three children of their own and her cousin Richard, who became orphaned at a year old when his parents died in a car accident. Alexandria had been twenty-two and her parents were too busy jet-setting around the world to start over raising a one-year-old, so she and David had taken him in. At seventy years old now, Alexandria only had her business and her island now. David and their three children, David Jr. twenty-five, Samuel twenty-one, and Dorothy nineteen, had all perished in the same sailing accident as Richard. She had never remarried.

Thinking about the Gardiner family tragedies reminded her of her losses and the loneliness she felt. She felt a strange comradery with Alexandria even though she had never met the woman. Jessica gathered her belongings and headed down to her car as the ferry docked at Orient Point.

Driving off the boat, she headed toward East Hampton. Along the way, she passed a few antique shops and farm stands. It reminded her of home. She had plenty of time until her meeting at the café, so she took a quick detour to the next antique shop she spotted.

Pulling into the dirt parking lot of an old Victorian-style home. It had an open flag attached to one of its porch pillars and an oak sign with the word Antiques burned into it, hanging above the porch steps. Jessica wondered what treasures she might find inside. She loved antiques and old architecture and this place had both, so she was smiling as she walked up the steps and opened the door. As she stepped inside, she heard a small bell jingle at the top of the doorway, signaling there was a customer entering. A small elderly gentleman with a crooked smile sauntered over to her with his cane. His eyes twinkled.

"What can I do for you, young lady?"

"I am just looking. If I find something, I will let you know."

He nodded and sauntered back to a little counter with an old-fashioned cash register. There was a small stool he sat on and a small old transistor radio playing all the latest hits. The music seemed out of place with its surroundings and Jessica chuckled to herself as she walked into another room. It was filled with antique milk bottles and canning jars. There were various pieces of antique furnishings, a hutch, a dining room table and chairs, an old student desk with an attached chair, and an old-fashioned washbasin.

They filled the next room with books and record albums. She thought to herself, *jackpot*! Her hobbies besides photography were reading and listening to her parent's old record collection. She looked through the titles to see if any caught her eye. Within twenty minutes, she had already found six books and ten albums. She finished perusing the rest of the antiques in all the rooms of the Victorian house and brought her finds up to the counter to pay the elderly gentleman.

"Did you find everything you were looking for?"

The man had lit a pipe that was hanging out the side of his mouth.

"Yes, thank you. I could have stayed in that one room with the books and records all day. You have an extensive selection!"

Smiling, the elderly gentleman nodded.

"That was my wife's favorite room as well."

The man's gaze glazed over as he finished ringing up her order and Jessica could tell that he had become lost in a memory. She understood the feeling well. When she spoke of her parents with her friends, she would catch herself reminiscing about her childhood and then would snap back to reality by one of them shaking her out of the memory.

She left the man in his memory and tiptoed away. As she opened the door and the bell jingled, she looked back and noticed he had snapped out of his daydream. He looked at her and nodded with a smile, and she nodded back as she walked out the door.

East Hampton wasn't far, and she made it there around one o'clock. She decided to just go to the café early and grab a bite to eat. It wasn't hard to find and was a quaint little place with an outdoor dining area with wrought-iron tables and chairs, and an inside dining area with two corner booths and several square tables. As Jessica walked in and sat down at one table, she noticed an older woman, maybe in her mid-fifties, and another woman in her early forties. They seemed to stop talking as she walked in and then leaned in and whispered to each other. Probably sizing up her white t-shirt, blue flannel long sleeve shirt, blue jeans, and work boots compared to their tailored skirts and blouses with high-heeled shoes.

The waitress, a woman about Jessica's age, brought her a menu.

"Can I get you something to drink, for starters?"

"A water and an unsweetened ice tea please."

"Sure thing."

As Jessica waited for her drinks to come, she noticed another sharp-dressed woman walk into the café. The woman took off her sunglasses as she entered, noticed the other two women, and shifted her demeanor from being relaxed to guarded. The older woman at the table spoke first with a wry smile.

"Good afternoon Mary, what brings you to the mainland this afternoon?"

"Not that it's any of your or your daughter's business, Rita, but I have an important meeting later in the afternoon."

The woman curtly turned towards Jessica's table and then halted. After a brief pause, she continued past Jessica.

Wow, whatever relationship these women had, it was definitely not a friendly one. The tension felt in the café was thick enough to be cut with a butter knife. Jessica also felt uneasy as she felt the woman called Mary seemed to be startled by her appearance.

She ordered some clam chowder and a sandwich and continued to people watch as she ate her lunch. Rita and her daughter seemed to enjoy a leisurely afternoon and were engaged in a conversation that only occasionally brought their gaze back to Jessica. Several times she caught Rita's daughter looking at her and shaking her head. Jessica was feeling a little self-conscious. When all the woman's attention, including her own, diverted when a tall man with brown hair neatly combed to one side walked in.

Jessica felt the temperature in the room rise by what seemed like ten degrees as she felt her cheeks flush. She couldn't remember the last time a man instantly attracted her. This guy was definitely in that category. She couldn't tell whether it was his broad shoulders underneath his sports coat, his firm looking buttocks in black jeans, or those emerald green eyes that seemed to shoot right through her when he looked at her. *Wait, why is he staring at me?* Jessica asked herself when she noticed the man staring directly at her.

The man walked right over to her table, which made Jessica feel thankful she was sitting down because she felt very weak.

"Jessica Greenhall?"

Startled that this gorgeous man seemed to know her name, Jessica paused before answering him.

"Yes, that is my name. But, who may I ask are you?"

"Oh, I am sorry. I should have introduced myself first. My name is Timothy Sullivan. I am the journalist writing the National Geographic article you are taking the pictures for."

Timothy seated himself across from Jessica at the table.

"Timothy Sullivan, yes, that sounds familiar. I have never seen a picture of you, but I have read several of your articles. You are very talented."

"Not as talented as you. I have been a big fan ever since the Amazon jungle pictures. That's one reason I specifically requested to work with you on this assignment."

"I am flattered. What are the other reasons?"

"Well, my friend Arthur also requested you. It appears you have more than one fan."

As the waitress came over and took Timothy's order Jessica was reeling with the realization that this gorgeous man who was already making her feel things she hadn't felt in a while was going to be working side by side with her the next couple of days. It was going to be difficult to stay focused on this assignment, with him being a distraction. The two of them had garnered more whispers between Rita and her daughter, making Jessica feel like she was in a fishbowl.

Soon Arthur Brockton joined them, Alexandria Cromwell's lawyer, who would accompany them to the island. Arthur already knew Timothy, so the two men quickly started talking logistics of the assignment while Jessica listened intently. Their conversation abruptly came to a halt when

Mary approached their table, sat down, and introduced herself to Timothy and Jessica.

"I am Mary Gardiner, Lady of Gardiners Island and the manor house. Arthur, Alexandria has notified me you and your two guests will stay at the manor house while they do their assignment on the island. I expect my privacy and just know if I had MY way you all would not set foot on the island, but as you know so well, Arthur, I have no say."

The four of them finished up the planning stages of the assignment and then made their way to the private ferry that would take them over to the island. This was turning out to be one of the strangest assignments Jessica had ever accepted. She was going to spend a few days on an island with a gorgeous man, a crazy lady that doesn't want them on the island, and a lawyer in charge of keeping the peace.

Chapter Four

The secret

Mira and Lena returned to school at St. Catherine's, and Mira found it hard to concentrate on her studies. She wrote Richard her first letter.

Dear Richard,

I miss you. All I can think about is our time together, so I can't concentrate on my schoolwork. I know you are married and I know we will never have a future together, but I can't help but love you. When can you sneak away and come visit me?

Love always,

Mira

She mailed her first letter and waited patiently for a reply. It was a week later that Mira received a letter back.

My Dearest Mira,

I miss you too. Even though our love is forbidden. I can not stop thinking of you, either. Next week, I will meet with your father to discuss insurance. I have arranged a tour at St. Catherine's, setting up a scholarship fund. I will drive my Mercedes. On Tuesday at 3:00 pm, I will be there. Can you sneak out of your dorm and sneak into my car? We can go for a drive in the country. I will return you later that evening to your dorm.

Love always,

Richard

Her heart skipped a beat or two. He was coming to see her! He wanted to see her. Their love wasn't her imagination. She sent him a quick note back that she could sneak away with him and she was looking forward to seeing him. She could focus on her schoolwork, knowing she would be in his arms again soon.

Lena had noticed something had distracted her friend and now she had focused again. She figured Mira had just been dealing with leaving her first-ever crush and had finally gotten over him. Even though Mira had a relationship with Richard over the summer, Lena wasn't aware of it. She was only aware Mira had a crush on him. Lena had met a teenage boy named Steven, and they had spent a lot of time together, leaving Mira alone. Lena had apologized profusely to her best friend, but Mira reassured her every time she was okay. Little did she know that when she was off with Steven, Mira had been off with Richard.

Tuesday came, and Mira made sure no one would miss her. She told Lena and other friends she was feeling under the weather and was going to skip dinner and just go to bed. Mira made it look like she was in bed with pillows and blankets, and then she snuck out her dorm window, leaving it open a crack so she could sneak back in. She then made her way to Richard's Mercedes, which she found unlocked and waiting for her.

Richard entered the car and leaned over to kiss Mira. He then started the car and drove them to a secluded dirt road. He parked the car and took a blanket, a picnic basket, and candles, and set them up in the field on the side of the road. Then he went back to the car and opened the car door for Mira, holding out his hand for her to take. They walked hand in hand to the blanket where they spent that early evening together, eating the dinner he had packed and loving each other fully and completely. As they lay on the blanket embraced in each other's arms, Richard stroked Mira's long, curly hair. He whispered as he brushed his lips over her forehead.

"I wish we could be together like this forever."

"I do too. My parents would never approve, and you are married. Mary would never let you or the island go."

Mira looked at Richard longingly.

"When you are eighteen, I will divorce her, and we can get married and be together."

"Oh Richard, she will take you for everything you own."

"It would be worth it all because I would have you."

He passionately kissed her, and all those feelings of the first night together in the Gazebo came flooding back. She would be his forever in two and a half years. They would be together forever. They had a future together. The stars in the sky above them seemed so much brighter, and Mira was content in knowing the man she loved for eternity would reciprocate her love.

It was late in the evening when Mira and Richard gathered their things and went back to the car. Richard drove Mira back to her dorm and helped her sneak back in through the window. Richard made weekly trips to see Mira always using the scholarship fund or talking insurance with Mira's father as an excuse to get away.

Mary never seemed upset at her husband's trips and frequently used those times to go to New York City for the day. She loved shopping on fifth avenue and catching a Broadway show while she was there. Lunch was always at The Tavern on the Square because that was where anyone who was anyone went to eat. She would meet up with friends, both male and female. The tabloids frequently photographed her escapades and plastered the pictures all over their pages with solicitous gossip about her and her absent husband.

Mary loved to be the center of attention, even if it was negative attention. Alexandria warned both Mary and Richard that the negative press was tarnishing the family name and reputation, however, neither heeded her warning. Richard's love for Mira was his focus. He ignored his wife's constant need for attention. Mary, sensing his disconnect, sought connection elsewhere and didn't care about the ramifications.

On one of her trips into the city, Mary met Benjamin Timmons, a wealthy entrepreneur who enjoyed sailing. Their friendship blossomed, and he frequently accompanied her on trips to the city. The tabloids were eating up their friendship and soon rumors were swirling of a romantic affair between the two. This infuriated Alexandria and she set up marriage counseling for Richard and Mary in the name of saving the family name and reputation. Out of respect for the cousin who raised him, Richard agreed to go.

My dearest Mira,

I want you to know I love you deeply and always will. I promise you, when you are eighteen, we will be together. Until then, I need to keep the peace with my cousin and keep up the appearance of a happy marriage with my wife. I am sure you have seen the tabloids and the rumors being spread about Mary and our marriage. While I truly do not care about what she does and who she is with, I care about the family name and reputation. I also care about you, and if the tabloids start following me around, that could be a disaster for both of us.

I love you enough to let you go, for now. We must not see each other for a while.

Love always,

Richard

As she read the letter, Mira's eyes filled with tears. She couldn't breathe. She felt dizzy and nauseous and she ran to the bathroom and vomited. Lena found her resting her head on the toilet bowl and sobbing uncontrollably.

"Mira, are you okay? Do you need me to get the headmistress?"

"NO, no Lena. I will be okay."

"Are you sure? You don't look okay. You look pale, you are shaking, and you are crying."

"I just don't feel well. I will be okay."

"Why are you crying?"

Mira reluctantly handed over the letter and watched Lena's eyes widen with the realization of what she was reading. She then violently vomited again. Lena rubbed her friend's back and sat in stunned silence. Neither girl could talk about what the letter meant. Lena helped soothe Mira and get her cleaned up for dinner that evening at the mess hall. Mira still looked pale when they made it to the table for dinner, but at least she was no longer shaking and you couldn't tell she had been crying for several hours. Mira slowly picked at her dinner of meatloaf and mashed potatoes as her stomach was still feeling queasy. Lena worriedly watched her friend and felt a tad bit guilty for her misery. If she and Steven hadn't left her alone so much this summer, maybe this would never have happened.

That same afternoon, Richard and Mary sat in their marriage counselor's office in New York City. They both played the part of the ignored spouse well and begrudgingly agreed to spend more time together. Mary even suggested they sail together and Richard agreed he would go into the City to see a Broadway play or two with her.

The counselor seemed pleased with the progress they made in their first session. After an evening dinner, they spent the night wrapped up in the sheets together. It had been months since they had been with each other that way and Richard caught himself fantasizing about Mira the whole time and on more than one occasion caught himself almost moaning her name. Mary, who was usually a stickler for Richard using protection, insisted on him not wearing a condom this time, saying she was ready finally to settle down and start a family with him.

Thanksgiving break came and Lena and Mira hugged goodbye as they both went to meet their parents at the pickup area. Lena was worried about her friend. It had been a month since she had received the last letter. Mira had not responded. She didn't know what to say, and she was afraid of the tabloids following Richard and finding out about them. She wasn't eating, though. Lena had noticed her appetite was very poor, and Mira had become very picky about what she ate. She couldn't tolerate pizza. Mira would have one bite and she would go running to the bathroom to vomit. Lena was worried her friend was having an eating disorder. Mira kept assuring her she was fine. She just still had a nervous stomach over the breakup with Richard.

Mary set the table for her and Richard. He would be home soon, and she couldn't wait to share the news with him. She rubbed her belly, smiling. She would always be the Lady of The Manor house on the island now.

Richard sat in his car in the driveway. In the dining room, he could see Mary's shadow. He hadn't heard from Mira since his last letter. It devastated him, thinking he broke her heart or worse, that she hated him now. It had been a month since he sent the letter, 5 weeks since he had held Mira in his arms last. Oh, how he missed running his fingers through her long, curly hair. It was always so silky to touch. Her milky white skin that he loved to taste. And her eyes were a green that reminded him of the ocean. As he thought of her, he became more aroused and he ached to be with her again. He needed to release the sexual tension he was feeling, so he went inside and wrapped his arms around his waiting wife.

Mary felt Richard's arms wrap around her from behind as he nuzzled into her neck and started planting kisses there. She turned in his arms to face him and saw his eyes burning with passion, and she let him take her right there on the dining room table. When he finished, she tidied herself up and then presented him with the pregnancy test with two lines showing.

Richard went numb. How could he divorce Mary in two years and be with Mira when he and Mary had a child together? He had always wanted kids, but Mary hadn't until recently. What about Mira? His mind was swimming, and he walked out of the room, out the door, and down to the beach where he sat down, put his hands in his head, and mourned the loss of Mira.

Mira walked down to the pharmacy and bought what she had come to get, the cashier eyeing her carefully as she put the item in a paper bag. Thankfully, her father was at work and her mother was at her studio. She could be alone. When she got home, she took the item out of the bag and went into her bathroom. As she waited, she felt a wave of nausea that had become all too familiar the last month. She looked at the item on the counter and saw to her horror the two lines confirmed her suspicions. Turning to the toilet, she vomited, another thing she had become all too familiar with over the last month. *What was she going to do? An unwed teenager, pregnant with a married man's child. There go her dreams of being a lawyer.* What would she tell her parents? She couldn't tell them it was Richard's. This would ruin Richard. She had to tell him, though; he had to know.

Dear Richard
I still love you. My period is two months late. I took a test.
I am pregnant.
Love always,
Mira

Richard had limited his trips to the PO Box to weekly the first month after writing his last letter to Mira, although after Mary's pregnancy announcement, he had resigned himself to once a month. When he opened the P.O. Box and saw the letter sitting there, his heart skipped a beat. When he looked at the envelope and realized the postmark was from a month earlier, he tore it open. As he read the words on the page, he couldn't believe what he was reading. Both Mira and Mary were pregnant with his child. What was he going to do?

Chapter Five

The manor house

Jessica had to leave her car in East Hampton since the private ferry could only handle one car at a time. Unloading her photography gear into the van that had brought Mary over earlier was a task made easier with the help of Timothy and Arthur. Mary just seemed annoyed at the lot of them. With all their baggage loaded, they all climbed into the van and boarded the small ferry. The crew instructed them to stay in the van while they crossed Gardiners Bay, which made Jessica very uneasy and claustrophobic.

She was never so happy to be docked on land when they pulled off the small, rickety ferry. As they drove the bumpy dirt road that took them up to the manor house, the sight that lay before her took her breath away. She felt transported back in time as the building was a red-bricked Georgian-style plantation home set amongst beautifully landscaped gardens. She could feel the history of the house swirling around her, and she couldn't wait to set foot inside.

"Martin, the butler will show you each to your rooms. He will take your baggage up as well. Stella, the cook, will prepare dinner, which she will serve promptly at 5:30 pm in the dining room. Martin will show you where it is. Betty is the housekeeper and will provide you with towels or any other amenities you might need. Unfortunately for you, we can not provide you with more appropriate attire."

As she finished her speech, she glared at Jessica and looked her up and down.

Martin, a greying gentleman in his sixties, exchanged glances with Stella and Betty as they surveyed their guests and listened to their mistresses' welcome. Stella, a short plump older woman in her fifties, seemed to be intrigued by Jessica and seemed to look her up and down and shook her head as she turned to follow Mary back into the house, shuffling behind. *Probably not impressed with my attire either,* Jessica thought to herself. Betty, a tall, rather gangly woman, turned abruptly and followed Stella. Leaving the three guests with Martin. Timothy leaned toward Jessica and whispered as he nudged her with his elbow.

"I find your attire quite suitable."

Feeling the heat in her cheeks and not knowing what to say back, Jessica grabbed some of her gear at the protests of Martin, smiled at Timothy, and walked into the foyer of the manor house. She could hear the clanking of some pots and pans coming from the back of the house down the hall and assumed that was Stella working in the kitchen. Martin came into the foyer carrying more of her gear and showed the guests up the stairs and to their rooms.

The room Jessica was to stay in had a queen-sized four-poster canopy bed that was covered with a white lacey bedspread and several pale pink throw pillows. There was an oak vanity with an oval mirror on the wall opposite the bed. The door to the left of the bed led to a closet and a door to the right led to a bathroom. The bathroom wasn't fancy, but it had a tub and Jessica could already tell she would soak away the tension tonight.

As she walked back into the bedroom from the bathroom, it startled her to find Betty standing in the doorway to the bedroom.

"Sorry, ma'am, for scarin' you. I was just comin' up to check on if you were needin' anythin'?"

"I am fine, thank you. No worries about startling me, just new surroundings and all."

"How come you not sharin' a room with your handsome fellow you with?"

Betty inquired, raising her eyebrows and wiggling them a bit.

"Oh, Timothy, I just met him today. We are working together, that is all."

Jessica felt her cheeks blush as she thought about Timothy.

Betty turned into the hall smiling as she walked towards Timothy and Arthur's rooms. Jessica didn't like how flustered she got thinking about the gorgeous man staying down the hall. She needed to pull herself together and focus on her assignment. She went for a walk to get a feel for the house and its gardens.

The house was vast, and she found herself a little lost at the end of a hallway. Here on the wall was a painting of a gentleman with icy blue eyes in a tuxedo sitting next to a much younger version of Mary in a blue gown. There was a small engraved plaque attached to the frame that stated Richard & Mary, 1991. Wow, what a handsome man Richard was, Jessica thought to herself. As she looked at the picture, she felt a sense of familiarity, as if she had seen this man before. *Impossible! He died when you were two years old. There's no way you could have ever met him!* She shook her head as she turned around to find her way back to her room.

She found herself face to face with Timothy and bumped into him. Her hands landed briefly on his chest, and she felt a jolt of electricity run through her fingertips. As she looked up at him and tried to stammer an apology, she wound up gazing into his emerald green eyes and noticed the similarity in shape and intensity between his eyes and Richard's eyes. The only difference was the color. That must have been the reason she had the sense of familiarity.

As she pushed herself away from him, she apologized profusely.

"I am so sorry, I got lost and went to head back, I didn't even hear you come up behind me, again I am so sorry."

"I'm not. I was hoping to bump into you before dinner, not literally, but I wanted to discuss some ideas for tomorrow."

Timothy was smiling wryly at her.

"Well then, glad I could oblige you. Let's find a place to discuss those ideas."

Jessica felt more than her cheeks getting warm and she realized his gaze and smile were heating her. They found the staircase leading back downstairs and found a sitting room off to the side. It had an antique sofa that

Jessica automatically recognized as the one Richard and Mary had sat on for the portrait she had seen upstairs. Timothy must have recognized it too and strode over to it and sat down the way Richard had been sitting in the portrait. He reached up and grabbed Jessica's hand as she attempted to walk over to another chair and guided her to sit next to him instead. She laughed as she tried to pose how Mary had sat in the portrait. Sitting this close to Timothy, she felt the heat again. She turned to start the conversation about the next day when he reached over and put his hand against her cheek while he leaned in gently to kiss her lips. The soft tenderness of his lips on hers electrified her.

She felt herself lose control and kissed him back. His arms wrapped around her in an embrace as he pulled her into him. All her senses took over her mind. The feel of his velvety soft lips pressed against hers. His musky cologne heightened her arousal and made her want him in ways she had never been with a man before. The strong, yet gentle feel of his hands caressing her back and slowly moving along her body excited her.

One of his hands moved to the front of her shirt and cupped her breast and she felt a rush of unbridled desire flood through her body as she explored his body with her hands. He maneuvered their bodies onto the sofa and her eyes jolted open and she pushed him away.

"I can't. Not that I don't want to. Believe me, you do not make it easy to say no."

Jessica hastily straightened herself up and fixed her clothes and hair.

"Then don't say no. We can skip dinner and take this upstairs."

Timothy leaned in and brushed her lips with his.

"No, no, no, this can't happen. I am adopted, and I know nothing about my biological parents. I don't know if I have brothers and sisters, especially brothers."

She rapidly explained and trailed off her sentence with pleading eyes, looking right into his.

He didn't seem wounded or dejected like every other man she had told this to. Instead, there was a heavy sigh and a bit of sadness in his eyes, yet she could also see a hint of understanding.

"I understand. All too painfully. You were the first woman I felt I could get through my block with relationships. I too am adopted and know nothing about my biological family or if I have sisters."

Timothy frustratingly ran his fingers through his hair.

"I felt instantly attracted to you though and felt there is no way we could be siblings if I felt such a strong connection to you."

"I am so sorry. I shouldn't have kissed you back, but I felt an instant attraction to you this afternoon also, and I have been fighting the urge to kiss you all day! My DNA kit went in the mail this morning to see if I can find my biological parents or any family connection. Have you thought about sending yours in?"

Timothy laughed.

"Coincidently, I sent mine in yesterday! Maybe in four weeks, when we both have our results, we can resume what we started."

"If we are not siblings, it's a date!"

They discussed their failed attempts at finding their biological parents and found out that the same lawyer's office that had handled Jessica's adoption had handled Timothy's. Similarly, they had lost his file in the fire years ago too. The conversation flowed effortlessly between them, and Jessica felt more relaxed than she had ever been with a man. Discussing the assignment and how they were going to use a hunting blind to get close to the osprey nests so Timothy could observe and write and Jessica could get the best shots. They could agree on rules that she usually had trouble getting writers to agree to. Her top priority was always working in silence. She found it was the best way to get the best shots of wildlife blending in, and he had agreed.

Martin came and found them and showed them to the dining room. The dark wood table and chairs gleamed with the light of the chandelier above. The table had dishes set eloquently, and the food smelled delicious. Timothy pulled out her chair for her and she sat down. He took the seat next to her that was across from Arthur's. Mary was sitting at the head of the table.

"I trust your rooms are to your liking and you have everything you need?"

"Yes, indeed Mary. Thank you. I spoke with Alexandria this afternoon, and she will join us tomorrow evening. She wants to meet both Timothy and Jessica."

"Great! More unwelcomed company."

Mary's response was full of sarcasm as she rolled her eyes.

At the news of Alexandria coming to meet her and Timothy, Jessica grew excited. She had already felt a kindred spirit connection with the old lady just knowing the tragedies she had endured, but also knowing she was a very successful businesswoman, excited her as well. Mary seemed more than annoyed. She seemed angry and scraped her fork against her plate aggressively. Mary made Jessica very uneasy. The woman seemed to glare at her with disgust and disdain. When dinner was over, Jessica went up to her room and took a nice relaxing soak in the tub.

The warmth of the water instantly relaxed her body and drew all the tension from her muscles. She slid down in the tub and tilted her head back while closing her eyes. She heard the bathroom door open and as she opened her eyes; the lights went out. As she struggled to find her towel in the darkness, instead she felt gloved hands on her body, pushing her under the water. Struggling, she tried desperately to release the person's grip. Her lungs were burning, and she started feeling dizzy. She knew in a matter of seconds she would lose consciousness and she would then drown. Someone was calling her name. Someone was knocking on the bathroom door. The person holding her under the water released her and as she came up gasping for air, the bathroom door busted open and Timothy threw on the lights.

"What was going on in here? I heard thrashing. The door wouldn't open, and you weren't answering when I called out to you. Mary will not be happy I broke the door. Are you okay?"

Timothy rambled as he grabbed a towel and helped wrap it around Jessica as she climbed out of the tub, shaking, still gasping for air.

"SOMEONE TRIED TO DROWN ME!"

"Jessica, you are the only one in this bathroom. There is only one way in and one way out, which is through the door that was locked!"

"I am telling you, someone else was in here. They turned out the lights, they locked the door, they pushed me under the water and tried to drown me."

"What's all this racket and why is this door broken?"

Mary angrily came into the room.

"I am sorry, Mary. I broke the door, but it somehow locked without Jessica's knowledge. Jessica wasn't answering when I called her name, and I heard a thrashing coming from inside. I will pay for the door."

"Someone tried to drown me, Mary. I want to talk to your security now!"

Security came and took Jessica and Timothy's statements and said they would give the information to the mainland police in the morning. They reassured Jessica they found no evidence of anyone else being in the bathroom. The chief security guard, Jimmy, convinced Jessica that she had probably fallen asleep, slipped under the water, and had a nightmare that she was drowning because she probably was. The only thing that bothered her was that she knew she wasn't the one that turned off the light or locked the door.

It was late by the time Jessica had settled into bed. Timothy offered to stay in her room with her, and she agreed. He made her feel safe. They talked about hopefully getting the assignment complete tomorrow so they could get off the island. They both fell asleep in the wee hours of the morning.

Chapter Six

The agreement

Alexandria listened intently as Richard held his head in his hands and explained the situation he had gotten himself into. He told her how he loved Mira with his whole heart and truly wished to be with her when she turned eighteen. Alexandria had been calm and understanding. Her demeanor unsettled Richard even more.

"I will take care of everything. I will contact a lawyer friend to put together a closed adoption for the child."

"Will the child be able to track us down when it is of age?"

"We can have that clause put in the adoption paperwork that when the child turns eighteen, the records will be unsealed. If that is what you want."

"Good, I want to know, my child."

Richard helped steer Mira's parents stealthily in Alexandria's lawyer's direction to set up the adoption of Mira's child by introducing them to him at a gallery showing of Kathleen's artwork. The lawyer and the Kennedys quickly became friends. Her parents did not know Richard was the child's father.

Mira hid her pregnancy from those at school by being diagnosed with mono and being homebound tutored. She had told her parents she had gone to a party where a few boys from the St. Joseph's Preparatory school were and had gotten drunk and had sex with one of them.

They pressed her to tell them which boy, however; she lied and said she didn't even remember. This almost blew up on her when her parents wanted to find the boy and charge him with rape. She assured them it was consensual, and she felt the boy was the same age as her, so there was no reason to get the law involved. Her parents agreed to let it go as a teenage mistake when the lawyer found a couple willing to adopt Mira's child. They were also good friends of the lawyer.

Alexandria visited Mary more frequently throughout her pregnancy. The extra attention from her made Mary uneasy. She felt Alexandria scrutinize every detail she told her about her pregnancy, from the morning sickness, to how quickly she showed, and how she seemed to be bigger than her expected due date would actually put her.

One afternoon in late March, Alexandria had stopped by unannounced and surprisingly found Mary's friend Benjamin Timmons paying Mary a visit. As she entered the parlor, she found the two laughing while sitting close together on the sofa.

"Well, what may I ask brings you around here?"

"Mary asked me to come for a visit. She wants me to teach Richard and her how to sail."

Benjamin hastily replied as he got up from the sofa and gestured to Alexandria to take his seat.

"Richard agreed months ago to learn how to sail together. Benjamin is an excellent sailor."

"Did Richard agree to HIM teaching you both?"

"Well, no, but I am sure he will be agreeable to Benjamin teaching us."

"Mary, I don't know what you are up to. However, just know, I am watching carefully and will not let the Gardiner name get tarnished. Take this as a warning."

Alexandria stood up and walked out of the room.

Against Alexandria's advice, Richard and Mary started going sailing with Benjamin every weekend. Richard seemed to really embrace the freedom he felt on the ocean and seeing him happy relaxed Alexandria a bit. As Mary's pregnancy progressed, she stopped going on the sailing trips with Richard and Benjamin. The two men became good friends, which made Mary uneasy.

Mira's pregnancy progressed and Lena came to visit her friend every chance she could get, filling her in on all the gossip at school. Thankfully, none of the gossip revolved around Mira. Lena and Steven had broken up, and Lena was now dating one of the St. Joseph's boys. It did not thrill her parents, as they were worried she would meet the same fate as Mira.

After several meetings with the lawyer, who was setting up the adoption of her child. Mr. Gilman, the lawyer, offered her a file clerk job, knowing Mira wanted to go to law school, eventually. As soon as she recovered from giving birth, she would start working and would work through the summer and during all school breaks. When Richard heard from Mr. Gilman that Mira was going to be working for him, he was happy to know he hadn't ruined her life.

It was an early June morning when Mira awoke with the tightness in her belly. As it eased and subsided, she got up to use the bathroom. As she stood up, she felt the warm gush of fluid soak her legs and feet. Her belly tightened again, and she doubled over with the pain and the realization that her baby was coming three weeks early.

That same morning, in a private birthing center in New York City, Mary checked in, as her contractions were five minutes apart. Richard had gone on a business trip, so he was rushing to find a flight home from San Diego.

Mira's parents brought her to the Day Kimball Hospital, and they admitted her to labor and delivery. Her mother stayed with her and helped coach her daughter through the difficult delivery. She used a wet washcloth and lovingly wiped her daughter's forehead. Part of her felt guilty for making her daughter give up her child for adoption. However, she knew it was the best thing for all involved. The adoption would give the baby a chance at a better start in life. The couple who were adopting had tried to have their own child for years and were unsuccessful. Mira could follow her dreams of becoming a lawyer because of the adoption.

Mary struggled with each contraction. The nurses were wonderful and helpful. They felt for Mary going through the delivery of her child by herself, although Mary assured them her husband was loving and would be there as soon as he could. When it came time to push, Mary bore down and pushed with all her might, however the baby just wouldn't budge and the baby's vitals dropped dangerously low. They rushed her to the closest hospital and into an operating room. They gave her an emergency C section.

Alexandria made it to the hospital well ahead of Richard, as he was stuck in Chicago. He had missed his connecting flight and was trying to get another flight into New York. As she walked into Mary's hospital room, she almost felt sorry for her. Then she remembered how she had deceived Richard and the family for months. It was only a month ago she had found out the truth.

When she had caught Mary and Benjamin in a romantic embrace and had told Mary she would keep her secret from Richard if she would agree to an amniocentesis to determine her baby's paternity. She had agreed, and so did Benjamin. Alexandria was the only one other than Mary and Benjamin that knew the baby was not Richard's. They had made an agreement to never tell Richard the truth. Alexandria slipped paperwork out of her purse, had Mary tearfully sign them, and walked right back out of the hospital without uttering a word.

By 10:00 pm Mira had given birth to a healthy 5-pound 4-ounce baby girl who measured 18 inches long. She held her briefly before the nurses took the baby to the nursery to care for her. It was the first and last time she would see her baby girl. The tears streamed down her face as she grieved the loss of her baby. Her mother held her tight and stroked her daughter's hair.

At sixteen, Mira experienced love and loss that most adults don't even go through. She longed to be in Richard's arms at that moment instead of her mother's, but knew that wouldn't even happen when she turned eighteen. Richard had written to Mira and told her about Mary also being pregnant and that he could not walk away from his child and divorce her. She clutched her mother and sobbed, grieving the loss of both her daughter and her lover.

The next day, Richard walked into Mary's hospital room and gathered her up in his arms. They both sobbed as grief overcome them at the loss of their baby boy. Mary had told Richard the night before when he had called from the Chicago airport that their baby had died during birth. The baby boy had been 7 pounds, 8 ounces and 20 inches long.

They agreed to name him Richard Gardiner, Jr. Mary told Richard she had planned for the baby to be cremated and interned at the family cemetery on the island. He went home that evening and mourned the loss of both of his children. The only consolation was that hopefully when Mira's child was eighteen they would be told the truth about their adoption. With the revealed truth, if they had his name, he prayed the child would seek him out.

Four days later, they laid to rest Richard Jr.'s remains among the family's ancestors. The family, close friends, and, of course, the island servants all gathered around the infant's grave. Mary, dressed all in black in a wide-brimmed hat draped with a black veil, could barely stand without help. Richard sobbed openly. Benjamin, who had befriended Richard through the sailing lessons, embraced his friend and sobbed with him.

Weeks passed and Stella, the cook, asked if it was okay to bring her newly adopted baby to work with her. Mary agreed and swooned over the baby, filling the void in her heart. While Richard begrudgingly agreed, he slowly warmed up to the child.

He took the boy on little walks through the garden, always secretly wishing it was his kid he was walking with. Someday he hoped to walk through the gardens with his child, maybe even walk her down the aisle. He had found out Mira had given birth to a baby girl.

Chapter Seven

The meeting

The sun peeked through the shade of Jessica's window and landed on her eyelids with its warmth. She slowly opened her eyes, blinking the sleep from them. At first she forgot where she was, and then she felt the warmth of the body cradling her protectively. She smiled and wearily let herself enjoy the comfort of Timothy's arms around her. *God, please don't let us be brother and sister!*

She slowly peeled herself out of his arms and quietly snuck into the bathroom to take a shower. She closed the broken door and stared down at it. As she remembered the event of the night before, she shuddered to think of what would have happened if Timothy hadn't broken down the door.

She looked around the room. *How could anyone have gotten in and out without Timothy seeing or bumping into them?* She wondered to herself. There was a window, however, they were on the second story and there was no way someone could get in and out without making a sound. Jessica opened and closed the window, just to be sure. The old window stuck as she pushed it up and struggled to pull it down, confirming there was no way the window could have been an escape. She opened the narrow linen closet. It had shelves with towels, cleaning supplies, and toiletries. There was no way someone could have hidden in there.

Realizing she still had an assignment to fulfill, she took a warm shower, got dressed, and quietly headed down to the kitchen for some breakfast. As she approached the kitchen, she heard voices talking. The female voice spoke first.

"It's eerie the resemblance she has to her."

"Is that why Ms. Mary seems to dislike her?"

She recognized the male voice as Jimmy, the head of the island's security team.

"I suppose, wouldn't you be unsettled if someone who looked like your deceased husband's lover was staying under your roof?"

Wait? Who are they talking about? Who looks like Richard's lover? Richard had a lover? Jessica sat frozen in the hallway, listening and processing what she was hearing. *Are they talking about me? I am the only other female staying under her roof. They must be talking about me.* Jessica felt as if they had transported her to some horror story. She was stuck on an island with a crazy lady who was associating her with her dead husband's lover. *What have I gotten myself into?*

Jessica took a deep breath, controlled her shock at what she just heard, and entered the kitchen. As she set foot in the room, Stella and Jimmy both looked startled to see her. Stella rubbed her hands on her apron and started busying herself with preparing breakfast for the house guests. Jimmy brought his coffee cup up to his lips and took a sip, swallowed, then cleared his throat.

"Ms. Greenhall, how did you sleep?"

"After almost being drowned? Just ducky. No pun intended."

"Now, Ms. Greenhall, we discussed this last night. You most likely fell asleep and were dreaming you were being drowned because you were drowning."

Jimmy tried to be reassuring.

"We went over the bathroom with a fine-tooth comb. There was no evidence of another person besides your companion, Timothy, anywhere near the bathroom. By the way, how well do you know him?"

"Timothy? I just met him yesterday. We are working together on an assignment. He is a writer for National Geographic and I am a freelance photographer."

Is he insinuating Timothy was the one that tried to drown me? Jessica thought to herself.

"Do you usually sleep with strange men the first time you meet them?"

Jimmy was peering over his coffee cup at Jessica.

Jessica was getting furious at his line of questioning. She needed a cup of tea and some food.

"Not that my personal life is any of your business, but no, I normally do not sleep with strange men the first time I meet them. After he saved me from a near death experience though, I felt safer with him near me while I slept."

Briskly answering the question, then she turned to Stella.

"Could I please have a cup of tea and may I ask when breakfast will be served?"

"Why, of course dear, I will pour you a cup of tea, and I will serve breakfast in about 20 minutes. My Jimmy doesn't mean you any harm or to upset you. He is just asking you questions and looking at all angles like a good detective would."

Jimmy finished his coffee, put his cup in the sink, kissed Stella on top of the head, and walked out of the kitchen.

"Your Jimmy?"

"Yes, my husband and I adopted him twenty-five years ago. He is such a good boy. He grew up on this island and now he protects it and everyone who lives here."

Stella handed Jessica her tea and brought her sugar and creamer to put in it. Jessica thanked her and took her tea with her while she went outside to walk in the gardens. She couldn't help feeling unsettled after overhearing the conversation between Stella and Jimmy. Jimmy's line of questioning towards her also unnerved her. *How could he even suspect Timothy as the one who tried to hurt her? Timothy saved her, didn't he? Maybe I was sleeping? Maybe I was drowning and dreaming someone else was drowning me? Sounds more plausible than Timothy trying to.* She had so many thoughts running through her head. *At least I know why crazy Mary dislikes me. I remind her of Richard's lover.* Jessica chuckled at that one.

As she strolled through the gardens, she came across a gazebo covered in dying vines. She imagined in spring and summer the vines had flowers that bloomed from them, however the breezes of fall were now rustling the dying leaves. She sat down in the gazebo and sipped her tea in the peacefulness.

"There you are. I have been looking all over for you!"

Timothy came striding over to Jessica in the Gazebo and took a seat next to her.

Her heart skipped a couple of beats, and she felt that warm feeling washing over her again. She took a deep breath and tried to keep her composure around him.

"I am sorry. I got up early and didn't want to disturb you. After you saved me last night, I figured letting you sleep was the least I could do."

"I forgive you."

He leaned over and kissed her forehead.

The warmth of his lips on her forehead brought back the rush of feelings from the previous afternoon in the parlor, and she struggled not to throw her arms around his neck and kiss him on the lips passionately. Instead, she abruptly stood up, spilling the rest of her tea, and explained they needed to get going to set up for the photo shoot and his article.

They both awkwardly sat through breakfast with Mary and Arthur. Arthur said that Alexandria would be there this afternoon to meet with Jessica and Timothy. Mary seemed to seethe with anger towards Alexandria and she seemed to shoot daggers at Jessica every time she looked at her.

After breakfast, Martin brought them out to the barn where there were ATVs that they could use to get around the island. Timothy packed their gear on two of them, and Jessica helped make sure everything was secure. Martin introduced them to a man named Samuel, who was to show them to the osprey nests.

Samuel walked with a limp and had visible burn scars on his hands and face. He also seemed to look at Jessica with disdain. *What is it with everyone on this island? Why do they all seem to dislike me?* She wondered to herself.

They all climbed on their ATVs and headed out to set up their observation camp. They had been on one trail for about five minutes when Jessica's ATV sped up. It only took her seconds to realize the throttle was stuck, as she swerved to avoid hitting Samuel in front of her and tried throwing it in park while turning it off simultaneously. She found herself and the ATV tipping over and rolling down a hill.

As she lay at the bottom of the hill with the ATV next to her and thankfully not on top of her, she took an assessment of herself and if she had any serious injuries.

She looked up the hill and saw both Timothy and Samuel sliding down it to see if she was okay. The look of absolute terror on Timothy's face melted her heart and made her smile.

"I'm okay!"

"Are you sure? Don't move until we can make sure."

Timothy demanded as he reached her.

"Hmf, a woman shouldn't be driving ATVs."

Samuel was mumbling as he stepped over Jessica and went to the ATV to assess the damage.

This infuriated Jessica and even though Timothy was trying to make sure she was okay, she gingerly stood up, walked over to Samuel and the ATV, and made sure none of her equipment had broken.

"For your information, Samuel, I ride an ATV at home almost daily on my fifty acres of land, where I also hunt and fish. The throttle stuck on this ATV. You could have been on it or Timothy."

Jessica looked Samuel straight in the eyes with an edge of annoyance in her voice.

"Are you sure you are okay?"

Watching her roll the ATV left Timothy visibly shaken.

"I am fine, really, just a little bruised and sore. Let's get my equipment up the hill and on the other ATV. I am going to have to ride with you the rest of the way. Let's get this assignment over with so we can get off this godforsaken island."

"I don't mind sharing my ATV with you. I like your arms around me."

Timothy smiled as he helped her and the equipment up the hill. Jessica laughed as they put her equipment on the other ATV and went on their way. As she wrapped her arms around Timothy and leaned her head against his back, she felt her heart race again and she struggled to keep her composure.

They set up their camp for the day by the osprey nests and worked in silence as they had both agreed upon the day before. They worked well together, respecting each other's craft. Jessica felt she was getting some amazing shots. They ate the lunches Stella had packed them and as the day went on, Jessica felt her muscles ache more and more from the tumble with the ATV.

What is it with this place? Two days in a row, I have had near-death experiences. Jessica was feeling a little paranoid. She wanted to finish the assignment and get off this island tonight. She looked over at Timothy, who was observing the osprey and writing fervently. He was so handsome, and it mesmerized her watching him. As he wrote, she noticed he bit his bottom lip in concentration. She couldn't help but think that just looked so sexy. She sneakily took some photos of him like this as he worked.

It was about 4:00 when they both agreed they had what they needed and they packed up the ATV and headed back to the manor house. When they got back, Timothy insisted on unpacking the equipment and told Jessica to go rest. As she headed into the house, Jimmy met her.

"Samuel says you had an ATV accident."

"Yeah, the throttle stuck."

"Sure, it was an accident. Samuel says your companion Timothy was over by the ATVs and was the one who packed the gear."

"You are insane. Timothy wouldn't want to hurt me."

"He seems to luck out whenever you have bad luck. I saw how you were holding on to him as you rode in on his ATV, and the grin on his face."

Annoyed with his insinuations again about Timothy, she pushed past him and headed to her room to get cleaned up for dinner. When she got to her room, it startled her to find a dress and matching shoes lying on her bed. There was a note with it.

Dear Jessica,

Please wear these gifts for dinner tonight.

Regards,

Alexandria

Wow, Alexandria is here, and she brought me a dress amazingly in my size, Jessica thought to herself.

Jessica soaked in the tub, with her eyes wide open this time. She couldn't help but feel as though she was being watched. As she got out of the tub and dried off, she tried to shake the unsettled feeling that was creeping back over her. For two days she experienced near-death accidents. *Were they accidents, though? Why is Jimmy trying to implicate Timothy in these accidents? Could Timothy really be trying to hurt me? He was there both times. He knew who I was and what I looked like. Could he be a crazy stalker? Could I have angered him by rejecting his advances?* Her mind swirled with questions, and she wondered if Jimmy was right about Timothy.

Slowly she got into the emerald green cocktail dress that had been on her bed. It fit like a glove. The dress had long sleeves, which she was thankful for because they covered the bruises from her earlier accident. She put on some makeup and pinned up her hair in a messy bun. She pulled a few curls down to frame her face. Jessica couldn't remember the last time she dressed up like this and she felt a little out of place.

There was a knock on her bedroom door, and she went to answer it. As she opened the door, it took her breath from her. Timothy stood before her in a black tuxedo. He stood there looking her up and down and let out a whistle.

"I see Alexandria gave you a gift as well. You look better in yours, though."

"No, Timothy, you look absolutely stunning."

She felt the blush spreading over her cheeks.

He offered her his arm as he escorted her down to dinner. Alexandria made sure Arthur was in a tux as well. While Mary was in a cocktail dress. Timothy pulled the chair out for Jessica and then sat down next to her again. Mary was not sitting at the head of the table tonight. Arthur explained Alexandria would join them momentarily. She was getting a briefing on the incidents that had happened the last two days.

When Alexandria entered the room, she was wearing a silver cocktail dress that matched her silver-grey hair. She looked eloquent and stunning for a woman in her seventies. As she came into the room, she was smiling. She came right over to Jessica and gave her a hug.

"I am so sorry you have had the experiences you have had here on the island. I hope you are okay, and I hope you will not hold it against us."

There was genuine sincerity and compassion in her voice.

"I am sure Jimmy told you they were just accidents. I am fine though, thank you for asking. Also, thank you for the beautiful dress."

"You are welcome, my dear. I am just glad you are okay."

Jessica felt that comradery with Alexandria and as they chatted through dinner, it appeared Alexandria felt connected with Jessica as well. She asked Jessica about her childhood and about her parents and she seemed very interested in her adoption. Mary seethed with anger the more Jessica talked about her life.

Alexandria pulled Timothy into the conversation also, and her interest in him being adopted piqued her curiosity even more. It shocked Jessica, though, when Timothy said his birth date was June 7th, 1992. That was her birth date also! They hadn't discussed that the day before. Alexandria was very interested in the fact they were born on the same day. They were born in different hospitals, though, in different states. She was born in Connecticut and he had been born in New York. This was good news in Jessica's mind. The chances of them being related were very slim.

Mary seemed to come out of her angry mood and slipped into a glazed stare into her plate at the mention of June 7th. Jessica thought she glimpsed a tear in her eye before she abruptly excused herself from the table and said she was going to bed.

After dinner, Jessica realized it was too late to take the small ferry back across to the mainland and she would have to spend another night on the dreadful island. The only consolation was she would spend another night with Timothy. They excused themselves from the table, and Timothy escorted her upstairs to her room.

Timothy closed the door behind them and locked the door. He turned to Jessica, wrapped his arms around her waist, and drew her towards him. She relaxed at his embrace and leaned into him, and kissed his velvety lips. He returned the kiss with passion and fire burning through his veins. He scooped her up in his arms and carried her over to the bed, where he gently placed her down. They embraced each other and explored each other's bodies with their hands while passionately kissing.

As they removed each other's clothes, they heard a scream and a thud. Scrambling to fix their clothing, they got up and ran to where they found

Alexandria bleeding from the head at the bottom of the stairs. They immediately called for help and applied direct pressure to the wound. They life-flighted her off the island to the nearest hospital. Jimmy and Arthur left the island to be with Alexandria and to see how bad her injuries were.

It visibly shook both Jessica and Timothy up with all the evening's events. They went back to Jessica's room, got cleaned up, and then just held each other until they fell asleep.

Chapter Eight

Status quo

Richard and Mary stopped going to marriage counseling. Mary slipped into a deep depression after losing their child. The only time she seemed to come back from her depths of despair was when Stella brought her baby around. The little baby boy would snuggle into her arms as she rocked him to sleep and she would hold him for however long he napped. Stella didn't seem to mind the amount of attention Mary gave the little one. When the baby wasn't around, Mary was miserable with everyone, including Stella.

Benjamin resumed the sailing lessons with Richard. Richard tried to be there for Mary and tried to be a loving husband. He begged her to come sailing with him and Benjamin to get her out of the house and back into living life. She finally agreed and the more and more she went, the happier she seemed to be.

After a few weeks, Mary seemed to come out of her depression. Richard tried rekindling the romance in their relationship. He brought her flowers, took her into the city for a Broadway play, and took her out to dinner at her favorite restaurant. When they got home, he led her up the staircase to their bedroom and gently kissed her. She pulled away, went into the bathroom, and got ready for bed. This frustrated Richard. It had been months since he had made love to his wife and even longer since he had been with Mira.

The thought of Mira made him hunger for her touch. He went for a walk down by the beach. Sitting there in the darkness listening to the waves crash upon the shore, he decided he would send a letter to Mira. He was sure she wouldn't respond. *Why would she? I ruined her life before it even really began. I broke her heart.* He missed her, loved her, and wanted to be with her. He had to tell her exactly how he felt and let the chips fall where they may.

Mira had recovered from giving birth and was working at the law office as a file clerk. She was a quick learner and soon was also covering for the receptionist and helping some secretaries with letters that needed to be typed. Downstairs in the file cabinet room, as she filed away files, she came across a file with her name on it.

She knew she shouldn't open it, however, curiosity got the best of her. It was the file regarding her daughter's adoption. It had all the information in it, who adopted her, and where they lived. Her heart ached thinking about her daughter, and a tear rolled down her cheek. Mira wiped it away and made copies of everything in the file. She didn't know what she was going to do with the information. Mira wanted the information to keep for her own records.

Mira continued with her work filing and came across another familiar name. Mary Gardiner. *It couldn't be. Why would Richard's wife have a file here?* She thought to herself. Mira slowly opened the file and realized it was adoption records, just like hers, except the birth certificate listed the father and it wasn't Richard. When she saw the birth date, her hand went up to her mouth in shock. Her heart broke for her ex-lover. His wife had made him believe their child had died. In reality, she had given the child up for adoption to cover her infidelity. She missed Richard and still loved him. She made copies of Mary's file as well.

When she got home, she hid the copies she had made in a shoebox in her closet. She took a walk that night and tried to figure out what she should do with the information she had. Her mind was swirling even when she got back and went to bed. She needed to talk to Richard.

Mira opened the mailbox a week later and saw the P.O. Box return address. It shocked her. She ran upstairs to her bedroom to read the letter.

Tears streamed down her face as she read the letter. He still loved her and she hadn't even told him what she knew about his wife.

Dear Mira,

I know I have no right to contact you because I know I hurt you and our child. I feel like I have lost everything that I ever really cared about or loved. You, our baby, and my son. I still love you and I always will. I would give up everything to be with you again. Mary doesn't love me and I don't love her. I can come to see you anytime.

Love you always,

Richard

She knew she had to tell him. It had to be done in person, though. He needed to see the information she had for himself. She sat down and wrote him a letter in response.

Dear Richard,

I forgive you and I still love you too! I need to see you.

Love you always and forever,

Mira

Richard checked the P.O. Box daily and held his breath each time. A few days went by and he was nervous when he saw Mira had sent him a letter back. As he opened the letter, he took in a big breath and braced himself for her response. When he read the words she wrote, his heart burst with joy. Over the next few weeks, Mira and Richard resumed their love affair. They renewed their commitment to get married. After Mira turned 18, Richard would file for divorce. They were careful not to get caught and in the meantime, Richard never let Mary know he knew the truth about their child.

Mary continued the sailing lessons with Benjamin, even when Richard couldn't join them. Without Richard there, Benjamin and Mary resumed their affair. For appearances, especially around Alexandria, Richard and Mary played the part of a loving married couple. Mary didn't care that Richard was taking more and more business trips out of town, since it gave her the opportunity to spend time with Benjamin.

On one of Richard's business trips, he orchestrated a get together with Glen and Noreen Greenhall. He had set up the meeting under the pretense of buying a piece of their property. The Greenhalls were a delightful couple, and they quickly felt comfortable with Richard. They decided they did not want to subdivide their property of fifty acres. However, they did own another lot down the road that they agreed to sell him.

At the closing, they had to bring their daughter with them because they couldn't find a babysitter. Richard, being compassionate and empathetic, asked his lawyer if it was okay if his file clerk could watch the Greenhall's daughter for them during the closing. He agreed it would be the best for all involved. They introduced the Greenhalls to Mira, and Mira took their daughter into the other conference room.

Mira closed the door to the conference room, and she showered the baby, her baby, with hugs and kisses. The tears rolled down her cheeks. She hadn't seen her daughter since the day she was born. The 9-month-old had little red-haired curls and green eyes, just like she did. The baby laughed and giggled as Mira played with her.

After about an hour, Richard entered the room where Mira and the Greenhall's baby were. He quickly closed the door and scooped the baby up and hugged her. Mira stood up, and Richard pulled her close. The baby squirmed and giggled.

"Someday, I promise we will be a family again."

Richard whispered to them both as he turned and brought the baby back to the Greenhalls.

Summer quickly came, and it was time for Richard and Mary to host their annual start of summer-party at the manor house. An invitation went out to Mira's parents, along with Mira herself. Richard also had befriended the Greenhalls and invited them and their now one-year-old daughter. Mary spent most of her time chasing after James, Stella's one-year-old, and didn't notice the time Richard spent doting on the Greenhall's daughter. She also didn't notice how her husband orchestrated for Mira to babysit the Greenhall's daughter for the day.

Mira held her daughter's hand and walked her through the gardens to the Gazebo covered in flowering vines. Shortly, Mary and James joined them, who were also walking through the gardens.

"What is your daughter's name?"

"She isn't mine. She is the daughter of the Greenhalls. Her name is Jessica."

Her words stung her heart as she spoke them.

"Oh, I just assumed she was yours. She looks just like you."

"It's okay. How old is your son?"

"Oh, he isn't mine. He is our cook's son. He is just a year old, though."

"Wow, they are roughly the same age then."

Mary got bored with talking to Mira and walked James back to the house. This relieved Mira. She didn't enjoy being anywhere near Mary. Richard made his way through the gardens and found Mira and Jessica playing in the gazebo. The memories of the first night he met Mira two years ago and their first encounter in the gazebo came flooding back to him. He sat down with the two loves of his life and put his head on Mira's shoulder. She gave his forehead a quick kiss and then got up to bring Jessica back to the Greenhalls. She knew being seen together would ruin all their plans.

As the months passed by, Richard gathered evidence of Mary's infidelity. He knew he couldn't use the information Mira had found without getting her in trouble. His goal was to file for divorce in April so that when Mira turned 18 in May and graduated in June, they could get married by the end of the summer. He couldn't wait to start their lives together.

Chapter Nine

The revelation

Jessica awoke and realized Timothy had already gotten up. She felt a little dejected that he wasn't lying next to her. As she moved to get up, her whole body reeled from the pain she felt. She quickly remembered the accident she had the day before and cringed as she gingerly got herself out of bed. The shower felt good, and she almost didn't want to get out, except the sooner she got out and got dressed, the sooner she could leave this place.

When she had gotten dressed, she packed up her overnight bag. She put the dress and shoes in the dress bag. As she did so, her thoughts went to Alexandria. She hoped she was okay. The fall that Alexandria had taken the night before still terrified her. Seeing her frail crumpled body at the bottom of the stairs and her head bleeding was a sight she knew would take a while to get out of her mind.

Making her way downstairs for breakfast, it alarmed her to find State Police officers at the bottom of the stairs taking pictures. She stopped midway on the stairs, not knowing if it was okay to come down, and looked over to see Timothy talking to one officer. He caught her gaze, smiled, and gestured for her to come over. The officer looked up also, nodded, and gestured for her to come over. She excused herself past the officers taking pictures and joined Timothy.

"Jessica, this is Officer Stanton. Alexandria is alive. She has several broken bones and a severe concussion. She is claiming someone pushed her down the stairs last night. That is why the police are here investigating. They need a statement from you, and then we are free to leave the island."

"Thank God she is alive! Why would anyone want to hurt her? I will do whatever I can to help with the investigation."

Jessica and Officer Stanton went into the parlor, where he asked her where she was when Alexandria had her accident. If she was with anyone else, and if she had heard or seen anything unusual leading up to Alexandria's accident. She felt her cheeks blush as she recalled what she and Timothy were doing when the accident occurred. She felt bad that she couldn't provide any pertinent information. Officer Stanton also asked her about the two incidents she had while on the island and she gave him all the information about what had occurred. When they finished, Jessica joined Timothy in the dining room for breakfast.

Timothy stood up and pulled out the chair next to him for Jessica to sit in. Arthur was still at the hospital with Alexandria and Mary had not yet come downstairs. Stella served them both breakfast and somberly walked out of the room. Jessica broke the silence.

"I still can't believe someone would try to hurt Alexandria."

"I can't either, or why anyone would want to hurt you."

"Well, I overheard yesterday morning that I look like our ungracious hostess's dead husband's lover. So that's why she seems to hate me. However, I don't think that would make her want to kill me."

"WOAH! Richard Gardiner had a lover? AND she looked like you? YOU'RE adopted, Jessica. You told her that the first night we were here. That gives her a plausible motive. You could be her dead husband's daughter."

Timothy pushed back his chair and ran his fingers through his hair.

Jessica dropped her fork on her plate as Timothy finished his statement. She was shocked. The thought of her being Richard Gardiner's daughter never crossed her mind. It made sense why Mary seemed to hate her. *Would it be enough for her to want to kill her, though?* Her mind was still swirling when Mary entered the dining room, looking quite distressed.

Stella followed her in and helped her get seated at the head of the table. *Could this frail-looking woman actually be a sociopath capable of attempted murder?* Jessica quietly observed Mary. Mary was shaking. She seemed mentally distraught and physically weak. *No, there is no way she could have been the one who attempted to drown me in the tub the first night I was here. Besides, she wouldn't have had time to change clothes before coming into the bathroom. She would have been soaking wet from the struggle I gave. When Timothy and I are alone, I need to remind him of that fact;* she thought to herself. Mary was the one to break the silence after she regained a bit of composure.

"I assume you two will leave promptly after breakfast."

"Absolutely! We want to leave before another tragic accident befalls anyone."

Timothy replied while side glancing at Jessica.

"I may not like having company on my island. However, I assure you, I dislike the fact that there have been three accidents in the two days you have been here. It's very unsettling."

"I know it's been unsettling for me, being involved in two of the accidents. Why is it so unsettling for you? You have made it clear from the start of your disdain for me. It was very clear about your dislike of Alexandria. So why would you care what happens to us?"

"Well, my dear, yes, it's true there is no love lost between Alexandria and me. However, a little known fact is, when she dies, the island will revert ownership over to the town as a nature preserve and I can no longer live here."

"So you don't care about Alexandria, you just care about losing your home?"

They could hear the disgust in Timothy's voice.

"What about me? Why do you hate me so much? I have never met you in my life."

"I don't hate you. You just remind me of the person who stole everything I ever loved and cared about."

Jessica briefly felt sorry for Mary. It must have been devastating to find out her husband had an affair. She couldn't imagine the betrayal she must have felt.

"I am sorry that I remind you of someone that hurt you. Please realize I am not that person."

"I know you are not her. I do not know whether you are her daughter, though. And I do not know if you are my husband's daughter. All I know for sure is my husband filed for divorce a month before his tragic accident. It wasn't until after his death I found out he had changed his will and had taken me out of it. When I went through his things, I found a picture of his mistress. You look so much like her. Remarkably."

"I hate to ask. Do you still have the picture?"

"Actually yes. It's in rough shape. Many times I have attempted to get rid of it. I always change my mind. I don't know why I torture myself."

Getting up from the table, Mary left the room to retrieve the photograph. Jessica looked at Timothy, who seemed astonished at the frank discussion that the two women had just had.

"I don't think she is the one who tried to drown me. They hurt her. However, I don't think she is a psychopath. She has no motive to hurt Alexandria either if what she says about the island being turned over to the town is true. Besides, she wasn't wet the night of my almost drowning."

"She may not have been the one to physically hurt you, but she could have put someone else up to it. She still has a motive for not wanting you alive, right?"

"Does she really have a motive? If I am Richard's daughter, that makes me the one legal heiress to this island. Even if I die, and Alexandria dies, she loses her home. It makes no sense. I understand her anger towards me if I am her husband's daughter. I don't think that would make her want to kill me, though."

"True."

Mary entered the room holding a small photograph that definitely looked beaten up. She handed the photo to Jessica, who covered her mouth as she looked in awe at the woman in the photograph. They could be twins! It was a school photo and on the back, there was cursive writing. It stated:

To my love Richard,
Here is my senior portrait. I can't wait till we can be together forever.
Love always, Mira
(1994)

Jessica noticed the date, two years after she was born. *Could they have carried on an affair behind Mary's back for over two years?* The more she looked at the picture, the more the woman in it seemed oddly familiar. Besides looking like her twin, Jessica felt she had met her before. *There is no way I could have met her before,* she told herself. She realized it was the same familiarity she felt about the portrait of Richard upstairs. *No way, there is no way I could have known these two people,* she thought as she shook her head.

"Penny for your thoughts?"

Timothy could see the pensive look in Jessica's eyes.

"This picture is from two years after I was born. I can understand why Mary thinks I look like her. We are almost twins. And oddly, the woman seems familiar to me, just like the picture of Richard upstairs gave me the same feeling. My adoption was closed. They adopted me a day after I was born. There is no way I could have met either of them."

Jessica continued to stare at the photograph, feeling baffled.

This time it was Mary's turn to be astonished as she sat down and covered her mouth with her hand herself.

"Does this manor house or the gardens give you the same sense of familiarity?"

"Actually, now that you mention it, the gardens and around the gazebo seem very familiar too."

Abruptly, Mary got up and left the room, mumbling something like I will be right back. Leaving Timothy and Jessica looking at each other, puzzlingly. When she came back, she had a photo album labeled Summer of 1993 Party. She frantically flipped through the pages to find the photograph she was looking for. She always had pictures taken at their parties, usually of the different families. Finally, she found the picture she was looking for and placed the album in front of Jessica. Mary sat down and sobbed uncontrollably.

When Jessica looked at the page, two pictures jumped out at her. One labeled the Greenhalls, which had a picture of her and her adopted parents, and the other labeled the Kennedys, which had the young woman named Mira in it. *I have been to this island before AND I have seen Mira and Richard before;* she told herself.

"Mary, are you okay?"

Mary shook her head no and tried to compose herself. When she finally did, she explained how, after Jessica said that she felt the familiarity of the gazebo and of Mira and Richard, it jogged her memory. She recalled how she had been walking with Stella's son, Jimmy, and had encountered Mira with Jessica. She had forgotten all about the encounter until this morning.

"I am so sorry that I have brought up more terrible memories. Can I keep these pictures please? It may help me answer some questions about who my biological parents are. "

"Sure."

Mary handed Jessica the pictures. She closed the album and walked to the doorway of the room. She turned and looked at Jessica and Timothy.

"I hope you find closure. Please let me know what you find out."

Mary walked out of the room, leaving Jessica and Timothy in awkward silence.

Chapter Ten

The fire

There was a knock at the manor house door, and Martin answered it for Mrs. Gardiner. It perplexed him it was a sheriff.

"May I speak to Mary Gardiner?"

Martin summoned the sheriff into the foyer and went to get the lady of the house. Mary walked into the foyer.

"Are you Mary Gardiner?"

"Yes, I am."

"You have been served."

The sheriff handed her a big manila envelope. He turned and let himself out of the manor house.

Mary stood holding the envelope in absolute shock. She went into the parlor and sat down as she opened up the envelope. Inside were divorce papers. Richard was filing for divorce? As she read the paperwork, it enraged her! He was filing based on infidelity, which nullified her getting anything from him according to their prenuptial agreement. She was seeing red; she was so angry! There was no way she was going to lose her island, her manor house, or her status in the Hamptons.

Richard felt free already. Knowing Mary was being served with the divorce papers made him feel like a new man. He couldn't wait to start his new life with Mira. He knew the divorce would be messy. Alexandria was already furious with him because of the ramifications to the family name this would cause. He had already discussed with her, giving up his portion of ownership of the island, although no specifics were discussed yet.

Mira had gotten accepted into Harvard and she would start in the fall. They were going to move to Boston as soon as they got married. She knew he had filed for divorce and Mary was getting served. She couldn't wait to start her life with Richard.

Mary had calmed down and thought more rationally. She made a phone call and poured herself a glass of wine. After the phone call, she was feeling much better, and she knew everything would be okay. She would not be losing her island, her manor house, or her status among the elites in the Hamptons. They set the plans to ensure her name stayed untarnished in motion.

Richard was thankful he had business trips planned that would keep him away from Mary for a few weeks. He knew her temper, and he knew the divorce papers would set her off. The only thing that disappointed him was he wouldn't be able to see Mira during that time. He missed her when he was away, so he called up Mr. Gilman and made an appointment that afternoon to discuss some legal issues so he could get a quick visit in with Mira while he was there.

At Mr. Gilman's office, he was busy with another client when Richard got there. As he sat in the waiting room, he heard heated voices coming from behind the conference room door. Richard recognized both men's voices. One was Benjamin's, and the other was Mr. Gilman's. Whatever they were discussing, Benjamin was furious. As he slammed the door open and stormed out of the office, he didn't even realize Richard was sitting there.

"Hey Richard, sorry you had to witness that. You can't please them all."

Mr. Gilman walked out to shake Richard's hand.

"Wow, I have never seen that side of Benjamin! I don't think he even noticed me sitting here."

"You are lucky he didn't recognize you. Your soon to be ex-wife sent him to intimidate me into giving him information about who you are claiming she is having an affair with. Don't worry, I didn't break and give him any information."

Mr. Gilman explained as they walked to his office and sat down.

The two men sat for an hour discussing the divorce proceedings, updating Richard's will, and discussing the possibility of Richard giving up his share of the island to Alexandria.

When they were done, Richard sat across the street in his car until he saw Mira leave the building to go to her car. When Mira saw Richard parked next to her, she smiled and quickly jumped into the passenger seat. They went for a drive to a secluded spot where they could be all alone.

As they passionately embraced, they heard sirens howling in the distance. They looked out the windshield and could see a glow in the sky. Something was burning. Curiosity got the best of them both and they drove towards the glow. Horror struck them as they realized it was Mr. Gilman's office. Flames fully engulfed the building.

Richard pulled up near Mira's car so she could get home before her parents heard about the fire and worried. As he pulled out of the parking lot, he saw a man standing on the corner facing the fire with a smirk on his face and his hands in his pockets. It was Benjamin!

It was then that Richard realized Mary was playing for keeps and would stop at nothing to get what she wanted. He also realized he needed to make sure Benjamin felt safe and make him think he didn't suspect him as Mary's lover.

Four hours later, when he got to his hotel room. He made a phone call to his friend Benjamin. After a few rings, the phone picked up.

"Hello."

"Hey Ben, it's Richard. A friend would be great to talk to. Mary has been having an affair with someone else. I don't know with who. She received divorce papers today. I won't be home for a few weeks. I have business to attend to out of town, but when I get back, maybe we can go on a sailing trip."

Richard smooth talked Benjamin, hoping it would lull him into a false sense of security.

"Oh, hey Richard, I am so sorry to hear that, pal. Definitely, when you get back, we will set up a trip."

Benjamin smiled wryly on the other end of the phone.

"Sounds like a plan. I will call you when I get back to town."

"Sure does."

Benjamin hung up the phone. As he did, he breathed a sigh of relief. Everything was falling into place.

Benjamin made another phone call before he went to bed. He knew he would have sweet dreams of a future with the love of his life, Mary. They would own Gardiners Island together in the end. It was only a matter of time.

Mary went to bed in a much better mood than she had been earlier in the day. She was feeling hopeful about her future with Benjamin. She would have everything she ever wanted or cared about. Her island, her manor house, and her reputation with the Hampton elite would still be intact.

It shook Mira up about her boss's business burning to the ground. Her parents were thankful she wasn't in the building. It was fortunate that nobody was. When she was sure her parents were in bed. She closed her bedroom door and took the shoebox out of her closet. She was thankful she had made copies of the two adoption files when she first found them. Somehow, someday, she hoped her daughter would search for her and she would have all the documentation and proof to prove who she was. As for the other file, it may serve a purpose someday. However, she didn't know how or when.

Richard went to bed feeling free and knowing Mira would be his wife as soon as his divorce from Mary was final.

Chapter Eleven

The visit

As Timothy and Jessica loaded the van with their things. Timothy's cell phone rang. He recognized the caller's number. It was Arthur, and he answered it immediately.

"Hey Arthur, How is Alexandria doing?"

Jessica couldn't hear the response from Arthur, however, she saw the concern on Timothy's face.

"Sure, I can. I can't answer for Jessica though. I will ask her."

Timothy turned to Jessica.

"Hey, Arthur is saying Alexandria is stable right now and is asking specifically to see us. Are you up to traveling to the hospital to visit her?"

"Absolutely!"

"Okay, Arthur, she is up for the visit. Send me the directions to the hospital via text and we will be on our way."

The two of them finished loading the van and then climbed inside. The driver took them to the rickety ferry and across to the mainland, where they left their cars parked. After transferring their things to their respective cars, they took Timothy's car to the hospital to visit Alexandria.

It was going to be an hour and a half drive to Nassau University Medical Center, where Alexandria was being treated for her injuries. That was with no traffic, which would take a miracle out on Long Island. Jessica and Timothy discussed the revelations that Mary had told them this morning.

Neither of them could believe that Jessica had been on the island before as a child and that she might have actually met her biological parents.

They both figured that it made sense if Mira was underage that they kept the pregnancy a secret and put the baby up for adoption. What made little sense, though, was the fact the adoption was closed. *How did her adoptive parents end up taking her to the island that summer? They swore they didn't know who her biological parents were. They wouldn't have lied to her, would they?* Jessica's mind filled with so many questions.

She felt so many emotions all at once. Part of her was excited that she might finally have a lead who her biological parents were and part of her was feeling a bit betrayed that her adoptive parents might have known all along. In what seemed like no time at all, they were pulling into the hospital parking lot.

Timothy opened Jessica's car door and helped her out. He could tell she was still sore from her ATV accident. He could also tell the information Mary had given them earlier was weighing heavily on her mind.

"Hey since you are here, maybe you should get yourself checked out with all those bumps and bruises."

"I am fine, just sore. I want to visit Alexandria."

As they walked into the lobby of the hospital, Arthur and Jimmy met them. They both looked equally worried, which made Jessica and Timothy both uneasy.

"Is everything okay with Alexandria?"

"She is still stable."

"Then why the concerned looks on your faces?"

"Well, it looks like I owe you an apology. After your statements to the state police, they went over the room you were staying in. Especially the bathroom. They found a secret door in the linen closet. It led to a ladder that led to the attic. There is a back staircase that leads to the kitchen by the back door that also leads to the attic. Anyone could have snuck into the bathroom, locked the door, and try to drown you if they knew about that passageway. Even after living on the island my entire life, I never knew about it! I failed my job. I am sorry."

Jimmy stammered out his words.

Jessica felt dizzy and reached for a chair to sit in. *So someone was trying to drown her! Who would want her dead?*

"Who would want to kill me?"

"I don't know, but I am determined to find out."

Jimmy looked Timothy in the eyes.

"Also, I owe you an apology. I am sorry. I thought it was you trying to scare her so she would look at you as her hero."

"No problem, man, you were just doing your job."

"Let's go visit Alexandria and we will worry about all this later."

Interjected Arthur, who was anxiously awaiting visiting with Alexandria, knowing she really wanted to see Jessica and Timothy.

The four of them got visitor passes and got in the elevator. Jessica disliked elevators, however, she hated looking like she was weak more, so she quietly kept her anxiety at bay for the ride up to Alexandria's floor. When they got to the room Alexandria was in, it shocked Jessica to see a State Trooper standing outside it. Arthur simply said they were all with him and they could enter.

Alexandria smiled when they walked in.

"There you all are! I have been waiting to see you!"

"Oh, I am so glad you are okay! I was terrified seeing you at the bottom of those stairs last night."

Jessica leaned in and gently hugged her.

"Doctors said if it wasn't for your quick thinking and first aid skills, I might not have made it. I am not out of the woods yet. I have some bleeding on the brain they are watching. That's why I need to talk to all of you. I need to get some things off my chest. There are some heavy family secrets that I carry. I lived my life worrying about my reputation and my family name and now, at the end of my life. I have no family that knows me, and all I have is my reputation. It's a lonely place to be."

"You are going to be fine. You are a strong woman. And just because we aren't blood doesn't mean we can't be family."

Jessica squeezed her hand and tried to hold back the tears forming in her eyes.

"That's just it child, two of you in this room very well might be family by blood. My pride in my reputation and worrying about the family name made me make some choices I regret. After losing my entire family, I have tried for years to find the two children I orchestrated the adoptions for all in the name of saving the family name. What is a family name without a family? I pray I have found you. I fear I am running out of time. If I am right, Jessica, you are the daughter of my cousin Richard Gardiner and his mistress Mira Kennedy. As for you, Timothy and Jimmy, I don't know which one of you might be the son of Mary Gardiner and her lover Benjamin Timmons. Benjamin Timmons was also Richard's half-brother. When I forced Mary to have an amniocentesis, I found out. I had Benjamin provide DNA to prove he was Mary's baby's father. I had Richard provide a DNA sample to prove the paternity of Mira's baby before adoption and to rule him out as Mary's baby's father. That's how I found out they were half-brothers. Richard never knew that Mary's baby was not his. He also never knew that the baby was born alive and given up for adoption. I am the only one who knew Richard and Benjamin were brothers. I know this is a lot to ask. Can you all provide a DNA sample? I have a lab that will give us the results in two hours."

As Alexandria rambled, Jessica, Timothy, and Jimmy stood there in stunned silence.

Jimmy broke the silence first.

"Woah, that's a lot to process, Ms. Alexandria. I have lived on Gardiners Island my entire life and now you are telling me I might actually be a Gardiner?"

Timothy chimed in next.

"Let's do this. I am hoping I am not a Gardiner. No offense, because if Jessica is a Gardiner and I am too, that means I have no chance of a relationship with her!"

"Well, after the information I got from Mary this morning and hearing this. I want to know, so sign me up."

"What information did Mary give you?"

Jessica and Timothy filled in the others on the information Mary had given them. Jessica pulled out the pictures to show. After seeing the pictures, they all agreed that Jessica was probably Mira and Richard's daughter.

Arthur made a call and soon a lab tech came in to take DNA samples to run. Arthur pulled out copies of Richard's DNA and Benjamin's DNA reports from his briefcase for the lab tech to compare the samples to. Now it was just a waiting game. Arthur, Jimmy, Jessica, and Timothy let Alexandria get some sleep and they went to have dinner.

They ate in awkward silence. Jessica pushed her food around on her plate and barely ate anything. Her stomach was in nervous knots. She was possibly on the verge of knowing who her biological parents were. The sad part was if Richard was her father, he was dead, and no one knew where Mira Kennedy had ended up. At least she potentially had names.

Jimmy tried to eat his burger and fries. He was having a hard time wrapping his head around the fact he might be Mary Gardiner's son. He had known the woman his entire life. *Did she know? Did his adoptive parents know?*

Timothy had his own thoughts running through his brain. He kept thinking there was no way Jessica was his cousin. He couldn't have an attraction to a relative. Then the horrific thought crossed his mind: *what if they were cousins? Did that make him sick because he might have a crush on his potential cousin?* It turned his stomach so much that he couldn't finish eating.

They all got hotel rooms for the night because, by the time they received the results, it would be too late to drive back to the Hamptons and Gardiners Island. While at the hotel, Arthur received a phone call from the lab.

When they got back to the hospital and up to Alexandria's room, the lab tech was already in there, going over the results with her. She had tears streaming down her face. She quickly wiped them away as they walked in.

"Arthur, we must draw up a new will immediately. I am leaving my entire estate, including Gardiners Island to my two sole heirs, Jessica Greenhall, the daughter of the late Richard Gardiner, and James 'Jimmy' Driscoll, the son of the late Benjamin Timmons (Gardiner)."

Jessica went numb. This was the moment she had been waiting for the last six years. She had family. Two members that were in the same room as her currently. What she never expected was to become an heiress to a million-dollar fortune and a private island. She finally knew who her biological parents were!

Jimmy seemed stunned. He knew about his adoption. He never questioned who his biological parents had been. Having the information now seemed a betrayal to his adoptive parents. He couldn't believe he was an heir to a fortune and the island he grew up on, too.

The news elated Timothy! He now knew 100% without a doubt there was no relation to Jessica, which meant he was free to pursue his romantic feelings toward her. He walked up to her and wrapped his arms around her. Taking his cue, she wrapped her arms around his neck and planted a kiss right on his lips. She pulled away.

"We will continue this later in private. Right now, I have a family to get acquainted with."

Chapter Twelve

Charades

Richard returned to the manor house after a few weeks of business trips to find Mary had all of his things moved to another bedroom furthest from hers. He honestly didn't mind, as he was planning on doing just that when he got home, anyway. All pretenses about a blissful marriage were gone now as well.

Alexandria was furious with Richard for filing for divorce and he knew he was going to have to work really hard at smoothing things over with her. He would talk to Benjamin about that sailing trip and see if Alexandria and her family could join them. Some quality family time might just do the trick.

He called up Benjamin and asked to meet him at one of the local bars to talk. Benjamin agreed and that afternoon they sat there laughing and having a good ole time drinking some beers. Casual observers would have thought they were best friends. They were both good at putting up the false façade.

When they left the bar, they shook hands and patted each other on the shoulder, as good friends would. As each of them returned to their prospective cars, though, they each had a wry smile on their face thinking they had just pulled a fast one over the other.

Benjamin got back to his house and quickly made a phone call. The conversation with the other person was short and to the point.

"We need to meet tomorrow. Usual spot. Usual time."

After, he went down to his dock and boarded his sailboat.

He loved his boat; it was his pride and joy. The twinge of sadness he felt when he thought about not owning it soon crept over him. Telling himself it would be all worth it in the end. He would have something so much better, his Mary.

Back at the manor house, Richard was walking in the door as Mary was heading up the stairs to go to her room. Part of him felt guilty. He knew he hadn't been faithful in their marriage, either. Then he remembered the ultimate betrayal Mary had pulled, making him believe she was pregnant with his child and that their child had died. That was unforgivable.

Mary didn't even look back down the stairs when she heard the door open. She knew it would be Richard. She wondered what had happened to them both. They had been so in love when they first married. They were the talk of the Hamptons and everyone aspired to be like them. Now, they would be the laughingstock, thanks to him and his blasted divorce. Not if she could help it, though. She was still hoping to get out of this mess without a tarnished reputation and hold on to the manor house and the island.

In Connecticut, Mira was helping her boss, Mr. Gilman, set up his new office. It had taken a couple of weeks to find a suitable place, however, he finally found the perfect setup. Mira was just happy to be back working and doing what she loved, learning about the law. They had ruled the fire arson. However, there were no leads. Richard gave an anonymous tip to the police about Benjamin Timmons, yet they had no evidence linking him to the actual fire.

When they questioned Benjamin about the fire, he was very cooperative. He had admitted to having a heated argument with Mr. Gilman earlier in the day. He had also admitted that he had gone back to apologize when he came upon the fire scene. After the police had left him, Benjamin was fuming.

The thought that someone that knew who he was seeing him at the fire bothered him. He had noticed no one who was familiar. He tried to remember back to that day and he tried to remember if there was anyone else in the waiting room when he left. All he could remember was his anger and storming out.

He didn't trust Mr. Gilman, the slimy sleaze ball of a lawyer that Alexandria had forced Mary to work with for the adoption of their son. A son he never got the chance to meet or hold. He had no say in the entire process.

Alexandria had all the proof she needed to take them both down and ruin their lives, yet she hurt them in the worst way possible to save her precious family name. Oh, how he hated her for the hurt she caused Mary. Soon, he hoped he could repay the favor.

On May 2, 1994, Richard made a trip to Connecticut to see Mira. It was a special day as Mira turned 18. Mira had told her parents she was taking the day off and going to the beach as a cover for meeting up with Richard and spending the day with him. They took a small road trip to Newport, Rhode Island, where they figured it would be safe for them to have an actual date finally.

They enjoyed the day as any normal couple would. Holding hands and stopping for a kiss or two as they walked together and did some sightseeing. They toured some mansions and in one garden of Hammersmith Farm, Richard knelt down on one knee and proposed to Mira.

Of course, she said yes. They were so happy together and they both noted the irony of getting engaged at a former Kennedy estate and her having the last name of a Kennedy.

The proposal overjoyed Mira. The gorgeous ring Richard had picked out overwhelmed her. She knew she was going to have to be very careful not to wear it in public just yet. For today, though, she was enjoying being the future Mrs. Richard Gardiner.

On the way back to Connecticut, Richard stopped at a quaint roadside motel and rented a room. They had never shared a bed. It had always been too risky for him to be seen with an underage girl. Now that Mira was eighteen, they were safe.

Before Mira entered the room, Richard set it up with candles, roses, and even a bottle of champagne. When she entered, the romantic gestures he had made filled her with such joy. As Richard shut the door behind them, he stepped forward and embraced her in a passionate kiss. The fire she had felt the first time they had kissed that night in the gazebo raged fiercely in her veins. They spent the rest of the afternoon and early evening wrapped up in the sheets, making passionate love. When they parted ways later that evening, Mira wanted Richard to know exactly how she felt.

"You have made me the happiest woman in the world. Today was the best day ever! I love you forever, Richard."

"I Love you too, Mira."

By the time Richard got back home to the manor house, it was late evening. Mary was already in her room for the night, although little did he know she was not alone. As he walked down the hallway, he heard a male's voice. At first, it startled him, and then he just smiled, because he realized they were getting bold. He eavesdropped on the conversation and he was very glad he did. After overhearing their plans, he had to figure out what he was going to do next. They were playing for keeps, and he had to as well. A few days later, he visited Mira again and told her of their plans. Their plans horrified her.

"Richard, you can't go on that trip! You can't let Alexandria and her family go either!"

"I can't back out of the trip. They will suspect something is up. I am their primary target. I will do my best to make sure Alexandria and her family don't go, even if it means having her hate me for the rest of our lives. Don't worry, we will use their plans to our advantage. It will all work out."

Richard hugged Mira tight and ran his hands down her hair.

Of course, the trip they were talking about was the sailing trip that Benjamin and Richard had been planning on taking on Mother's day. Since Alexandria had been the only mother Richard had ever known, he thought it would be nice to take her and her family out sailing with Benjamin. Now, he had to get Alexandria so mad at him she would refuse to and refuse to allow her family to go. He had to keep them safe at all costs. The alternative was too awful to even think about.

Richard knew all too well how to rile up Alexandria, so he set himself to call her.

"Hey Alexandria, It's Richard. I hope I am not catching you at a bad time. I need to talk to you about my divorce from Mary and the future of the Island."

"Hello Richard, I am kind of busy with the business. What is it now with the divorce? I hope there are no snags and it is quick and quiet. You know we don't need any bad press. Have you relinquished your half of the island totally to me?"

"Well, not exactly. I want to keep my half of the island and actually, Mira and I want to get married at the manor house gazebo as soon as my divorce is final. Mira deserves a big, beautiful wedding. I want to give that to her."

Richard then held his breath for the fury he knew would come.

"What? Are you crazy?? A big wedding, immediately after they complete your divorce, to an eighteen-year-old!! The press will have a field day!! No way, no how!!! And you want to keep your half of the island! What happened to you wanting to live a life of seclusion after your divorce?"

There it was, the fury, the response he knew he would elicit. After a few more back-and-forth remarks and no compromising. Alexandria told him in no uncertain terms would she or her family be going sailing with him on Mother's Day and that if he went with the big wedding on the island, she would disown him.

Hanging up the phone, it satisfied Richard that his plan had worked and at least his family would be safe from Mary's and Benjamin's wrathful plans. He felt guilty making Alexandria mad, and he made an appointment with Mr. Gilman to discuss drawing up legal documents to give Alexandria his portion of the island. It wasn't much for the pain she would experience soon, but he knew it would console her somewhat.

Mother's Day morning came and Richard headed to the dock where Benjamin kept his sailboat moored at. As he walked towards the vessel, he saw Benjamin, who waved enthusiastically towards him. Stepping onto the boat, he saw his three cousins sitting comfortably, ready to set sail.

"What are you three doing here? I thought your mom said you all weren't coming."

Richard's heart raced with panic. David Jr., Alexandria's oldest son, was quick to explain to his cousin their presence on the boat.

"Mom isn't coming, but the rest of us decided she can stew in her anger. We are not missing out on a fabulous sailing trip. Dad is below deck putting his things in his bunk."

Richard felt sick. *No, this is not how this is supposed to go! Alexandria will never forgive me.* He didn't know what to do. He couldn't call off the trip and couldn't contact Mira. Richard felt helpless to stop what was going to happen.

"What's the matter there, bud? You are looking a little green around the gills? Everything okay."

Benjamin patted Richard on the back.

"I am fine. Must have eaten something that didn't quite agree with me."

"Glad you all could make it. It's a shame Alexandria couldn't come. It will be a pleasant couple of days for sailing."

Benjamin finished his sentence and then started getting ready to set sail. Richard knew there was no turning back. He prayed God would forgive him and that someday Alexandria would, too.

That evening after dinner, Richard went to his bunk early, with the pretense of feeling under the weather. The others stayed up later, drinking and playing cards. He couldn't sleep. He prayed the others could.

In the morning, news spread fast about the tragic explosion that engulfed the sailboat, killing all souls on board. It devastated Alexandria, her entire family gone in one fell swoop. Mary was told of the death of her husband and she fainted. Everyone in the Hamptons felt sorry for both Alexandria and Mary. Tragedy always seemed to befall the Gardiners.

Chapter Thirteen

Family

Jessica sat there getting to know both Alexandria and Jimmy in Alexandria's hospital room until the nurses kicked them out. There were hugs and tears as they said goodbye. There were also promises of staying in touch.

The four visitors went back to their hotel rooms to get a good night's sleep. Jessica couldn't believe the events that had transpired over the course of the last three days. She unlocked her hotel room door and went inside. Shortly after, there was a knock at her door.

It was Timothy. She smiled and opened the door. As she did, he scooped her up, placed her gently on the bed and began making passionate love to her. Jessica lay breathless in his arms. She had never felt so content and happy in her life.

Timothy rolled up on one side and looked down at Jessica.

"Will you marry me, Jessica?"

"What?"

Jessica bolted upright in bed.

"I know it sounds crazy. We only met four days ago, but I know I love you and I want to spend the rest of my life with you."

"Timothy, I love you too. I am just overwhelmed by everything that has occurred over the last few days. Let's take it one day at a time and see how it goes, okay?"

"I will wait till the end of time for you, Jessica."

Timothy sat up, pulled Jessica towards him, and kissed her gently on the lips. Electricity ran through Jessica and she succumbed to round two of passionate lovemaking. They fell asleep in each other's arms.

In the morning, Jessica and Timothy joined Jimmy and Arthur for a farewell breakfast. Jimmy would head back to Gardiners Island to help with investigating the accidents that had occurred. He also had to give the news to his adoptive parents that he knew who his biological parents were. Then there was the matter of confronting his birth mother.

Arthur would stay near Alexandria until her release from the hospital. He would also make sure things at her business ran smoothly while she was away recovering from her injuries.

Timothy and Jessica would head back to East Hampton so Jessica could get her car and head back to Connecticut. Timothy would head back to his place in Riverhead. On the drive back, they would have plenty of time to discuss their blooming relationship and how to make it work long distance. Each of them had very successful careers that could take them anywhere in the world at a moment's notice. It would be challenging, however, they both felt it was worth trying to make it work.

At the manor house, Mary was pacing back and forth in the parlor. The revelations of the day before still reeling in her mind. That Richard was bold enough to bring his mistress to the island infuriated her! Right under her nose, too! She couldn't be mad at Jessica. An innocent victim in all of this. She was also the only potential heir to Gardiners Island if, in fact, she was the child of Richard and his mistress. So Mary needed to stay on her good side if she wanted to remain in the manor house and keep her lifestyle on the island.

Then there was the matter of the phone call from Jimmy about the three accidents over the last few days and the finding of the passageway. He had changed his mind and was leaning more towards the accidents being planned and attempted murder. He would work closely with the State Police. Everyone on the island was being interviewed. She couldn't think of anyone on the island that would want to kill Alexandria. They all knew that if she died, without an heir, they would turn Gardiners Island over to the Town and it would become a nature preserve. It made no sense.

As for someone wanting to hurt Jessica. The only people on the island that knew about her finding the photograph of Richard's mistress were Stella and Betty. They had found her sobbing on the floor the night she found it. They were loyal to her, they always had been, but she didn't think either of them would have hurt Jessica. Did Stella tell Jimmy? Jimmy had been very critical of Jessica and her writer friend, Timothy, the whole time they were here. No, she couldn't see him hurting her, either.

There were other workers on the island and their families. None that she was that close to and would know her business. At least not anymore. She couldn't think of anyone or any reason anyone would want to hurt either Jessica or Alexandria. Just thinking about it all was giving her a headache, and she left the investigation up to Jimmy and the police.

Jimmy walked into the kitchen of the manor house and found his Mom cooking. He sat down at the counter and poured himself a cup of coffee. It was difficult for him to start the conversation about his biological parents. He didn't want to hurt her.

"What's got you stewing, Jimmy?"

She could always tell when something was weighing heavily on her boy's mind.

Jimmy smiled, just like her to always know. She wasn't his biological mom, but she was in tuned to him since day one.

"Well Mom, I don't know how to tell you and I don't want to hurt your feelings. I love you and dad so much. I found out who my biological parents are. It wasn't my idea to find out. There was a reason, though."

Stella dropped the spoon she was holding onto the stove and turned to face her son.

"I knew this day might someday come. I've tried to prepare myself for you to come and ask if it was okay. The expectation was never for you to find out first and then tell us. I am not hurt. You have a right to know where your roots are from. Your father and I know nothing about your birth parents. Ms. Alexandria knew we had been trying for years to have a child of our own and she knew an adoption lawyer, Mr. Gilman. He found us you."

"So you do not know who my biological parents are?"

"No, Jimmy. I never really cared much to know. You were ours from day one. The timing was really difficult on Ms. Mary though as she lost her only child the same day you were born. You helped her heal, though. She always loved doting on you."

"Yeah, about that. Mom, I need you to have a seat before I tell you what I found out."

Jimmy pulled out a chair and helped the only mother he had ever known sit down. He then told her everything he had found out. When he told her about Benjamin actually being Richard's half-brother and that he was now one of two heirs to Gardiners Island, Stella gasped.

"Does Ms. Mary know?"

"No, Ms. Alexandria does not want her to know about Benjamin's lineage or that I stand to inherit half of the island. I can tell her I am her biological son, however, until we find out who pushed her down the stairs, who attempted to drown Jessica, and who rigged the ATV throttle to stick, its safer that no one else knows."

"My lips are sealed, Son. I do not want you to be hurt. So Jessica was Richard's daughter? Isn't that something? That's why she looked just like his mistress. It's crazy you were born on the same day, too."

"She is pretty cool, Mom. I guess it's cool to have a cousin my age. Well, I guess I better go track down Ms. Mary and have a talk with her and then get to work."

Jimmy got up, kissed his mom on the forehead, and went to look for Mary within the manor house. He found out from Betty that Mary was up in her bedroom resting, so he checked out the passageway the State Police had found in the linen closet. He couldn't believe he missed it when he did his investigation.

After coming down the back staircase, he headed outside to where they stored the ATVs. The police had taken the one Jessica had crashed on. They wanted to examine it for prints. He found Samuel, the resident island handyman, working on one tractor.

"Hi Samuel, need a hand there?"

"No thanks, kid, I got it."

"How was it around here yesterday while I was gone?"

"Besides the police hounding everyone about those broads' accidents, it's been quiet."

"They weren't accidents Samuel, the police, and now I believe they were intentional."

"That's crazy man. Just clumsy, accident-prone broads, that's all. How is the old bat, anyway?"

"Samuel, I know you don't like Ms. Alexandria. However, calling her an old bat is just plain disrespectful. She is stable. They think she will recover fully, although it will be a long road."

"Good for her. Now, if you don't mind, I work better without distractions."

Jimmy left Samuel working on the tractor and went back to the manor house to see if Mary had come down from her room yet. Martin informed him she had, and she was sitting in the parlor. As he walked into the parlor, he found Mary sitting on the sofa, looking at an old photo album. The album had *The Summer of 1991* written on the spine.

"Good evening, Ms. Mary. May I come in and have a word with you?"

Startled, Mary looked up and smiled at Jimmy. He always brought comfort to her. She closed the album and gestured for him to sit down next to her.

"Of course Jimmy. I always have time for you."

Jimmy took a seat next to her and searched his mind for how to start the conversation with her. Finally, he just figured he would be straightforward.

"Ms. Mary, as you know, my parents adopted me. I just recently found out who my biological parents are."

"Yes, Jimmy, I am aware of your adoption. Your mom and dad have always loved you as their own, though. Why would you want to know who your biological parents are? Aren't you afraid you might hurt your mom and dad with that information?"

"Well, I already told mom. She was surprisingly okay with me knowing. She was just as surprised to know who they are."

"Why are you talking to me about this then, Jimmy? I figured you were coming to me for advice about whether you should tell your mom or dad."

"Ms. Mary, or should I say, Mom, I am coming to you because I am your son. The one that they forced you to give up for adoption because my father was not Richard."

"Oh my. I am so sorry, my Son!"

Mary hugged Jimmy and wept. Jimmy explained how he had found out the night before from Alexandria. She had kept the DNA records from the amniocenteses and the lab could check his DNA against it. He also confirmed her suspicions about Jessica being Richards's daughter. Jimmy kept the part about Benjamin and Richard being half-brothers from her. At this point, he didn't know who to trust. If the island was the motive for the attempted murders, he needed to keep his identity as an heir secret.

Chapter Fourteen

Memorial service

It was a few days after the tragic sailing accident that they held the memorial service for all that lost their lives that fateful day. They held the service at the family cemetery, where they attached an engraved plaque to a lighthouse monument with the names of the dearly departed. There was nothing to be buried since they found no remains.

Mary's attire consisting of black clothes from head to toe, including a hat with a veil covering her face. Alexandria's formal wear was also black from head to toe, minus the hat and veil. Both widows were distraught with grief. Hundreds of mourners attended the service.

Some people who the two women knew well, and others from the community who just came out to support the grieving wives. Many of Richard's friends and business acquaintances attended to pay their respects. Including the Kennedys, the Greenhalls, and Mr. Gilman.

Mira gave her condolences to both women alongside her parents. She also offered to watch little Jessica for the Greenhalls which they were more than grateful for. Seeing her daughter lifted the sadness of the day from Mira's heart. Richard was gone forever.

Lena and her parents were there, too. Lena caught up with Mira and walked with her and Jessica through the Gardens. She felt so sorry for her best friend. She knew with Richard gone, this would most likely be the last time Mira saw her daughter. Mira had told Lena how she had found the adoptive parent's identity and how she and Richard had planned at times to see her under the guise of other things.

As the afternoon turned to evening, the mourners thinned out and Mira's parents were ready to go. She said goodbye to the Greenhalls and Jessica, then got in the car. The long ride home was torturous. As soon as she got into her room and closed her door, she fell on her bed and cried herself to sleep.

Mary, being surrounded by people, was comforting to her all day. She barely could remember all the names and faces. She recognized some. Others, she did not know who they were. Probably business associates of Richards. One such gentleman, she couldn't remember the name he introduced himself as, wore a jet-black suit and sunglasses. He had jet-black hair and his voice cracked as he gave the two women his condolences. He must have been a close associate because he seemed pretty distraught over the loss of Richard.

She tried to seek him out again to make sure he was okay and to find out his name, however; he had vanished among the mourners. Later, she would look at the book that mourners had written in to see if any of the names jumped out at her as his.

Those wishing to comfort her as well surrounded Alexandria. They couldn't believe she lost her entire family in one tragic accident. The more people said it to her, though, the more she had wished she had gone on the trip and perished too. She didn't know how she was going to live without her husband, her three children, and her cousin, who was more like a son.

She, too, couldn't remember the names and faces of all those who came to share in her grief. There was one gentleman that never approached her or Mary. He had stayed in the distance, on the edge of the mourners. Dressed in a black suit, as most of the male mourners had. The only difference was he wore a cowboy hat, sunglasses, a bandana around his neck, and black driving gloves on his hands.

When Alexandria went to look for him to approach him, he had vanished. She would never know who he was or how he knew her family. She was just grateful for the outpouring of support she and Mary were receiving. They were both going to need it to get through their grief. If they ever would.

She had decided it was best for her to stay at the manor house for a few weeks. The thought of going home to an empty penthouse apartment in the city was just too much to bear. Then there was the matter of settling Richard's estate. She knew that would not go over well with Mary. Richard had only made the most recent changes to his will after filing for divorce. She knew Mary would try to contest it.

Mary was exhausted. Mentally, physically, and more so emotionally. She made her way upstairs to her bedroom and soon found herself fast asleep.

Alexandria barely slept and soon the sun came up and it was time to go down for breakfast. She didn't want to get out of bed. Closing her eyes tight, she tried wishing away the nightmare she was living. When she opened them and realized the nightmare was still her reality, she broke down into a sob. She didn't want to live without her beloved husband and children. Why did she let Richard push her buttons? She should have been on that boat with them all. She should have perished along with them.

Mary awoke feeling a bit refreshed from her sleep. Stella would serve breakfast shortly, so she dragged herself out of bed and got herself showered and dressed. She truly felt sad at the loss of Richard and the others. The only consolation was she could remain here on the island, in her manor house, and keep her reputation intact with the Hampton elites. The divorce never went through. As Richard's spouse, she would inherit his share of the island.

Mira awoke the next morning. She got up, showered, and got dressed. In a few weeks, she would be graduating. Mr. Gilman had helped land her a secretarial job at a law office close to Harvard. On this particular day, her parents were driving up with her to find an off-campus apartment close to both school and work.

She had convinced them she would focus on her schoolwork more if she had an apartment all to herself instead of sharing one or having to live in the dorm. They were a little leery, especially because of her past. In the end, she used reasoning to persuade them. She used the fact that for the rest of her High School years; she didn't have a boyfriend, she worked, and she received top honors. It was hard for them to dispute any of it. They joked she would make an excellent lawyer someday.

When only Mary came down for breakfast, Stella and Betty went upstairs to check on Alexandria. They found her sobbing on her bed. They helped calm her down before they coaxed her to take a shower and get dressed. When she was done, they escorted her down for breakfast and doted on her more than usual. Mary had told Martin she was going for a walk on the beach. They felt sorry for both women and did what they could to help them in their time of grief.

Mary came back from her walk and she looked calmer and less distraught than the day before. To cheer up Alexandria, she tried to suggest that she, too, should take a walk down by the beach. That it might clear her sadness and bring some peace. However, Alexandria just went upstairs to her room and locked the door.

She didn't want to be bothered and certainly didn't want to walk on the beach and see the water that her loved ones perished in. She didn't want to be coaxed into eating or dressing. Her will to live was gone.

Mira and her parents found the perfect apartment for her. It was within walking distance of the school and her new job. The best feature for her parents was it was a second-floor apartment, which meant less of a chance of anyone breaking in through the windows. They were still nervous about their baby girl living all by herself in a big city. She assured them she was going to be fine. They put a deposit down on the apartment and made plans to move her in two days after graduation.

It took several days before Alexandria came out of her depression. Everyone gave her space to grieve in her own way. Stella had been leaving food trays at her bedroom door at mealtimes. Each day, she noticed that more and more food was being eaten. Alexandria would take a bath daily and when she did, Betty would freshen up her sheets and straighten up the room for her.

It was a Friday morning when Alexandria joined Mary for breakfast. Mary was looking chipper, as if nothing had happened. While Alexandria was still looking like she had gone through hell and back. As Mary finished her breakfast, she left the room and went for her daily walk down to the beach. Alexandria still could not bring herself to go down by the water. She did, though, manage to take a walk through the gardens and to the gazebo.

As she did, she remembered how her children and Richard played in the gardens as kids. They played hide and seek. And of course, their favorite game was to pretend the gazebo was Captain Kidd's pirate ship, and they were pirates. She smiled, remembering how they loved the island and playing amongst the many gardens. It brought her a little peace.

When she went back into the house, she was a bit surprised to see Mr. Gilman with Martin in the foyer. Until she remembered that today was the reading of Richard's will. There was no way to prepare for this. They sat in the parlor and waited for Mary to get back from her walk on the beach. Alexandria knew, no walk on the beach would prepare Mary for what she was about to be told. Part of her felt sorry for her. The other part of her didn't.

Mary came back from her walk, looking even happier than the day before. She sat down in the parlor along with Alexandria and Mr. Gilman and prepared to hear her husband's will read.

"Ladies, I know this has not been a simple time for either of you. As executor of Richard's will, it is my duty to see that I carry his wishes out. This is never a straightforward task. There will always be those who have high expectations that do not materialize."

Alexandria shifted in her seat. She knew he was trying to soften the blow to Mary. Mary seemed to sit on the edge of her seat and was quickly becoming impatient with Mr. Gilman's monologue.

"Can we just get on with it? Just read the will and be done. How difficult of a job can it be?"

"As you wish, Mary."

Mr. Gilman read Richard's will. Mary sat intently listening until he read the Disposition of the property part. *Had she heard that right? She couldn't have?*

"Could you please read that again? I am not sure I heard you correctly."

"You heard it correctly, Mary. Richard bequeathed his share of the island to his cousin, Alexandria. His business and personal assets are to be liquidated and then divided up between you and the St. Catherine's Preparatory Scholarship fund."

"WAIT, I don't get his share of the island? I don't get to live in the manor house? Where will I live? This can't be. We were still married! We did not complete the divorce!"

Mary became irate at the revelation she would lose the island and the manor house along with it. She stormed out of the parlor and out of the house. This was not how it was supposed to be. She wasn't supposed to lose everything.

Chapter Fifteen

Home

Jessica pulled down her driveway and was so happy to be home. It had been a whirlwind couple of days. On the way back to her car, she had made plans with Timothy for him to come out to her house in a week. They needed to coordinate his article with the pictures she took. The week would give him time to compose the article and her time to develop the pictures.

She smiled to herself, just thinking about Timothy. What a difference it was to feel feelings for someone without the thought of whether there was any relation to you. Finding out who her biological parents were, and Timothy was no relation, was freeing. She thought, *this is what true love must feel like*. Whatever it was, she liked how it felt.

Unpacking her car went quicker than usual, since she had a little more pep in her step just thinking about him. By the time she got everything in the house and brought her gear into her photography studio, it was dinnertime. She looked in her freezer and found leftovers she had put in there before she left. While she waited for her meal to heat in the microwave, she put one album on that she picked up at the antique store.

She laughed to herself as the song *You're The One That I Want* sung by Olivia Newton-John and John Travolta from the *Grease* album blared from her record player. She fantasized she was Olivia Newton-John and Timothy was John Travolta as she danced and sang in her kitchen.

Meanwhile, back in Riverhead, Timothy was busy getting to work on his article. The sooner he finished it, the sooner he could see Jessica again. He could not believe how he felt. He had never felt this strongly about any woman before. Then again, he also never was 100% sure he was no relation to any of his past love interests like he was now with Jessica. This was unfamiliar territory, and he loved it. He ordered himself a pizza and once it came; he sat down to get to work.

Jimmy had a pleasant talk with his dad, John Driscoll. He was very understanding and not hurt by the information Jimmy had told him. The man had been the head of security on the island for thirty years. He had just recently retired and was proud that Jimmy had become his replacement.

Arthur sat faithfully by Alexandria's bedside. She seemed to do well, and he was relieved that his friend should be okay. As she was resting, he nodded off, too.

After dinner, Jessica took her film into her darkroom to develop. She still used some old 35mm cameras when she went on assignments along with using the digital counterparts. She found sometimes the older film cameras were better for capturing certain perspectives. This was the most time-consuming process of her job.

She was immersed in her work when the ringing of her cell phone jolted her. Recognizing the name of the caller, she smiled to herself.

"We haven't been apart for more than a day and you are already calling?"

"I needed to hear your voice and also take a writing break. Figuring you might need a pause, too. I know we are both workaholics."

"It is nice to hear your voice, and yes, I probably should take a rest once in a while."

"See, I am already so in tune with your needs."

She chuckled and remembered the night before and said to herself, *Oh; you are definitely in tune with all my needs.*

"Yeah, if you are so tuned into my needs, what do I need right now?"

"Since we are so much alike, I would have to say you are probably needing a repeat of last night."

As Timothy finished his sentence, he realized just how much he really needed a repeat of the night before.

"Ah, you would be correct, Timothy, however we both agreed to get our work done first, then we can meet up."

Jessica paused.

"Ah shit, power just went out."

"Jessica, are you okay?"

"Yes, just a typical Preston power outage. Hang on while I go outside and start my generator."

"Okay, take the phone with you just in case."

"In case of what? I do this all the time."

"Jessica, please."

"Okay, okay. Not sure what the fuss is all about."

Timothy listened intently as Jessica made her way through her back door and outside. As she walked, he could hear her breathing. He could hear her put the phone down. He heard something that sounded like a switch, and then he heard the roar of the generator.

"I am back, all set. I have power now."

"You are a pretty remarkable woman, Jessica."

"Thanks, I don't see myself as remarkable. I see myself as self-sufficient."

"Now that you have power and you are back in the house. I will let you get back to work. So we can see each other sooner. Goodnight, Jessica. I love you."

"Goodnight, Timothy. I love you too."

Jessica was just about to go back into her darkroom when she heard her generator sputter and then go quiet. Then came the darkness. She turned her flashlight back on and made her way back outside to the generator. It had gas. She couldn't figure out why it had stopped. Until she went to hit the switch to start it again. It was then she realized the switch was off. She quickly turned it back on and scanned her surroundings. She couldn't see anyone or hear any movement.

Going back into the house, she went straight to her gun safe and took her pistol out. She loaded it and walked back out onto the porch. Scanning the perimeter of the woods, she still couldn't see or hear anyone. She took the safety off her gun, pulled back the slide, and fired a round into the darkness.

"That's a warning shot! I am armed, willing, and able to protect myself! I don't know who you are or why you are playing games. Leave me alone or you will face the consequences."

She walked back into the house, locked all her doors, and went back to work. The thought crossed her mind to call Timothy back and tell him someone had shut down her generator, but she decided that would just cause him to worry. She brought her pistol with her wherever she went in the house for the rest of the night. Even when she went to bed, it was within her reach, in case she needed it.

Jessica was glad her dad had taught her how to use a gun at an early age. She knew she shouldn't have fired the shot into the darkness. It was reckless of her to do so. She never felt as vulnerable as she did earlier though when she realized someone had turned off her generator. It was a feeling she wasn't familiar with and she didn't like feeling that way. Firing the shot gave her control over the situation. It had enabled her to take her power back.

Thinking about her dad got her thinking about her biological parents. She had names, and she had faces. Sadly, her biological father had died when she was about two years old. Her mother, though, as far as anyone knew, was still alive. She would do some research on the genealogy website in the morning. She had her name. It was a start. Jessica drifted off to sleep.

The next morning, Jimmy was making his morning rounds on the ATV around the island. He saw nothing out of the ordinary. The rickety ferry boat was just docking, and he recognized Samuel's truck. He must have had to go onto the mainland to get parts, Jimmy thought to himself. Samuel was always fixing something around the island, so it wasn't unusual for him to go back and forth to the mainland.

Jimmy hadn't slept well the night before. He felt bad about not believing Jessica at first and for suspecting Timothy of taking advantage of the situation. He could not think of anyone on the island with the motive to hurt either Jessica or Alexandria. An outsider getting on the island was nearly impossible as well. None of it made sense to him. He was missing something, but he didn't know what.

Timothy woke up and got straight to work on his article again. He hadn't been able to really get much done after his phone call with Jessica.

He just couldn't get her out of his mind. It was difficult for him to not call her. She was right, though. They needed to focus on their work first, then they could meet up again. Just the thought of holding her in his arms again drove him crazy.

Awakening to the sputtering of her generator again, Jessica bolted upright and reached for her pistol. Realizing it was daytime already made her relax a bit because that meant the generator was most likely out of gas. She got dressed, made sure she had her pistol, and went outside to check on the generator.

It indeed had run out of gas. Before refilling it, she flipped the transfer switch to see if they had restored the power. Thankfully, it had been. She looked around to see if there was any evidence of the person who shut off her generator. After three full walks around the house and finding nothing, she went inside to have breakfast.

Arthur awoke in his hotel room with the grim realization he was going to have a long day making notifications. He had gotten very little sleep the night before. The beeps and alarms that went off when Alexandria had gone into cardiac arrest had startled him from his nap the evening before. The scene that unfolded before him was something he would never forget. Nurses and doctors rushed into the room to revive her. Someone ushered him into the hallway. He still couldn't believe she was gone.

As Jessica opened up her laptop and typed in the genealogy website, she looked at the photos Mary had given her. She still couldn't believe she had spent time with her biological parents as a child. Of course, she was too young to actually remember, but the photographs were proof.

When she typed in Mira Kennedy, tons of information popped up. Now to narrow it down. She knew Mira was sixteen in 1992. That meant she would have been born in 1976. Jessica assumed Mira was born in Connecticut as well. A birth record for a Mira Kennedy popped up with a birth date of May 2, 1976. She saved it as a potential match. Next she found a marriage record for a Mira Kennedy to a Mathew Brockton in Cambridge, MA, October 5, 1994. Another maybe. She had leads. Cambridge wasn't that far. She could make a day trip and do some research, but first she needed to get her work done. She powered down her laptop and went to work downloading and editing her digital photographs on her computer in her studio.

Timothy felt good about getting the first draft written. He definitely felt he had extra motivation with this assignment. At the suggestion of Arthur, he requested to work with Jessica. He knew her photography work was top-notch and was a fan of her work, but he never expected to be attracted to her. A break was in order and he heated some leftover pizza and cracked open a beer.

Finishing his noontime ride around the island, Jimmy approached the rickety ferry dock and noticed the ferry incoming with Arthur's car onboard. He got a bad feeling in the pit of his stomach. Arthur had said he planned on staying close to Alexandria, especially until they found out who had pushed her. Him being on the ferry meant one of two things. Either the police figured out who had pushed her or she had taken a turn for the worse. His bet was on the latter of the two.

Chapter Sixteen

The move

Mira was excitedly packing up her room into boxes. She had graduated the night before and would move into her new apartment within the next couple of days. Her parents still didn't like the fact she would live on her own. They felt she was too young, however; they knew their daughter was stubborn as a mule.

Mary had gone on strike and had locked herself in her room. She wasn't leaving her house and island. She was contesting the will and set out for a long, drawn-out fight for her share of the island. Stella and Betty resumed the routine they had used with Alexandria during her depression.

As for Alexandria, she had snapped back from her depths of despair and had moved back to her penthouse in the city. She left Mary to wallow in her misery. The business she and her husband had built needed her to be strong and take charge, so that is exactly what she did.

The days flew by till it was moving day. Mira packed boxes in her car and her dad helped the movers pack her furniture into the moving truck. They assured him he didn't need to help, but he insisted.

Mira's parents followed the moving truck while Mira followed behind them in her own car. She felt such a sense of adventure and freedom. Anything was possible in her mind. Her life was just beginning. She looked down at her left hand and smiled at the ring she had slipped on before driving.

Traffic was light, and they made it to her apartment in what seemed like no time at all. When Mira stepped out of the car, she stood there for a moment, looking up at the apartment building. She took a deep breath, slipped off the ring, put it in her pocket, and closed the door. The sounds of the city were invigorating to her. Cars honking, kids playing on the sidewalks, and taxi cabs driving by. The city was full of life and she felt alive with it.

The movers and her parents helped her get her things to her apartment. Her mom ran to the grocery store to stock her cabinets while her dad helped to rearrange the second hand living room furniture a half a dozen times until Mira decided she liked it the way they had first had it. Her parents were just about to leave when there was a knock on the apartment door.

When Mira answered the door, there was a man holding a pizza and a bottle of soda, smiling from ear to ear.

"Oh, we didn't order a pizza."

Mira said to the man as her parents peered over her shoulder.

"Indeed, you didn't. It is my welcome to the building gift. My name is Mathew Brockton and I live across the hall. I saw you moving in today and wanted to introduce myself and welcome you."

Mira's father ushered Mathew in and introduced himself and his wife. He let Mira do her own introductions. Mira thanked him for the pizza and offered for him to join them in eating it. Mathew declined the invitation, saying he didn't want to intrude, and that he had already eaten his dinner.

After Mathew had left, Mira and her parents sat and ate dinner together.

"Nice fellow there. Seems like quite the gentleman."

"I don't know. He seems so much older than Mira. I don't know how I feel about her living across the hall from a single man."

"Geez, Mom, he doesn't seem that much older than me. Besides, as dad said, he seemed very nice and gentlemanly."

They said their goodbyes after dinner and tears flowed down her mom's face. Mira couldn't believe the big deal her mom was making over leaving her until she remembered the last time she saw her own daughter. She hugged her mom tight and told her she would be fine.

Shortly after her parents left, she heard another knock on the door. When she opened it, there was Mathew standing there with a popped bag of microwave popcorn and a movie. She smiled and invited him in. She spent the first night in her first apartment on a first date with Mathew Brockton.

Coming out of her office, it surprised Alexandria to see Mr. Gilman and another man standing at her receptionist's desk.

"Mr. Gilman, did we have a meeting I forgot about?"

"No, Alexandria. I am turning over my practice to Arthur Brockton, my nephew. It's time for me to retire and enjoy life to the fullest."

Alexandria welcomed both men into her office, where she got to know her new lawyer. It was Arthur who brought up the workable compromise with Mary. Alexandria could let Mary live on the island in the manor house until she remarried or died. She agreed, except she added one clause. The clause stated that in the event Alexandria died and Mary was still unwed and living, she would have to vacate the island because it would revert over to the town as a nature preserve.

The phone call with her lawyer wasn't exactly what she expected, however Mary thought it was a suitable compromise. She took a walk down by the beach to think more about it and the ramifications. When she came back, she called her lawyer and said she would agree to the compromise.

Mira started work the Monday following her move. Mathew surprised her at her door when she got home and invited her over to his apartment for dinner. She accepted. The candlelight dinner he had prepared mesmerized her. They ate and talked about her first day. She told him how much she enjoyed her job and couldn't wait to start school in the fall. He talked about his business dealings and his plans for expansion.

After dinner, they watched another movie together. Mathew put his arm around her and she snuggled right into his chest. It was comforting to just curl up and watch a movie in his arms. She closed her eyes and breathed in his cologne. She felt the rise of desire building inside her. When she opened her eyes and looked up at him, he was looking back at her with the same intense desire flickering in his eyes. He gently lifted her chin and kissed her lips ever so softly. She responded with more intensity than she had expected, and soon he carried her to his bed.

Mathew and Mira settled into a nightly routine of dinner, a movie, and passionate lovemaking. Soon they started discussing moving in together. They knew they had to tell her parents about their relationship before they took that step, though. They planned a trip home to Mira's parents for Labor Day Weekend.

Classes were starting the week before, so the quick break would help ease her back into school. Her parents were excited to see her. They hadn't been able to make a visit up yet because of their busy schedules. When she said she would bring her boyfriend home also to meet them, there was silence at first on the other end of the line. She assured them they would love him as much as she did.

"Love. Did you just say you loved a man you have only known for six weeks?"

"Yes, Mom, I did. I feel like I have known him for years, though. Everything just comes naturally with him."

Mira was smiling when she got off the phone with her.

Labor Day weekend came and Mathew turned on the charm to win Mira's parents over. It wasn't hard with her dad. Her mom was not comfortable with the age difference at all. Her husband kindly reminded her there was a ten-year difference between her and him and their relationship was great. By the end of the weekend, Mathew had asked her parents for their blessing in asking Mira to marry him, which they gave, and then Mira told them of their plans to move in together.

They set their wedding date as October 5th. Mira was looking through bridal magazines when nausea overcame her. She barely made it to the bathroom when her lunch decided it wasn't staying down. Mathew came home to find her hugging the toilet bowl. He rubbed her back and held her hair. When he asked her if there was anything he could get her, she simply looked at him.

"A pregnancy test."

Mathew happily went down to the drugstore and got the item she requested. He also stocked up on ginger ale and saltine crackers. He had heard that helped to ease morning sickness in pregnant women.

Mira brushed her teeth to get the taste of vomit out of her mouth as she waited for the results of the pregnancy test. Two minutes later, Mathew was lifting her up in his arms and swinging her around. She protested mildly because it made her queasy. They were both extremely happy they would get married and start a family all at once. Mira suggested they hold off from telling anyone about the pregnancy until after the wedding, though. She didn't want any wrinkles in her day. She knew she wouldn't be showing, so it wasn't a big issue not telling anyone.

The wedding was a small gathering of mostly Mira's family and Mathew's business associates. She insisted that the wedding venue have a gazebo and that the ceremony would occur there, much to the dismay of her mother, who wanted her to have a more traditional church wedding. They decided they would wait until her semester was over before they went on their honeymoon.

At Christmas time they sprung the news of the baby on her parents. They had excitement and concern. They were afraid she was going to throw her education away. She assured them, as did Mathew, that her education would continue and she would still keep her job until she had to take maternity leave.

On May 2, 1995, on her nineteenth birthday, Mira gave birth to a healthy 6lb 6oz baby boy. She insisted on naming him Richard Mathew Brockton. She was so happy the day they left the hospital together. The sadness she felt knowing she had missed that with her daughter passed as she stared down at her perfect baby boy sleeping in her arms.

Her daughter would turn three soon. It had been almost a year since she saw her. She yearned for that contact. She had the address of the Greenhalls and she sent a birthday card to her daughter anonymously. It made her feel better knowing she was doing what she could to keep that connection open, hopefully.

On June seventh, she baked a cake and sang happy birthday to her daughter while tears streamed down her face. Mathew sang with her and hugged her tight. Little Richard was already a month old and was growing like a weed. He was 12 lbs. 5oz. She cherished the time she had with him and relished in each milestone, no matter how tiny. She had missed all of that with her daughter, and she would not miss them with her son.

She found a home daycare close by that had room for Richard when it was time for her to go back to work. It was very hard saying goodbye on the first day. As she got back into the swing of things at work and when school started back up, it got easier to leave Richard in the competent hands of the daycare provider.

Mira was happy with her life. She had a loving husband and a beautiful son. There was nothing more she could ask for, except more kids. She loved being a mom. Mathew convinced her they should wait until Richard was at least a year old before they should have another child. He was concerned it would be too much for her with school, work, and being a mom. Mira, though, seemed to thrive with the challenges of her crazy schedule. She made the dean's list every semester and received a promotion as the senior partner's secretary.

Chapter Seventeen

Bad news

Jimmy waited at the ferry dock for Arthur to drive his car off. When he drove up, he saw the grief written all over his face. Arthur and Alexandria were more than just lawyer and client. Over the years, they had become companions. Not lovers though, Alexandria could not open her heart up to any potential love interests after losing her whole family in one day. Arthur had fallen deeply in love with Alexandria and was content to just be her confidant and companion for all these years. Jimmy felt bad for him, his pain must have been unbearable.

Arthur and Alexandria had hit it off immediately when he had taken over for his uncle's law practice. They both had lost their spouses and children in tragic accidents. Arthur's had perished in a house fire two years before Alexandria's family had lost their lives in the sailing accident. Their losses brought them together, since each could relate to what the other had gone through. Together, they were a force to be reckoned with in any of Alexandria's business dealings.

As Arthur pulled his car off the ferry, he drove right up to Jimmy, standing by his ATV. Getting out of the car, he was visibly distraught and Jimmy could tell he had been crying. Jimmy pulled Arthur to him in a big bear hug, and as Arthur hugged him back, he sobbed uncontrollably.

Regaining his composure, Arthur pulled away and wiped the tears from his face.

"I am sorry. I don't know what came over me and I don't know why I am blubbering like an idiot."

"No apologies necessary. Arthur. You loved her. It's a tough loss for all here on the island, however, it's much greater for you,"

"Thank you for understanding. Now, speaking of those on the island. They need to come to the manor house immediately. I need to tell them all together. I need to assure them Alexandria had changed her will and they all will continue to have jobs and their houses here on the island."

"Yes, sir!"

Jimmy climbed onto his ATV to fulfill Arthur's request.

Arthur took a deep breath and climbed back into his car. He drove to the manor house where he would be the one to tell everyone of Alexandria's death. He would tell Mary before the others, so she had some time to process the news before she had to face all the employees on the island. Phone calls had to be made as well.

Timothy heard his cell phone ringing. It was surprising to see Arthur was calling him. He hit the green button.

"Hello Arthur, how is Alexandria doing? Good news, I Hope."

"Good afternoon, Timothy. I am afraid it is not good news. Alexandria had a heart attack last night. They could not revive her."

Arthur tried to hold his composure.

"Oh, Arthur, I am so sorry to hear that. She seemed to be such a nice person. Is there anything I can do?"

"Thank you. Yes, she was a wonderful woman. I will miss her dearly. There is something you can do. Could you please let Jessica know? I think she might take it better coming from you. Poor kid, just finds some family, and in an instant, one member is gone."

"Sure thing Arthur. I will call her as soon as we get off the phone. You take care, and if you need anything else, please call and ask."

"Thank you. I will let you know as soon as we make the funeral arrangements."

The two men hung up the phone. Timothy had no problem calling Jessica. He was dying to talk to her again, anyway. Although he had resigned himself to trying to wait, this gave him the perfect excuse to hear her sweet voice again.

Jessica was working on some digital editing when her cell phone rang. She picked it up and smiled when she recognized it was Timothy. Ironically, the pictures she had been editing were the ones she had snuck of him writing.

"Hey, we will never get to see each other in person if we keep taking breaks and talking on the phone."

"I know, I know. But I had to call you. I just got off the phone with Arthur. He asked me to call you."

This was going to be harder than he thought. He really wished he could tell her in person. He wished he could hold her and comfort her. This long distance stuff sucked.

"Wait, Arthur asked you to call me? Please do not tell me something bad has happened to Alexandria."

Jessica's stomach knotted up. Tears welled up in her eyes in anticipation of potential bad news.

"I am so, so sorry, Jessica. My wish is I could be there right now with you. I hate having to tell you this over the phone. Alexandria had a heart attack last night. I am truly sorry. Do you want me to come there? I can take the next ferry across and be there in no time. I can finish the article there."

Timothy's words rambled. He felt so awkward telling her like this. All he could hear on the other end of the phone were quiet sobs.

"Jessica, Jess, are you okay? I am so sorry. Please say something."

"I am here. Please come, I need you, Timothy."

Jessica could barely choke out the words. She felt lost. Life was just too cruel, and it felt as though every time things seemed to look up, fate pulled the rug right out from under her. She barely knew Alexandria, however she had felt that kindred spirit with her from the beginning and then learning she was family. Real biological family, it was hard. Gaining family and losing them all in a matter of days. Timothy would be there that night. He would hold her in his arms and comfort her. That was unquestionably a comforting thought.

Timothy hung up the phone after assuring Jessica he would be there that evening. His packing was done, and he was ready to go in less than a half hour. Getting a reservation on the next ferry wasn't as easy. He drove to the ferry terminal and waited in the stand by lane, hoping to get on the next available ferry.

In the parlor of the manor house, the residents and employees of the island had gathered at the request of Arthur. Mary sat composed on the sofa. Jimmy was standing, making sure everyone was present. He was observing them all. Everyone in this room was a suspect in the murder of Alexandria in his mind. He noticed Samuel was missing and took Arthur aside to tell him he wasn't there. Arthur told him he had already informed him. He had seen him getting off the rickety ferry as he was waiting to get on. Samuel had said he had parts to get.

"I am sure you are all wondering why I have called you all together. You are all aware our beloved Ms. Alexandria had a dreadful accident the other day. I am deeply saddened to tell you all that last night she suffered a major heart attack. Our beloved Alexandria is at peace now with her loving family."

There were audible gasps around the room. Many employees, including Stella and Betty, wept openly. Someone made a statement.

"What does that mean for us?"

Arthur continued.

"I know that everyone here knew that Alexandria had planned on bequeathing the island to the town and having it turned into a nature preserve when she passed. Recently, she changed her mind. The reading of the Will will take place after her funeral. I assure you, no one will leave the island. The new owners have already stated they want things to remain exactly the way they are."

They heard a collective sigh of relief around the room, along with murmurings of who the new owners would be. Considering as far as they all knew, there were no living heirs, they were all thoroughly confused. Arthur guaranteed they would all find out who the new owners would be after the funeral. Then he set tasks to be done to complete the arrangements.

Timothy boarded the four o'clock ferry at Orient Point, heading to New London. He was eager to get to Jessica's house to comfort her. He knew he had a two-hour ride across the Long Island Sound, so he set up his laptop and started working on his article.

Mid way through the trip, his work immersed him, and another passenger losing his footing and bumping into it rattled his table.

"Sorry, man, I didn't mean to bump into the table like that. Guess my sea legs aren't as good as they used to be."

As Timothy looked up to acknowledge the gentleman, it surprised him to recognize him as the grumpy Samuel from Gardiners Island. The one that had shown him and Jessica to the Osprey nests.

"No problem, hey aren't you Samuel? You took me and my photographer friend out to the osprey nests on Gardiners Island."

"Yeah, that's me. Where's your photographer friend?"

"I am actually going to see her. What brings you out this way?"

"Oh, she lives out this way? I am on a hunt. For tractor parts that are scarce. Hoping to get lucky and find them in Connecticut."

"Yeah, she is from Connecticut. Good luck with the parts search. Oh, sorry about the loss of Alexandria."

"Thanks."

Was all Samuel responded with as he swayed while walking away.

Jessica couldn't concentrate on her work. The sadness she felt at the loss of Alexandria was too much for her to bear. She knew it would be a few hours before Timothy would be there. So she went for a ride through her trails on her ATV. Riding always seemed to clear her mind and her heart because it brought her out into nature, where she felt most at peace. She rode to one of her favorite spots.

A downed tree ripped from the earth from one of the many storms that had gone through her town in the past. It sat precariously parallel to the ground. She pulled herself up onto it at the base where the roots were showing and climbed up on it. Walking as if on a balance beam slowly, she walked the slight incline of the trunk to sit where she could nestle herself between some branches. It wasn't very high off the ground, maybe eight feet. However, the view of the nearby meadow from her spot was always breathtaking and calming. Many times she had sat in this very spot and witnessed does grazing as their fawns frolicked.

As she sat perched in the tree, she leaned back against the branch and closed her eyes. They snapped open when she remembered she would now inherit the island and Alexandria's business, along with Jimmy. She knew nothing about real estate, especially in a big city like New York. How the heck was she going to manage that? She was sure Jimmy had no clue either and figured he would feel more comfortable handling the island. Thinking about having to take over Alexandria's business, Jessica realized she needed to finish up her last assignment. She climbed down from the tree and rode back to the house to get back to work.

Timothy had finished the final draft of his article while he was on the ferry. He was happy to complete his portion of the assignment so that he could focus his energy on helping Jessica through the loss of Alexandria. As he descended the steps of the ferry to get into his car, his thoughts went to the night they had found out there was no possibility of them being relatives. Making love to Jessica that night was amazing. He was still shocked to find out that was her first time. He understood her reasoning, about not getting into a physical relationship with being adopted and all, however he had had a few drunken encounters over the years where he gave in to his primal desires. Holding Jessica in his arms again was the only thing he desired at that moment in time.

As he drove off the ferry and across the train tracks, he heard a thump, thump, and soon realized he had a flat tire. Pulling over to the side of the road, he put the car in park and cautiously got out of his car to check the tire. Yup, it was flat, and he didn't have a spare. He called AAA, and it frustrated him to find out it would be at least a half hour.

Timothy called Jessica to tell her there was a delay. She offered to come help, and he refused, saying she could use that extra time to get the pictures ready for the assignment. In the end, she agreed and got back to work.

Jessica finished picking the photographs she was going to submit with Timothy's article within forty-five minutes of Timothy's call. She was happy she stayed and finished her work. Knowing it would be another half hour before Timothy would pull into her driveway, she went to go sit out on her porch swing to wait. As she opened her door, she found an envelope on the front steps. She had heard no car drive up her driveway. And heard no one go onto her porch. She opened the envelope and found a typed note.

If you return to Gardiners Island, you will never leave. Don't go back.

Chapter Eighteen

Lena's wedding

Three years had flown by since the tragedy that had taken six lives. Life had moved on for those most affected. Mary was an exception. She became almost a recluse, staying on the island and rarely going to the mainland. No more trips into the city, or Broadway shows. She received many invitations to all the Hampton elite gatherings. She declined every single one. The island became her sanctuary and her life. She no longer hosted the summer gathering either and tightened up access to the island by outsiders. The last time anyone from the public without ties to the island was on the island was for the memorial service.

As Mary rummaged through her mail and sorted the invitations that had come in for various events, she came across one from her cousin Rita, inviting her to her daughter Lena's wedding.

You are cordially invited
To witness the nuptials
Of
Lena Duvall
Daughter of
Rita and Thomas Duvall
Of East Hampton, NY
To
Steven Weston

Son of
Peter and Cynthia Weston
Of East Hampton, NY
On
Saturday July 5th, 1997
At
2 O'clock in the afternoon
At
Triune Baptist Church
33 Eastville Ave
Sag Harbor, New York
Reception immediately following at
The Hedges Inn
74 James Lane
East Hampton, NY

When they were younger, Rita and Mary had been close. They were almost like sisters instead of cousins. Rita was 6 years older and had been the rebellious one in the family, leading to an unplanned pregnancy at 15. Lena had been the child born out of wedlock and Mary had babysat her frequently for Rita.

Rita was supposed to give Lena up for adoption. However, after seeing her precious baby alone in the nursery, she changed her mind. It had been a hard path. Rita had navigated single parent life well and had successfully attended Community College getting a paralegal degree.

Mary reminisced about those times. It was the summer before she went off to college that their friendship and closeness ended. They had both attended the annual Gardiner summer kickoff party on Gardiners Island. Alexandria's parents hosted. They were rarely home, except for their traditional parties.

Both girls had a big crush on Richard Gardiner, as did most of the debutantes from the Hamptons. His icy blue eyes mesmerized them all. They had agreed, a pinky promise though, that neither would pursue him out of consideration of the other's feelings.

Mary broke that pact the night of the party. They had all gone down to the beach and started a bonfire. Richard started flirting with Mary, and

Mary flirted back. By the end of the night, they were the latest couple of the Hamptons and Rita hardly ever spoke to Mary again. The invitation to Lena's wedding was purely out of obligation.

She almost tossed it in the trash when she remembered Lena had attended St. Catherine's school. The same school where the photograph of Richard's mistress was from, Mira. *Could they have been friends?* She needed an escort. She couldn't go alone and knew exactly who she would take. He owed her.

She had hired Samuel to be the island mechanic and handyman about a year after Richard's death. Mary felt sorry for him. He had suffered burns on his hands and face in some accident that he rarely would speak about. She gave him the job on the island and he fixed up one of the old servant's cabins for himself to live in. She also paid for cosmetic surgery to help with the scarring of his face. He owed her. Even with the scars, he was a handsome man, so that was another bonus for her taking him to the wedding. He would serve a purpose as an air of mystery, which was perfect for her return to the Hampton social scene.

Mira was excited to see Lena again. She had come to East Hampton for the bridal shower and her last fitting for her Matron of Honor's dress. The last time she had been in the area was for the memorial service. The thought of that day brought back a flood of emotions. She said goodbye to Richard and her daughter that day. Wiping away the tear that fell down her cheek, she turned into the driveway of her friend's beach house. Holding onto the wonderful memories would always help her get through the bad ones.

The two women hugged in the driveway and Lena took her friend's hand as they walked up the steps and onto the wrap around veranda. Around back Rita was sitting sipping lemonade almost exactly as she had the first time Mira had met her. The three women sat and caught up on all the latest news in each others lives all afternoon.

In the morning, Lena and Mira met the other bridesmaids at the dress shop for their final fittings. Mira, being four months pregnant and showing, was stunned that her dress was getting tight and wasn't zipping up all the way. She burst into tears. The seamstress, working on her dress, handed her some tissues and reassured her she could fix the dress so it would zip and wouldn't be too tight.

That evening, the bridal party took Lena out on the town for her bachelorette party. Since Mira was pregnant, she was a designated driver. The women showered their friend with drinks and helped her celebrate the next milestone in her life.

Thankfully, the bridal shower for the next day was in the late afternoon, so those that had partaken in too much alcohol had time to recover. Mira, who had not drank was up early getting the final touches finished on her friend's bridal shower. She smiled as she remembered her own wedding three years ago and how Lena had been her Maid Of Honor.

Sure, her wedding had been small and occurred rather quickly, to the dismay of many friends and family. However, it was a beautiful day that she would cherish forever. She and Mathew were happy. They had built a significant life for themselves in the last three years. They were expecting their second child. Mira was still doing great in school, working towards her law degree, and they had promoted her to a paralegal at the law firm she worked at.

The bridal shower went on without a hitch. Rita fawned over Lena and all the fabulous gifts she received. It would set Lena and Steven to start their new life together in their new home, thanks to the generosity of their guests. One invited guest who didn't show up was Mary. She hadn't sent a gift either.

Mary had thrown the invitation to the bridal shower in the trash. She hadn't even RSVP'd to it. She was planning on making a grand entrance at the wedding. Waiting till the last minute to even respond to the wedding invitation. She was glad that the RSVP date was after the bridal shower. It helped to make her attendance at the wedding more of a surprise.

The day of the wedding arrived and Mary walked into the church, accompanied by Samuel. As one groomsman ushered her down the aisle to her seat, she was fully aware of the turning of heads and the whispers behind hands. She smiled calmly as she took her seat, and Samuel slid into the pew alongside her. The reactions were exactly what she expected, and had wanted. The rush she got from the attention made her feel alive.

She perused the program that was handed to her, listing the names of the bridal party, what readings would take place, and the hymns that they would sing. As she did, the name she was looking for jumped out at her.

Mira, Mira Brockton, listed as Matron of Honor. She couldn't wait to see the bridal party walk down the aisle so she could verify it was the same girl from the picture. Then she noticed another name that enraged her. Richard, Richard Brockton listed as the ring bearer. It had to be her, Richard's mistress. Had she been pregnant when he passed away?

The processional music started and the wedding party started down the aisle as the Groom and his Best Man stood waiting at the altar for his bride. As Mira walked down the aisle holding her son's hand, she smiled at all the guests. Then, as she passed Mary, they briefly locked eyes, and Mira felt a cold shiver run down her back. The look on Mary's face was one of recognition that filled Mira with confusion.

Her mother Rita and her father Thomas escorted Lena down the aisle. Mary smiled and gave a small little wave as Rita caught her glance. Rita smiled back, although she was seething underneath the fake smile. She couldn't believe Mary had the audacity to actually show.

After the ceremony, the bridal party lined up outside the church so that guests could congratulate the newlyweds. As Mary made her way down the line with Samuel, Rita watched her. The mystery man that was with her cousin intrigued Rita. He was tall, bald and had grey eyes. He had some scarring on his face and hands, yet it didn't diminish his appearance in the least. She found him quite alluring.

Mary got to Mira in the reception line and leaned in, and whispered in her ear.

"I know who you are. You whore."

Then continued down the line to congratulate her cousin's daughter on her marriage.

Mira was a bit stunned, yet she kept her composure after what Mary had said. Smiling and greeting all the guests while gripping her restless two-year-old's hand. She wouldn't let anyone ruin her best friend's wedding and she certainly would not engage her ex-lover's widow in any drama.

At the reception, after a few glasses of wine, Rita got the courage to interrupt Mary and Samuel dancing and asked if she could cut in.

"I pinky promise it's just for one dance."

She said to Mary as Samuel took her hand and started the next slow dance with her.

Mary understood the reference and went back to her table, annoyed at both Rita and Samuel. Why Samuel was obliging her cousin's whim perplexed her. Whose side was he on, anyway? She drank some wine as she loathingly watched Samuel and Rita enjoying their dance together. Then she noticed Mira dancing with whom she presumed was her husband. As she watched them, she couldn't help but feel like she knew him. He seemed very familiar with his jet-black hair and his mannerisms.

She finally remembered where she had seen him before. It was at the memorial service! When the dance ended, she walked up to the man and introduced herself.

"Good afternoon, my name is Mary Gardiner. My husband was Richard Gardiner. I believe you attended his memorial service three years ago."

"Why yes, I am so sorry for your loss. Richard had been a business associate. He was a good man. Great golfer too. We played several times together."

"Thank you. And your name is?"

"Oh, I am sorry. I forgot my manners. Mathew Brockton and this is my lovely wife, Mira and our son Richard."

"We met in the reception line. Your son is adorable. So, how did you two lovebirds meet?"

Mathew indulged Mary in the story of how he and Mira had met after she moved into his apartment building. Soon Mary became bored with the conversation and looked for Samuel. She found him standing at the bar, engaged in what looked like a flirtatious conversation with Rita. As she walked up, Rita edged closer to Samuel and placed a hand on his chest as she was laughing.

Mary, recognizing what Rita was trying to do, walked up to Samuel and grabbed his hand.

"There you are, dear. I have been looking all over for you. I think I am ready to go home and make this a private party for two."

Samuel smiled and shifted his body toward Mary, causing Rita's hand to drop from his chest.

"Dear, that sounds like an amazing idea."

They said their obligatory goodbyes and headed back to the manor house and Gardiner Island. Mary felt she had made her presence known and once again felt more alive than she had in the last three years.

Mira felt sick to her stomach. It wasn't pregnancy sickness either. The words Mary had whispered in her ear ran through her mind. The fact she approached Mathew and recognized him being at the memorial service made her stomach do even more flips. She told Lena she wasn't feeling well, and they left the reception a little early and headed to their hotel room to get some rest. They would head home in the morning.

Chapter Nineteen

Reunited

As Timothy drove up the driveway of Jessica's house, he understood why she loved the solitude of her surroundings. He thought that where he lived in Riverhead was rural, especially compared to the city, but seeing where Jessica lived, he realized he was wrong. This was rural.

Jessica sat on her porch swing, waiting for Timothy. She was debating whether she should show him the note she received or tell him about the generator issue. This wasn't the first time she had dealt with a stalker. After the Amazon pictures had earned her awards and more notoriety, she periodically dealt with these types of situations. This time it was a little more unnerving, though, with the incidents that had occurred while she was on Gardiners Island. They could be coincidences or they could be connections. She didn't know what to think.

The note mentioned Gardiners Island, however stalkers have mentioned places she had been on assignment before. She let it all go and would not tell Timothy about it. Her focus needed to be on grieving Alexandria's death and preparing herself to help run Alexandria's business.

The sound of Timothy's car startled her out of her thoughts. Calmness enveloped her as she realized it was him. The thought of being able to hug him again brought a smile to her face. As she put her foot down to stop the swing, Timothy's car came to a stop.

Timothy hopped out of his car and made quick work of the steps of the porch. Jessica had barely stood up when she found herself wrapped in his powerful arms. She felt safe with him, a feeling she hadn't noticed she didn't feel until she met him.

Tears came quickly for Jessica, and Timothy let her get them out. He knew she needed to grieve. She would grieve more than just Alexandria. She would also grieve the lost family connection that she had just made and also her former life. Taking over Alexandria's business would be a huge undertaking.

She regained her composure and showed Timothy her home. When they got to her studio room, she showed him the photographs to go with the article. He agreed they were the perfect pictures.

They read and edited his article, added the pictures, and sent the assignment off to the editors at National Geographic. With the assignment finally done, they turned their attention to their budding relationship. They went on an actual date.

With Timothy not knowing the area, he let Jessica plan their date. She took him to The Harp and Dragon Pub for dinner and planned on taking a walk down at the Norwich Marina afterward.

She drove her car and was lucky to find a parking spot out front. Jessica watched Timothy's reaction to the little city atmosphere. She could see the amazement that within a matter of minutes, they went from a very rural area to this mini city. It still differed from the big city hustle and bustle of New York City. They sat at a high top table for two.

Timothy was aware of Jessica watching him. He loved how she smiled at his reactions. It definitely amazed him at how diverse the region was that she lived in. Jessica seemed to know several of the regulars in the pub as they waved or shouted hello to her. Timothy felt a brief pang of jealousy when he realized that most of them were men.

The waitress came over to get their order. They ordered a couple of beers, pretzel bites, and cheesesteak sliders to start. Their conversation flowed so easily from one subject to another. Jessica reflected on how easy this all seemed with Timothy. She had never had this type of relationship and she was really liking it a lot.

They both ordered the prime rib special for dinner. The tenderness of the meat blew Timothy away. The fact Jessica could finish the king sized meal was astonishing. She laughed at his astonishment and teased him he must be used to some prim and proper model types.

As they left the pub, they held hands and walked to the marina, where there was a gentleman with a telescope set up to view the stars. They paid the man ten dollars to look through the telescope. The clarity of the stars they could view fascinated them. As they continued to walk around the marina, the air got chilly and Jessica visibly got cold. Timothy put his arm around her to warm her up. They headed back to her house.

Back home, Jessica made Timothy a cup of coffee and herself a cup of tea. They sat and watched a Netflix movie and warmed up. Timothy put his coffee cup down, took Jessica's cup out of her hands, and gently pulled her towards him. He kissed her passionately with all his pent up lust for her over the last few days. He felt as if he was going to explode.

Jessica's response to his kiss was just as explosive. She felt the rush through her body. The hunger to have him hold her skin to skin. To feel his heartbeat against hers. The desire to feel as though they were one. She took his hands and led him to her bedroom, where they fulfilled each other's desires all throughout the night.

In the morning, Jessica awoke nestled in Timothy's arms. A strong feeling of contentment overcame her it actually brought tears to her eyes. Feeling a teardrop falling on his arm alarmed Timothy that he had done something wrong.

"Jessica, are you okay?"

"I am fine. Actually, more than fine, I am absolutely wonderful."

Jessica wiped the tears and rolled in his arms to face him.

"Then why are you crying?"

"They are happy tears. I have never felt more happy and content in my life. As I do, right now, right here, in your arms."

Timothy held her tighter and kissed her gently on her forehead.

Timothy's cell phone ringing startled them out of their embrace. When he grabbed it and answered it, Jessica rolled out of bed and put a bathrobe on.

"Good morning Timothy, it's Arthur. I just wanted to update you on the funeral arrangements for Alexandria."

The two men conversed, and Arthur told Timothy Saturday morning on Gardiners Island they would hold the funeral. And they would do the reading of the will on Saturday evening. Arthur also expressed that Mary had said they were more than welcome to stay at the manor house for the weekend. Timothy told Arthur he would give the information to Jessica and they would let them know their decision on where they would stay before they came.

Jessica bristled at the thought of going back to the island and staying in the manor house. She resigned herself to staying there one night. They agreed they would get a room at an area bed-and-breakfast for Friday night and Sunday night. She almost brought up the note and the generator issue, however, she kept that to herself, for now.

Timothy didn't like the thought of going back to the island and staying at the manor house, either. It was still unsettling about Jessica's near drowning and ATV accident. He knew he was going to be by her side the whole time because he wanted nothing to happen to her. He couldn't help but feel she was feeling uneasy too, even as she was trying to reassure him that everything would be okay.

Jessica took Timothy on a tour of her property on her ATVs. She showed him the tree and the meadow. The realization that she was opening up a part of herself she had never opened up to anyone else hit him. They spent the whole day just enjoying each other's company. Timothy fell just as much in love with Jessica's property as he had fallen in love with her. Jessica was falling in love with Timothy, fast and hard.

The young couple spent the next few days exploring various sites together. Each time Jessica brought Timothy to a new place, he fell in love with her more. He loved how she enjoyed the outdoors and couldn't believe the amount of places she took him hiking. It was when she took him to Mohegan Sun Casino and they bar hopped he realized just how diverse a woman Jessica was. She could have fun anywhere.

Time seemed to travel so fast when they were together. Soon they packed Timothy's car to head to Gardiners Island for the funeral. Timothy tried to keep conversations light to help ease Jessica's anxiety about the will and her inheritance. Spending time with Timothy had all but erased any of Jessica's concerns for her own safety, and she concluded in her mind that her stalker had probably moved on, as was usually the case.

They made it to Long Island and took the scenic ride to East Hampton where they were staying at a bed-and-breakfast for the night. After checking in, they went to the small café they had originally met at to have dinner. When they walked in, Jessica noticed a large party sitting in the back corner.

She recognized two of the women as the two that had been in the corner watching her the first time. She also recognized the young woman who had waited on her for the first time in this café. The others facing her she didn't recognize, however; she assumed the men sitting next to each woman were their husbands. There were five people with their backs to her. A man with black hair, a woman with long curly red hair, a young adult male with strawberry blonde hair, a young adult woman with long curly red hair, and a teenage boy with strawberry blonde hair. They gave her the impression of a family and she felt a pang of longing, which led to feelings of grief.

It wasn't until they all got up to leave that she could see their faces. As she recognized the woman walking out the door as an older version of the young woman in the photo Mary had given her, she dropped her fork to her plate. Her stomach did flips, and it paralyzed her with excitement and fear. Jessica realized she missed her chance as the family climbed into their car and drove away outside of the café.

"Are you okay?"

"Yeah, did you see how much that woman resembled the picture Mary had given me of my mother?"

"Yes, I also noticed the resemblance to you of the younger woman, who I presume was her daughter, possibly your half-sister."

"Why didn't I get up and ask her who she was?"

"You were afraid of rejection? Afraid she wanted nothing to do with you after all these years. Afraid her family wouldn't accept you either."

"Maybe. I just froze."

"Maybe we can track her down. She is obviously in the area."

"Yeah, maybe we can."

Jessica and Timothy finished their dinner and drove back to the bed-and-breakfast they were staying at. They had become all too familiar with sharing a bed and drifted off to sleep, discussing the possibilities of moving in together.

Chapter Twenty

Going home

Mira started the pot of coffee and retrieved the morning paper off the front step as she had for the last 20 years. Picking up the paper, as she closed the door to the suburban neighborhood they had settled in, she opened the paper to the business section. It had been her morning ritual for as long as she could remember, opening to the business section and putting the paper next to Mathew's breakfast plate for him to read when he came down.

As she opened the paper, she met with the headline, *CEO, and President of Cromwell Realty and Investments Group, Alexandria Cromwell Dies After Tragic Fall*. Her hand covered her mouth as she sat down to read the rest of the article. The tears fell. She knew this day would come at some point in their lives. She just never expected it to be this soon.

Mathew came downstairs, fixing his tie. As he walked into the dining room and found his wife crying. He rushed to her to find out what had upset her. All she could do was point to the article. He sat down, put his head in his hands, and sobbed.

They both knew the death of Alexandria heralded a day of reckoning for them. They would finally reveal truths and they would hopefully learn to forgive themselves for their pasts. The funeral would be Saturday, and they made plans to attend. First, they had to sit down and explain everything to their three children.

Richard was their oldest. He was twenty-two years old and had just moved into his own apartment with a bunch of friends. He was working as an advertising executive for a social media company. Samantha was their middle child. She was twenty and was still going to college and working part time as a waitress. And then there was David, he was eighteen and fresh out of high school. With no job and no desire to even go to college.

Later that evening after dinner, Mira and Mathew sat their children down to tell them about their older sister and why they needed to attend the funeral of a woman, they had never met before. They were stunned at what they were told.

Richard was the first to react, and it wasn't what either of them was expecting. He got up silently, went to the door, and opened it. As he walked out the door, he looked back with contempt and disgust on his face while shaking his head. It was like a knife was driven straight into Mira's heart. She cried. Mathew put his arm around her and tried to soothe her.

Samantha sat there, not knowing what to say or think. All this time, she thought her family was perfect. Her mother was a successful lawyer. She had worked hard to get her own practice. To find out she had a child as an unwed teenager and had an affair with a married man was hard to wrap her head around. The only exciting part of all this was she had a sister! A big sister at that. Samantha had always wished for a sister and when David was born, she was very mad at her parents for weeks. How could her parents keep these secrets for so many years, though? They weren't the people that they portrayed to the outside world. Her dad held the darkest secrets, and that part scared her. She understood Richard's reaction.

David focused on the fact that the heirs to Alexandria's estate would inherit her real estate empire and Gardiners Island. He rushed to his room to google as much information as he could about the island and the business.

They all begrudgingly agreed to attend the funeral with their parents after a day or two of cooling off and processing the information they had. The only good part of the trip was they would stay with their mother's friend Lena, whom they all adored and called Aunt Lena. Although that was getting awkward for Richard as he was finding out he was having potent feelings for her daughter, Danielle. If they ever started a relationship, he would have to stop calling her mom Aunt Lena.

They all arrived at Lena and Steve's house in East Hampton on Thursday night. Lena cooked them a big pasta dinner and then they sat out on the deck overlooking their private beach with a view of the Atlantic ocean. Danielle and her two sisters, Erica and Stephanie, led Richard, Samantha, and David down to the beach where they could sit and enjoy time away from their parents.

Richard filled in Danielle and her sisters as to the news that his parents had told him and his siblings only a few short days prior. Their eyes bulged and their hands went over their mouths. Samantha gave Richard a glaring look. Danielle was the first to say something.

"I think I met your big sister two weeks ago. She was in the café I work at. I waited on her. My Mom and Grandma were in that day too and they told me later that they couldn't get over how much she looked like your Mom. And now that I think about it, she looks just like you, Samantha. She seemed really nice."

"What about everything else I said? Doesn't any of that bother you at all?"

"Secrets are big around here. Everybody has them, some bigger than others. Honestly, any secret that sticks it to Mary Gardiner is okay with me. She is the biggest bitch around."

"But.... what about the accident? What about the lies? Doesn't any of that sit wrong with you?"

"Well, yeah, but look where it all leads. You are sitting here with me."

Danielle smiled and stood up. She reached for Richard's hand and they took a walk down the shoreline as the waves crashed toward them.

The next night, they all went to dinner at the café Danielle worked at. When Jessica walked in with Timothy, Danielle immediately recognized her. She mentioned nothing because she didn't know how Richard would react. She assumed that her mother and grandmother either didn't recognize Jessica this time or they didn't want to say anything either.

It wasn't until they were all leaving that it appeared it startled Jessica to see her family for the first time. Danielle heard the fork crash against the plate. So did Richard, and at that moment, she saw recognition in his eyes. Danielle pushed him through the door and the two families got into their separate cars to head back to the house.

"She was in there!"

Richard looked back as they pulled away.

"Who was?"

"Jessica! Your daughter!"

"Really? Should we go back?"

"Yes!"

Richard, Samantha, and David were unified in their response.

"No. Tomorrow we will all meet her at the funeral. She will have too many questions that we can't answer until tomorrow."

Mira knew Mathew was right. They had to wait one more day. A silent tear rolled down her cheek. She had waited twenty-three years to see her daughter again. She prayed she would forgive her. Starting tomorrow, no more secrets and no more lies. Tomorrow, hopefully, they could start fresh, as a complete family.

The next morning, they all got ready to attend Alexandria's funeral. All the attendees were being shuttled over in vans to the island on the rickety old ferry. The shuttles started at 7 am and didn't stop until 10:30 am. Hundreds of friends, acquaintances, and business people came to pay their respects.

Chapter Twenty-One

Alexandria's funeral

Sleep was hard for Jessica. She kept thinking about seeing her Mom and her potential siblings the night before. Her stomach had done flips all night long, and now she was downright nauseous. Alexandria's funeral was later in the morning, which added to the nervous stomach. She couldn't contain the nerves any longer and she bolted for the bathroom. Timothy awoke to the sounds of Jessica in the bathroom vomiting.

Timothy got out of bed and went to see if there was anything he could do to make Jessica feel any better. He rubbed her back and held her hair until she could stop, wishing there was more he could do. He didn't know how to help calm her nerves and he couldn't imagine all the thoughts running through her head at this moment.

They both showered, got dressed, and made their way downstairs to breakfast. Jessica picked at the scrambled eggs and bacon on her plate. Timothy encouraged her to at least eat the toast, which she got down.

After checking out, they headed to the island. Once on the island, Martin met them at the manor house, who showed them to their room for the night. Jessica was uneasy being back on the island and at the now creepy feeling house. Mary was a little friendlier, although she seemed on edge with all the hustle and bustle surrounding the funeral.

Jessica walked into the family cemetery where Alexandria's plot was dug and waited for her casket to be lowered into. The lighthouse monument that memorializes the six people who tragically lost their lives in the fatal sailing accident twenty-three years ago caught her eye. She was at that funeral with her adoptive parents, however; she searched the recesses of her mind and could not remember being there. Her biological father, Richard Gardiner, had perished in that accident. She would never get the chance to know him.

There was a small headstone for the baby that Richard and Mary had lost. She knew the truth that he had survived birth and was then put up for adoption. She knew that the child had grown up on this island and would share in the inheritance along with her. Jessica had already decided to let Jimmy control the everyday workings of the island. She was hoping they could get past their rocky start and work together as cousins to manage Alexandria's estate.

As the morning dragged on, people filled the garden where chairs sat waiting for mourners to fill them. They lay Alexandria out in her casket for people to pay their respects. Arthur was up front, greeting the mourners and sharing stories about his beloved friend. The habitants of the island all mingled with the other mourners from the mainland. There was a buzz amongst the mourners wondering who the new owners of the island were and several were very blunt in asking the inhabitants. All the inhabitants could tell them was apparently Alexandria had left the island and the rest of her estate to someone, however they weren't aware of who yet.

Promptly at 11:00 am, the minister asked everyone to take a seat. Arthur, Mary, Jessica, Timothy, and Jimmy all sat in the front row reserved for family. The sight of Jessica, Timothy, and Jimmy sitting in the front row set off a buzz of whispers behind them from the attendees.

As the minister spoke of the spiritual journey that Alexandria's soul would now embark on. He reminded the mourners that a chapter in her journey had ended and a new one had started. He also mentioned she was now reunited with those she had lost two decades ago and that those in attendance should rejoice at her reunion. His message continued mentioning it was up to them all to continue her legacy and to remember her by sharing their personal experiences and stories of her with each other. He then invited attendees to come up and share any memories or stories with everyone.

Arthur was the first to step up and share.

"Good Morning, and thank you all for coming to pay your respects to Alexandria. As many of you know, I have been her family lawyer for many years. Over those years, we had developed a fond friendship. Although we were not romantically involved, I loved her more than anyone could ever understand. We met at a time we were both grieving the loss of our families. We found comfort in our shared tragedies. All will miss Alexandria, however, not nearly as much as by me."

As Arthur finished, he broke down in tears. He sat down next to Mary, who handed him some tissues. Several friends and business associates stepped up next. Each taking their time to explain their relationship to Alexandria and how much they already missed her. Some people told funny anecdotal stories of outings with Alexandria, and others spoke of her business prowess.

Mary, feeling a bit obligated to say something, finally stepped up in front of everyone.

"It is no secret that there was no love lost between Alexandria and myself. However, I will forever be grateful to her for allowing me to continue living here after the death of my beloved husband. Losing him was the greatest loss I ever had to bear and losing my home also would have been even more unbearable."

Jessica didn't know what compelled her to get up next when Mary sat down. However, she got up to the small podium and looked out at all the mourners gathered to say goodbye to her cousin, whom she had just met. She didn't know what she was going to say, and as she stood there, the nervousness of her stomach returned. Then she looked out into the mourners and she was stunned to see her mother and her family sitting there. And she spoke.

"Good morning all. My name is Jessica Greenhall. Some of you might know me as an award-winning photographer. And you are probably wondering what I am doing here. Two weeks ago I had an assignment here on Gardiners Island. Before stepping foot onto the island, I had felt a connection with Alexandria. You see, we both have lost loved ones to tragedies. I won't go into details of my life because we are here to honor and remember Alexandria's life. I had the pleasure of meeting her while I was here on the island. That meeting solidified that connection. One of the last things she did while with us was to help me find out who my biological parents were. I will forever be grateful to her for that and only wish we had more time together to grow our friendship to the level as many of you had. I already miss her so much."

As she spoke, she watched her mother. Her mother dabbed at her tears when she spoke of having a connection with Alexandria and the tragedies they both endured. And she covered her mouth with the tips of her fingers when she mentioned Alexandria helped her find out who her biological parents were. Her mother looked at her husband and her husband looked at her and you could see her start to sob.

When she finished speaking, Jessica sat down, and Timothy wrapped his arm around her. He pulled her close, and she rested her head on his shoulder. She was exhausted, mentally and physically. Her mother seemed to have remorse for giving her up for adoption. At least, that was how Jessica took her reaction to her words. She was patiently waiting for the funeral to be over. She was hoping to talk to her mother and then take a nap.

Finally, it appeared everyone who wanted to speak had spoken, and the minister asked if there was anyone else that wanted to say something. It dismayed Jessica when she saw her mother's husband walking up to the podium. He was wearing sunglasses and a black suit.

"Good morning everyone, some of you know me as Mathew Brockton. No relation to Arthur there. You know me as a business associate or friend of Richard Gardiner. Today, though, you will all know the truth about who I really am. Out of love and loyalty to my dear cousin Alexandria. I hope someday when we meet again in heaven she will forgive me for my sins and for staying away so long."

As he ended his last sentence, the man at the podium removed his sunglasses and his jet-black hair wig. Revealing the piercing icy blue eyes and strawberry blonde hair of Richard Gardiner. He stood there alive and well, to the dismay of everyone in attendance.

Mary screamed and then fainted. Jimmy rushed to attend to his mother as Arthur rushed up to Richard and ushered him into the manor house. Jessica sat there, stunned. Her father, whom she just found out was biologically hers, who was supposed to be dead, was really alive. She felt a little faint herself.

Jimmy helped Mary to the manor house while the minister gained control of the attendees. The funeral proceeded, and they placed the casket in a horse-drawn carriage to make the small journey to the family cemetery. The mourners walked behind the carriage.

Mary and Jimmy returned to place flowers on the casket. Arthur also returned and placed two dozen red roses on the casket. Jessica couldn't see her mother or father through the crowd of mourners. The minister closed the funeral by inviting all the attendees to join for a lunch on the west lawn.

As attendees mingled and ate, there was definitely a buzz about the return of Richard. Jessica could not find him anywhere, though. She also could not find her mother or her siblings. She finally found Arthur and cornered him.

"Where are they, Arthur? Where is my family?"

"They are safe. I asked them to stay away until everyone leaves the island. You will get to be with them later. Be patient Jessica, this throws a lot of legal issues into the situation and the estate of Alexandria's. And we still don't know who pushed Alexandria down those stairs. Or may I add, who tried to drown you? Your father told me a story about how he survived that tragic sailing accident. If true, there are some legal ramifications there too. It's extremely complicated."

Jessica couldn't process any of what Arthur was saying. *Legal ramifications? How did her father survive? Why did he choose to pretend to be dead all these years?* She found Timothy and told him she needed to go rest. They went to their room in the manor house and tried to rest.

By 3 o'clock in the afternoon, all the mainland attendees were off the island and Arthur had told the inhabitants that the reading of Alexandria's will would have to be postponed. The return of Richard brought so much unease and uncertainty to all involved. Mary was on the verge of a nervous breakdown. *How could he have survived and Benjamin didn't?* That wasn't how it was supposed to happen.

Benjamin was supposed to survive. He was supposed to take the lifeboat and meet her at the beach. They were going to watch the sailboat burn together. However, something had gone horribly wrong and as she sat on the beach that night, she saw the boat and her dreams with Benjamin go up in flames. Benjamin never showed up at the beach. She checked daily for weeks and he never showed. If Richard survived, he had to have known their plan. If he knew, Mary was in serious trouble. She had to figure out what to do.

Chapter Twenty-Two

His story

When it was dinner time, Jessica and Timothy made their way down to the dining room. They were stunned to see Richard, Mira, and their three children sitting at the table along with Arthur and an uncomfortable-looking Mary. Jimmy was also sitting at the table. Arthur looked up as Jessica and Timothy took their seats at the table and addressed everyone.

"Now that everyone is here that needs to be here, I would like you, Richard, to tell us all your story."

"Thank you, Arthur. First, I need to address Jessica. I am so sorry your mother and I had to stop all contact with you. Until the sailing accident, we had made it a regular occurrence to spend time with the Greenhalls in order to spend time with you. We couldn't risk your life being endangered if anyone found out I was still alive. The sailboat fire was no accident. They planned it to kill me."

As Richard said that last sentence, he looked straight at Mary and continued with his story.

"My first wife, Mary, was not happy that I was divorcing her, conspired with her lover, Benjamin Timmons, to take me out for a sailing trip and set fire to the boat to cause an explosion killing me. I overheard their plan and made a counter-escape plan with Mira. The only wrinkle was that Alexandria's husband and children went with us, even though I had created a disagreement with her to persuade her not to go. I couldn't back out of the trip. Mary and Benjamin would know something was up. I only wish I could have saved them along with myself. They were the reason I could never face Alexandria with the truth and why I went into hiding as Mathew Brockton."

Jimmy sat listening to Richard's story and watched his biological mother, Mary, intently. Her body language told him everything he needed to know. Richard was telling the truth. She was an accessory to murder. And his biological father was a murderer. Unfortunately, there was no evidence of the allegations Richard was making. There were even no bodies found. Mary was a bundle of nerves that finally exploded.

"Never! I don't know what you are talking about! Yes, I was angry about the divorce and you accusing me of having an affair. The hypocrisy of that is sitting right before us."

She pointed at Jessica.

"To accuse me of conspiring to murder you is ridiculous!"

"I know at this point in time, I have no proof. It is my word against yours. So I am proposing this, in good faith. Sign the divorce papers, finalize the divorce so I am not a polygamist and I will allow you to continue to live on the island as Alexandria had agreed. My life is in Massachusetts now."

Mary knew he was right. There was no proof of the attempted murder of him and the actual murder of his family members. There was proof, though, sitting at the table with them, they both had been unfaithful in their marriage. She could still save face with the divorce since Richard had been MIA since the accident. Most importantly, she could still live in the manor house and keep her status on the island. She agreed to sign the divorce papers and complete the divorce after twenty-three years.

Jimmy was fuming. He was angry to know that there was nothing he could do to prove or disprove his biological parents had murdered four innocent people. He couldn't even stand sitting next to his mother and he didn't know how he felt about her still living on the island. *Was she the one that pushed Alexandria? Was she the one that attempted to drown Jessica?* He couldn't hold in his emotions any longer. He stood up briskly, knocking his chair over, leaned on the table and directed his comments at Arthur.

"Wait! Don't Jessica and I have a say in who lives on the island and who doesn't as heirs to Alexandria's estate? What if we don't want Mary living here?"

Jimmy's outburst shocked everyone. Especially Mary, who burst into tears that her son would not want her on the island. Jessica was still processing the fact her biological parents were sitting at the same table as her. She realized Jimmy had a point. It was their island, too. They had a say. Richard looked at Jimmy perplexed

"Who may I ask are you and why would you inherit Alexandria's estate? Jessica, I understand. And yes, I should have asked your opinion on the matter. I apologize."

As he finished, he looked directly at Jessica.

"Who am I? Well. Let me enlighten you. My name is James Driscoll. Stella and John Driscoll adopted me twenty-five years ago. Until last week, I never knew, or cared, to know who my biological parents were. Alexandria suspected who they were since she orchestrated the adoption. She had done research and orchestrated the three infants born on the same day twenty-five years ago to be reunited. We were all adopted through private closed adoptions through the same law firm. She then had us all tested to prove two of us were of Gardiner lineage. Jessica and I both have Gardiner blood. Jessica through you, Richard, and I through your half-brother, Benjamin Timmons, who fathered me with your wife, Mary. So, Uncle Richard, the decision is not solely yours to make. And until we know who killed Alexandria, I am not making any promises to anyone."

As he finished speaking, he looked at his biological mother and walked out of the room.

Richard sat there, stunned. He knew of the child Mary bore with Benjamin. He also knew of the adoption. They still had the copy of the adoption paperwork that Mira had copied as a file clerk. What he didn't know was Benjamin was his half-brother. This was new information that he had to process. His father had been unfaithful to his mother, just as he had been to Mary. Then the last sentence Jimmy uttered hit him like a ton of bricks. They killed Alexandria. The obituary never mentioned that.

Mary, still crying, now uncontrollably, ran out of the room and they heard her running up the stairs, presumably to her room. Jessica felt bad for her to some extent. She was still numb about her parents, though. Her siblings, who were sitting there through all this, seemed dazed and confused by all that was being discussed. It felt like they were living in some strange twilight zone. Timothy also seemed a little dazed and confused, although he never let go of Jessica's hand the entire time. He was lending her silent support through it all.

Richard slowly overcame his shock.

"Is what he said true? Was Alexandria murdered? And was Benjamin really my half brother?"

"Yes, Alexandria claimed someone pushed her down the stairs. We have found no evidence linking who might have done it. And now that she is dead, all we have is her initial statement. And yes, Alexandria knew Benjamin was your brother and that he was the father of Mary's child. I find it interesting that you didn't specifically ask about whether Jimmy was really Mary and Benjamin's son. Why is that?"

"Arthur, I didn't ask if that was true because I knew that part years ago. Mira worked in the law office that handled the adoptions. She saw the files and told me. She knows what she did, as a minor, was wrong. We never used the information, except to start a friendship with the Greenhalls getting close to our daughter Jessica. Even if we couldn't be her parents, we wanted to watch her grow up. We planned on approaching the Greenhalls when she turned eighteen to see if they would allow us to tell her we were her biological parents. And then the sailboat accident happened and things had to change."

"Well, Richard, your nephew is correct, though. You are not the sole owner of the island. Jimmy and Jessica are the sole heirs named in Alexandria's most recent will. Technically, since you are still alive, your will is void, so you still own your share of the island. I am going to leave you for now because you all have a lot of catching up to do with your daughter. Jessica, I formally introduce you to your father, Richard Gardiner, your mother Mira, your brother Richard, your sister Samantha, and your brother David. Gardiners, meet Jessica, your daughter and sister."

"Thank you, Arthur. We will discuss the legal matters later. I do want to get to know my daughter."

Jessica looked at Arthur as he got up and mouthed the words, "thank you".

The butterflies in her stomach were returning. She didn't know what to say or do. After what seemed like forever, Richard and Mira both got up and walked over to Jessica. They bent over and tried to hug her, which just seemed awkward all around. So Jessica got up out of her chair and hugged them both. Tears streamed down her face. Samantha was the first of the siblings to get up and hug Jessica, too. She started crying.

"I always wanted a sister."

The next sibling to get up was David. He came over and gave Jessica a big bear hug.

"Welcome to the family, sis. So how did you get so good at photography? And how do you like being famous?"

Her brother Richard still seemed a bit unnerved by the whole situation and begrudgingly got up and gave her a hug. He then locked eyes with Timothy.

"So who the hell are you, and where do you fit into this whole crazy situation?"

"Me? Well, I guess you might say I am your sister's boyfriend. At least I think that's where our relationship is heading. My name is Timothy Sullivan. I am a writer for National Geographic magazine. They assigned me to write an article about the ospreys on the island and I requested your sister take the pictures. That's how we met two weeks ago, and it's been a whirlwind since that first day."

"Hey, just because you are my brother doesn't mean you can shake down and interrogate my boyfriend."

Jessica chided, as she nudged her brother Richard with her elbow.

"That's what brothers do."

Responded Richard and David simultaneously, then laughing.

They had broken the ice. They spent the rest of the evening getting to know each other better as a family. When it was time for everyone to go to sleep, Samantha begged Jessica to have a slumber party in her bedroom with her. Jessica obliged and went to Samantha's room. The one she had been told she could stay in for the evening. Timothy jokingly teased Jessica he would be lonely without her and she kissed him goodnight and said he would be fine.

Timothy was nervous not having Jessica by his side in this house. He was worried about her safety. The allegations brought against Mary by Jessica's father didn't sit well with him. He replayed the evening that they almost drowned Jessica in his mind. *Could Mary have been the one to try the drowning? She had plenty of motives. She also had the motive to kill Alexandria.*

Chapter Twenty-Three

Confessions

Mary locked herself in her room and threw herself on her bed. She was heartbroken. The way Jimmy now looked at her with disgust and contempt was unbearable. She had to think of a way to get back in his favor. She didn't know how she was going to do it, though. He had worked security on the island since he was eighteen. He took his job seriously and believed in law, order, and justice.

She opened a bottle of wine from her private stash and poured herself a glass. When she had drank half of it, her nerves had settled a bit and she felt calmer. She had to think rationally. Her home and lifestyle depended on it.

It was generous of Richard to offer her to stay on the island in exchange for the divorce. She only wished she had known that Benjamin was Richard's half-brother when he was alive. If they had known that, things could have been different. Why had Alexandria kept that a secret all these years? *Damn bitch, had messed up so much of her life*. Making her give up her only child for adoption.

As she finished her first glass of wine and poured herself another one, she thought taking a relaxing bath would help her think. She placed the bottle of wine and her full glass on a chair next to her tub. She turned the water on and let the tub fill. Her cell phone rang in her bedroom and she went to answer it. There was no one on the other end, so she hung up. She went to go back to the tub, and it rang again, so again she answered it and no one was there. Annoyed, she turned off her phone and went back to the tub.

She drank more of her wine and undressed. Stepping into the tub, she wobbled slightly, feeling off balance. As she slid herself into the tub, the warmth of the water enveloped her. Relaxing more and more, she finished her second glass of wine and poured herself a third. After a few sips, she felt drowsy, and she closed her eyes.

Soon she was dreaming of her and Benjamin and the life they had wanted together. The dream morphed. In the dream, she was on the beach. Jimmy was sitting next to her, and she was trying to explain to him why his father and she had planned to kill Richard. Alexandria's family was just collateral damage. She had felt guilty about that for the last twenty-three years. She had lost Benjamin, too. Wasn't that enough punishment?

In the dream, she pleaded with Jimmy to forgive her and to understand. He was angry and refused to forgive her. He accused her of trying to drown Jessica and of killing Alexandria. She denied having anything to do with those instances, however; he refused to believe her. He told her he was going to go to the police. She couldn't bear the heartbreak and she couldn't bear him telling the police.

She picked up a rock next to her and hit him in the head with it. As he slumped over, she kept repeating.

"I am not a murderer!"

Then everything went dark.

In the morning Stella was quietly making breakfast for the houseful of inhabitants. Jimmy had filled her in on what had transpired the night before. It still disgusted him with the knowledge his mother had conspired to kill people. All for prestige and money. He hated the thought of becoming like that.

One by one the Gardiners awoke and came down for breakfast. They were all very polite and appreciative of the home cooked breakfast and coffee. Jessica and Samantha came down together, giggling like schoolgirls. Shortly after, Arthur and Timothy emerged from their rooms to dine with the rest of them.

The only inhabitant that did not come down for breakfast was Mary. Stella sent Betty to go check on her. And within minutes, they could hear blood-curdling screams from Betty throughout the house. Chaos erupted as everyone went running to find out what brought on the screaming.

To everyone's horror, they found Mary dead in her bathtub. On the chair next to the tub was an empty wineglass, an empty bottle of wine, an empty pill bottle, and a note written by Mary to Jimmy.

My Dear son Jimmy,

I am sorry I am a murderer. I love you with all my heart and always have. The thought of you hating me is one that I can not bear. I would rather be dead than see the disgust and contempt for me in your eyes anymore. I helped to conspire to kill my husband, Richard. Benjamin was not supposed to die. We were supposed to live happily ever after on the island together. Instead, I lived a lonely existence for the last twenty-three years. Alexandria's family was not part of the plan. Unfortunately, they became collateral damage. I tried to drown Jessica the first night she was here. I also tampered with the throttle on her ATV. And yes, I pushed Alexandria down the stairs.

Someday I hope you will forgive me and understand. I will always love you.

Love your MOM.

Jimmy read the note with tears in his eyes. Then he called the State Police.

Richard and Mira sat with everyone in the parlor. Their first questions surrounded the confession about Jessica almost being drowned and the ATV throttle. It mortified them their daughter was the target of a psychopathic murderer. The police came and the coroner came.

The police interviewed everyone in the house. With the note, the empty wineglass, the empty pill bottle, and the empty bottle of wine and no evidence of the contrary, the police ruled Mary's death a suicide and entered her note into evidence in Alexandria's case. With her confession, they were going to close the case. They also closed the investigation into the incidents with Jessica.

The mood in the house was a somber one and for the second time in two weeks, they planned a funeral on the island. Jessica didn't want to stay on the island. She used the excuse that she and Timothy had already booked the room at the bed-and-breakfast. She couldn't shake the feeling that something was off about Mary's death, but she couldn't put her finger on it.

She needed to get off the island. Her parents understood. They were feeling creeped out about staying in a house that someone had just died in and they stayed at Lena and Steve's until they could have Mary's funeral.

They all hugged Jimmy and Arthur and told them if they needed anything to call them and headed for the mainland. The revelations still shook Jimmy in the note and the death of his biological mom.

At the bed-and-breakfast, Jessica could finally express her feelings to Timothy about Mary's death.

"None of it makes sense. How could she have been the one to drown me? She would have been wet, right? There wasn't enough time for her to go through the passage and change clothes before entering the room, was there? I feel like that night is becoming a blur. So many revelations in such a short time. I can't even think straight."

"I don't know, Jessica. It seemed like an eternity to me when I was trying to get inside the bathroom. She confessed, though. Jimmy and others verified it was her handwriting. Why would she confess to something she didn't do and then commit suicide?"

"Something just doesn't seem right. I don't know why, but something seems off about it, that's all. I think I just need some sleep."

They both agreed a good night's sleep away from the island and the manor house would be beneficial to them. Jessica filled Timothy in on her slumber party with her sister and how she actually had fun. She fell asleep telling him how happy she was that she finally had found her biological family and she would do everything in her power to help him find his.

Timothy wasn't sure he wanted to know about his biological family anymore. Seeing everything Jessica had been through in the last two weeks, he couldn't imagine having to go through it all himself. Plus, he was content with starting his own family with Jessica. He didn't need anyone else.

After breakfast the next morning, Jessica and Timothy met Lena and Steve. Lena apologized to Jessica for watching her and whispering about her in the café when she and her mother first saw her. She explained she just couldn't get over how much she looked like her mom.

Rita stopped by and was visibly upset about her cousin Mary's death. Lena filled in Jessica about the relationship between her mother and Mary. She also found out about Rita having Lena at a young age. Lena quietly whispered to Jessica. She wished she knew who her biological father was. However, her mother was always tight-lipped about that.

They all did some shopping at the outlets in Riverhead. While they were there, Timothy and Jessica snuck away to his house for a bit. Jessica found it spotless in his bachelor pad. It was small, but quaint. It seemed to work for him, considering he traveled a lot for his different writing assignments. He had a small yard, and the house was a two-bedroom ranch. After a brief discussion, Jessica convinced Timothy that they should just stay at his house until Mary's funeral in two days.

When they told the others they wouldn't be returning to East Hampton until the funeral, there was a disappointment by Richard and Mira. However, they remembered young love and the desire to shut the rest of the world out. They said their goodbyes, and they told each other they'd see each other in a few days.

The further Jessica got away from the island, the more relaxed she felt. Timothy cooked a nice romantic dinner and even lit candles on his table. They settled in on the couch after dinner and watched a movie. Jessica felt so at ease with him. She couldn't believe they had only met two weeks ago.

Timothy's phone ringing interrupted their solitude. It wound up being his editor telling him about an assignment he was being sent on in the everglades of Florida to do an article on the snake overpopulation. He tried requesting Jessica be his photographer again, but his editor stated they already had a photographer lined up. He would leave the day after Mary's funeral.

Jessica was okay with not going, considering the snakes petrified her. Oddly, she received a phone call from her agent about an assignment for her to photograph the Cliffs of Moher in Ireland. She needed to leave the day after Mary's funeral as well. Sadness overwhelmed her, and she cried. She knew she needed to work and Timothy did, too. The thought of being so far away from him even for a few days, though, really was difficult to work through. This would be the first test of their relationship and their careers.

Knowing it would be one of the last nights in a while they would be together, they spent the night making love to one another.

In two days, they made the drive back out to East Hampton and back to the island for Mary's funeral. It wasn't as big or as well attended as Alexandria's had been, but it was big enough. There was still buzzing about the return of Richard. News had spread fast about Mary's suicide and that she had confessed to the attempted murder of her husband. Knowing that helped people to understand why Richard had gone into hiding under a different alias.

When Jessica told Arthur that she would leave the country the next day, it flustered him. They still needed to go over Alexandria's will and get her estate straightened out. They decided that they would have to read the will after everyone left Mary's funeral.

Chapter Twenty-Four

The will

Before the reading of the will, Arthur, Richard, Jimmy, and Jessica sat down to discuss the logistics of how they were going to work together to manage the island. With Mary being deceased, that meant the manor house was empty. Jessica had no desire to live on the island or in the manor house. She felt Jimmy should be the one to live there since he had the most connection to the island.

Richard agreed. His life was in Massachusetts with his family. He felt confident Jimmy could run things on the island and also felt he should live in the manor house. Richard would remove any of his belongings, if any remained. He assumed, though, that Mary had gotten rid of them years ago.

Jimmy was agreeable to running the island. He just wasn't sure how he felt about living in the manor house. His mind was still processing all that had transpired over the last two weeks. Finding out who his biological mom was and losing her in a week's time was overwhelming. Not to mention finding out both his biological parents were murderers. It made him question whether he had any psychopathic tendencies. He could not share those thoughts with anyone for fear of others thinking he was dangerous or incompetent. He agreed to at least try living in the house for a period.

There were still things that made Jessica nervous about telling the island inhabitants who Alexandria's heirs were. Mary's suicide still didn't sit right with her. Neither did her confessions. It did not convince her they were safe.

"Arthur, is there any way we can keep our lineage to Alexandria a secret? Or at least Jimmy's?"

"I suppose we could, but why should we?"

"To be honest, there are things about Mary's death that don't sit right with me. I can't pinpoint what exactly it is. I just don't feel that we are safe."

"Jimmy, what are your thoughts?"

Jimmy was listening to the conversation between Arthur and Jessica. He thought he was the only one that questioned Mary's death. Hearing Jessica's concerns made him feel a little less crazy.

"I agree with Jessica. I can't pinpoint what isn't settling right with Mary's death, either. However, I do not feel as if we are safe. I feel Jessica and Richard are safer being away from the island. So I agree, not telling everyone that I am actually a Gardiner is the safest bet."

They all agreed they would not disclose the lineage of Jimmy. Jimmy left the meeting to tell everyone it was time for the reading of the will. The others joined the rest of Richard's family and Timothy and explained to them quickly what they were going to do.

Once everyone came together, Arthur addressed the group.

"Good evening all, thank you for being patient and waiting for Alexandria's will to be read. I am going to ask you all to remain quiet while I read the will and explain things. When I am done, you can ask questions you may have."

He then cleared his throat and continued.

"The last will and testament of Alexandria Cromwell. The declarations state: This is my will. All previous wills and codicils are void. I live in Manhattan, New York. I am widowed. Nomination of executor: I nominate the individual or bank, or trust company below as the first choice as executor to carry out the instructions of this will. No bond or other security of any kind will be required of any party acting in a fiduciary capacity for my estate/ or any trust created through my will. I grant to my executor the following powers. The power to exercise all powers of an absolute owner of property. Power to keep, sell at public or private sale, exchange, grant options on, invest and reinvest, and otherwise deal with real or personal property. The power to borrow money and pledge any property to secure loans along with the power to divide and distribute property in cash or in kind. The power to compromise and release claims with or without considerations. Power to pay my legally enforceable debts, funeral expenses, expenses of last illness, and all expenses in connection with the administration of my estate and the trusts created by my will. The power to employ attorneys, accountants and other persons for services and advice and any other powers conferred upon executors wherever my executor may act. If the first choice does not serve, then I nominate the second choice to serve. My first choice is Arthur Brockton, my personal attorney. My second choice is Allison Simmons, my friend and CEO of Cromwell Real Estate Investments. The disposition of property. Specific gifts of cash. I make the following cash gift (s) to the following person (s) or organization (s) named below. I initial my name in the box next to each gift. To Stella and John Driscoll, I leave $100,000. If Stella and John Driscoll do not survive me, I leave this gift to their heirs-at-law. If they have no heirs-at-law, they shall distribute the gift as residue of my estate."

Arthur continued listing each employee of the island, except for one. He continued reading the will.

"I leave the whole of my company Cromwell Real Estate Investments and Gardiner Island to my heirs at law. I leave in place the agreement with Mary Gardiner as to her living on the island. Residuary Estate. Except for specific gift (s) made above, I leave my residuary estate, after the payment of any estate tax, as follows, and I initial my name in each box after each gift. I leave a third of my residual estate to Arthur Brockton. To Jessica Greenhall, I leave 33.34% of my residual estate. To Jimmy Driscoll, I leave 33.34% of my residual estate. If any beneficiary of this gift does not survive me, I leave his/her share to their heirs-at-law. If there are no heirs-at-law, then their share will be distributed as residue of my estate. General provisions. Severability. If any provisions of this will are deemed unenforceable, then the remaining provisions shall remain in full force and effect. Survivorship. I shall deem no beneficiary to survive me unless such beneficiary remains alive 30 days after my death. Any beneficiary prohibited by law from inheriting property from me shall be treated as having failed to survive me."

As Arthur finished reading the will, the room was abuzz with conversation among the inhabitants. One inhabitant walked out of the room without saying a word to anyone. The only one that seemed to notice was Jessica. She had been watching the reactions intently of everyone in the room. Everyone seemed pleased except for the one person not mentioned in the will, Samuel.

Jessica approached Arthur and quietly asked him.

"Why wasn't Samuel mentioned in Alexandria's will?"

"Samuel was not and is not an employee of Alexandria. Mary hired him and she paid him. I need to catch up with him and discuss that with him. Jimmy has said that he wants to keep him on and take over paying his salary. Do you agree with that?"

"Yes, I absolutely want to keep him on. I hope Alexandria did not slight him by not gifting him money like the others, though?"

"I will let him know. Mary's lawyer has also already informed me she left him a sizeable gift in her will, so I will inform him of that as well."

"Thank you, Arthur, I must be saying my goodbyes for now. I have to get home and pack for my assignment in Ireland. I leave tomorrow."

Timothy and Jessica said their goodbyes and headed back to Jessica's house in Connecticut. They both would catch flights to their respective assignments the next day. Jessica was forlorn that she did not have more time to spend with her family, however, she felt hopeful that when she returned, they could get together.

The inhabitants seemed happy with the fact they left Jimmy in charge of the island. They explained that both Richard and Jessica, the only known heirs-at-law of Alexandria, had requested that Jimmy would be in charge of the island. It was also explained that Jessica had asked Alexandria to name Jimmy as a residuary recipient to compensate him for his work of running things on the island. Everyone seemed pleased with this explanation. All the inhabitants went to their homes, content that their jobs and homes were secure.

Richard and his family headed home to Massachusetts. Richard and Mira felt freer knowing the truth was finally out there about them. Their adult children were in shock at the events that had transpired over the last several days. They were happy though that they got to meet their big sister. Even Richard Jr. had warmed up to her.

Arthur caught up to Samuel and explained why there was no mention of him in Alexandria's will. He also explained Mary's will. Samuel seemed surprised that it named him in Mary's and Arthur seemed to think it made up for not being named in Alexandria's. The two men parted ways and went about their own duties.

The silence in the manor house was deafening to Jimmy, who, after everyone had left, was alone. He worried he might go insane being all alone with his thoughts in the big house. *Is that what happened to Mary?* Thinking about his biological mother lead to him remembering the conversation with Jessica earlier. He went up to Mary's room to look around.

Shivers ran down his spine when Jimmy walked into Mary's room. They had left everything the way they found it that fateful morning. When he went into the bathroom, he remembered what he had missed in the bathroom during the investigation into Jessica's near drowning. Opening the linen closet, he found that there indeed was another secret passageway leading up to the attic. There were passageways from every bathroom to the attic. He wasn't sure what the original purpose was, however; he knew they made it easy for someone to sneak around the house undetected.

The question in his mind, though, was, could Mary have attempted to drown Jessica, sneak back to her room, change clothes, and then reappear with no one noticing? He was determined to test the theory and gathered the items needed to simulate the situation. He attempted to submerge a makeshift dummy, escape, change clothes in Mary's room, and then reappear as if nothing had been done. The first attempt was an utter failure. After locking the door and turning off the lights, it was nearly impossible to move around the bathroom purposefully. She would have had to have had night vision goggles.

Every member of the security team, including himself, had a pair, so borrowing or finding a pair was not impossible. He used his pair for the next attempt at recreating the scenario. No matter how many times he attempted the scenario, he could not escape, change out of the wet clothes, and reappear in less than 20 minutes. Far longer than it took for Mary to appear that night from what Timothy and Jessica had stated.

According to this information, Mary could not have been the one to attempt drowning Jessica. Even though she confessed to doing so in her suicide note. If Mary didn't do it, then maybe she didn't actually commit suicide. How would Jimmy prove that, though? He would discretely keep digging and investigating everything that occurred in the last two weeks. If Mary was not the murderer, then he or she was still walking amongst them. He had to be very careful with who he trusted any information with as well.

For now, he decided not to tell anyone else.

Chapter Twenty-Five

Family Thanksgiving

Weeks went by and Timothy and Jessica moved in together. Jessica precipitated the decision coming home from her Ireland assignment to find her house broken into and ransacked. They took nothing of value, although the one thing that was taken Jessica hadn't told the police, her family, or even Timothy.

Things had been so quiet since Mary's death that she didn't want to upset anyone. She didn't even know the significance of the stolen item. It was the note she had received prior to going back to Gardiners Island for Alexandria's funeral. Nothing had happened to her when she returned to the island, so she felt it had been one of her many crazed stalker-type fans.

Still, the break-in made her feel vulnerable and unsettled and that helped push Timothy into the decision to move in with her. Timothy put his house on the market and moved in with Jessica.

Jessica made a weekly trip to Manhattan to sit in on the board meeting of the Cromwell Real Estate Investment Corporation. She was grateful for the CEO, Allison. Alexandria knew how to hire the right people to get the job done.

Allison was intelligent, resourceful, and was always full of innovative ideas. Jessica admired her and felt very confident in her running the company. Richard also attended the weekly board meetings, along with Jimmy.

Afterward, the three would meet to discuss the island and how things were going there. Jimmy was managing things there well and still hadn't told the others he had figured out about Mary's death and confession not being plausible. He was still doing information gathering.

A week before Thanksgiving, Jimmy invited the family to the manor house to have a traditional Thanksgiving dinner. They were all planning on attending and all were going to stay at the house. Jimmy had told everyone that for safety and security reasons, he had installed a padlock on the kitchen door to the attic and he was the only person with a key as an added measure.

The night before Thanksgiving, they all returned to the island. Stella was busy preparing some of the dinner dishes and baking several pies. The aromas made everyone's mouths water with the anticipation of the next day's feast. If anyone dared enter the kitchen though to steal a taste, she met them with a tap of a wooden spoon to their hands.

Jimmy had converted the parlor into a den. It had a pool table and a ping-pong table in it. He replaced the antique sofa and other furniture with more modern comfortable couches and chairs. The family approved, and they all enjoyed challenging each other to both games.

The next morning, Stella cooked up a grand breakfast to start the morning festivities. She made all the different pancakes, eggs, bacon, and sausages. The entire family enjoyed every morsel.

Jessica had never had a big family. She also never had a big traditional Thanksgiving. While it was all new experiences for her, she was soaking up all the fabulous memories they were all making.

Mira was content knowing all her children were finally all together with her and Richard. She watched as her children bonded with their older sister more with each passing day. There were so many blessings to be thankful for this Thanksgiving. She knew she would etch this in her memory as her favorite holiday memory.

When they all sat down to dinner, they said a blessing, shared what they were each thankful for, and then ate. Richard was happily sitting at the head of the table. He was glad to be with his family, however, he still had pangs of guilt and sadness regarding Alexandria and her family. He missed them all.

Sitting at the table he had grown up at brought back all those bittersweet memories. This is what he had always wanted for himself, though. A family of his own, sitting enjoying a holiday meal together. He knew soon the family would expand as his children settled down. As he looked at his son Richard with his girlfriend Danielle sitting next to him and Jessica with Timothy sitting next to her. He wondered which couple would get married first.

Danielle and Richard had known each other for years and just recently became a couple. Timothy and Jessica had only met months ago and had dove headfirst into their relationship. He couldn't judge either couple. He had done the slow and steady with Mary and the fast and furious with Mira. All he wanted for his children was for them to be happy and healthy.

After dinner, the family retired back into the den. They had a ping-pong tournament going, that was getting pretty competitive. Jimmy was currently in the lead. He was glad everyone was enjoying themselves. He also felt confident in all his security measures. There had been no strange accidents or deaths in the month following Mary's apparent suicide and confession. It was good to see everyone relaxed and having fun.

Timothy and Richard had left the room briefly and, on their return, were both smiling wryly. Jessica was playing a fierce game of ping-pong against her sister Samantha, in which she was narrowly winning. When she had won, Timothy approached her, grabbed her arm and raised it in the air, proclaiming her a winner. As he dropped her arm, he dropped to one knee and continued holding her hand.

"Jessica, it's been a whirlwind ride for the last several weeks, but there is no one else I would rather spend the rest of my life with. Will you marry me?"

"Yes!"

The entire room erupted with excitement and congratulations. Mira had tears of joy. Richard proudly smiled and slapped Timothy on the back in congratulations. Samantha couldn't wait to help her sister plan her wedding. David and Richard Jr. welcomed Timothy as their brother-in-law to be. Jimmy congratulated the couple and offered for them to hold the wedding on the island if they wished.

Emotions overjoyed Jessica. A few months earlier, she hadn't even known who she was. She had no family that she knew of and, by a weird twist of fate, she had found them. She also had found the love of her life. Something a few short months ago she had not even thought possible.

Nothing could take the smile off her face. The rest of the weekend, the family helped Jimmy decorate the manor house for Christmas. They even went to a local Christmas tree farm and cut the biggest tree they could find.

As they decorated the tree, they made plans to spend the Christmas holiday together at the manor house. They also discussed possible wedding dates. Jessica and Timothy decided on a July wedding. They thought having the wedding in the manor gardens would be simply wonderful, as they forgot all about their first few times on the island and the bad luck that had befallen them.

Soon, it was time for them all to leave and head home. The family thanked Jimmy for his hospitality and said their goodbyes to each other. They all left the island with hope in their hearts that the tragedies of the island's past were all behind them. Jimmy breathed a sigh of relief as they all drove away to the rickety ferry that he had kept them all safe this time.

There were no signs of trouble the whole long weekend. He had the security team on constant patrols. No one had reported seeing anyone or anything out of the ordinary. He thought Mary had been the intended target all along. That all the other accidents and near-death experiences were to frame Mary. Jimmy couldn't think of a motive, though.

Mary had left everything to the one employee she had hired on the island, Samuel. He wasn't aware he even stood to inherit anything until after her death. That meant inheritance could not be a motive. Samuel had been angry at first with not receiving anything from Alexandria's estate, but then learning he had inherited everything from Mary, made up for it. Mary had always treated him well, and he was grateful for that.

Mary's death nagged at Jimmy. He knew he was missing something, but he couldn't figure out what. Every day, he made his usual rounds on the island. He would stop at the beach she frequently sat at, waiting for his father to return after the fateful boating accident. He still couldn't believe they had conspired to kill Richard. It made him mad his parents were capable of such atrocities. He was madder with himself for caring about who killed his mother, but he told himself it was his job to know and keep everyone safe.

That's what he would focus on now, keeping everyone who stepped foot on the island safe. As he did his evening rounds, he looked at the rickety old ferry and decided at their next meeting he would suggest replacing it. He knew Jessica would probably agree since she always complained about how it made her nervous.

He would talk to Captain Bill, who drove the ferry, and get his recommendations. Jimmy felt they should do it before Jessica and Timothy's wedding. He wanted his cousin's day to be just perfect. They had grown quite fond of each other over the last few months, despite their rocky start.

Jessica and Timothy got home, and they sat together on their couch, looking at wedding websites on Jessica's laptop. She couldn't believe they were planning their wedding. She didn't want it to be too fancy, although with it being on the island, she knew there would be a slight air of fanciness. Her sister and her mother were already texting her all kinds of wedding ideas. She felt grateful she could share her excitement with them. She also knew that Timothy had no family to share his excitement with.

Jessica was even more determined now to find his family. She encouraged him to log in to the genealogy website he had submitted his DNA to months ago. When his results had first come in over a month ago, there were several hundred distant cousins and some 4th cousins. However, there had been no closer relatives. This time, when he logged in, there was a match with a second cousin. He messaged the person to find out as much information from them about their family as he could. And then came the waiting game for a response.

Timothy didn't know what he would do with the information, since he did not know what part of this family's tree would be a help to him. He made a promise to Jessica to check his messages daily and his matches. Together, they were determined to find out who he was.

Chapter Twenty-Six

In the shadows

When they heard the family was coming to the island for Thanksgiving, they grumbled. There wasn't enough time to really plan any proper welcoming. The anger was brewing and there was no release.

Finding the padlock on the kitchen door to the attic increased their anger. Why was it padlocked? *Damn it, Jimmy. You and your high horse security measures.* They mumbled to themselves. They would have to resort to spying on the family from the outside of the house this time. Until they could figure out a more sophisticated way to hear what was going on.

As the family arrived on the island, the hatred for them all simmered. Revenge would be sweet, eventually. They would bide their time and plan carefully. Calculating every move they made. Everything that was to occur had to be planned just right.

Watching the family the first night was nauseating. Their laughter carried away from the house as they watched from the shadows of the gardens. It was tempting to ruin their fun with a few scare tactics. Patience was not their strong suit, however, they resisted.

The worst was watching through the windows as they decorated the Christmas tree. That reminded them of their childhood and the Christmas mornings they endured. That was if their mother even was sober enough to realize what the date was. Or if she wasn't busy entertaining one of her gentlemen friends.

After the family left for the weekend, they had heard rumors they would be back for the Christmas holiday. That gave them time to do some planning. Not much time, however, enough to do some prep work. They also heard about the wedding in July. No actual date, though. That was disappointing. They secretly hoped for the fourth of July.

That would be poetic justice. They smiled and laughed at the thought. Fireworks and explosions would make a perfect distraction. Rubbing their hands together with anticipatory excitement, they started making plans.

This will be an epic ending for them and a beautiful new beginning for me.

Erasing Secrets

The Lyons Garden Book Two

D.M. Foley

Remember My Roots Press

"Believe me, every heart has its secret sorrows, which the world knows not, and often times we call a man cold, when he is only sad." HENRY WADSWORTH LONGFELLOW

Chapter One

Winter Chill

Winter on Gardiners Island started early, with the first snowfall in the first week of December. It began by lightly covering the ground and the treetops. The soft sea breeze carried the fluffy snow into little drifts here and there, mimicking the dunes along the beach. Bundled up, Jimmy rode his ATV around the island, doing his security rounds. Occasionally stopping to drink from the thermos full of hot coffee Stella had made for him. The coffee did wonders, warming him from the inside out.

It had been weeks since Mary had committed suicide, and someone had pushed Alexandria to her death. The hush of the snowfall amplified the quiet stillness that had encompassed the island since those tragic events had unfolded. He had no evidence that Mary hadn't actually committed suicide. However, the investigation he had done refuted that she was the one who almost drowned Jessica. So Mary's confession to that act still did not ring faithful to him. This made him question her apparent suicide. None of it proved out. No rationale why Mary would confess crimes she could not have committed. However, his daily remorse over her suicide was a completely different story. His disdain for her past transgressions had led her to make the very permanent, rash decision to end her life. She was his biological mother. That truth had been the ultimate shock, and it was still hard for him to fathom.

Jimmy had known Ms. Mary his entire life. The adoptive son of Stella and John Driscoll, growing up on the island as he walked through the Manor house gardens with the woman he knew as Ms. Mary. His parents worked on the island while he spent time with her. She had loved him even when she didn't know he was indeed her son. Giving up her child caused her immense grief, but ironically, the same child later became the source of her healing. Without the understanding, the child was hers.

After making his morning rounds, he wound up at the family cemetery. Jimmy placed a small bouquet on Mary's grave after wiping the accumulation of snow off her headstone. It was her birthday. Compelled to pay his respects to the woman that had given him life. He let a single tear roll down his cheek.

The eerie silence with snow falling, compounded by realizing the tragic losses the cemetery had held, sent a shiver up his spine. Then, turning to leave, he noticed a new memorial box lovingly left recently at Alexandria's headstone. Jimmy smiled, knowing that it was Arthur who had put it there. Arthur visited Alexandria weekly and did a great job honoring her by taking care of her plot and headstone.

Jimmy had noticed the change in Arthur since Alexandria's death. His usual cheerful demeanor had turned glum and depressive. His conversations were short and sweet. They mostly filled those talks with business issues or legal issues that needed to be handled. Jimmy tried to help by inviting him to the family Thanksgiving he had hosted. However, Arthur didn't feel very festive and declined the invite.

The hope that Christmas would be different, Jimmy had already extended the invitation for Arthur to join the family for the holiday coming up. Arthur said he would think about it. Jimmy had already bought gifts for the family, making trips to the mainland. The presents piled up fast from him.

He had found some pretty cool filters and lenses for Jessica. He knew she would enjoy using them in her photography. It still amazed him they shared a birthday, and they were cousins. Neither of them had known their biological families until a few months ago. It had been a whirlwind discovery that had thrown them into the throes of owning and running the island and a multimillion-dollar real estate company.

His life on the island hadn't changed too much. Other than moving from his parent's small farmhouse to the Manor house on the island. He had stayed the head of security. The only difference was the weekly trip into the city to sit on the real estate business board meeting. That aspect of the additional responsibilities was demanding. In keeping Jimmy's secret, the reasons for him being there were wearisome. Lies told to the inhabitants, and even the board members, were burdensome. He was thankful for his Uncle Richard. He had more business prowess and understanding than Jimmy or Jessica would ever have. It made managing the business easier for them both. Jessica had expressed to him frequently that she was also thankful that her father was also savvy with the company. It gave her the freedom to continue doing her photography business.

Jimmy knew planning her wedding with Timothy also took up a lot of Jessica's time. They had picked the date of July seventh to be wed on the island in the Manor house garden at the gazebo. It thrilled her parents that they had made that decision and were excitedly helping with the plans. Jimmy, though, was apprehensive. The information he knew about Mary's death and confession weighed heavily on his mind and worried him.

The only consolation was the knowledge that it would be a relatively small wedding party and reception. Jessica had asked her sister Samantha to be her maid of honor. Timothy was still searching for any trace of his biological family. Sadly, despite having a second cousin match on the genealogy website, there had been no response to his inquiry. To complicate matters Timothy had no brothers through his adoptive parents. Not having many close male friends compounded the situation. So Timothy asked her brother Richard to be his best man. Being adopted and having no siblings, Jimmy could relate and sympathize with Timothy's plight.

Jimmy found it sad Timothy's adoptive parents were angry with him for attempting to find out who his biological parents were and had disowned him. Even the news of him meeting Jessica and asking her to marry him hadn't softened their hearts to their perceived betrayal by him. Timothy had expressed feeling blessed over meeting Jessica when he did. Their relationship had started only a few months prior and had blossomed quickly. Feeling graced with the supportive and loving adoptive parents, Jimmy empathized with Timothy.

Timothy and Jimmy had quickly become good friends after their rocky start. They could laugh now at the fact Jimmy thought Timothy was the one behind Jessica's near-drowning and ATV accident. Those events that occurred were perplexing to them all. The peculiar way they had brought together the family was a silver lining to the chaos.

Walking into the Manor kitchen to grab some breakfast from Stella, Jimmy continued contemplating the last few months of his life.

"Morning, my son. You look down on this beautiful day."

"Thinking about the last few months. The craziness of it all. Feeling blessed for you and Dad, but also feeling sad about Ms. Mary."

"Ah, I know your life has changed, and I know you must still grieve the loss of Ms. Mary, your mother, but she would want you to move on, son."

"I know, Ma, it's just hard. I feel guilty, you know. If I hadn't had such a powerful reaction, she wouldn't have killed herself."

"Son, it wasn't your fault. You reacted the way anyone would have in your shoes. She reacted the way she felt was right for her. Ms. Mary always only thought of herself and how things affected her. It was her biggest fault and was her downfall."

"I know all of that, but it doesn't change the way I feel."

"It's okay to feel a little guilty, and it means you are human and you care. I would worry if you didn't feel a bit of guilt. However, don't live there in guilt. Feel it, acknowledge it, forgive yourself, and move on from it."

"Thanks, Mom. I love you. Please never change. Remember, you and Dad will always be my number one parents. No matter what. I know I am feeling the loss of my mother, but I am thankful for you."

Jimmy finished his breakfast and headed back out into the swirling snow.

Samuel, the mechanic, passed by Jimmy as he climbed back onto his ATV.

"Morning, Jimmy."

"Good morning, Samuel. It's a cold one today."

"Yup."

"Stay warm. Stella's got coffee brewing in the kitchen. You can help yourself to some."

"Thanks, maybe I will. Later."

"You are welcome. Have a good day."

"You too."

Jimmy could tell he was busy fixing something because grease covered his overalls. Samuel, a quiet man, could restore any machine on the island. This made him a valuable asset to the island's operations. An employee for the last twenty-two years. With no family ties to the place. Unlike most of the other inhabitants who had grown up on the island their entire lives, like Jimmy. As he watched, Samuel climbed into his pickup truck and headed toward the ferry to the mainland. Jimmy figured he was on the hunt to get some parts. This was a common occurrence.

At the security shack, Jimmy met up with a few of his security crew. Zach was a twenty-year-old who had joined the security team when he graduated from high school two years prior. His father, Matt, was also a member of the crew. They were both sitting, monitoring the radio chatter of the rest of the team. Four team members were out on two boats patrolling the island perimeter from the water. Four other members were out on ATVs roaming the vast acres of the island. Today, with the snow falling and the wind blowing, it wasn't a fun job.

Most days, though, they all found their job to be exciting. They routinely caught teenagers coming ashore by boat to party on the beaches on the island. After reading about Captain Kidd burying his glory on the island, some searched for pirate treasure. Then there were the regular tabloid journalists who always dogged the family. Since Richard's mysterious return to the island after Alexandria's death, and Mary's suicide, the tabloid journalists had been more frequent. He hoped the change in the weather would curb the influx, though. Most journalists seemed to be fair-weather friends, so Jimmy and his crew looked forward to a much-needed reprieve.

"Hey, boss. When is the Gardiner family coming out for the holidays?"

"A few days before Christmas Eve."

He raised his eyebrows.

Zach was usually shy and rarely asked questions about the comings and goings of anyone on the island. Jimmy was curious why now he seemed interested in the family's arrival.

"ALL of them are coming, right? Even Samantha."

He was smiling from ear to ear.

There it was. Zach had a crush on Samantha. Jimmy laughed and patted him on the back. Jimmy was a sucker for immature love.

"Yes, Samantha will be here. Do you want me to introduce you to her?"

Zach got extremely quiet, blushing, and shook his head yes.

"Get spruced up for the party. I will definitely introduce you to her."

"Sounds like a plan, boss. Now don't forget."

"How could I forget to introduce two potential love birds?"

The plan was to introduce them during the Christmas Eve open house. He was planning on hosting it for the island inhabitants and the family. Matt, Zach's father, just chuckled and shook his head at the two men's exchange. Secretly, he was hoping his son would hit it off with the younger Gardiner daughter. Relation to the family through marriage wouldn't be a bad thing.

"Hey Zach, if you play your cards right, you may end up part-owner of the island."

"Dad, don't rush things. Samantha is a mainlander and you know how they can be towards us."

"Don't sell yourself short, son. You have what it takes to win her heart."

"Ah. I hope so. I don't want to be a part-owner. That is just way too much responsibility. I want to know the green-eyed beauty with red flowing hair."

Matt chuckled again. He had grown up on the island. Both his parents grew up there, got married, and raised their family. He was the only one who stayed and had gotten a job himself on the island, raising his own family. His wife helped take care of the gardens.

Many older families like him found it harder and harder to convince their children to stay and continue living there. He was happy Zach enjoyed working for the security team alongside him. His college daughter had no aspiration to come back. Few jobs available made living on the mainland more appealing to the younger generations.

"Don't run off with the mainlander and leave your parents."

"Why would I leave here? I have the best job!"

The biggest job was security. The wives of the security team worked the sprawling gardens around the Manor house. There were a few specialty jobs. Stella was the Manor house cook, Martin the butler, and Betty, the housekeeper. Captain Bill, the ferry captain, had a small crew that helped him run the ferry to and from the island. Jimmy knew losing the family atmosphere on the island was inevitable. How soon that occurred was the question. For now, he was thankful that he had Zach and Matt.

"This party will be different."

"I am excited to take part in festivities instead of being outsiders, looking in."

"I am glad you are excited. I hope others are as well."

"Oh, others definitely are! It is the talk of the island! You are doing good, Jimmy. I am proud of you."

Matt was hoping for a change on the island. Maybe that would bring his daughter back. He hoped she would hear of the changes and give it a shot. The thought of his family's legacy on the island eventually dying out saddened him.

"I am making it a family atmosphere. Instead of us vs. them. The younger family members are unique. Maybe since they didn't grow up knowing they were part of the Gardiner family."

"I hope so, boss. I want to know them better. Especially, Samantha."

"I think you are going to like them all, Zach. Not just Samantha."

"Well, I am only interested in her. I am sure they're all nice."

"You realize being friends with her brothers will be a benefit to you, right?"

"Yeah, I am aware. I need to know her first. She may not even like me. No sense wasting time befriending her brothers."

"You have a point there. Don't forget, she has a big sister too. And from what I have learned about her, she is feisty."

"Honestly, I am not worried about the big sister. I am used to big sisters. They don't scare me."

Jimmy just shook his head at Zach. Not wanting to think about the changes or Zach's sister. The changes would come, though. It was inevitable.

They would have to replace people when they retired with others from the mainland. Something he didn't want to do. He knew bringing more mainlanders onto the island would eventually taint the entire island. Ultimately the newcomers would want to usher in mainland ideas to the tranquility of the island. Samuel mentioned to Jimmy the island would make a great tourist resort on several occasions during their conversations.

While he understood Samuel's idea, he knew Samuel didn't understand the love of the island most of the inhabitants had. It was history. It was untouched by the outside world. In places on the island, one could feel transported. Native Americans had lived there. They could feel the spirits of the generations of ancestors from the past. Jimmy found many arrowheads and other artifacts. He couldn't imagine desecrating the island with a resort.

With his head still deep in thought Jimmy left the security shack and started his afternoon rounds. He noticed the snow had stopped falling. They had received about three inches of accumulation throughout the morning. He could hear the roar of a truck engine coming up the road. Jimmy recognized it as Samuel's.

When Samuel got out of his truck, he headed towards the cemetery instead of the barn. Jimmy noticed the bouquet in Samuel's hands. He watched from a distance as Samuel placed the spray of white roses at Mary's grave. It was touching to watch someone else pay their respects on her birthday.

It made sense Samuel would, considering Mary had hired him. Moreover, she left him a sizable chunk of her estate so that he might have felt a sense of obligation towards her. Whatever the reason, it warmed his heart that someone else remembered his biological mother's birthday.

Chapter Two

Secrets

The most minute detail could spoil the best-laid plans. An early snowstorm was a stark reminder of that. The layer of snow would make it hard not to leave a trace. They had done well until now, hiding their comings and goings.

In a few short weeks, the family would return. However, plans formed made them feel that revenge would bring them elation.

The cage of crows crowded the back bedroom. Their cawing had become loud and annoying, so they threw a sheet over the cage to quiet the noise. Smiling, they couldn't wait till they could silence the lot of them for good. In due time, the blasted birds would serve their purpose.

As they sat thinking about the crows, a childhood memory crept into their mind. They had been out on a walk and found a fledgling that had fallen out of its nest. Finding the nest had proven fruitless. They brought the fledgling home and put it in a shoebox hoping to care for it until it could be released back into the wild.

Mom had become irate in a drunken stupor, yelling, "Why did they carry another mouth in the house to feed?" She could provide little for them as it was. Her gentleman caller had taken the shoebox from their tiny shaking hands. They remembered how he grabbed the fledgling with aggression from the box and snapped its neck. Right there, in front of them all. Their mother was not fazed by the violent act and seemed relieved that the problem of another mouth to feed had been eliminated.

This hadn't horrified them either, even though they were a young child. The many gentleman callers of their mother had shown them all sorts of violence over the years. Instead, the finality and swiftness of it all fascinated them. One minute the fledgling was alive, and the next, it was lying limp with its head hanging. The power that this man had displayed lit them on fire. Did they hold the same power? To control another living being's life and subsequent death?

As they sat contemplating that thought, a cockroach crawled from behind the couch. Reaching for it and grabbing it, they held it between their fingers and twisted it. They kept rotating until the creature was in two parts. This act ignited a sense of life they hadn't felt before. Until that point, they had just existed for ten years. Not living, just surviving. The school they attended was boring, and they had no real friends. Not even the other children on the island. This senseless violent act had now given them a purpose, though. They could choose what lived or died or who.

That memory made them smile. They have come far since that day. With each kill, they felt stronger. When they took each creature's life, something transferred its essence to them. The power they expected to feel in the future excited them. They needed patience for it all to work out.

The snow posed a problem. They had to spy on the family without being caught. Jimmy locking the kitchen door to the attic had taken some wind out of their sails. They used those passageways for years, spying on the inhabitants. They knew all the family secrets, good and bad.

Their mother was one of the dirty little secrets. It was by following her one day that they discovered the passageways. Mom got dolled up. She said she was going out and had left a plate of food on the table. A piece of stale bread and a slice of bologna. They hadn't been hungry and curiosity had gotten the better of themselves. Their mother had crept through the darkness to the back door of the Manor house. She stealthily opened the back door and then went through the attic doorway directly across the entryway. They had lagged behind so as not to get seen but continued to follow their mother. That was when they had found their mother in the Lord of the Manor's bed. Their first glimpse of the darkness. They were six and didn't quite understand what the two naked adults were doing. Curiosity engulfed them, they became interested in the physical interactions between the two.

After that night they followed their mother regularly and came to understand in a very basic way what their Mother's purpose was, servicing the Lord with the Lady away. In return, she could live in one of the servant's homes on the island with her child. He gave her a day job to obscure her actual occupation. There wasn't love, at least not from him. However, the way their mother kissed this man was different than how she kissed her gentleman callers. It was clear she cared more about him. Clear even to a young child. Although it was also clear the man was dismissive towards her. It was pure desire, though when they were together. The pleasure expressed by both participants was so intense that it bordered on abuse.

From that first night forward. The passageways themselves were used to gather all the secrets they could. There were plenty with the Gardiner family. The outside world thought the family had perfect lives. They came to know the brutal truth. As a child, they didn't quite understand the power these secrets wielded. The older they got the more they appreciated the potential the secrets held.

Many times a phone call to the tabloids would have ruined the family in its entirety. They didn't, though. Instead, they gathered and documented everything they could and kept the secrets hidden from everyone. The unknown, known to them, and holding the key to a whole family's destiny, felt powerful. The power they craved and lived for. The energy they killed for and would again.

The family had done an excellent job of unearthing several secrets. Richard, coming out of hiding, had been a big one. They hadn't seen that one coming. One secret they hadn't known. The entire world had thought he died in the tragic sailboat accident. Instead, he survived and started a new life with his mistress of several years. That life was happy until Alexandria's death.

Much as her death had given them such a sense of power and purpose, it was incidental. Not planned, at least not so soon. They had tried to start a discussion with the old bat. Tried to reveal one secret they knew to be the truth. She hadn't wanted to listen, even when they tried showing her proof. They had tried to grab her to stop her from walking away and had made her lose her balance. She had fallen down the stairs in a crumpled mess. Surprisingly, she survived for a few days. She had told the police someone pushed her. However, she hadn't said by whom. That was the most bewildering part. She had known. That is one secret she kept till her death.

Her death had become a catalyst for so many of the family's unearthed secrets. How Mary's betrayal of Richard's trust had revealed the truth about their lost child. That child, who was not Richard's, was also a Gardiner descendant. Just another of the dark secrets. Very few knew about Jimmy. Only the Gardiner family themselves, Arthur and Jimmy's adoptive parents, and them. Knowing this brought a flutter to their heart and a gleam to their eyes. That secret would be useful. When the time came. It would come. Secrets were powerful weapons used at the right time. They could serve them well. Mary's secrets had benefited them well a few months ago. They had gotten the police off the island.

The police presence had made them paranoid. They hadn't expected the authorities to become involved, even with the accidents that had occurred. All explainable as accidents. The old bat told police someone pushed her down the stairs. That's when things changed. They devised a plan to get the police off the island. It could have been bad if they had stayed and investigated longer.

However, Richard's return caused the chaos of unearthed secrets which had set up a perfect scenario to remove the police. Mary's reaction was predictable, which helped them get rid of her. That night had worked out perfectly. Mary had locked herself in her room and started drinking, which was her standard practice when upset.

They had seized on the opportunity and snuck through the passageway. Mary set up the bathwater, as they watched, giving them the perfect setup to stage her suicide. They had added a few pills to the wine glass when they distracted Mary with the cell phone calls. Then waited until she was incoherent to be coached to write the note. They had added the rest of the pills to her last glass of wine and watched as she drifted into unconsciousness. As Mary slipped under the water, they remembered watching the bubbles from her nose and mouth end. She served her purpose well. They smiled again at the thought of every secret serving a purpose.

Lunch break was over. They had to get back to work. The mundane chore of their everyday existence bored them. They needed to release some pent-up frustration, needed a power rush before returning to work, and needed to feel alive.

The covered cage of crows was tempting. They thought about just taking one. Would it matter if they killed one earlier than planned? Could the remains serve a purpose if it was decomposing already?

Out of the corner of their eye, they saw a field mouse scurry across the counter. They mused at the perfect timing. With swift experience, they caught the mouse and hung onto its tail. The mouse struggled to get out of the grip of their fingers.

Slow and calculated. Fast and furious. Those choices they had to make. Each had its pros and cons. Each also had its satisfying reward. They went slow and calculated and filled the kitchen sink with water.

As they lowered the mouse headfirst into the water, the sound of its frantic squeaks filled the air. Just as it seemed to give up the fight, they yanked it back out of the water. Then, as it caught its breath and wriggled to life again, they lowered it again into the water. They repeated the process until the mouse no longer regained its breath and was lifeless in their fingers.

They tossed the dead mouse into the trash, sighing. They washed up, put their coat on, and headed back to work, feeling alive with energy. The rush never got old. The small kills didn't give a big lift or energy boost as the big kills, though.

They needed a hunt for a more significant kill. Later, they would see if they could get a kill out in the fields. One to hold them for longer. They needed to hold out a few more weeks. To plan was crucial, anticipating snow a few days earlier, they had ordered a drone to assist them in spying on the family. It came quickly and would help them gather more secrets. The more secrets they had, the more power they held. They had plenty of time to learn how to use it. Maybe they would take it hunting with them later. That helped solve the problem of leaving tracks in the snow while spying outside. Then they had the brilliant idea of bugging rooms in the

Manor house. Technology was becoming their best friend. They would order the necessary equipment later that night.

The rest of the afternoon was routine. They went about their work as normal, seeing Jimmy doing his rounds on his ATV. They watched and pondered how he would react when his secrets came out. He wouldn't be able to deny them. There was too much proof. His secrets would play a vital role in their plans for the family.

With the darkness, they would erase every family secret, except one.

Chapter Three

Family Tensions

Jessica was watching the snowfall out her window as she drank her cup of tea. The weekly board meeting was canceled because of the impending storm. So she found herself with nothing planned for the day and time to kill. She was lonely with Timothy being away for the next week on an assignment. This would have been their first snowstorm together and she was a little wistful thinking about all the fun, romantic things they could be doing together.

Seizing on having nothing planned; she looked at wedding dresses online. There were only eight months until she and Timothy would say their nuptials. She wanted nothing too frilly or too girly-girl. It couldn't be too long or too short, it had to be just right. Dresses were not her forte and the thought of all eyes on her while wearing one terrified her. So it was imperative that she find one that she would be comfortable in.

The wedding would be outside, in the gazebo of the Manor house in July. Comfort was her principal goal, with a splash of elegance and primary simplicity being her prominent style. Her mother, Mira, wanted her to wear grace and frills, more of a princess-type gown. The thought annoyed Jessica. She wasn't good at pretending to be something she wasn't. Elegant was not a quality anyone knew Jessica to be. The thought was downright laughable. She drank with the guys she hung around under the table, belched with the best of them, and downed shots like there was no tomorrow.

This difference in styles and personality traits had added some tension to the whole wedding planning with her mother. Especially after Jessica's parents presented her to her biological grandparents, Brad and Kathleen Kennedy. They were the epitome of materialistic snobs. They had gushed over finding Jessica, apologizing for having Mira give her up for adoption, yet claiming it all had worked out for the best in the end. The shock for them was learning the truth about Mira and Richard's relationship and that Richard was Jessica's father. Their anger subsided when the realization came that they were related through marriage to a wealthy and influential family, the Gardiners.

The more Jessica got to know them, the more she despised them. This made her feel guilty since they were family, after all. She just couldn't understand their materialism. Every week, her grandmother would call her up and invite her to go clothes shopping with her mother and sister. When she went the first time, she couldn't believe the number of clothes they all bought compared to what she wound up buying. She needed a couple of new pairs of jeans and a few sweaters. That was the difference, though. She needed what she had purchased, and the others just bought it because they wanted it. She had visited her parent's home after that first shopping spree, and her sister had shown her a closet full of clothes with the tags still on them. This had dumbfounded Jessica. She couldn't fathom owning so many clothes, let alone not wearing half of what she owned.

Raised by the Greenhalls, Jessica had learned humbleness and thankfulness for everything. They had never gone without. However, they didn't live with excess either. Instead, they had shown her how to live off the land. They gardened and grew most of their fruits and vegetables, canning and freezing to use throughout the year. Deer hunting was a big thing for them, filling their freezers every year with enough game to last until the next season.

The first time Jessica had her biological family over to her house for dinner, she cooked some venison steaks marinated in raspberry vinaigrette. They all ate it and commented on how delicious the meal had been. When they asked where she had gotten such flavorful steaks, though, horror filled them finding out they had eaten deer meat that she herself had killed. Afterward, her grandmother had gone on a two-week vegetarian cleanse diet to purge her body of the *Bambi* meat, as she had put it.

Jessica chuckled to herself when she remembered their horror. The wedding planning caused tension, and more than once, she suggested they take a trip to Vegas and elope. Timothy reminded her, though, that they planned on getting married once, so they should do it the way they wanted. He figured out how to keep her calm and rational. One of the many reasons she had fallen in love with him. Thoughts of him now only made her miss him more.

Despite hoping to find her perfect dress online, she realized her search was fruitless. She had hoped to find one online to get out of shopping with her sister, mother, and grandmother. Samantha set up an appointment at a dress shop in Boston. It would be a chance to look at bridal and bridesmaid dresses in person. She was nervous about shopping with the three of them present. However, she hoped to find the perfect dress.

She reached up to the back of her neck and felt the tightness in her neck muscles. Relaxation was necessary to ease the anxiety and tension she was feeling. Jessica bundled up, took one of her cameras, and went outside. Taking pictures of the falling snow, she loved catching the shimmer of sunlight reflected off the snowflakes. Along the edge of her yard, there was a row of cedar trees whose boughs and branches were bending with the weight of the falling snow. They created a brilliant winter wonderland tunnel.

Through the tunnel, walking, she got some pretty exceptional shots. Jessica loved to get different perspectives while taking pictures, so she lay down in the snow and took pictures of the snow tunnel from different angles. When she finished, she was wet and cold. She decided it was time to go inside. As she shed her wet coat and snow pants, her cell phone rang. She smiled as she answered it.

"Hello, my love, I miss you."

"Ah, I miss you too. That is why I called. I needed to hear your voice."

"It's snowing here. You are missing our first snowfall. It's beautiful. I took a bunch of pictures just so I can show you."

"I can't wait to see the pictures. I am sure they are not as beautiful as you, though."

"You always make me blush. How is the writing going?"

"I do my best to let you know how much I love you. I am lucky to have found you. The writing is going well. I am learning from the crocodile guides down here. Like, how not to get eaten alive."

"I love you too and feel the same. Please take heed of what those guides tell you. I don't want to be a widow before we're married."

"I will be careful. Hey, speaking of the wedding. Do you think we could add crocodile stew to the menu? It's croco delicious!"

Jessica spit out the sip of tea she had just taken. She could just see the looks of horror on her grandparent's faces if she mentioned crocodile stew was on the wedding menu.

"Hmm, maybe turtle soup as the appetizer?"

"Catepiller crepes for desert!"

Both of them burst into full belly laughter at their diabolical minds melding into one.

One thing was for sure. No matter what, they were decisive to have their wedding how they wished. They didn't care what anyone else thought. As they hung up the phone, Jessica felt better than she had felt earlier.

It still amazed her how much Timothy completed her life. She couldn't wait to be his wife. The thought of being the mother of his children also excited her. She knew the challenge of bringing up their children as she had been. Especially now that she had found her biological family and had inherited a multi-million-dollar real estate company. Determination ran through her veins, though. She saw the differences between herself and her siblings, wanting her kids to be like her.

Timothy had expressed the same desire. He didn't like the materialism of her family. Their kids would work for what they needed and wanted in life. Even though his adoptive parents had disowned him for looking for his biological family, he was still grateful for his upbringing.

Jessica's heart ached for Timothy. She couldn't understand how his adoptive parents would disown him. Trying to help him find his biological family had become a priority for her. She wanted him to have family members at their wedding. Yet, they had very few leads.

One second cousin matched on the genealogy website a few months prior and Timothy had messaged the person and had gotten no response. This perplexed her. Jessica logged onto the genealogy website and logged in to Timothy's account. She inspected the second cousin's tree. It was public, so she could try to disseminate information.

Going over the tree, a name jumped out at Jessica. Allison Simmons, could it be the same Allison who was the CEO of Cromwell Real Estate Investment Corporation? The same Allison that she sat across from at the board meetings? She wrote down the tree information and would ask Allison more about herself and her family at their next meeting. Was there a family connection for Timothy right under their noses? Nothing surprised her anymore after what she had been through finding her own family. She would keep the relationship a secret until she could verify or deny it. Not informing Timothy would be difficult. However, she wanted to spare him any potential disappointment.

Two days later, she was sitting in a meeting across from Allison. Discussing the latest project for the real estate company, acquiring an older building in Manhattan, and debating whether they wanted to demolish it and build brand new or renovate it.

"Can we get a cost analysis? I would like to see the difference between the cost of renovating the existing building, and demolishing it to build new."

"Hmm, it might be a wise decision. I don't see why we can't."

It surprised Richard Jessica wanted the cost analysis. However, she was leaning more towards the renovation because it was an older type of architecture. Her fondness for architecture made her appreciate the art in older buildings compared to the shiny tall buildings that marked the surrounding skyline. Maybe it was her photographic eye, or her affinity towards preserving history, that made her that way.

Allison was more inclined towards the demolition and rebuilding option.

"We have always demolished and built new in the past. It is better for resale value."

"I disagree, Allison. Having been to Dublin, I have seen how they blend old architecture with new."

In addition, her world travels had given her a different perspective than Allison. The latter had lived and worked in New York City her entire life.

Richard, Jessica's father, was on the fence. He agreed with Allison about resale value. However, he listened to Jessica's impressive arguments. He did not realize she knew about architecture. Wanting a cost analysis on both options showed him she was learning this business fast.

Jimmy, being inclined to preserve history himself, was leaning toward Jessica's idea of remodeling the building. Willing to wait until they do the cost analysis to decide, though.

After the meeting, Jessica tried to strike up a casual conversation with Allison.

"Hey, Allison. I realized the other day that I know little about you. Even though we work with each other. So do you mind me asking you some questions? To get to know you better."

"Not at all. What do you want to know?"

Jessica, treading lightly and not getting too in-depth or personal. She wanted to know everything she could. She had to figure out how to ask her. So she went with the relatable approach.

"Well, I have three siblings I never knew I had. I am adjusting to having a big family coming from a small one. So, do you have siblings?"

"Yeah, I know your family story. That must be difficult to navigate. I have two older brothers, Thomas and Robert. We were close growing up. However, now that we are older, we have our own lives."

"Oh, I am sorry. I didn't mean to bring up any bad feelings about your family."

"It's all good. My brothers are both married and have children. Me, I haven't found Mister right yet. I am married to my work. And I have no children."

"Well, I hope you find your Mister right. I feel blessed I met mine! I am grateful you're married to your work! This business needs you."

"I appreciate you saying that. Alexandria taught me well. I miss her, as I am sure everyone else does. She was like a mother to me."

Jessica smiled as she finished talking to Allison. She had gotten the confirmation she needed. It related Allison to the DNA match to Timothy in the family tree! Now to figure out if Allison and Timothy matched. Of course, she had to prove it, too. Could she even be his biological mother?

Chapter Four

Siblings

Samantha was excited about her sister's visit coming up on the weekend. The dress shop in Boston had to have the perfect bridal gown for Jessica. Despite her sister's pickiness in choosing a dress style, confidence filled her. She knew she could help Jessica find the right one while simultaneously satisfying their mom's wishes. These thoughts ran through her head as she was getting ready for her Thursday night shift at the restaurant where she waitressed at. Samantha divided her long red hair into three sections and braided it. The servers had to wear black fitted skirts cut above their knees and a white top. Many of the girls she worked with hated the outfits for various reasons. Not her though, she loved showing off her long legs with the skirts. She knew men found her attractive, and she used that to her advantage. Flirting with the male customers had become an art form to her. Treading light when the men accompanied women, though.

It was never her intent to come between any couples. She wanted money to move out on her own. Not that she had to move. Her parents welcomed her to live at home as long as she wanted to. She just wanted some privacy. Being an adult and living at home had some downfalls. The main pitfall was dating. Samantha's parents would give her the third degree over every guy she even mentioned or hung out with. A multitude of questions would berate the poor guy as well if she happened to bring him home. These situations always led to awkwardness. So she flirted and got big tips, which she put in a jar in her closet. She could ask her parents for the money to move out to be independent. They would give it to her. However, since meeting her big sister, she realized how privileged she had been. Determined to do this one thing on her own to prove she wasn't a spoiled rich brat.

Thursday nights were her favorite shift. Several regular customers would ask to be seated in her section. One guy about her own age was her favorite. A cheeseburger, fries, and soda were his regular meal. He was always so polite when he ordered, saying little besides placing his order, even when she turned on the charm. He smiled and laughed plenty at her flirtatious demeanor. It was rare that he bantered back. His tips were always good.

When she got to work, the restaurant was already getting busy. She loved busy nights. Money filled her pockets on those nights. She was skilled at providing exemplary customer service, quickly turning the tables over. If the kitchen kept up the pace, everything ran like clockwork for her.

Her regulars came, and the hostess seated them. She went up to each table and took their orders. When she came to her favorite regular, she smiled with a sparkle in her eye and a flip of her braid.

"What can I get you today, handsome?"

"I'll take the 8oz steak with a baked potato and the mac and cheese, please."

Zach blushed as he answered.

"Ah, changing it up, I see. How would you like that steak cooked?"

"Medium well, please."

"You got it! You want your usual drink, or are you changing that up too?"

"The usual, thank you."

"Anything for you, sweetie."

Samantha turned to walk away. Zach lifted his head up from looking at the menu. He blushed and smiled. Then, as his knees shook under the table. He got the courage to reply.

"Anything? How about your number?"

His comeback surprised Samantha and stopped her in her tracks. He was so quiet and reserved. But she liked this new version. Of course, he still had his shyness, and she loved how she could make him blush. The quiet confidence he was getting, though, made him even more attractive than he already was. She turned back to him.

"I don't even know your name. You know my name, but I do not know yours."

"It's Zach."

"Well, Zach. It is nice to converse with you. But if I give you my number, you need to promise me you won't give it out or write it on the bathroom wall or anything."

"I promise, I would never do that."

"Okay, I will keep you to that promise. I look forward to talking with you more."

Samantha handed him a slip of paper with her number on it.

He blushed again while taking the slip of paper from her fingertips. Their hands brushed, and she felt a jolt of electricity run through her. This time, she blushed.

At the end of her shift, she felt exhausted. She had done well with tips, and she put the thousand dollars into her jar at home. When she closed her eyes to go to bed, her thoughts went to Zach hoping he would call. A first for her. She had never given her number to a customer. Plenty had asked. However, she either wasn't interested, or she just hadn't felt comfortable. It surprised her she was interested in him and felt secure with Zach.

Jessica arrived at her parent's house Friday evening. Their hugs comforted and their smiles were genuine. Mira was excited about dress shopping the next day. The conversation at dinner revolved around the wedding plans. Jessica appreciated the excitement and the interest in helping. Although, she couldn't help feeling overwhelmed by her mother's insistence on certain things being done her way. It appeared it focused her mother more on the big wedding on the island that she and Richard could not have. This made it feel more about her mother and father, rather than about her and Timothy.

The newness of their relationship made it hard for Jessica to stand up for herself and be assertive about her wishes. She didn't want to hurt her parent's feelings and was thankful for her brothers Richard Jr. and David changing the subject.

"Hey, Dad, David, and I have been doing some thinking."

"Yeah, we thought Jimmy could use some company in that big house on the island."

"I can work from anywhere, according to my employer. Plus, I could see Danielle more frequently."

"And I could help Jimmy bring the security on the island into the 21st century with cameras and more technology."

Jessica welcomed the reprieve from the wedding discussion. She thought her brother's idea was brilliant. Worry for Jimmy all alone in that big house had been on her mind. This would help ease it.

"What are your thoughts on this, Jessica?"

"I think it's a great idea! The boys could help share in the responsibility of watching over the island. But, of course, we would need to ask Jimmy his opinion too. He has a say in the matter."

"We can talk to Jimmy next week at our meeting. We will let you two know what he says."

Richard Jr. had fallen head over heels for Danielle. He just wanted to be closer. They had known each other their entire lives. Their moms were best friends from high school. Growing up, they had become best friends themselves. That friendship had grown. It blossomed into a romantic relationship, and they had dated for the last few months.

Danielle had been there for him when his universe turned upside down. The shock of finding out he had an older sister he hadn't known because his parents conceived her out of wedlock because of an affair. Also, not knowing his sister because of the adoption. He learned his father had been leading a double life. Still married to his first wife and his mother. This knowledge had thrown him for a complete loop.

He felt graced he had Danielle helping him through that tumultuous time. It was then he realized he could no longer hold back his true feelings for her. They walked along the beach that night. He had told her about his family's secrets. Hand in hand. He had felt in seconds they were one. The memories of that evening flooded his mind. When she halted, turning to face him, and wrapping her arms around him, hugging him. The tension in his body melted being held like that. That's when he got the courage to kiss her. He had swept her long dark hair out of her brown eyes, leaned in, and kissed her soft lips. She tightened her hug and reciprocated the kiss with a little more fire than he had expected. He smiled, remembering how she had pulled away saying.

"It's about time you made that first move!"

They have been a couple since. However, the long-distance relationship made it hard to see each other regularly. He was having thoughts of marriage and family with her. The distance, though, brought doubts into his mind about their relationship. This was why he wanted to move closer to her.

David just wanted a purpose. Fresh out of high school with no job. It was hard to figure out life. The knowledge of being a Gardiner had sparked an interest in his family history. He wanted to preserve that history and help protect the island and his family. He had no desire to get involved in any relationships like his siblings. David wanted to have an established career first before getting involved with another person. Life was muddling enough. Without bringing another person's drama into it all. His inner feelings were confusing to himself as well without bringing another person into the chaos. Something attracted him to women. However, he felt he connected deeper with his male friends. He felt that soul connection. David didn't feel this with any female yet. This made him question his sexuality. The soul connection excited him differently than his attraction to women. This was difficult for him to talk about to anyone. He felt that living on the island with Jimmy and his brother Richard might help him untangle his inner feelings. In addition, he knew his vast knowledge of computers and technology would help enhance security on the island. He was sure Jimmy would feel the same and welcome David and Richard onto the island.

The rest of the evening, discussions fluctuated between the wedding, the Christmas holiday coming up, the family business, and the boys moving to the island. Jessica felt a little inundated since she still was not used to the dynamics of a big family.

The tub called to her tired, tension-filled body. She drew the water, calling Timothy as she waited for it to fill the tub.

"Hey, beautiful. I am so glad you called. How is your visit home going?"

"It's going okay. I am just getting ready to take a tension-relieving bath."

"I wish I was there to massage that tension right out of you."

"Me too. Tonight, the bath will have to do."

Just hearing his voice soothed her soul. She shared the conversations of the evening with him. He agreed that Richard Jr.'s and David's plans to move to the island and the Manor House were great ideas.

They said their goodbyes, and she slipped into the tub to relax. She tried to close her eyes, yet the heart palpitations started, and she had to open them back up. The PTSD from almost being drowned made baths less relaxing. She couldn't talk to her family about it. They would not understand. Timothy was the sole person who knew about her PTSD. The apparent quiet on the island since Mary's suicide eased her anxiety. This made it okay for her to be wed on the island. Getting out of the tub and settling into bed, more relaxed, she dozed off, thinking about going dress shopping in the morning.

The sun was bright. It was the wedding day. Chairs formed rows with an aisle running down the center leading to the gazebo. Vines of clematis and roses entwined the gazebo. Something obscured the faces of the guests. At first, she thought it was because of her veil, then she realized she was lucid dreaming. It didn't feel right. Dark clouds came and covered the sun. Timothy was waiting at the gazebo for her. As she reached him, his hands were outstretched towards her. Thunder boomed and lightning flashed. No, it wasn't thunder. It was gunshots. The smell of sulfur burned her nose, and she looked down and saw the gun in her hand. Timothy lying at her feet in a puddle of blood. Her hands shaking, she dropped the gun and fell to her knees.

Jessica bolted up in her bed. Thank god it was just a nightmare! It had been years since she had a bad dream. This was upsetting. She dwelled on the meaning as she rested her head back on her pillow. She loved Timothy with her entire being. Why would her subconscious have her kill him? Jessica wanted to hold Timothy. She trembled at the fear of what the dream meant.

The last time she had a lucid dream, she had lost her adoptive father in a horrific car crash. She had the knowledge he passed before she even received the phone call. Was this an omen she would lose Timothy?

Praying. She asked God to please not take him from her.

Chapter Five

New & Old Love

It was Saturday, Jimmy's day off. However, he was a creature of habit and was so used to his daily routine that he rode his ATV around the island, even on his days off. The melting snow from earlier in the week provided plenty of muddy trails for him to ride on. This was one of his stress relievers. Going fast through some of the deeper puddles making a wake of muddy water behind his rear tires and sliding around some of the bigger curves in the trails. Slowing down off one of the beaten paths, heading toward Willow Brook. He drove across and headed towards the two lookout towers on the island's eastern side. In the winter months, the woods were less dense, making it easier to ride through them with the ATVs.

As he maneuvered down the less worn path he could see something fairly large lying in his way up ahead. He slowed to a crawl as the realization hit that it was a deer carcass. It was rare to find any wildlife dead around the island. Especially deer, since there were very few natural predators in the area. Those who hunted on the island hunted for food, not sport, and would never leave a carcass to rot.

As he approached he realized it was a few days old. The putrid stench was the first giveaway which got worse the closer he got. Flies and maggots crawling all over the body were the next telltale sign. He covered his mouth and nose with the scarf he had around his neck. This gave him a bit of relief from the stench.

It was a decent-sized buck, at least an 8-pointer. There didn't seem to be a gunshot wound or an arrow wound. Upon closer inspection, Jimmy realized the gruesome truth. This deer had its throat slit and its heart removed. *Who would do such a thing?* He thought to himself.

He used his radio to call for a security team to come and bury the poor animal. Then, taking out his phone, he took pictures of the scene. There were no visible signs of anyone being around the carcass other than his footprints. However, he knew very well that the perpetrator could have snuck onto the island despite their best security efforts. No one on the island would have done this in his mind. They were all connected too much to the land, and even though few had ties to the Native American ancestry of the island, they still respected it. This was a violation of that connection. Zach and Matt showed up from the security team to help dispose of the deer. What they saw was shocking to them. Matt stepped closer.

"Who do you think did this, Jimmy?"

"Don't know. It makes no sense. No one on the island would do such a thing."

Zach stepped forward to inspect it closer.

"What a waste of a magnificent deer! That would have provided a couple of months' worth of meat."

"Exactly! That's why it makes no sense. Someone from the outside must have somehow got on the island. Maybe they took the heart like some sort of sick souvenir."

The men dug a hole and buried the deer. They were somber as they worked. Growing up on the island, they all respected the wildlife that lived alongside them. This was a stark reminder that some did not have that same respect. It was also a crisp nudge that their security wasn't foolproof. The security team was going to have to step it up a bit to ensure the safety of the wildlife. In addition, security rounds would have to be expanded to include more of the secluded interior aspects of the island. The thought gave Jimmy an instant headache. They were already a skeleton crew regarding the size of the island. There were few people on the island they could hire as added security. This was going to be a logistical nightmare for him. He hopped back on his ATV and continued his ride hoping it would clear his head a bit. Thoughts went to the deer. He wondered if he should mention it to Jessica and Richard at this week's meeting. Things had been so quiet, he really didn't want to bring up the memories of the past couple of months. At that moment, he really didn't think there was any connection between the past incidents and this one. Deciding to keep this under wraps for now, he drove back to the security shack to come up with some tentative plans for increased security. Zach and Matt were both back at the shack. It was their lunch break. However, neither was all that hungry after dealing with the deer carcass. So instead, Matt read the local paper, trying to erase the images from his mind. While Zach focused on his phone. They both looked up as Jimmy entered the building. Zach and Matt shook their heads. They knew he was not visiting on his day off. The guy was a workaholic, and they all knew it. Jimmy noticed Zach had stopped typing on his phone.

"Don't let me interrupt your lunch break conversation. I just need to work out some logistics regarding upping security around here."

"Do you need any help, boss? You shouldn't be doing all this on your day off."

"I appreciate your offer, Zach. Enjoy your lunch break. I haven't seen you smile like that, ever. So whoever you are texting is clearly more important, especially after this morning. You deserve the escape."

Zach blushed.

"It's Samantha Gardiner. I have been going up to Boston to eat at the restaurant where she works for weeks now. Thursday nights, since I have Thursday and Friday off. I finally got the courage to ask her for her number. We have been texting on and off since. So, I guess you don't have to introduce us at Christmas."

"My man, good for you! Just don't hurt her. You know she has siblings. Not to mention, it's my job to protect her."

Jimmy patted Zach on the back.

"I have no intentions of hurting her! You forget it's my job also to protect the Gardiners!"

Zach was smiling from ear to ear. Zach's happiness meant the world to Jimmy. They were like brothers, both growing up on the island. They went to school together on the mainland. Their fathers both worked for the security team. The differences in their lives were Zach had a sister, Jimmy had no siblings, and Jimmy was 5 years older. But he had no doubts that Zach would be good to Samantha.

Thoughts about Zach and Samantha got him thinking about his own love life. It was pretty nonexistent. When Zach's sister Melissa moved away to college, his hopes of love and marriage were shattered. They had dated throughout high school. Both being from the island made it hard for them to fit in with the mainland kids. They had grown up together. Jimmy and Melissa weren't always friends, though. As kids playing after school, he recalled they were often outright mean to one another. Sometimes pushing each other into Willow Brook or even putting frogs down each other's pants. She had been more of a tomboy back then.

Till puberty hit them both. That's when Jimmy and Melissa both noticed each other in a peculiar light. During freshman year, they had dated, and they stayed a couple till graduation day. That's when she broke up with him and told him she was leaving for college in the fall. When she told him she had no plans to return to the island, it devastated him. He had thought she was the one and thought they would be like their own parents, getting married and living on the island. She had kept her word, too. In the seven years after leaving, she hadn't come back. Not once. Her family visited her once or twice a year in upstate New York. Jimmy had tried to move on. He dated a few women here and there from the mainland. But, unfortunately, his mind always wandered to Melissa. He compared every woman to his lost love. No matter what, he could not get her out of his mind.

For now, he was content with his bachelor's lifestyle. He enjoyed living by himself in the big old manor house. Even though sometimes it was lonely and boring. The thought struck him that maybe it was time he tried his luck on the mainland scene again. He decided to go to the mainland for dinner at one of the local bars and see if he could find someone who could erase the memory of Melissa from his mind. This would be a tall order to fill. However, he was on a mission.

Jimmy finished his preliminary plans to beef up security. He left the security shack late afternoon and headed to the Manor house. He gave Stella the night off from cooking dinner, then let her know he was going to the mainland to catch a bite to eat. She was happy her son was taking a much-needed break from the island. When Jimmy got to the bar, he faced indecision on whether he wanted to sit at the bar or a table. Since his primary goal tonight was to erase the memory of Melissa from his mind, he decided on the table. It gave him a better vantage point to see the women in the bar.

There were plenty of attractive women. Most were in groups of 3 or more. There were also plenty of other men searching for their match. This intimidated Jimmy. Being rejected by a woman in front of her friends terrified him. Vying for attention was not one of his strong suits. When the waitress came to his table, he ordered his dinner and a beer. He needed some liquid courage. The beer came before his dinner, and he drank it rather quickly. By the time his dinner came, he was on his third beer, and he had the start of a good buzz. Then, having a clear view of the door, he noticed a couple more women walk in.

He shook his head to get his vision clearer because he wasn't sure whether his eyes were playing tricks on him or he was experiencing a new type of beer goggles. There was no way beer goggles would make a woman look like Melissa, though. Could she be here? He hadn't seen her in 7 years. Was his mind playing tricks on him? The woman who looked like Melissa locked eyes with him. Those amber brown with flecks of golden eyes had a flicker of recognition in them toward him. Then there was the sheepish smile and a small wave. It was her. Now she was walking toward him. His heartbeat was fast in his chest, and he hoped she couldn't tell.

"Hey, Jimmy, long time no see. How are you doing?"

Melissa leaned on his table with both arms.

He couldn't believe she was right here. His hands slipped onto his legs under the table, wiping the sweat off his palms and pinching himself. He realized he was not dreaming. Shockingly, the one person he was trying to forget was now facing him. But how could he ever forget her? Her flowing dirty blonde hair and her dimpled cheeks when she smiled. Was it the alcohol, or was he still profoundly attracted to her? He honestly couldn't tell. All he knew was it was taking every ounce of restraint for him not to gather her up in his arms and kiss her. But, at least he had sense enough to know that would probably not turn out too well for him.

"Oh, hey, Melissa. Yeah, long time. I am doing well. How the heck are you doing?"

Jimmy acted nonchalantly.

"I am doing well. I am working on my doctorate in psychology now. Dad and Zach told me you are head of security on the island and living in the Manor house. That's quite an accomplishment."

"Yeah, the new owners didn't want to live in the Manor house, and they didn't want it left empty, so they offered to let me live there. Kind of like extra compensation. Your father and brother didn't say you were coming for a visit."

"They don't know I am here. Could you be a doll and not tell them you saw me, please?"

"Sure, I guess. Why wouldn't you want to see your family, though?"

"I refuse to step foot on that cursed island! I don't understand why anyone would want to stay there. If I told them I was out here with friends, they would guilt me into going to see them. I have worked hard to distance myself from the shadows of that place. No way do I want to go back."

"That's too bad. Many people miss you and love you there."

"As much as I miss the people and love them too, I need to preserve my sanity and my life. It's been good catching up with you, Jimmy. I hope you continue to be well. I need to get back to my friends."

Melissa finished speaking and turned to walk away. Not knowing what came over him. Jimmy scrambled out of his chair and caught up to her, gently grabbing her arm and turning her to face him. It shocked her when he embraced her and passionately kissed her. Jimmy didn't want to let go, and he certainly didn't want to stop kissing her. The taste of her sweet lips again rekindled the smoldering fire within him that had been burning for so long. Melissa wasn't resisting and seemed to melt into his embrace. He ended the kiss and looked her in the eyes.

"When you are ready to come back to the island and be my wife. I will be waiting."

Jimmy let go of Melissa, put a hundred-dollar bill on his table to cover his check, and walked straight out of the bar. He couldn't believe he had just done that. Boldness had never been part of his repertoire. *Did I just ask Melissa to marry me?* He thought to himself.

Melissa just stood there, mouth agape, watching Jimmy walk out the door. *Did he just ask me to marry him?* The kiss had stirred up old feelings she had fought for seven years to repress. Then, her friends came up to her, asking her too many questions about Jimmy. She quickly told them he was an ex-boyfriend and then continued her evening out. It wasn't until later she replayed the interaction with Jimmy in her head while lying in bed. *Damn it, Jimmy, why did you have to kiss me?* She remembered how he took charge and went after what he wanted at that moment. She just wished he would leave the island and go after what he wanted, which was clearly her.

She hadn't resisted his kiss. In that instant, she didn't want it to end. It had transported Melissa back in time in that brief minute. Earlier in their lives, all she wanted to do was be with Jimmy and love him. Tonight taught her one thing. She still loved him, and she knew he still loved her from his actions. Now the only problem was figuring out what to do about it. She would not be returning to the island. That was a definite no for her. So, the only solution was convincing him to leave the island. That would be almost impossible. She fell asleep dreaming of being in Jimmy's arms once again.

Chapter Six

Sisters

With the obnoxious beeping of her alarm clock, Jessica rolled over and begrudgingly turned it off. She hadn't slept well after the nightmare. She rubbed her eyes to help wake herself up. Jessica realized how much she hated waking up without Timothy by her side. Her sister Samantha was stirring in the other twin bed in the room. Jessica could tell she wasn't a fan of alarm clocks, either. The pillow was being used to cover her head.

They both knew they needed to get up and get dressed. First order of business for the day, the girls had a breakfast date with their mother and grandmother. Then they were all going to head to the dress shop to pick out Jessica's wedding gown. Jessica was not looking forward to shopping. She rolled over on her back and pulled the covers over her head. Procrastination was her superpower when she really didn't want to accomplish a task.

Samantha slowly got out of bed herself and got motivated. The more she moved around the room, her excitement built. She looked forward to helping her sister pick out her wedding dress. Something that Samantha had never thought would happen a few months ago. But, when she found out she had a big sister, the feeling of winning the lottery overcame her. Samantha jumped on the twin-sized bed her sister was lying in with the covers over her head.

"Rise, and shine, sleepyhead! Today is the day you say yes to the dress!"

Jessica just groaned, throwing the covers down off her head. Then she saw her younger sister with her hands and knees on the bed bouncing with child-like excitement. This made her smile and bust out laughing. She had never had siblings before. This was all new, and she felt as though both were catching up on the things in childhood they never got to experience together. A light bulb went off in her mind, and in one swift movement, she sat up and grabbed her pillow. A little more vigorously than she expected, swinging and knocking Samantha off her bed with the first hit. Samantha grabbed her pillow and retaliated. They both became breathless with laughter and the exertion of the pillow fight. Jessica felt less anxious and tense afterward. She could perceive the excitement of the day that had been radiating off her sister.

When they came bounding down the stairs together, they found their mother and grandmother waiting for them. Mira just smiled at them both as she could see that bond growing between her two daughters. She felt blessed that their family had finally become whole after not having Jessica with them for so many years. Their grandmother just looked at them scornfully.

"It's about time."

Jessica and Samantha brushed off her comment and didn't respond.

Mira looked at her mother.

"Mom, let the girls have their fun. We are not running late."

Kathleen Kennedy didn't appreciate frolicking or fun. She was a serious woman who only cared about status and prestige. In her eyes, her granddaughter's behavior was annoying. It seemed childish, and they weren't children. They weren't even teenagers. They were adult women. In her eyes, they should act decently.

When they got to the diner. Both Jessica and Samantha ordered a large stack of chocolate chip pancakes at breakfast. They smothered them with butter and maple syrup while their grandmother frowned in disgust. She had ordered scrambled eggs, toast, and two sausage links. The girls giggled as they ate, daring each other to be the first to finish their plate. As they both struggled to eat all the pancakes, they joked that they would have difficulty trying on dresses with such full bellies. This did not amuse their grandmother at all, either.

Jessica finished all her pancakes, and Samantha ate about three-quarters. After using the ladies' room to wash up from the sticky syrup, they were on their way to the dress shop. The nervousness had returned to Jessica. She prayed everything would go smoothly.

The dress shop was a bridal boutique, one of those fancy shops with dresses and mannequins in the windows. They had an appointment, so they had the whole place to themselves. This was a saving grace for Jessica. She certainly didn't want anyone to see her try on dozens of dresses.

Her mother and grandmother were already oohing and aahing over several big poofy princess-style dresses displayed on the racks. Finally, they both picked a dress for Jessica to try on. The boutique attendant was hyping up both dresses as beautiful choices. Jessica took the dresses into the dressing room. Samantha went inside with her to help her get into them.

As Jessica slipped into the first one and looked in the mirror at herself, she suppressed a laugh and pursed her lips. This was definitely not her style. The sleeves were long and puffed up over her shoulders, starting just above her elbows. The scalloped neckline was uncomfortable, and the train was eight feet long. Bustled up, the train made her butt look twenty times bigger! It was hot and bulky, which would never work for a July wedding. She indulged her mother and grandmother and showed them the dress.

They gushed over her and the dress and said she looked perfect. The attendant also agreed with them. Thankfully, Samantha reminded them all it would be a July wedding, and this dress was not a practical choice. Reluctantly, her mother, grandmother, and the attendant agreed.

Dress two was just as horrendous. It, too, had long sleeves, although no poofy shoulders. The neckline went straight across. It had lace that went up and encircled her neck. She felt as though she was being strangled by itchy hands. This dress also had a long train that when bustled made her butt look awkward.

Again, when she stepped out of the dressing room, her mother and grandmother loved the dress. This time, the attendant stepped up and reminded them of the season the wedding would occur. Samantha and Jessica sighed with relief that they didn't have to bring it up this time.

Jessica's mother, grandmother and the attendant scrambled, looking for other dresses. Samantha helped Jessica out of the second dress and then looked for the perfect dress for her big sister. Finally, she found one that she thought would look elegant but simple for her sister. She brought it to the dressing room.

Looking at the dress on the hanger, Jessica could not believe Samantha had found the perfect dress! Now she was just praying it looked just as beautiful on her as it did just hanging there.

Stepping out of the dressing room in the third dress, she felt as if she was the center of the universe. Usually, that would make her uncomfortable. Notwithstanding, this dress, it felt magical. She could walk, twirl, sit, and just move, which felt absolutely fantastic in a dress.

Eyes watering, Mira covered her mouth with both hands. Jessica was elegant in the simple dress. Samantha had found the perfect one for her sister. Still, the dress wasn't a distraction from Jessica's natural beauty one bit. On the contrary, it only enhanced it one hundred percent.

Kathleen scowled. She felt the dress was too simple and a bit more revealing than a bridal dress should be. The attendant rebutted her and said that for a summer wedding, less was more.

Samantha beamed with pride at her sister in the dress she chose for her. It was perfect! No fuss, no muss, but absolutely elegant on her.

The dress was simple on the top, with three-inch sleeves off the shoulder and two straps coming up and over the collarbones. Two sides came together above the breastbone along the neckline, with a small broach. The bottom of the dress came up a few inches under the kneecaps in front and tapered down around the legs to the floor behind.

With Jessica's long, curly, red hair flowing down over the white dress, it was a picture of simplicity and breathtaking elegance. This was the dress. When Jessica told the attendant it was the one she wanted, Samantha squealed and hugged her! Then, hugging her sister back, they both got misty-eyed.

Now it was time to pick out Samantha's maid of honor dress and the mother of the bride's dress. Her grandmother also needed to find something suitable to wear. They spent the rest of the morning helping each other find the perfect dresses with the help of the attendant.

It was lunchtime when they finished. The women went out for lunch before heading back home. Jessica and Samantha were chatting about the wedding and various ideas for centerpieces in the back of the car. Then Samantha's phone buzzed, startling her, and notifying her of an incoming text message.

As she read the message, she smiled and replied. Noticing the difference in her little sister's demeanor, the way her smile was radiating, and the twinkle in her eye, she nudged her sister's elbow. She didn't say a word to her. Samantha looked up from her phone, and Jessica nodded at the phone, smiling. She shrugged, and mouthed the words, "New guy friend."

Jessica left her sister texting for the remainder of the car ride. She thought about all the sweet moments they had had that day. Two sisters who a few months ago never knew each other existed. Now bonded for life. Jessica couldn't imagine her life without her little sister.

When they were alone later back at the house, Jessica pressed her sister for more information on her new guy friend.

"So, tell me more about this mysterious guy you were texting throughout lunch today?"

"Well, for starters, I have known him for a few weeks now. He is one of my Thursday night regulars. He has always been shy, but this week he actually asked me for my number."

"And you gave it to him? Do you usually give your number out to strange guys at work?"

"Yes, I gave it to him. And, no, I have never done it in the past. He gives off a trust me vibe. So I did. We have been texting on and off since."

"Okay, so what else do you know about this guy?"

"His name is Zach Zimmerman. Are you ready for some irony? He works with Jimmy on the security team on the island."

"Wait, what?"

Jessica was getting a red flag warning.

"He saw me at Alexandria's and Mary's funerals. Then he found out where I worked and drove up here on his days off, just to see me."

"That's kind of creepy and sweet at the same time. What else do you know about Zach?"

"He grew up on the island. He has an older sister who coincidentally dated Jimmy throughout high school. Unfortunately, she broke his heart and went off to college. She hasn't been back on the island since."

"Wow. There is so much we do not know about our cousin. So what does he look like? Give me the scoop, little sis."

"He is cute. His hair is this brownish-gold. It's not cut short, more than a little above shoulder length, straight-ish, and falls just so when he runs his hand through it. It's more of a tousled look. But, ugh, his eyes are to die for. They are brown with these flecks of gold."

Jessica watched her sister as she described Zach. This guy had her sister smitten already. She would have to interrogate Jimmy on this guy and make sure his intentions were pure with her little sister.

So much she had to remember for this week's meeting already. Foremost, she needed to find out if Allison or her brothers had a child twenty-five years ago. Next, she needed to find out that connection for Timothy. Then the discussion of her brothers moving into the Manor house with Jimmy needed to be brought up. And last, she needed to pull Jimmy aside and get the inside scoop on Zach.

The biggest thing, though, was she couldn't wait to get home and hug Timothy. Her dream had really shaken her up. Just thinking about it brought fear into her heart. She couldn't lose him. Not now. Never. The meaning of the dream eluded her. *Should they postpone the wedding? Did her subconscious have cold feet?* Maybe. Maybe not.

Chapter Seven

Connections

Timothy made it home before Jessica returned from her trip. He had bought a bouquet of wildflowers at a gift shop in the airport. In a vase, he arranged them, placing them in the center of their dining room table. He could not wait to see his beautiful bride-to-be. It had been a long week without her. The photographer who worked on the assignment with him this time had grated on his last nerve. Her incessant talking in her squeaky voice, while he observed and took notes, drove him insane. To top it all off, she had been immensely flirtatious towards him the entire trip. He didn't even think there would have been an attraction to her if he was single and drunk. Not that she was physically unattractive. Her personality irritated him too much. This experience was the icing on the cake for him. He insisted Jessica do photography for all his assignments in an email he composed to his editor. Not sure how receptive to his demand his editor would be. He was willing to risk losing his career to make sure he stayed sane. Time away from Jessica for work and paired with other annoying photographers, had him at his breaking point. He emailed and hoped for the best. He had a twinge of anxiety about how his editor would react in his gut. If he got canned, he could always just be a freelance writer. There were options for him, and he shouldn't have to back down from his convictions. Jessica was not due to arrive home until early afternoon, so he checked his genealogy account while he was on his computer. There was finally a message from the second cousin match.

Dear Timothy,

Thank you for reaching out to me about our match. I am sorry for the delay in response. I tried to do as much digging as possible into the probability of you being part of my mother's side of the family. Since I know little about my father. I also have tracked down little information on my grandfather's family side. I asked my mom if she knew of her cousins giving up any children for adoption. She had no definitive answers. The only story about any of her cousins she could remember being a big deal was when her cousin Allison spent over a year in a psychiatric facility. She didn't know why her cousin was there. All she knew was ever since, she had not been the same. Her cousin never married and had no children. I wish I could give you more information that was helpful. In the meantime, I would like to get to know you better since we are cousins. So maybe we can meet up soon and talk.

Your cousin,

Jack Martin

Timothy digested the message and then checked the family tree of this cousin. There was one Allison. The name rang a bell, Allison Simmons. Then he realized Cromwell Real Estate's CEO was Allison Simmons. She worked for Jessica. *Could this be the same Allison?* He sent Jack a response. Hopefully, he could get an answer quicker this time.

Dear Jack,

No worries about the delay in response. Thank you for the information you could provide. Every bit helps. I would absolutely love to meet up with you. It is cool to finally find a biological family member. I have one question, though, about your mom's cousin Allison. I noticed her name is Allison Simmons in your family tree. Do you know her occupation? Also, my fiancée has an employee by that name. I am curious to differentiate if it is the same person. Looking forward to your reply.

Your cousin,

Timothy

Patience waiting for a reply was going to be the hard part. It had taken months for Jack to respond the first time. Timothy did not know how long it would take this time. He was about to log out of the site when he received a message notification. It was a reply from Jack.

Hey man, I actually do know her occupation. She makes a big deal of it at every family function. She is the CEO of The Cromwell Real Estate Development Company in Manhattan. Let's figure out when we can meet up. I live in New York City. Where are you living?

Timothy's heart pounded as he read the response from Jack. Jack's mother's cousin was the same Allison working for Jessica! This was mind-blowing to him. He quickly typed another message to Jack.

Woah! Small world! That is the same Allison who works for my fiancée. My fiancée takes the train from New London into the city every week for a meeting. We live in Connecticut. I could go with her, and we could meet for coffee somewhere while she was at the conference. If that will work for you?

He couldn't believe that he was possibly related to Allison. The only way to prove or disprove being related to her would be through a DNA test. Timothy knew for sure was Jack was his second cousin. The question was whether he was kindred through Jack's father's side of the family or Jack's mother's side. They would have to use the power of elimination. He would have to ask Jack if his mother would do a DNA test to see if a connection with Timothy was there.

Dude! Your fiancée is a Gardiner? How lucky are you? I work nights waiting tables, so anytime you are in the city, I can pretty much meet up. When is the next meeting?

Timothy laughed to himself, reading Jack's response. I guess he never really looked at Jessica as a Gardiner. Maybe because they didn't even know she was one when they first met. Jack's response woke him up to the realization that others probably look at Jessica the same way Jack does. The thought was kind of sobering. He typed his response.

Yeah, she is. Although, when we first met, she was not aware of it, neither was I. So it's a kind of weird twisted story. I can tell you tomorrow if you would like. That is when the next meeting is.

Timothy and Jack exchanged a couple more messages to solidify their plans to get coffee and meet the following day while Jessica was at her meeting. He was excited about connecting with his cousin. Finally, a biological connection to another person, something he had longed for his entire life.

His adoptive parents had never kept it a secret about his adoption. On the contrary, they had reminded him relentlessly that he should be grateful they adopted him. They acted like they were his saviors, and he should be eternally grateful. He was appreciative. The life they gave him had been good. Despite his physical needs being met, there was always that lack of connection. Not necessarily a lack of love, but a lack of proper bonding.

There was always that notion that he owed them everything for adopting him. But, as he got older, he grew to resent it. That had been the driving factor in finding out who his biological parents were. He craved connection and the bond between a parent and child that he had never felt with his adoptive parents.

Timothy and Jessica had discussed this subject on numerous occasions since their introduction. She always expressed how truly blessed she felt growing up with her adoptive parents, the Greenhalls. She was always empathetic to him, though, knowing he did not have the same experience.

Thoughts of Jessica made him look at the clock. Any time now, she should be home. He couldn't wait to see her. She was his best friend and confidant. With the purr of her car coming up the driveway, he went out to meet her on the front porch.

Jessica noticed Timothy leaning against the post leading down the steps on their front porch. Her heart skipped a beat. She had missed him so much. A glimpse of him waiting there for her made her realize just how lucky she was to have him. Putting the car in park and shutting off the engine. It startled her at how quickly he made it to her car door. Opening it for her, he helped her out of the car and embraced her. The kiss he planted on her lips reminded her of just how intoxicating he could be. She felt drunk with desire for him and let her mind shut the rest of the world out. She rested her head on his shoulder as he scooped her up and carried her into their house. Drinking up his musky scent, she softly planted kisses along his neck. They made it as far as the living room floor before succumbing to both of their desires. When they finished fulfilling each other, they rested in each other's arms and filled each other in on the events of the day.

Jessica listened intently as Timothy explained the conversation with Jack. She told him she had confirmed that Allison was the same Allison in the tree. But, having said that, Jessica didn't want to get him too excited. She explained that was why she had said nothing yet.

They pondered together the plausibility of Allison being his mother. She was the right age to have had him as a teenager, which would make sense as to why she gave him up for adoption. It was Jessica who mentioned the story of being in a psychiatric facility could have been a cover for the pregnancy. They recalled her own mother's cover story of having Mono, which kept her out of school with a homebound tutor. Both agree Allison's story might have been a cover story.

Either way, Jessica was thankful she knew this information before talking to Allison about Timothy. With this knowledge, she had to tread lightly on the subject.

Jessica told Timothy about her visit home. They discussed again how her brothers wanted to move to the island to help Jimmy. It was during this conversation she mentioned a slight bit of apprehension. It might make Jimmy's job harder, having two Gardiners living on the island full-time. She also divulged that she still didn't feel that Mary's confession was genuine. She couldn't help but wonder if her brothers would be in danger.

Then she talked about the dress shopping experience, leaving details about the dress she chose out of the conversation. Timothy loved hearing the stories of her bonding with her sister. He laughed at the fact they were annoying her grandmother.

When she talked about the guy, Samantha had been texting and how he was from the island. Timothy expressed some concern about the stalking aspect of how they met. Jessica explained how she was already going to get Jimmy's take on the situation.

Their stomachs both growled. They laughed. Getting back into the clothes that they had shed. They got some pizza from Village Pizza. It was one of their regular go-to dinner spots when neither felt like cooking.

Timothy went to pick it up while Jessica unpacked from her weekend trip. She noticed the new flowers in the vase on the dining room table and smiled. He always brought her flowers when he came home from a trip. It was a subtle way of saying how much he missed being away from her. His sweetness was so endearing to her.

They knew they had an early morning the next day, so they retired to the bedroom after dinner. Jessica slept so much better when he was home. She hadn't told him of her nightmare. Snuggled up on his shoulder with his arm around her, she quickly dozed off to sleep. Timothy listened to the even breathing of Jessica as she slept. He kissed her forehead, and then he dozed off to sleep himself.

Chapter Eight

Meetings

Jimmy stumbled out of bed early on Monday morning. The room spun as he was still hungover from the weekend. The sight of Melissa had sent him into a tailspin. Saturday night, he had come home and drank more beers until he passed out. When he awoke Sunday afternoon, realized what he had done, and said to Melissa, he drank again. Every movement he made caused the pounding in his head to worsen. Nevertheless, he knew he needed to get motivated. They expected him at the weekly meeting this morning. The face in the mirror he hardly recognized. It was obvious that he hadn't shaved in a while, given the dark stubble on his chin and jawline. The pillow matted one side of his black hair, while the other side stood up. He splashed some cold water on his face, waking himself up a bit more. After shaving and showering, he was feeling better. The aspirin he took was helping take the headache away. Even so, his stomach was rumbling for some sustenance. Liquid meals were not very sustainable. Walking into the kitchen, Stella handed him a cup of coffee and a plate of scrambled eggs. He devoured the food faster than he had expected.

"Son, you look a little rough around the edges this morning. Are you okay to go into the city?"

"Yeah, Ma, I just need to shake this hangover."

"You haven't binged like that in a while, since Melissa."

Stella's words trailed off. She hated to remind her son of that painful time in his life. Worry, though, ran through her mind. They almost lost him during that time. She didn't want to journey down that path again. Reflection made her realize they had been very close to losing their only son. The drinking had led to him trying to numb the pain of his broken heart with more potent drugs. Thankfully, they were able to get him the help he needed. Ms. Mary had helped get him into a better rehab facility. Finally, he had gotten clean of the drugs. He still occasionally drank. This time he had fallen off the wagon hard. The first for him. Concern about what set him off floated through Stella's mind.

"I know, ma, don't worry. I am okay. Just saw someone I had been trying to forget."

"You saw Melissa?"

"Yeah, but you can't tell her parents, I promised."

"I won't tell, son. You know your secrets are always safe with me."

Jimmy filled in his mom about the chance encounter with Melissa and their interactions. It embarrassed him about the kiss and marriage proposal. Stella listened intently to her son explain what had occurred. Her heart broke for him. She knew he would never fully get over his first love. That connection ran way too deep. Stella filled a thermos of coffee for him for his trip into the city. He kissed her forehead and headed out the door.

Jessica and Timothy woke up early, gathered their things for the day, and headed to the train station in New London. This had become Jessica's weekly routine. However, Timothy had rarely joined her. It was a pleasant change of pace, having him to talk to along the way. They both had fun people-watching. Timothy had fun making up things about the people they observed. A woman possibly in her thirties or forties sat across from them talking loudly on her cell phone. Timothy speculated she was a spy using reverse psychology to bring attention to herself to blend in. Jessica joined, and it filled the entire morning with laughter and speculation between them.

When they made it to the office building, they kissed and parted ways. In the coffee break room, Jessica ran into Allison, preparing herself a cup of coffee. Jessica contemplated how to bring up Allison's potential relationship with Timothy. It was Allison, though, who struck up a conversation first.

"Was that your fiancée this morning?"

"Yes, that's Timothy. He also has a meeting."

"Very handsome. You are lucky. What does Timothy do for work?"

"Yes, and I feel blessed to have him in my life. He is my world. He is a writer for National Geographic. That's how we met. We worked together on the Gardiners Island story."

"Ah, sounds exciting. What type of meeting is he having here in the city?"

"Oh, it's not for work. It's a personal meeting. Ironically, being adopted, he just recently got in contact with a second cousin that he matched with on a genealogy website."

Jessica was observing Allison and her reaction.

"Wow, that's crazy that you are both adopted! I hope your fiancée has a good meeting with his new-found cousin."

"What is crazier is we both share the same birthday!"

"Really?? What day is that?"

"June 7th, 1992."

Allison had just taken a sip of her coffee. She seemed to choke on it and started coughing.

"Are you okay, Allison?"

"Yes, thank you. The coffee was just hotter than I expected."

She then promptly left the room.

Noticing that Allison had left her coffee cup on the counter in her hurry to leave, Jessica dipped her pinky into it. It was lukewarm. She thought this was interesting. That meant her reaction was to Timothy's birthdate and not to the coffee.

The board meeting discussed the preliminary cost analysis of the demolition and rebuilding or remodeling of the existing building they had recently gained. It showed that the costs saved by repurposing far outweighed rebuilding costs. Jessica felt good about asking for the cost analysis. The findings were surprising to Allison.

"It may cost us less to remodel, but in the long run, new is going to give us a bigger resale value."

"Honestly, Allison, no one can predict the market and resale value. You may find a client that cherishes the older architecture. Someone like me. Given the chance and choice, I would remodel all the old buildings to preserve the past."

The board decided to remodel the building to preserve the exterior architecture. Asbestos remediation would come first. The board will continue the discussion after finishing the asbestos remediation. Not knowing if unknown costs would add to the project.

When the board meeting finished, Richard, Jessica, and Jimmy stayed in the conference room to have their private consultation. Richard brought up the question of Richard Jr. and David moving onto the island permanently to live in the Manor house along with Jimmy.

The hair on the back of Jimmy's neck bristled at the request. Not because he didn't want to share the island with his cousins, he was just concerned about their safety. He had kept his concerns about Mary's death a secret until this point. He had also thought it was prudent to keep the deer carcass incident a secret. *Should I tell them?* He thought to himself. Jimmy decided not to voice his concerns.

"I could use the extra manpower on security. We always feel understaffed. If they will help, I gladly will welcome them into the ranks of the security team. I also wouldn't mind the company in the Manor house. That big old place gets lonely."

He needed the extra help with the security. Having them help, whereas they were vested in the island, could be beneficial. There wasn't much else to discuss with the island. Richard left to return to Boston. This left Jessica and Jimmy alone in the conference room. Out of respect for her sister's privacy, Jessica had not asked about Zach in front of her father.

"Hey Jimmy, what do you know about Zach on your security team?"

"He is a good guy. I have known him my whole life. I trust him. If this is about him talking to your sister, I already warned him."

"I hope you are right. Samantha is already head over heels for him. I don't want her heart getting broken."

"By the smile on his face when he was texting her Saturday, the feeling is mutual. I don't want Samantha to suffer the consequences of heartbreak, either. I know what that is like."

"Zach told Samantha about you and his sister. I am sorry she broke your heart."

"Yeah, me too. Me too."

Jimmy and Jessica finished their conversation and parted ways. Jessica was excited to find out how Timothy's meeting with Jack went. As she was leaving, she bumped into Allison again. Allison seemed a bit distracted. Her standard self-control and composure were shaky, and Jessica wondered if the board siding with her and not Allison caused it.

"Hey Allison, I hope the outcome at the board meeting today didn't upset you. I know you are for new construction. I hope there are no hard feelings?"

"Not at all. After seeing the cost savings, it's the better business decision, in the short term. I am just not sure it's the wisest decision for long-term investment. Researching Dublin, I see what you mean about the artistic blend."

"Okay, I just didn't want to step on your toes or upset you. I value you here. I don't want to do anything to lose you."

"I appreciate you saying that. My mind is elsewhere today. No worries though, I will get myself back on track."

"I noticed. That is why I am concerned. If you ever need to talk. About anything, I am here for you."

"Thank you. I will keep that in mind."

Jessica left the office building and went to meet up with Timothy. She hoped Jack was still with him. It was exciting for her to meet a biological relative of Timothy's. Then a terrible thought crossed her mind. *What if it didn't go well?* Anxiety built inside her.

Rounding the corner, she saw the coffee shop where the meeting was taking place. A little more reluctantly, she entered the shop and looked for Timothy. He was sitting, laughing, engrossed in friendly conversation with the man across from him. She didn't want to interrupt. Timothy looked her way. He stood up and motioned for her to join them.

"Jessica, this is my cousin, Jack."

"It is a pleasure to meet you, Jack. I am so excited for you both!"

Jack shook her hand when introduced.

"It is great to meet you too! Timothy has told me about you. I really can't believe how you too met."

"Yeah, definitely not your run-of-the-mill romance story. We didn't swipe left or right. Destiny, same place at the same time."

"Well, to be honest, it wasn't just destiny. I knew Arthur, and he knew I was a big fan of your photography. With Alexandria's urging, he recommended you to me and my editor for the Gardiner Island story. I didn't know it was all part of Alexandria's plan, though."

"Wow, still amazing! I guess I can admit I am awestruck. I have never met a multi-millionaire before."

"I don't look like one and I certainly do not act like one. Probably because I didn't grow up as one. Just treat me like you would any other human being, please. We are a family now. Or at least when Timothy and I get married we will be family. I can't get over how much you two look so much alike."

The resemblance was uncanny. Jessica commented they could pass as brothers. They laughed and agreed.

They talked about so many things that Jessica's head was spinning. Jack explained he had told Timothy that his mother had agreed to do a DNA test through the genealogy website. To help them narrow down which side of Jack's family Timothy was a part of. This news made Jessica so happy for Timothy.

Jessica filled them both in on the conversation with Allison and how she was acting differently afterward. They both agreed that it made things suspicious of her. They all held the same view. Since they didn't know the reason behind her psychiatric hospitalization, there could be a logical explanation.

It was getting late by the time they said their goodbyes. They made plans to meet up the following week. Timothy and Jessica headed to the train station to go home. It had been a productive day. Jessica had swayed the board to vote along with her idea, which impressed Timothy. The discussion also included the decision to allow the boys to move in with Jimmy. Jessica also filled him in on her conversation with Jimmy about Zach and Samantha.

It was late by the time they got home. They wanted to climb into bed and get some sleep. As Jessica lay nestled against Timothy, she looked up into his eyes. It surprised her to see a tear welling up in the corner.

"What's wrong?"

"Honestly, not sure. I am feeling overwhelmed right now. I am feeling nervous about finding my biological family."

"Oh, honey, I get it. I am right here by your side."

"I know you do. That helps so much. My fear is they will want nothing to do with me, like my adoptive parents."

Timothy choked out the last sentence. Jessica crossed her arm over his body and pushed herself up to look him in the eyes. He looked so vulnerable at that moment, and her heart just melted. She leaned over him and gently kissed his forehead. He reached around her and pulled her to him. Settling his head against her shoulder, he slowly stopped crying and started softly kissing her neck. They nurtured one another until they fell asleep in one another's arms.

Chapter Nine

Darkness

The listening devices they planted in the Manor house came in extremely handy. They relished in the fact that Jimmy had spilled his guts to his mom about Melissa. Oh, how that would be used to their advantage in the future. The knowledge that Jimmy had fallen off the wagon was another vital secret. How the Gardiner family always fell right into their best-laid plans amused them.

Then, hearing that the two Gardiner boys were moving to the island and into the Manor house, was the icing on the proverbial cake. The family was making things just way too easy for them.

The excitement of what was to come was building inside them. All of the ways in which they could tear the family apart were swirling in their brain. Who to target first was a big question. They still didn't know. They needed more information about the family. Their comings and goings.

With Richard Jr. and David coming to stay on the island permanently, that would be much easier. Maybe one of them would be the first to go. The girls, though, would be fun targets. Easy to terrorize. Maybe even torture. One thing they knew for sure was in their mind, Jessica would be the last to go.

The hatred for her seethed in their veins. From the moment Jessica had stepped foot on the island, there was something about her that just irritated them. Her beauty was mesmerizing. Albeit, that wasn't it. Aware of who she was, and that she was the heiress to the Gardiner fortune. That angered them. How she came to the island was a mystery to them. It had to be orchestrated somehow. They didn't believe in coincidences.

Of course, they thought there were only two other heirs, Jessica and Jimmy, back only a few months ago. They knew the family secrets that even those two hadn't known about themselves. They thought back then, getting rid of them would have proven to be more accessible.

They had almost succeeded that first night in getting rid of Jessica. Oh, how it angered them that Timothy had interrupted them. They had stolen a pair of night-vision goggles from the security team. They had snuck into the bathroom where Jessica was bathing. Turned off the lights, locked the door, and had pushed her under the water. They had barely escaped through the passageway when Timothy had busted through the door.

He would pay for taking that kill away from them. He would pay dearly. Perhaps he could watch Jessica die, or maybe he would be the one to kill her. They just couldn't decide yet. They had time to make those plans. Either way, he would suffer the consequences of his actions.

The plans for the family's Christmas visit were coming along nicely. They had gained the boxes needed for the families' Christmas gifts. Their imagination ran wild thinking about them all opening their packages on Christmas morning. It gave them such a rush.

Terror was their purpose for the gifts. Jessica had not heeded their first warning. The letter sat in a box, along with other items that would serve an essential purpose in the coming months. All that happened now was her fault. She should never have come back to the island.

Every life lost on the island, whether animal or human, was now her fault. They would make her feel the guilt. The thought of the darkness of guilt and shame enveloping Jessica made them feel jubilant.

A rumor went through the inhabitants about a deer carcass being mutilated and left to rot. Security felt it was someone that had snuck onto the island. They chuckled at the thought they had gotten away with another big kill. Right under everyone's noses, it emboldened them to do it again. They were waiting for it to be found.

It upset many inhabitants about the deer carcass. For most, it was such a violation of their way of life. They all embraced the Native American roots of the island. Respecting the land and the animals that lived on it. The inhabitants felt it had been a desecration. Not them though, they embraced a different aspect of the island's past.

They embraced the darkness. Early in life, their mother told them about the stories of dark witches who lived and worked on the island. They had descended from those bloodlines. Though their mother had never learned the craft, they had studied it. They were learning to perfect it and harness it.

Disgust filled them at the thought of their mother. Had she learned the craft and harnessed it, their lives could have been so different. They could have lived a life of privilege instead of a life of existence and servitude.

How else could they explain their lot in life? Being born to the mistress of the Manor house. Everyone knew their mother was promiscuous. What they didn't know was about her mistress status, though. Their birth known, their birthrights hidden. Their fellow inhabitants pitying them instead of respecting them.

When their secret becomes known, they will gain respect. The inhabitants would all know who they were, eventually. When they took their rightful place on the island. Revenge would be pleasant.

Patience was not their virtue. Still, they knew they needed to time things right to get away with what they were planning. They needed to make sure it pointed no fingers at them. The planning would point to someone else.

Christmas would be here soon. The entire family would be here. They could easily take them all out at once. Start a fire in the house when they were all sleeping. A tragic ending. There were too many variables in that plan, though.

Richard's survival of the boating accident taught them that. His survival had also taught them that plans needed to be kept secret. No accomplices. Richard survived because he had heard the plans to kill him. Then, knowing the goals, he hatched his own survival plan.

The family could escape a fire. Too much risk, not enough control in the outcome. Picking them off one by one would prove more complex. Notwithstanding, there was the assurance that the family would disappear for good.

Each individual kill would strengthen them. The power they would gain would be great. More significant than any they had ever felt. They could do anything they wanted to. They would have it all.

They would have the island, the respect, the wealth, and with all that, they could find someone to share it all with. Maybe even love. They were sure they could make someone fall in love with them with all the power they would possess.

Everyone loved power. They had seen it their entire life. Those that didn't live on the island coveted those that did. Because of the perceived strength, the Gardiner family held. Their wealth and prestige gave them that power.

Other people with prestige had flocked to the island events. This was where they had observed the attraction to power that led to love on so many occasions. Maybe it was the love that led to the control. This thought had crossed their minds on so many occasions. Although they knew little about love at all.

Love was an enigma to them. They hypothesized it led to greater personal power only by observation. It was an emotion that had been barren in their life.

Even though they had never really felt loved, it was the one thing they craved more than revenge. To be accepted for who they were unconditionally by someone. They had never felt that from anyone. Not even their own mother.

Their mother seemed to despise their existence in this world. She lived her existence properly, serving the family during the day and at night serving entirely differently. So she was too busy to be a proper mother.

She gave no nurturing moments growing up. No, I love you, no bedtime stories, and no tucking them in at night. Instead, they pretty much raised themselves. A wild child roaming the island. Just learning about those that lived there.

Their father had nothing to do with them. He knew. It was inconvenient and messy to acknowledge them, though. So there was no love there, no nurturing, no relationship.

They were always an outcast. Until they were of age to be of use to those who owned the island. Then they had a job, as all inhabitants on the island did.

Learning their job, they performed it well. Using it to their advantage of observing and gathering secrets of the family. It gave them a wage and housing. Modern-day slavery in their mind. They would break those chains in time.

The inhabitants were second-class citizens. Especially when they ventured to the mainland. Everyone knew who were members of the Gardiner family and who were not. If you were family, you were royalty. If you were not family, you were trash.

It was rare that an inhabitant would find themselves treated fairly by mainlanders. However, it happened occasionally, and that was how some mainlanders found their way onto the island. First, becoming an inhabitant through marriage. Then, quickly became indoctrinated into the culture of the island.

Their match had yet to be found. They didn't fit in with the inhabitants or the mainlanders. They were a lone wolf. Hunting through the darkness to feel loved and accepted. To feel loved would be the most significant power boost ever.

Chapter Ten

The Move

The week before Christmas, Jimmy was busy preparing for Richard Jr. and David to move in. He had updated the security team that their safety was the number one priority. They were going to be joining the security team as well. The pairing of Richard Jr. with Matt, and David with Zach seemed good.

He had let Betty know to make sure all the rooms were clean and ready except Mary's old room. Not knowing which rooms his cousins would choose to make their own, he wanted them all prepared. All except Mary's. It was the one room he had kept precisely the way it was when he first moved in. Not being able to bear the thought of anyone else occupying it yet.

Martin, the butler, was looking forward to the two Gardiner boys moving in. It was boring with only one person living in the Manor house. The years of dealing with Mary and her mood swings were long gone in his mind. He had enjoyed the change of pace with Jimmy and felt the addition of the other two males would bring some life back to the place.

He had felt outnumbered working alongside Stella and Betty in the Manor house for years. Especially after Richard had supposedly died. The only male in the house for too many years, he had become somewhat reclusive.

Now, though, he enjoyed shooting pool with Jimmy in the parlor most nights after dinner. The rapport they had made it fun to work for him. Martin had never felt that with any of the previous Manor occupants. Maybe it was different because Jimmy was just like him, still an employee of the Gardiners.

Jimmy had been rewarded, though, and allowed to live in the Manor house. Would that feeling of comradery disappear when the Gardiner boys moved in, though? That was his only fear.

The buzz around the island was filled with excitement and some anxiety. No one really knew the two Gardiner boys. Some of the older generations knew their father and had always held him in high regard.

When the moving truck pulled off the rickety ferry and drove up to the Manor house, everyone stopped what they were doing to observe the new residents. Two workers hopped out of the truck, and everyone went back to work, realizing they were not the boys.

Jimmy rode his ATV up to the truck and introduced himself to the movers. They explained the boys were coming across Gardiners Bay behind them in their vehicles. Since all could not fit on the ferry simultaneously, the boys had decided to go across last.

When the boys pulled up, Jimmy excitedly welcomed them home. He exchanged hugs with them both and patted them on their backs. He hoped his trepidation did not show. There were still many reasons for him to be uneasy about this move. Their safety was first and foremost in his mind.

"Betty will show you the rooms available for you to choose from for yourselves. So please make yourself at home! As always, Martin will help you with your things and help you get settled. And, of course, Stella will have dinner prepared by 5:30 pm."

"Thanks, Jimmy. David and I are both looking forward to shooting some pool after dinner! I am sure we are going to need the fun and relaxation after moving all our stuff in."

Jimmy hopped back on his ATV and resumed his rounds while the boys followed Betty into the house to choose their rooms.

As they walked past Mary's old room, Betty gave a warning to them both.

"Yous all should be mineful to stay outa thar. Mr. Jimmy don't want anyone goin' in and desturbin' that room."

Richard Jr. and David looked at each other and just shrugged. They figured their cousin would have reasons for not wanting Mary's room touched. They would not question it one bit. Neither of them had any desire to enter it, anyway.

They still etched the gruesome scene they had witnessed months prior in their minds. They both chose bedrooms as far away from hers as possible. The movers had to first remove the existing beds and bureaus. Since they both had furniture they had brought with them.

It was easier for the movers to put the unused furniture into the attic than in the basement. When all was said and done, it was early evening. When the movers finished and the boys were settled in. They were looking forward to the delicious home-cooked meal Stella had been preparing. The aroma had been wafting throughout the house, making their stomachs grumble.

As Jimmy was heading back to the Manor house to call it a day, he got a call from Zach on the radio to meet him and Matt out by the south end of Great Pond on the southern tip of the island. The shakiness in Zach's voice concerned him. It was rare that anything got Zach shaken up. He stopped quickly to let Stella know he would be late for dinner, told her not to hold things up, and headed to meet Zach and Matt.

It was dark, and their ATV lights were shining on what they had found. When he pulled up to the scene, Jimmy got the feeling of Déjà vu. It was another deer carcass. This time a doe. Killed the same way and mutilated. He took pictures, and they worked together to dispose of the body.

They worked silently together. They tried not to let the stench and decomposing body make them sick. Jimmy had hoped the first carcass was a fluke. Stupid teenagers pulling a prank or something. The discovery of this one made that scenario less likely. The timing couldn't have been less ideal.

The Gardiner boys had just moved in today. How was he going to keep this under wraps? He didn't want them to freak out. But, on the other hand, he certainly didn't need the family to back out of coming for Christmas, either.

"We have to keep this under wraps for a few weeks. You both understand, right? We can't have the family scared to come for Christmas. We may have to pull some double shifts, though, and increase patrols even more."

As Jimmy finished, he ran his hands over his face in frustration. He was mentally tired. His men were exhausted. They had beefed up patrols already after they found the first carcass.

"It's okay, boss. We will keep it under wraps, and we will do what needs to be done to keep everybody safe. Can I at least run some questions by Melissa about the type of person who might do this? She might be able to give us some insight. "

Zach looked at his boss sympathetically.

"That's a good idea, Zach. Your sister is a smart cookie. She might be able to give us a clue, Jimmy."

The mention of Melissa's name made Jimmy wince, but he knew Zach and Matt were right. She was smart. Psychology was the primary subject she was studying, and they needed some insight into the psyche of whoever was doing this.

"Mention the first carcass to her, not this one. Everyone on the island knows about that one. Ask her hypothetically what it would mean if someone were to do it again. And tell her I said hi."

Zach said he would call her later that night. Concern was all over his face. He was just as determined as Jimmy to sort this out. They didn't know if this person posed a threat to any human on the island. Yet, they were taking it as a threat and would do everything in their power to make sure everyone was safe.

By the time Jimmy got back to the Manor house, dinner was over. Stella had made him a plate of leftovers, although he wasn't hungry at the moment. She could tell something was bothering him. Still, she didn't ask. His body language told her he was in no mood to discuss anything.

Joining the boys and Martin in the parlor, Jimmy sat down to relax. They were already shooting pool and having a couple of beers.

"Hey David, aren't you a bit young for that?"

"If I was away at college enjoying the frat life, this is exactly what I would be doing."

David chugged the rest of his beer.

"Come on, Jimmy, have one with us! Let's celebrate our new brotherhood."

Richard Jr. threw another beer at David and one at Jimmy.

He caught the beer thrown at him. Jimmy knew he shouldn't drink it. He was not in the right frame of mind. His cousins didn't know about his past, so forgiveness could be given to them for their pressure. Not wanting to disappoint his cousins, he decided he could handle one.

They all enjoyed playing pool and hanging out until late in the evening. Martin was the first to turn in. Jimmy followed suit shortly after. He knew the next day would bring a deluge of problems to solve because that was just how things were rolling lately. The boys would be introduced to the security team and start their training in the afternoon. The boys stumbled to bed as well.

All was quiet that first night in the Manor house. Then, in the morning, Jimmy's alarm jolted him awake. As he slipped out of bed, he kicked a couple of empty beer cans on the floor. He stopped in his tracks. One, that's all he remembered having. Cleaning up the cans, he assessed himself. No hangover, no headache, no feeling queasy, and no spinning of the room.

He shook his head. He shrugged it off as a joke by his cousins. He proceeded to shower and get dressed, then head down for breakfast, he would ask them about it later.

Jimmy had just finished his eggs, bacon, and coffee when he heard a bunch of yelling coming from upstairs. He went to investigate. Jimmy found both of his cousins in towels as if they had both just gotten out of the shower, standing in the hallway. Both were pointing to their bedrooms, visibly freaked out.

"What's the problem?"

"Dude, what the hell is that on my pillow? It wasn't there when I got up. It was there when I got out of the shower."

David was the first to say something.

"Same in my room! What the hell is going on? Is this some sort of sick initiation thing?"

Jimmy peered into David's room first. As he got closer, he knew what it was, and his heart sank. His stomach wanted to heave. The formaldehyde was strong. There on the pillow was a heart. If Jimmy was a gambling man, he would bet that it came from a deer. As he went across the hall to Richard Jr.'s room and saw the same thing, he knew he was right.

He took pictures. He told his cousins he was sorry and would get to the bottom of this, then called Zach and Matt to the house. While his cousins went down for breakfast, they dusted for prints, took more pictures, and investigated as much as they could. Then they cleaned up the sheets. When they finished, Jimmy let Betty know both rooms needed new linens.

Before leaving for the security shack, he checked in on Richard Jr. and David to ensure they were okay. They both seemed less rattled than earlier, which eased Jimmy's mind a bit. As he left, he stopped in the kitchen to ask Stella if she had seen anyone in the Manor house that morning. The only person who generally wasn't in the place daily had been Samuel.

Samuel had fixed the dishwasher for her that morning. Then she remembered Betty had asked him to check out the washer and dryer while he was there, too. He had been in and out with tools and parts. Stella had been busy preparing breakfast, so she had paid little attention to his comings and goings. Nothing seemed out of the ordinary with him, though, she had added.

Leaving the Manor house, Jimmy paid Samuel a visit to his shop.

"Good morning, Samuel. What are you up to today?"

"Jimmy boy, I am working on this darned tractor again. It might be time to replace the old thing. Getting parts is harder and harder to come by."

"I heard you were up early fixing stuff at the Manor house this morning."

"Yeah, them women had me chasing issues they cause themselves. I know Stella is your mom and all, but I have told her a million times she needs to rinse the dishes before putting them in the dang dishwasher! She is constantly clogging the thing up! Then that Betty. Geez, overloading the washing machine and not checking the lint trap on the dryer. You're gonna have a fire if you're not too careful!"

Jimmy chuckled at Samuel's response. He was never too fond of the womenfolk. They all seemed to annoy him regularly. His presence in the house that morning seemed on the up and up.

"You didn't happen to see anyone else in the house that normally isn't there, did you?"

"Nah, just the usuals. Stella, Betty, and Martin. What's with the 3rd-degree boss?"

"Ah, nothing, just someone pulling some pranks on the Gardiner boys this morning. I am trying to figure out who is doing the hazing, so I can get them to knock it off."

"Not me, boss. I have too much to do around here than mess with those two. If I see anything out of the normal, I will let you know."

"Thank you, Samuel. I appreciate that."

Jimmy was perplexed. For the life of him, he could not think of anyone that would have done that to the boys. Then Jimmy got to thinking about the beer cans in his room. He had forgotten about them. Did he drink more than one beer? Could he have blacked out? It scared part of him to think he was heading down that dark road again. He needed to be more diligent and resist the temptation.

Chapter Eleven

Home Creepy Home

Timothy's phone rang. It was his editor. Timothy took a deep breath and steadied his resolve and thoughts before answering the phone.

"Good morning Larry. What do I have the pleasure of your call today?"

"Timothy, my reasons for calling are twofold. First, I understand your frustrations with being away from your lovely bride-to-be for a long time. Second, I also understand she is the best at photography. I have no problem pairing you up with her for all of your future jobs. As long as she is not working on another project."

"I appreciate your understanding, Larry. However, I also realize she is a freelance photographer, and she may get work that conflicts with our deadlines."

"I am glad we could reach a mutual understanding. I would hate to lose a talented writer. With that being settled, I have work for you and Jessica to do. Sorry, it is so close to the holidays and all."

After their conversation, he sent them both to Antarctica to do a piece on the hatching of penguin chicks.

The assignment being so close to Christmas was annoying to Jessica and Timothy. However, they figured they could get the work done and be home just in time. It just meant that their investigation into Timothy's biological family would have to wait.

A consolation for them both was, they invited Jack to the family Christmas Eve gathering on Gardiners Island. Jack was excited to attend. Jessica had also asked Allison to attend the party under the pretense of working with Jimmy, Richard, and herself. Mentioning Arthur's invitation, hoping it would entice Allison to attend.

Before heading on their trip, Timothy researched the weather in Antarctica. Antarctica in December was bearable for Jessica and Timothy, who lived in New England. Average daily temperatures in the low 30s were not unheard of in New England, which was the norm this time of year in Antarctica. So they packed their winter gear along with their equipment and were on their way for an adventure.

The helicopter blades whirred above their heads as they hovered above the scientific observatory camp they would call home for a few days. The brown tents and heavy machinery scattered around made the base look like a small military installment. They were shown both a cot and a footlocker to store their gear in the barracks. The mess hall was a small tent about 20 feet from the barracks. The latrines were situated around the back of the barracks.

Their accommodations took the wind out of their sails a bit. First, they realized they would not be bunking together. They bunked females on one side of the barracks and males on the other, with a fabric partition between them.

The first night was less than ideal. The food presented was meatloaf, mashed potatoes, and green beans. It looked like canned dog food, something with the consistency of oatmeal instead of mashed potatoes and some green smoothie puree. The texture and taste were less than desirable. They knew they needed to eat though and choked down the food given to them.

Their first-morning meal was not much better, and they ate as much as they could stomach. Then, the two bundled up for the first expedition out to the penguin nests. They were ready in no time. Jessica and Timothy wanted to get this assignment over with as soon as possible. It was the harshest in terms of environmental conditions either of them had been on in a while.

The guide showed them the best vantage spots to observe the penguins hatching. He was doing his scientific observations, so he stayed with them the entire day. All day, not a single egg hatched. This was the money shot Jessica was trying to get. She knew they couldn't leave until she got it.

It took three days of observing the penguins to catch the chicks' hatching. The shots Jessica captured of the chick's beaks emerging from the shells showed the miracle of their birth. She couldn't help but think it was ironic that these baby penguins were hatching for Christmas. The miracle of birth always had a soft spot in her heart.

She looked over at Timothy and watched him write. Her mind wandered to the thought of them having their own children together. Soon, but not too soon. They would make great parents. At least, that was how she felt. She envisioned Timothy holding their baby for the first time and smiled. Timothy looked her way and caught her staring at him with love in her eyes.

"What is that grin across your face for?"

"I am just thinking of you holding our own baby one day."

"Are you trying to tell me something?"

"Oh, no, not yet anyway! You will be the first to know, though. After me, of course!"

They finished up their work for the day, laughing. It felt good to get what they needed for the assignment done. They were thankful they could leave the following day. This would give them a couple of days to develop the pictures and for Timothy to write the accompanying article. Then they would be off to meet the rest of the family on the Island for the Christmas holiday.

Their first Christmas together. Jessica's first Christmas with her biological family. Timothy's first Christmas with his genetic cousin. There was so much to be excited about and thankful for. They kept talking about the gifts they had bought for family members the entire trip home. They couldn't wait for them to open them up on Christmas morning.

Both of them felt the childlike excitement of the holiday again, which added to their overall joyfulness. With the added motivation of the holiday approaching, Jessica and Timothy could get their assignment done in a day.

The editor was delighted with their work and how they had gotten it done in such a timely fashion.

Jessica got in touch with Jimmy and asked if they could arrive a few days earlier than planned. He was more than happy for them to come early. Although, at first, Jessica thought there was a slight hesitation in his voice. She shrugged it off as he was busy at work and getting everything ready for the rest of the family to arrive.

Delighted to hear that Arthur would join them for Christmas Eve, Jessica finished packing for their holiday getaway. Timothy packed his clothes and all the presents in the car, and then they were off to catch the ferry to Long Island.

The roads were snow-covered still from the minor storm that had pushed through the night before. Yet, sunshine glistened and sparkled off the snow-covered fields as they drove past. The untouched beauty was breathtaking.

The ferry service was running, despite being rougher than regular seas from the storm. They made it across the sound and headed towards the island ferry to cross Gardiners Bay. Jessica always dreaded that leg of the trip. The ferry was old and rickety. Jimmy was getting a replacement. Albeit, that would take time. Captain Bill always assured Jessica the vessel was seaworthy, rapping his knuckles on the bow.

Captain Bill was a little rough around the edges, with his long grey hair and beard, his weathered skin, and gruff voice. He wore a white captain's hat. A cigar was hanging out of his mouth. Not lit, he tended to just roll it back and forth in his mouth and chew on its end.

Growing up on the Island, his father had been a captain as well. When he was sixteen, they had hired Captain Bill as a deckhand. Working under his father had toughened him up a bit. There was no favoritism on board his father's vessel, and he ran a tight ship. Captain Bill did the same.

As they pulled off the boat, they saw David on one of the ATVs alongside another security member. They waved as they passed him. His smile showed how happy he was. This delighted Jessica. David was the one she worried about the most. He was young and had no compass where he wanted his life to go.

When they reached the Manor house, it only took minutes for Martin to welcome them and start helping them unload their car. Jessica noticed the difference in his relaxed demeanor now compared to the first time she had been on the Island. Although she also welcomed them, Betty was inside the house and was still standoffish. Before unpacking, Jessica detoured into the kitchen to say hello to Stella.

As always, the kitchen smelled of delicious aromas. Stella gave Jessica a big welcoming hug and snuck her a few of the freshly baked Christmas cookies she had made. This transported Jessica back to her childhood as she bit into the cinnamon-covered morsel.

She remembered, closing her eyes, how her Mom made it an annual tradition for them to bake cookies before Christmas. They would start the day after Thanksgiving and bake daily until Christmas Eve. They boxed up many cookies and gave them as gifts to friends and neighbors. A tiny teardrop escaped from the corner of her eye. Quickly opening her eyes and wiping the tears away, she thanked Stella for the cookies and headed to her room to unpack. Stella gave her a nod and squeezed her hand.

Martin and Timothy were just finishing bringing the bags to the room. They were talking about playing pool later after dinner. The atmosphere in the Manor house had gone through a significant overhaul since the last time she was here. The air of gloom and doom was gone. Hope and happiness replaced it.

The two places in the house that still gave her the creeps were the room she had stayed in the first time. The one someone almost killed her in. Also, Mary's room. Just walking past it gave her the chills and brought her memory back to that fateful morning.

Her thoughts went to Betty. It must be difficult for her to work day in and day out and walk past that room. She was the one who found Mary. Jessica was kicking herself for not realizing this earlier. She made a mental note to discuss it with her father and Jimmy when she got a chance. That could explain Betty's demeanor.

After unpacking, Timothy and Jessica had some time to explore the Island. Something they had yet to do. They got a couple of ATVs to do some riding. They met Samuel in the garage.

"Hi, Samuel. We are going to do some exploring with two of the ATVs. Which two should we take?"

"Those two over there are ready to go. Be sure to make sure everything works before you head out, though. We don't want any accidents occurring."

Samuel pointed his thumb over to two of the ATVs.

"Thank you. We will make sure the machines are working," Timothy said, a little more annoyed than he should have shown. "Even though that's your job."

Neither of them had an affinity towards Samuel. They got the impression the feeling was mutual. He hadn't been friendly towards them the first time they met, and his attitude hadn't seemed to change.

Jessica felt it was best to follow the trails already blazed through the snow by the security team. She didn't want to get stuck somewhere on the Island, not knowing how to get back to the Manor house.

Heading east from the Manor house, they followed a path that took them southeast and over Willow Brook Pond. They found themselves at Two Lookout Tower. Jimmy was there and welcomed them to the Island.

Showing them the view from the lookout tower, it amazed Jessica as the beautiful waves of the Atlantic Ocean crashed along the coast of the eastern beaches. The power that the waves displayed was spectacular.

Jimmy's radio crackled, startling them out of the quiet watchfulness they had been in. The voice on the other end was informing him he needed to meet them at Captain Kid Hollow. Jessica thought she recognized the voice as her brother Richard Jr., as Jimmy hopped on his ATV to meet up with the person on the other end of the radio. Jessica and Timothy hopped on their ATVs and followed suit.

When he pulled up to Richard Jr. and Matt at Captain Kid Hollow, Jimmy could tell by the look on their faces it wasn't good news he was being called out there for. He got off the ATV and walked up to them to another deer carcass. It was another doe mutilated, just like the others.

Jimmy rubbed his face with both his hands. He had already told David and Richard Jr. about the other carcasses after they found the hearts on their pillows that first morning. With Timothy and Jessica right behind him, he knew he would have to inform them of everything that had occurred.

Timothy hopped off his ATV, followed by Jessica. When they saw what the commotion was all about, they both stood with their mouths open. They were both accustomed to the views of nature. They had never been exposed to such grotesque disregard for life. Jessica was the first to lose her stomach contents, with Timothy following suit.

Jimmy coaxed them both to head back to the Manor house as it would get dark soon. He promised he would fill them in when he got back. But first, the security team would have to do a thorough investigation.

When Jessica and Timothy returned to the Manor house, they went straight to their room. Disconcerted by what they witnessed, Jessica paced.

"What the hell was that? Who the hell would do such a thing?"

"I don't know, hun. Jimmy will have some answers when he gets back."

"I sure do hope so! Did you notice how none of them seemed phased by it? Like it was an everyday occurrence or something?"

"Yeah, I did. The entire security team was all eerie calm. Even your brother."

"I have seen dead deer before. Hell, I have killed plenty, but that. That was a blatant disregard for that animal's life."

"Let's try to forget it for now till Jimmy comes back."

Timothy trailed off his sentence as he wrapped his arms around Jessica and just hugged her tight. She relaxed a bit and leaned her head on his shoulder.

"I will try, but just when I thought the creepiness of this place was gone, it goes and rears its ugly head again."

Chapter Twelve

Good Morning, Surprise!

Jimmy and the boys got to the house for dinner. They looked ragged and drained. Jessica let them eat dinner in peace without asking the nagging questions in her mind. It wasn't until later in the evening, when they were all relaxing in the parlor, Jimmy started the conversation.

"Hey Jessica, I need to say I am sorry first. I have been keeping some stuff from you and your father that has been occurring on the island. At first, I thought it was just some punks pulling sick pranks in my defense. Until your brothers got here, and the targeting occurred."

"Wait, what? My brothers were targeted? How? By who? When you say targeted, do you mean like I was targeted?"

Jessica's mind was racing. She had known in her gut Mary wasn't the one that had attacked her before. Despite her confession in her suicide note. Was Jimmy confirming that suspicion?

"Look, I don't know who. That is the most frustrating aspect of this whole thing. I have interviewed everyone on this island half a dozen times casually to not raise suspicion with any of them. No one gives me clues as to being able to do this. None give any inclination of dislike to the Gardiner family. On the contrary, they are all grateful for their livelihoods here. With no motive why someone would do these things, and no evidence leading to a suspect, my hands are tied."

"I got one question, Jimmy. And I want a straight-up honest answer. Do you think this is the same person who came after me?"

"Yes. Forgive me for keeping that from you, too. I investigated the theory of Mary using the passageway to get away after almost drowning you. There was no way she could do it and reappear in time. None. Things had been quiet, though, so I figured things were good. I am sorry."

"Hey, it's okay. But, yeah, am I a little freaked out. Absolutely. No one in their right mind wouldn't be. I trust you, and I know you are doing everything in your power to keep everyone safe and understand all this."

Jimmy took a deep breath in and released it, relaxing his shoulders a bit. They all agreed to keep all the incidents from Jessica's parents and Samantha. At least until they knew more. They were soon forgetting all about the latest find and playing pool.

Martin joined them, and they all had a few beers. Being cautious about drinking still, Jimmy set his mind on only having one. He held onto the one can all evening. Only putting it down when it was his turn to shoot pool.

When it was time to turn in for the evening, Jimmy marked his can before putting it in the recycling bin. Then, up in his room, he made sure there was no single can of beer empty or full anywhere. He even opened the little parsonage cabinet on the wall. There was not a drop of alcohol in his room.

This had become his nightly routine, and every morning he awoke to the same thing. Empty beer cans were strewn over his floor, and no memory of him drinking them. He checked them for fingerprints every time, using the primary dusting and lifting with tape method. The ones he found always seemed to be his.

Of course, he kept all of this secret and didn't ask anyone else to analyze the prints. He didn't want anyone to know that he was afraid he was relapsing somehow and not remembering anything. He had heard of psychosis causing memory loss. Using alcohol and drugs could induce psychosis.

He had a few episodes of psychosis after drug and alcohol use in the past. It was what led him to get treatment. He had been sober and clean for so many years. The thought of him relapsing without knowing scared him.

However, he didn't know who he could reach out to for help. He fell asleep after tossing and turning for what seemed like hours.

Morning came, and Jessica was the first to rise. She left Timothy sleeping and padded down to the kitchen. Stella was already making breakfast, stopping to make Jessica a cup of tea. Jessica loved Stella. She was always so cheerful and seemed to love cooking for everyone.

Betty came into the kitchen and seemed to be less than amicable.

"Stella, ya know if Samuel is out in thar shop yet? That danged washer's acting up again."

"I saw the light on when I walked past this morning, Betty. Get your coat and boots on and go see if he will come and fix it for you again."

Grumbling something about the cold, Betty followed Stella's instructions and headed towards the shop to get Samuel. Stella looked at Jessica.

"That girl is always breaking that machine. Samuel is going to throw a fit again. He is never happy when he has to tinker with stuff in the house. At least since Ms. Mary's passed. I think he had a soft spot for her. He never minded fixing things when she was here."

"Is that so?"

Betty was back in the kitchen, with Samuel following right behind within twenty minutes. Stella was right about one thing. Samuel did not seem amused at having to fix the washing machine again. As he walked through the kitchen and into the utility room, he grumbled under his breath.

Jessica couldn't hear what was being said between Betty and Samuel. She could tell that it wasn't a friendly conversation. Betty emerged from the utility room and stormed off to do her housekeeping duties.

Timothy was just entering the kitchen and was almost knocked over by Betty's departure.

"Wow, someone seems to have woken up on the wrong side of the bed this morning!"

"Ah, the washing machine is broken, again. Samuel is trying to fix it. But, despite that, he isn't too pleased to be tasked with the job."

Jessica shrugged.

Laughing, Timothy leaned over and kissed Jessica on the forehead.

"Sounds like an old married couple."

Samuel emerged from the utility room as they both laughed at Timothy's comment. Grumbling again, something about needing to go find Betty and apologize. This time, it seemed like something was wrong with the blasted machine and not an operator error.

Stella pointed him in the direction Betty had gone. While Jessica and Timothy sat at the island in the kitchen eating their breakfast, Jimmy was upstairs staring at the empty beer cans on his floor.

He had woken up hours ago, or at least that is what he thought. The appearance of the cans again was making him seriously question his sanity. His focus was trying to figure out how this kept happening. There were no physical signs he had drank more than one beer. No hangover and no after-effects. Could he be sleepwalking and drinking?

So entrenched in his thoughts, that he hadn't heard Jessica leave her room across the hall. He also didn't hear Timothy go a while later. Not even hearing Betty stomping through the hallway while doing her morning housekeeping duties. Or Samuel tracking down Betty and apologizing. Instead, Jimmy was lost in his own mind, trying to figure out if he was going crazy or not.

When Jessica and Timothy returned to their room, they were surprised to see the bed already made. They figured Betty must be in a frenzy this morning to get her work done. So Jessica got ready to take a nice relaxing bath and get dressed.

As she pulled back the shower curtain that surrounded the claw-footed tub, she jumped backward, finding what appeared to be a heart in the bathtub.

"WHAT THE HELL IS THIS?"

Her yelling snapped Jimmy out of his fog. He rushed across the hall to see what his cousin was hollering about. As soon as he looked in the tub, his stomach dropped. They called security to investigate, and Jessica and Timothy moved to an unfamiliar room so they could get showered and dressed in privacy.

The thoughts running through Jimmy's head were getting darker and more suspicious. He was questioning whether he was the one doing all these strange things. Could he be experiencing blackouts? Both his biological parents had been capable of murder. Could he have inherited those psychotic traits?

Another thought came rushing to his mind. Could he have been the one to almost drown Jessica? He felt like he was indeed going crazy. Fear gripped him. Was he a danger to those around him? Should he try to get some professional help? He didn't know what to do.

So he did the only thing he knew how to. He investigated the scene as thoroughly as possible. He interviewed everyone who had been in the house at the time of the discovery. But nothing was revealed to point him in any specific direction.

The lack of clues and evidence just added to his dread. Rousing from his thoughts when Zach started asking questions.

"Hey boss, you know, Melissa said that whoever is doing these things is a psychopath. Do you think they are going to hurt the family? Are the hearts some type of warning? The hearts were only presented to members of the Gardiner family. Wouldn't that point to them being targets?"

Jimmy hadn't heard Zach talk so much in his life. He rubbed his hands over his face and tried to answer his questions as best he could.

"Yeah, I know that's what you mentioned she had said. But, honestly, I don't know the answer to any of those questions. I am just as confused as you are. You bring up a point I hadn't thought about, though. There might be some sort of symbolism in the heart. We should look into that."

Was the family in danger? That was the big question. Jimmy could not ascertain the answer at the moment. There had been no direct threats. Did it appear the family was being targeted? Absolutely. By who, though, was the big question he could not answer.

There was no motive for anyone to target the family. He was the only member of the family not known about. Was that why he had not been targeted? He was contemplating calling off Christmas. He needed to talk to Jessica, Richard Jr., and David to get their thoughts.

"Samantha is coming today, boss. Is she going to be targeted next?"

"I don't know. There have only been three deer carcasses found, so only three hearts. Unless this sick bastard has another one stashed somewhere, she may be in the clear. Let's make sure we triple-check the island today, all remote areas. If we find a carcass, we know that the heart will be used to torment Samantha. We need to prevent that from happening."

"I will volunteer for 24-hour bodyguard duty."

"I am sure you would."

Jimmy laughed at Zach's suggestion, but he thought it might wind up being the best possible answer at the moment. They discussed the possibility of twenty-four-hour bodyguard protection for the entire family as well. This was something they had never had to do on the island.

However, they realized they needed to sit down with the others before implementing this. So they headed downstairs to round up the Gardiner siblings to have a frank discussion about the security threat they were facing.

Jessica and Timothy were still edgy about the heart in the bathtub sitting in the parlor. Part of Jessica just wanted to pack her things and leave the island for good. The creepiness had returned, and she no longer felt safe. Deep in her gut, she knew they were all sitting ducks.

Jimmy and Zach came into the parlor and sat down. Richard Jr. and David joined them, who had been getting ready for work. Jimmy took a deep breath and then addressed them all.

"I think by now we all realize this is not a prank. I think we all know we are dealing with some sick psychopath. What we don't know is what their end game is. We don't know why they are doing these things. And we certainly don't know who is doing it. Zach and I discussed the possibility of round-the-clock bodyguard protection as an added security measure for all family members. The only problem is we are already short-staffed. It would leave aspects of the island vulnerable. Patrols in the remote areas would stop. Today, though, we are going to step those up. If we find another carcass, we know the next step would be to target a family member. Most likely, that would be Samantha since she was coming today. Thankfully, your parents aren't arriving until tomorrow evening. Hopefully, we can piece together what is going on here and keep everyone safe."

David was the first to respond. He seemed eager and excited to express his opinions.

"I know it isn't a short-term solution, but I think we need to install cameras. Using a drone to search the island could also be beneficial. In the meantime, I agree with the suggestion of bodyguards. I could order the cameras today. No idea when they will get here, but I could install them. I already have a drone. It's upstairs in my bedroom. I could use it today to search the island."

"Wow, great ideas, kid! Get that drone and get searching! Order those cameras, and get as many as you think we need. Also, I need someone to research what those hearts may mean. Could there be symbolism somewhere?"

"Timothy and I can do some research on symbolism. I agree the bodyguard system might be needed. Let us see what the rest of today brings. Maybe we can figure it out together. In the meantime, we should not tell Samantha or Mom and Dad about any of this."

"I am going to head out on the ATV and do a more thorough search of remote areas. Then I will start up north and go back and forth. I will see if I find anything. David, radio me if you see anything suspicious with the drone," said Richard Jr.

"I will start at the southern end of the island and do the same thing," said Zach.

"Sounds like we have a plan. Keep in radio contact at all times. I will search the middle of the island. Let's make sure this son of a bitch can't mess with us anymore," Jimmy ended the conversation.

Chapter Thirteen

The Date

In researching the symbolism of the animal hearts, Jessica and Timothy found out that some forms of black magic or voodoo used them in rituals of revenge or vengeance. So they deemed it a threat.

David flew the drone over the entire island, going low in specific places to ensure he saw nothing. No dead deer carcasses anywhere to be found. He felt a little more at ease. Through the drone, he saw a herd of deer in a field. He flew it down to see how close he could get. It amazed him at how trusting the deer were. The drone got within feet of them before they got scared off by the noise it made.

Richard Jr. made a pattern of back-and-forth paths on the northern part of the island and found nothing out of the ordinary. When he was done, he radioed in the all-clear.

Jimmy made the same pattern of back-and-forth paths in the middle part of the island. He also observed nothing out of the ordinary. The all-clear for his sector was being radioed in.

Zach made the back-and-forth pattern on the island's southern end. He saw nothing out of place in his watch area either. His all-clear radioed in and headed back to the Manor house. He was excited to see Samantha. They had made plans to go out to dinner on the mainland for their first date tonight.

They Facetimed or texted every day since she had given him her number. Zach had continued to see her every Thursday on his day off, but since she worked till late at night, they never had time to go out afterward. Nerves were setting in. Even though they knew everything about each other, Zach couldn't help but think she was way out of his league.

Samantha pulled up to the Manor house and found Zach sitting on his ATV, waiting for her. He slipped off his ATV, meeting her at her car. He pulled a bouquet from behind his back to give to her before opening the car door.

Amazed they weren't the standard roses most guys give women. Samantha smiled when she realized he had gotten her carnations instead. This showed he listened when she talked. She reminisced about the conversation that contained the information about her favorite flowers.

She thanked him for the flowers, hugged him, and kissed him on the cheek. This made Zach blush. The way he blushed around her was such a charming quality to her.

Martin came out of the house and helped Zach carry Samantha's things up to the room she chose. Without letting her see what he was doing, Zach scanned the bedroom and adjoining bathroom to ensure no surprises were waiting for her.

When he felt everything was clear, he relaxed a bit more and started talking about his plans for their date.

"I get off work at 5:00 pm. So I will go home and change and pick you up around 5:30 pm if that's okay with you. I have a pleasant night planned for us, Samantha. I hope you enjoy it."

"Sounds like you have put a lot of thought into all this. That is so sweet of you. I can't wait!"

Zach hugged her, kissed her forehead, and headed back to work. Samantha finished unpacking her things and then tried to pick the perfect outfit for their first date.

Jessica had heard Samantha had arrived and saw that Zach had left to go back to work. Jessica went to see her sister. Finding Samantha looking at several outfits laid out on her bed.

"Need some help there, little sis?"

"Yes!! It's our first date. I want it to be exceptional and look good, but I want to be comfortable too. I can't decide!!"

"Okay, okay. Breathe first. I like this green knit v-neck sweater. I think it will offset your red hair and bring out your green eyes. If you are going for comfort, wear these jeans. Oh, and wear these knee-high black boots. I think all of that will look great on you."

Samantha took the outfit Jessica chose and put it on. Then, looking in the full-length mirror, she turned side to side and smiled. Next, giving her big sister a big hug and a kiss on the cheek.

"It's perfect! Exactly what I was going for! Thank you so much."

The two girls sat on the bed and discussed their blooming relationships. They were like two schoolgirls sharing their innermost secrets. Jessica felt blessed to have gotten to know her sister. It was as if they had known each other their entire lives. But she hated keeping the secret about the family's dangers from her. It was the best thing for now, though.

Zach was prompt. He was at the door at 5:29 pm, holding another bouquet and a box of chocolate. Martin let him in and called Samantha to let her know her date was here. Then, after some razzing by Richard Jr., David, Jimmy, and even Timothy, they set off for their date.

They took the rickety ferry to the mainland and drove to the Blue Parrot Mexican restaurant. He was enamoring Samantha with his efforts to make this a memorable date. Zach opened the car door for her and extended his hand, helping her out of the car. He held the restaurant door open for her and let her enter first.

Then he pulled her chair out for her and helped settle her in her seat before taking his. It was refreshing to be on a date with a polite gentleman. Even choosing her favorite type of food showed her he listened when she told him stuff about her.

They had a great time laughing and conversing as if they had known each other all their lives. Zach was becoming more and more comfortable around Samantha, and his shyness was disappearing. She could still make him blush though, which she loved doing.

When the night was over, Zach dropped Samantha off at the front door of the Manor house. As they stood at the doorstep to say goodnight, Zach held both of Samantha's hands.

"May I give you a kiss goodnight?"

"Yes, I would love that."

Samantha looked into Zach's eyes. Zach leaned in and kissed her lips. Samantha felt the warmth in her cheeks, and she felt faint. The night had been flawless, with the perfect ending. They said goodnight, and Samantha went up to her room to go to bed. Zach went home thinking the night went without fault. They both fell asleep thinking of love and marriage.

Samantha awoke to the sun, trying to shine through the slats of the blinds on her window. She rewound the memories of the night before over and over in her mind and smiled to herself. She had never had a more perfect night. Zach pulled her chair out for her, holding doors for her, making sure she was steady on her feet walking through the parking lot, charming her. The complete package she had always dreamed of. Spending so much time with him would be magical the next week.

She felt sad when she thought of going back to Boston after the holidays. She didn't know if she could handle a long-distance relationship. Then she had a fabulous idea to move into the Manor house! Her brothers had already moved in. Things were going well for them and Jimmy. She didn't see why anyone would object to her moving in.

Samantha remembered Danielle was a waitress at the café on the mainland. She knew she could get a job working there. However, she needed to secure that before presenting the idea to Jessica, Jimmy, and her brothers. Motivated, she got up and took her shower. She got dressed and went downstairs for breakfast.

It surprised Samantha to see Danielle downstairs in the kitchen. She and Richard were sitting eating breakfast together at the kitchen island. While Samantha and Zach were out on their date, Richard and Danielle had their own. Catching up with them about their evening over breakfast, Samantha offered to take Danielle to work.

This gave Samantha the chance to talk to Danielle about getting a job at the café. Danielle was excited about the possibility of Samantha working with her and her living at the Manor house. It would be fun to have another girl around to hang out with when she visited Richard on the island. Since there was so much testosterone flowing in the house, it was sometimes overwhelming for her.

Danielle introduced Samantha to the manager at the café and then started her shift. They offered Samantha a job on the spot, and she told the manager she would let her know for sure the next day. Going back to the island, she was confident in her plan to move into the Manor house to spend more time with Zach.

While Samantha was out of the house, Jessica, Timothy, Jimmy, Richard Jr., David, and Zach had a quick meeting. They had made the appraisal that there wasn't any inclination that there would be a threat toward Samantha so far. However, Jessica and Timothy were taking turns checking her room to ensure there were no surprises left there for her. The lack of evidence of another deer's carcass so far led them all to believe there would be no heart left for Samantha.

Jessica let the others know what she and Timothy had found out about the symbolism of the heart being connected to dark magic or voodoo. Jimmy remembered hearing stories as a child about a dark witch who had lived on the island many decades before. He could imagine no one on the island being into any of that.

David gave an update on the cameras he had ordered. The cameras would be in a few days after Christmas. They all agreed they would have to be even more vigilant about their security until then. They would scrutinize anything out of the ordinary.

He also told them how using the drone worked out well. In explaining how he used the drone, he also informed the others how close he could get to the herd of deer. They all found it fascinating. As they were finishing up their briefing, Samantha walked into the parlor.

"Hey everyone, glad you are all here. Especially you, Zach. I know I need to ask permission and make sure it's all okay with Dad, Jessica, and Jimmy, but I have decided that I want to move here to the island. I have already secured a waitressing job at a café on the mainland. So I guess it's up to you two and Dad, of course."

As Samantha looked at her sister and Jimmy, Jessica's heart sank. She didn't want to say no to her sister. The smile on Samantha's face said it all. This was putting her in a dire predicament. If she said no, it would break her sister's heart. However, it could keep her safer. If she said yes, she might just put her sister in harm's way. Looking at Jimmy, she could tell he had the same dilemma running through his head.

Zach just looked at Samantha and then looked at the others. His heart was skipping beats. He wanted to see Samantha more regularly, yet he was terrified of losing her to some psychopath.

Richard Jr. ran his hands over his face in frustration. He was picking up that trait from his cousin. Then he shrugged his shoulders and looked at everyone else imploringly.

"We have to tell her. She needs to know what she is getting herself into."

"What do you need to tell me?"

Zach looked at Jimmy and motioned for him to tell her. Jimmy looked at Jessica, who looked back at him, defeated, and nodded her head. Then Jimmy informed Samantha about everything. It well enlightened her of the danger she was stepping into moving onto the island.

"Mom and Dad don't know about any of this?"

"Nope. Do you think they would have allowed David and me to remain on the island if they had known? They can't know. And if anything occurs while they are here, we need to all shrug it off as some stupid fraternity-type hazing incident. You understand."

"Got it. So I can move in then?"

Jimmy and Jessica both shrugged their shoulders and nodded yes. There was nothing they could do or say to change her mind. She hugged them both and then ran over to Zach and planted a big kiss on his lips in front of everyone. Zach turned the brightest shade of red.

"Alright guys, it's time to head out for work."

While the others went off to do their security details, Jessica, Timothy, and Samantha played pool in the parlor. Martin came and joined them since he had finished his work for the day and was waiting for Mira and Richard to arrive.

Chapter Fourteen

Change of Plans

They were furious! Just when they were having fun torturing the family, the family had to fight back. The fact that the two Gardiner boys stuck it out and joined the security team irritated them. The younger Gardiner boys' ideas of cameras and drone use would cause a problem or two. This needed to be addressed.

The added security had made it harder to hunt for the more significant kills. This was causing them to be agitated. Their hatred for the family grew bigger daily. The fact they weren't scared off yet made them seethe.

They had the crows. It was close enough. They could start eliminating them one by one. It would give them power and a way to relieve the stress and aggravation they were feeling.

The culling of the crows gave them great satisfaction. They decided on a unique method to extinguish the life force within the creature with each one. As they did so, they imagined each bird as a member of the Gardiner family until they were all lifeless. The rush of power had soothed the anger inside them, for now.

At least the listening devices in the house were coming in handy. They could hear all the new security plans, including potential round-the-clock bodyguards. This would be problematic in knocking them off one by one. The idea of eliminating them all at once crossed their mind again.

Nope, they knew that wouldn't work either. So they were going to have to back off a bit. To give the family a false sense of security would benefit them much more in the long run than keeping up the torture.

Dejected, since they couldn't torture Samantha like they had tortured the other siblings, they hatched a plan that would make up for it. The blossoming relationship between the young security guard Zach and the young Gardiner girl gave them more ideas. They knew their power would grow soon enough.

They had to have patience. The thoughts of how, when, and who to eliminate first raced through their mind. They zeroed in on the who. Now they just needed to gather more information to figure out the how and when.

The timing was everything. They could not point fingers at them. It was imperative to their survival that all roads led to someone else, if at all. If things could look tragic, that would be best.

If a few lives were to become collateral damage it wouldn't bother them one bit. It just meant more power to feed the darkness inside them.

They drew an upside-down pentagram on the wood floor and placed the lifeless bodies of the crows at the point of each triangle and one in the center. They added black candles and lit each one as they chanted an incantation. Each crow would hold a curse. The curses were to aid them in their mission against the family.

Their studies of dark magic had provided them with a wealth of knowledge. It was useful in their purpose against the family.

When they were done with their ritual, they prepared the family's gifts for Christmas. Then they blew out the candles, buried them in the backyard, and erased the pentagram off the floor.

Since they knew the family had connected the hearts to black magic or voodoo, they needed to be more careful. They should find no trace to tie them to any of what had occurred or what was to happen.

They had to stay one step ahead of the family at all times and all costs. For their plan to succeed, no one could suspect them. They felt they were flying under the radar for the time being.

Samantha moving into the Manor house would make gathering information on her much more accessible. Sometimes it was comical how much the family played right into their master plans. But, unfortunately, they would be the reason for their demise in the end.

The listening devices helped them listen in on Jessica and Samantha's conversations, which already had proven to be helpful. Their bond was the strongest out of the siblings. That information would be beneficial. They could use that to hurt one or the other. Or even use it to break them both.

Both the girls were head over heels in love with their men. Their men seemed to reciprocate those feelings. However, they wondered if the seeds of doubt were planted, what would the outcome be.

They imagined the heartbreak they could cause, laughing. Messing with others' emotions had been a fun game they had learned long ago. They had even chased a few people off the island using those tactics. It was fun making people doubt their own emotions and their sanity.

They wondered how long it would take poor Jimmy to go off the deep end again. Awareness of his weaknesses was so valuable. The most significant defect was his undying love for Melissa. She had left the island seven years ago and had yet to return. Consciousness about Jimmy and Melissa's chance encounter and the subsequent marriage proposal gave them a brilliant idea.

Arranging Melissa's need to come to the island would set Jimmy up for more heartache in the end. This would have to fit into their plans somehow.

They needed to get back to work. If anyone noticed them gone, it would send up a red flag of suspicion. So they hid the presents and went back to doing their assigned tasks.

As they worked throughout the day, they gathered information. Using this knowledge, they continued to formulate their plans. Finally, they would take a break from torturing the family after Christmas. It would warn thoroughly the family of their fate. What the family did with that information would be interesting. The family would not escape the plans, but eventually, the entire family would be gone. Every one of them, even Jimmy.

Recognition from experiences in the past, the police would not be involved. The family liked to handle things on their own. They didn't know whether this was an ego thing or just a power trip. Either way, it played into their plans beautifully.

Chapter Fifteen

Empty Nest

Mira and Richard pulled up to the Manor house just before dinnertime. The car behind them was Mira's parents. Martin came out to meet them all and to show them to their rooms. Jessica and Timothy greeted them also and helped with the grandparent's luggage.

By the time they were all in their rooms, it was time for dinner. Sitting down for dinner, Richard sat at the head of the table as he had years ago with Mary. It was a strange feeling sitting there with Mira and all of their children. A dream he had once had with Mary. To have family dinners nightly in this very dining room, as he had growing up.

Thoughts going back to his younger years, he was naïve to believe he and Mary would have lasted. They were so different in so many ways. He had loved the island and living there, but she loved it for the prestige it brought her, not like the connection he had.

While he wished they could have divorced amicably and avoided the tragic circumstances of their actions, he felt content with where his family was now. Richard missed his cousin Alexandria and her family. The memories of his childhood were vivid in this house. That guilt he carried with him daily. Being back in the Manor house amplified those feelings.

Mira was beaming with happiness. She had missed her boys and was still adjusting to their decision to move to the island. At least Samantha was still living at home with her and Richard. It was nice to be eating dinner together as a family again.

Mira had never felt comfortable on the island, especially knowing she was of a different social class than Richard had been. Although her parents acted pretentious as if they were the same, they felt like they and their daughter belonged on the island. Her parents sat at the dinner table pretending as if they had belonged there their entire lives.

The conversation flowed from discussing who would attend the Christmas Eve open house the next night, to how the wedding plans were going. Jessica bristled at the many questions about the wedding and the onslaught of suggestions from her grandmother. Timothy sensed her feelings of tension.

"Jessica, you haven't told them the main course is going to be crocodile stew yet?"

Jessica almost choked on the mouthful of food she was chewing and nudged him with her leg. All except her grandparents found the suggestion amusing. Jimmy and the others followed Timothy's lead and started suggesting the most outrageous foods they could think of.

"I vote for Rocky Mountain oysters."

Becoming a sort of game with them all. Even her parents chimed in.

"Your mother and I suggest Fried Silkworm."

The grandparents didn't see the humor in any of it. Instead, they grumbled and commented on how uncivilized today's youth were.

When dinner was over, they all retired into the parlor. Jessica's grandparents hadn't been to the Manor house in many, many years and were not at all impressed with the changes Jimmy had made to the parlor. Their comments were it made it look like commoners lived there. Jessica and her siblings rolled their eyes at each other. Jimmy shrugged off the comments.

Zach stopped by to visit Samantha and became inundated with questions from her parents and grandparents. They were like piranhas on a piece of meat. Now Jessica understood why Samantha wanted to move out. But, thinking about that, Jessica wondered when Samantha would spring that revelation on her parents.

As if Samantha had read Jessica's mind.

"Hey, Mom, Dad, I have some great news. I got a new job working with Danielle at that little café on the mainland. I am moving in here with Jimmy, Richard, and David! Isn't that great?"

Richard looked at his youngest daughter and then looked at his wife. Mira had tears welling up in her eyes. She knew someday she would have an empty nest. She just never expected it to be so soon and so sudden. They had just become a whole family again, finding Jessica. Mira was not ready for all her children to fly on their own. He put his arm around his wife to comfort her.

"Is this because of this young man?"

"Partially, Dad, I have been saving up to move out on my own for a while now. But, yes, I want to be closer to Zach. It's not like I will live by myself. I got these guys to keep me safe and out of trouble."

"Your mind is set? Just know if it doesn't work out, you can always come back home."

Samantha gave both of her parents a big hug.

The grandparents thought it was a crazy idea. They didn't understand the rush of the youth of the day to move out and be on their own. Finally, they were tired and said goodnight to everyone else and went to bed. Soon after, Mira and Richard retired to their bedroom.

Everyone else stayed up playing pool and drinking beer. Jimmy had one and only one. That morning was the first in a while he hadn't woken up with beer cans strewn all over his floor. The irony of not discovering a deer carcass or deer's heart wasn't lost on him with the absence of the beer cans. He wanted to make sure none of those things returned, so he was diligent about only drinking the one.

The next day would be hectic, and he wanted to make sure he was at his best mentally. However, the planning he had done for weeks for the Christmas Eve open house would hopefully go smoothly. His only concern was that security would be not as tight as usual since they had invited all team members to attend.

They all had agreed to treat it as an undercover-type assignment and take turns patrolling outside so everyone could enjoy themselves. Jimmy had already vowed to himself he would not have a drop of alcohol, just to be sure he stayed alert.

He turned in earlier than the others. Although his body ached with exasperation, sleep eluded him for the first few hours. Anxiety filled his mind. The party would be the first big event on the island in years. Success, or failure, depended on so many things. Keeping everyone safe was the number one priority. The only problem he had was figuring out who he was trying to keep everyone safe from.

The nagging in the back of his mind whether he could be the one doing the tormenting scared him. He loved his cousins and would never knowingly or consciously want to hurt them. Although it was his subconscious, he was concerned with. That part of himself that he knew could lose touch with reality.

Seven years was a long time, though, to go without an episode. Could the events of the last few months have triggered something in him? He hadn't talked to his therapist in three years. The need to continue therapy wasn't there, and even she had agreed he was doing so well. Maybe it was time to resume.

Even though Mira and Richard had gone to bed hours before their children. They had lain awake discussing the turn of events. Shocked that all three of their children had decided to move to the island, they were trying to come to grips with it all.

Both were not fully accepting of their children's decisions. Mira was having a hard time thinking she would come home to an empty house from now on. Her heart hurt. As a mother, she knew her children were supposed to move on with their lives. She just didn't want it to be now.

Richard understood the allure of the island. He had grown up there. But, although he had wanted to raise his family there, fate had seen fit to ensure that did not happen. Or, more appropriately, Mary had been determined to ensure that did not happen.

As he held Mira in his arms and discussed their feelings on the matter, Richard could not help but feel a bit of remorse at how they had handled Mary and Benjamin's plot.

Maybe he should have gone to the authorities with the plot to kill him. Would they have believed him, anyway? He had regrets. His actions had caused the death of his cousin's family. That was something he could never forgive himself for.

Their children were good-hearted people. They were just ready to spread their wings sooner than either of them wanted to acknowledge. Richard pitched the idea of Mira and him moving into the Manor house as well. Mira couldn't. The idea of living in the same place that his ex-wife was willing to kill for creeped her out.

Staying at the house for even a few days was difficult for her. There were times she felt every portrait on the walls watching her every move. She even thought she could hear whispering about her as she walked the halls. But, if you let it, one's imagination could also convince one of the most nefarious things. Mira's imagination did just that in the Manor house. They eventually fell asleep.

Jessica and Timothy said goodnight to her siblings. They went to their room and got ready for bed. Laying in Timothy's arms, Jessica let the tension of the day slip away. He kissed her forehead and dropped asleep. Jessica found her own eyes heavy with sleep and followed suit.

Richard Jr. and Danielle had retreated to his room for the night. She was spending more and more time at the Manor house. This was the second night she had felt too tired to make Richard Jr. drive her home. He was more than happy to share his bed with her, in all honesty.

They hadn't yet actually made love to one another. Richard felt that the time would be soon to take that next step in their relationship. Sleeping with her in his arms, though, made restraining himself difficult. He didn't want to push it. She was his best friend, and if something went wrong and they broke up, it would devastate him to lose her. They fell asleep rather quickly, content in each other's arms.

Samantha and Zach were the last ones awake. They sat together on the sofa, discussing how excited they both were that she was moving to the island. Zach held one of Samantha's hands while sitting with his arm around her. She leaned her head on his shoulder. The scent of her hair smelled of lilacs, and he let go of her hand to sweep a strand of hair out of her eyes.

Samantha had never dated a guy as sweet as Zach. Most of the men she dated in the past were looking for a quick fling. Something she utterly despised. They made her feel like a slab of meat at a market. Zach was so different.

His touch was always so careful and gentle as if she was fragile like fine china, and he didn't want to break her. This was so adorable to her and was one thing she loved most about him. The way he actually listened to her talk. And how he remembered what she had said in previous conversations were other traits that just made her fall in love with him.

It was late, and although Zach didn't live far from the Manor house, Samantha convinced him to stay the night with her.

"It's late. You are tired. Come upstairs and sleep in my room," Samantha said while getting off the sofa and pulling Zach with her.

"Samantha, there is something you should know," Zach said, standing firm where he was.

"What's that?"

"I never have... what I mean... I'm a virgin."

"Yeah, so? I am too. We don't have to have sex if we sleep together. When we are both ready, when the time is right, then we can take that next step."

Zach smiled and blushed while letting Samantha lead the way to her bedroom. He was nervous about sharing a bed with her.

The first time he had seen her, he had known he wanted her in the worst way, at Alexandria's funeral. That desire had fueled his trips to Boston to eat dinner at the restaurant she worked at. Then, it fueled him to ask her for her number despite feeling she was way out of his league.

Now, knowing she was also a virgin just made him want her more. He wanted their first time to be special. That would take some planning and a lot of self-control. The self-control part would be the hardest. Making sure he didn't go too far too soon. Just the thought of being with her intimately someday aroused him.

At the doorway to her bedroom, she paused. Samantha looked at him and smiled while turning the doorknob. Then she led him in and closed the door behind them. Samantha could tell he was nervous. What he didn't know was she was just as scared.

Sharing a bed with a man was something she had never done before. Appreciation that he was a virgin too, eased her mind. There were no expectations between them and no one to compare her to. She didn't know if he expected anything to happen, but she didn't want to rush into anything.

Samantha grabbed a t-shirt and sweatpants, going to the bathroom to change.

Zach sat on the edge of the bed. While taking his shirt off and contemplating whether he should sleep in his pants.

When Samantha came out of the bathroom and saw Zach without his shirt, she felt the heat in her cheeks rise.

The sight of his chest, along with his chiseled abdomen, tempted her to run her hands over his bare skin. Instead, biting her lip, she averted her eyes from him and concentrated on the lamp on her bedside table.

This might be more difficult than she thought. The view of Zach sitting on the edge of her bed, looking completely vulnerable yet gorgeous, made her want him.

Trying to keep her composure.

"You can make yourself comfortable. I have two brothers. I have seen guys in their underwear before. So if you want to sleep in your underwear, feel free."

He took in Samantha, walking out of the bathroom as she put her hair up in a bun. Zach could see the outline of her body through her white t-shirt. This was not helping him keep himself in check.

He noticed her cheeks flush when she saw him sitting shirtless. Which also was not keeping him from feeling as if he wanted to do more than just sleep with her. When she told him he could sleep in his underwear, he thought he might lose control. How could he expect to sleep next to her, almost wholly naked, feeling nothing at all?

With a bit of trepidation, Samantha slid under the covers of her bed.

He struggled to hide his nerves. Zach went to the opposite side, slipped his pants off, and quickly slipped under the covers. It was awkward for both of them. They both felt the desire inside them. Yet, they were both trying not to act on it. Finally, Zach rolled over to face Samantha and kissed her forehead.

"Goodnight Sam, is it okay if I call you Sam?"

"Goodnight. You can call me anything you want, dear."

Samantha leaned over and kissed Zach softly on the lips. Tasting her soft rose-colored lips on his did him in. He pulled her towards him and kissed her back, longingly and deeply. Then, Reciprocating, she explored his body with her hands.

"I want you," he said.

"I want you too."

"Now?"

"Yes."

"Are you sure?"

"Yes."

"I love you, Sam."

"I love you too, Zach."

Chapter Sixteen

Preparations

In the morning, Jimmy was the first to awaken. As he swung his legs out from under his covers and onto the floor, it thrilled him to find no traces of any beer cans. He breathed a sigh of relief.

There was much to do, so he quickly showered and got dressed. Stella was already busy in the kitchen preparing the family their morning breakfast. He ate his breakfast, drank his coffee, and then reminded her she had off in the afternoon and evening. The caterers would be here at noontime to prepare for the party.

As he finished up his coffee, a van pulled into the driveway. He went out and met with the driver and his passenger. They were the party decorators. Then another van with a trailer came up behind them. It was the tent he rented to be set up in the gardens. Jimmy showed them where everything was supposed to go, and they set out to get it all set up.

Next on his agenda, were morning rounds, and heading to the security shack. He was always the first one to come and relieve the night crew. Those who had worked overnight usually filled him in on any unusual occurrences, of which there had been none. The day shift crew was trickling in.

At the Manor house, Zach woke up to his phone alarm going off. He fumbled around to grab his phone out of his pants pocket on the floor. The beeping silenced, Zach turned to see if it had woken up Samantha. He felt horrible when he realized it had.

He leaned over and kissed her on the forehead.

"I am sorry, didn't mean to wake you. I hate to leave, but I have to get to work. Thank you for last night. I love you more than anything."

"It's okay. I need to get up and get ready for the day, anyway. I wish you could stay, but I understand. Thank you for last night. I love you too. I will see you tonight, right? At the party."

"Yes, I will be here for the party. See you tonight."

As they finished their conversation, Zach threw on his clothes from the night before. He knew he didn't have time to run home and shower and change. So he, in haste, made his way downstairs and through the kitchen. He grabbed a freshly baked cranberry muffin Stella had cooled on a rack and a quick cup of coffee and headed out the door.

Stella raised her eyebrows at seeing him in her kitchen and smiled.

Zach made it to the security shack before Richard Jr. and David. He full tilt went to his locker, where he always had an extra pair of clothes, and grabbed them. Zach switched clothes in the bathroom and stashed his dirty clothes in his locker before either of Samantha's brothers made it to work.

He was hoping they hadn't seen him leave their sister's bedroom or the Manor house. That was a confrontation and conversation he did not want to have.

Jimmy had seen Zach come in through the doorway of his office and watched him go wild, changing so no one would realize he spent the night with Samantha. He thought it was pretty comical and debated whether to have some fun at Zach's expense or not. Deciding to forego having fun, he figured he would keep Zach's secret for now.

Richard Jr. left Danielle sleeping soundly in his bed. He wrote her a sweet note telling her he would see her later at the party. He watched her sleep in his bed peacefully, making him want to crawl back into bed and snuggle up to her. But that would be a mistake because then he would be late for work. So, he made it down to the kitchen for breakfast before David and figured he would meet him at the shack.

David got up and headed downstairs for breakfast. He loved Stella's cooking and always looked forward to having an excellent, warm breakfast before heading off to work.

His mom was never big on cooking, so it was something he loved about living on the island. In addition, Stella was always so friendly to him, which made the mornings much more enjoyable. There were no expectations of her and no judgments.

"Stella, thank you for always making such delicious breakfasts. They help me start my day off."

"You are welcome. It's my job to make sure everyone in the house eats. Even the stragglers."

"Stragglers?"

"Yeah, you don't have any yet, but it seems each of your siblings has one."

"Oh, you mean boyfriends or girlfriends. Yeah, I don't have one of those yet. Not sure I will have one anytime soon."

"Why not? You are a handsome young man. I am sure the ladies adore you."

"Well, the ladies adore me. I am just not sure I adore them."

"Oh. Regardless of who adores you or who you adore, you will find your soul mate someday. You will see."

"See, that's the problem, Stella, and I haven't ever uttered these words out loud to anybody before. I am physically attracted to women. Yet my soul finds a connection with men. It's so confusing. I don't know if I will ever find the one."

"Oh, dear boy. That sounds confusing and burdensome. Just try to stay true to yourself, and whatever comes will be. It will all work itself out. Take your time to find out who you are and what you want. Then the rest will fall into place."

"Thanks, Stella."

Soon the day crew was all at the shack, including David. They had their morning briefing before heading out on their various patrols. Jimmy sensed most of the staff were excited about the party later and were not focusing as they usually did. So he headed out on patrol, stopping at the Manor house to check on the preparations for the party. Everything was going as planned.

There was excitement in the air among everyone on the island. The family awoke and made their way downstairs for breakfast. There was a bustle of activity outside the Manor house and even inside. The professional decorators made sure the place was festive, looking inside and out.

Jessica noticed her sister, Samantha, had an extra bounce in her step. She attributed it to her sister moving onto the island. She felt thrilled for her. It was lovely watching her siblings spread their wings. She had been on her own for a few years now, so observing them change as their lives evolved was interesting.

They had all had the shock of learning about their parent's pasts a few months prior, and Jessica couldn't help but think that learning the truth had shaped all of their futures. It seemed to have jump-started them all into making some significant changes in their lives for her siblings. All of them moving away from their parents was a noteworthy change. A change she was curious to see how her parents would genuinely handle.

Danielle needed a ride home, so Samantha offered to bring her there. Jessica asked if she could tag along, and both the other girls agreed. Once they were all in the car, Samantha spilled the beans about Zach spending the night.

"Oh my god, guys, I have been dying to tell somebody all morning! Zach and I slept together last night!"

"Wait, did you sleep together, or did you SLEEP together?"

Danielle felt jealous that Samantha and Zach might have gotten more consequential than she and Richard had gotten.

"Woah, little sis. I hope you aren't rushing into this too fast."

"Well, we didn't intend to do anything but sleep. Since we were both virgins and all, we wanted the first time to be special."

"WERE virgins! That means you two did more than just sleep!! So, how was it?"

The jealousy was hard to suppress for Danielle.

"So WAS it special?"

Jessica was concerned at the fast course their relationship was taking.

"Yes! It was magical in every way!! I mean, I don't know how it was supposed to feel, but that's how it felt to me. But, of course, I have nothing to compare it to being a virgin and all. He was so gentle and fulfilled my desires. It was the best early Christmas present I have ever received!"

Danielle was happy for Samantha that her first experience with Zach was good. Jealousy was flowing through her a bit, though, since she and Richard had been dating for far longer.

Then Danielle thought about how long it took for Richard to first kiss her. She had started to have feelings for him long before he had feelings for her, or at least long before he showed those feelings.

If they were going to move to the next level of their relationship, she felt she would have to make the first move. As she got out of Samantha's car and said goodbye, her thoughts went to when she would make her move on Richard. After the party, later tonight would be perfect.

Jessica couldn't believe her little sister was talking to her about having sex for the first time. It felt awkward at first. But then, she appreciated the fact her sister felt comfortable enough to share private information with her. It was a testament to the unbreakable bond that had formed so quickly between them.

She remembered the first time she and Timothy had made love. Smiling to herself, she realized she couldn't be so critical of her sister. She and Timothy had known each other far less than Samantha and Zach.

They got back to the Manor house around the same time the caterers arrived. The place was still bustling with preparations for the party. Arthur had come while the girls were gone, and with him, he had brought Allison.

Jessica was happy to see them both. She knew Arthur had been having a hard time after the death of Alexandria, and she felt being around the family would help him. Jessica hoped to piece together more clues about Allison and her possible relationship with Timothy.

Timothy, Arthur, and Allison were in the parlor chatting when Jessica walked in. It seemed that Timothy and Allison had hit it off and were engaged in conversation. So she sat across from them and observed and listened to them both. The first thing she noticed was they both had green eyes. The shape was contrasting, but the color was the same.

Their conversation paused, and they both looked at Jessica. As they did, she noticed their jawlines were similar. Both of them had the same shaped nose as well. Jessica believed in her heart that they somehow were related.

"Don't let me interrupt."

Timothy smiled at her and turned back to the conversation he was having with Allison. Allison seemed genuinely interested in Timothy and his life. Especially his work as a writer. A slight twinge of jealousy ran through Jessica's mind. Then she reeled those thoughts in quickly. She knew Timothy had no romantic interest in Allison. She also felt Allison knew she was old enough to be his mother.

The irony of that last thought struck her instantly. Holding in all her questions for Allison was becoming increasingly more complex. Knowing she had to tread lightly with her, though, was what kept her from unleashing her inquiries.

Arthur started a conversation with Jessica and drew her attention away from Timothy and Allison. She welcomed the reprieve.

"How are the wedding plans going, Jessica?"

"They are coming along. I picked my dress. Samantha did a great job of helping me. Since fashion is not my thing."

Richard and Mira joined everyone in the parlor as they had come back from doing some last-minute gift buying on the mainland. Mira joined the conversation between Arthur and Jessica.

"She chose the most beautiful dress."

"I know Alexandria would have loved to be a part of that."

Jessica reached over and squeezed Arthur's hand. He appreciated the sentiment.

Everyone decided it would be wise to get ready for the evening's festivities late afternoon. Betty showed Allison where she could freshen up and change into the outfit she had brought.

Before Timothy and Jessica headed to their room, Martin brought another guest into the parlor. It was Jack, Timothy's cousin. Jessica welcomed him and then excused herself to go get ready. Timothy showed Jack up to a room that he could use to get changed for the party.

"I am so glad you could join us."

"I wouldn't miss this for the world. I can't believe I am here. On Gardiners Island, with my cousin."

Chapter Seventeen

The Party

Jimmy had gotten off from work and dressed in a formal suit for the party. He felt out of place since he lived in his work clothes ninety percent of the time.

The Gardiners had thrown lavish parties, though, and he wanted to live up to that reputation. With a bit of a twist, though. Those who worked on the island performed their duties at these events. But not this time. He made sure everyone on the island who worked or lived there received invitations and was welcome.

This had indeed improved morale on the island for the few weeks leading up to the party. Jimmy had hired all outside help for the evening. He wanted everyone who attended to enjoy themselves as much as possible.

He was the first to be ready and stood in the entranceway, prepared to greet guests as they arrived. People showed up at 5 o'clock on the dot. The first few guests were some inhabitants of the island. They all seemed beyond doubt excited to be included on the guest list. Some families from the mainland also arrived.

The great room on the Southern end of the house served as the prominent gathering place for the party. The French doors opened up to the gardens, covered by the party tent. They dispersed propane heaters throughout the tent area to give guests warmth.

Knocking on her door, Jessica checked on Allison to show her down to the party. Looking unsure of herself, Allison opened the door.

"Everything okay?"

"Yeah, I just get nervous in new surroundings. I am not one for enormous crowds and such."

"Stick with me. I am still new to all of this, too. But we will get through it together, okay?"

"Thanks! Being a grown woman and not feeling comfortable in large gatherings, I feel silly. Having an ally helps."

"No worries! Let's go have some fun!"

The two women went downstairs and into the great room together. Jessica spotted Timothy and Jack over in a corner, talking. Jack's back was to them as they walked up to the pair.

As Allison recognized Jack, she froze. She couldn't fathom why her cousin's son had an invitation to the party. Jack turned just as she froze. He took a sip of his drink and stopped when he saw his cousin's reaction to him being there. Then, making quick work of the distance between them, he walked up to Jessica and Allison.

"Hey cuz, fancy meeting you here. I see you look shocked at my presence."

Jack hugged Allison.

"Well, yeah. This party is for the Gardiner family, friends, and employees. So, how the heck did you get an invitation?"

"I can answer that," Timothy said. "Jack and I just of late connected through a genealogy website. We are second cousins. He is the only biological family connection I have so, Jessica and I invited him."

"Oh. Jack, is he related to you through your father's side or your mother's side?"

Allison had some trepidation in her voice.

"We don't know, but my mom sent in her DNA to either confirm or deny whether it related him through her side or my dad's. Seeing we don't know about my dad or his side of the family, it's the easiest way to help narrow down the search."

"Ah. I see. Well, I hope you all figure it out. I am parched, so I am going to find myself something to drink at the moment."

They watched her walk away, and Jessica looked at Jack and Timothy with raised eyebrows. She explained how she felt in her gut that Timothy and Allison had some kind of connection. Both the men agreed. However, they all decided not to pursue any more information from Allison until the results from Jack's mom's test came back.

The rest of the guests were mingling along with the family members. Lena and her family had arrived and were busy catching up with Mira and Richard. Even Lena's mom Rita had tagged along since her husband Tom was on a business trip and would be home first thing in the morning.

Everyone seemed to have a great time. Samantha was hanging out with Zach and his parents. Jessica noticed how Samantha and Zach were holding hands. She thought it was so sweet-looking. She wondered if she and Timothy gave off that same glowing aura of love and happiness when they were side by side.

There was less public display of affection between her brother Richard and Danielle. Although you could see their mannerisms and how they looked at each other, they were indeed in love. Then there was David. He seemed lost in the sea of people.

Jessica saw the uneasiness in his stance. His hands were in his pockets and then out of his pockets. He shifted his weight from one leg to the other. Danielle's sisters, Stephanie and Erica, seemed to keep engaging him in conversation or even getting him out on the dance floor. Yet, he showed no genuine interest in them. Observing her little brother, she sensed his awkwardness around the two women who seemed enamored by him.

What was refreshing to see was the workers from the island interacting with everyone and having a great time. Watching Samuel and Betty both at the bar, impressed Jessica at how elegant they both looked. Samuel was wearing a nice suit, and Betty wore a red cocktail dress. The scooped neck of her dress added some dimension to her tall, skinny figure. Neither of them stayed at the bar for long. Jessica watched as David walked up to the bartender.

"Can I have a beer, please?"

"Can I see your ID, please?"

"Sorry, I don't have it on me at the moment. I am David Gardiner, though. I live here."

"Oh, my apologies, sir."

The bartender handed David the beer, and David thanked him. Then, standing next to the bar, David made quick work of the first beer and asked for another one.

"Easy there. You may want to slow down some, man."

"I know, I know. I just need something to calm my nerves and all."

"What's got you all in knots?"

"People, I just feel so alone, even in this sizeable crowd."

"You? Alone? Dude, you have so much going for you. You are handsome. You are rich. And you have several beautiful young women following you around tonight."

"Yes, even with all that going for me, I feel alone. But wait, how do you know about the women following me?"

"Um, well, I noticed you right away. As I said, you are handsome. So I was watching you. I hope you don't mind?"

David didn't mind. He found it comforting that he stood out to someone out of all these people. It didn't bother him that the bartender was another man.

He stood at the bar most of the evening, getting to know the bartender, named Joe. Stephanie and Erica came up, trying to get David to leave his post and go dance with them. They succeeded once, although he headed back to the bar when the song was over.

Jessica noticed the difference in David as he stayed at the bar talking with the bartender. She didn't know whether it was the alcohol he was consuming or the potential friendship he was making. The reason didn't matter. What mattered was her brother's happiness.

Jimmy was mingling with everyone and having a great time. He felt the event was an immense success. Cracking open a beer and toasting with David for a great night. In the back of his mind, though, he was determined to only have one beer.

As the evening got later, guests left. Arthur and Allison said their goodbyes and thanked the family for the invite, then headed on their way home. The stragglers were the family, some workers, and Lena's family.

Rita was at the bar next to Samuel. Samuel recognized her from the wedding he had attended with Mary many years ago. He thought that night would have started a beautiful relationship with Mary. She wasn't interested in having a relationship with a lowly mechanic. She just used him for her needs and cast him aside.

When Mary had gotten drunk, she would go to his place and get what she wanted from him. He supposed her way of thanking him was leaving him a sizeable amount of money in her will. Seeing Rita again brought back memories of how flirtatious she had been with him that night. Striking up a conversation with her, he hoped she would be just as flirtatious.

"Remember me, darling?"

Rita remembered Samuel. His allure attracted her to him at her daughter's wedding. Although, she realized a lot of the enticement towards him was that he had accompanied her cousin Mary to the wedding. Her husband was away on business, making it a straightforward decision for her to go along with his flirting and see where it led. Her marriage had been all but dead for several years now. They stayed together because it was the easiest thing to do.

When Lena was ready to leave, she couldn't find her mother anywhere. Calling her cell phone, she located her. Within minutes Rita appeared, coming down the stairs. She told her daughter the downstairs bathroom was being used, so she had found the one upstairs to use.

Jack left after Lena's family, and Timothy and Jessica headed upstairs to their room. It surprised them to meet Samuel in the hallway leading towards the stairs. As he walked past them, he grumbled something about having to use the bathroom.

When they got to their room, they found a gift addressed to Jessica with instructions not to open until the following day. The hair was raised on the back of her neck. Timothy didn't like the looks of this gift. They knew the rest of the family was still downstairs, so they made haste to everyone's rooms. Just as they suspected, there was a gift for each family member. They gathered them all up and brought them to their room.

They did not want to ruin everyone's festive mood. So Jessica and Timothy hid the gifts in the bathroom closet and did not tell anyone else about them. They thought that tomorrow morning after they had opened up all their presents, something would be said if the surprises were from someone in the family. In that case, they would bring the gifts to everyone. If no one mentioned them, they would let Jimmy know and investigate further.

The last guest left late in the evening, and Jimmy supervised the clean-up. The decorators would leave the decorations up for a couple of days and also the tent. After that, it would be easier to take it all down during daylight hours.

Much to Danielle's dismay, when her mother and father left earlier, they insisted she go home with them. So Richard Jr. went to bed alone, and her plans to take their relationship to the next level were foiled.

Samantha and Zach had waited until everyone else had gone up to their rooms, except Jimmy. Then they snuck up to her room to be alone for a bit before Zach went home for the evening.

David had enjoyed hanging out with Joe. They had struck up a friendship. So they made plans to hang out on their next day off. David didn't know where the fellowship would go. He just knew they seemed to hit it off.

By the time Jimmy had finished up, the entire house was quiet. Everything had gone off without a hitch. He felt a bit more relaxed that whoever had been tormenting the family had stopped. It was a peaceful Christmas Eve, and as he looked out the window, he noticed snow falling.

It was beautiful to see it come down. There was a tranquility that seemed to envelop the house. Jimmy could only pray that the following morning would be just as serene. He went to bed the most relaxed he had been in days. Soon he was off to dreamland, where his mind went to Melissa and his true heart's desire.

Chapter Eighteen

Christmas Morning

Stella was up early and over at the Manor house, making a big Christmas breakfast for the family. The aromas of eggs, bacon, sausage, chocolate chip pancakes, regular pancakes, French toast, and waffles wafted up to the second floor and aroused the house's occupants out of their slumbers.

As they awakened, one by one, they made their way down into the dining room, where Stella had arranged chaffing dishes on the sidebar. Each one served themselves and sat at the table, eating the delectable foods Stella had prepared.

Before Jessica and Timothy went downstairs, they ensured the gifts they had found were secure in the closet from the night before. They were there all right, and Jessica couldn't help but have an ominous feeling about them. Praying she was wrong, they made their way down to breakfast with the family.

Jimmy was one of the last ones to arise. As he slid his feet onto the floor, it horrified him to find empty beer cans strewn over his bedroom floor. He knew he had only one beer all night, or that is what he could remember. Panic filled him with what awaited for the day. He realized that the beer cans coincided with ominous events.

Joining the family downstairs for breakfast, he scanned faces to see if anyone seemed alarmed or distressed. Everyone seemed joyous and content eating the fabulous food his mother had prepared for them all. He saw nothing unusual in any of them.

The family had their fill to eat by mid-morning and settled into the parlor to exchange gifts. They were all excited to see how their loved ones liked the presents they had picked out for one another.

Jessica opened her gift from Jimmy first. When she opened it and realized he had gotten her a bunch of different filters for her camera, she became misty-eyed. The last time anyone had bought her a Christmas gift that had to do with photography was the last Christmas with her adoptive dad. So getting the thoughtful gift from Jimmy meant the world to her. She gave Jimmy a big hug and thanked him.

Next, Samantha opened her gift from Jessica. It was a snow globe with two girls holding hands. A ribbon on the front said, *Having a Sister Means Having A Friend Forever.* Samantha was in love with the gift from Jessica, hugged her, and said thank you. Carefully, she wrapped it back in the tissue paper and placed it in the box, so it would not get ruined before she could bring it up to her room.

Jimmy had gotten both the boys a crossbow to learn to hunt with. He also had paid for hunting courses for them to take. Both of them thought it was the most incredible gift ever. They couldn't wait to learn how to shoot the crossbows. But when they lifted them and acted as if they would shoot them, it was distressing to their grandparents.

Grandma and Grandpa Kennedy had gotten the girls a cardigan sweater, a Michael Kors handbag, and diamond earrings with a pendant necklace. In addition, they bought each of the boys a cardigan sweater, a men's Michael Kors wallet, and a Rolex watch. Materialistic items that were not unique or personal for any of them. The gifts were impractical for them all in their careers. Their grandparents did not understand the lives they lived.

Mira and Richard had gotten each of their kids a picture frame that said, *family*. They requested they get a family portrait done while they were all together during the week. It was a sweet, sentimental gift for them all, which had more meaning now that they were all not living at home. Jessica told them she could easily set her equipment up to take a timed picture. They had gotten them many other items that weren't highly extraordinary.

Richard Jr. and David had taken the easy way out and bought everyone gift cards. Everyone laughed because they gave simple gifts.

However, they had wrapped them in the most creative and challenging ways. They had covered the gift card in a box for Jimmy with several other packages. The boys wrapped each one in a complicated manner to be unwrapped. They covered one in duct tape and another in zip ties.

The family all laughed at the creativity and the challenges. They had sent Jessica and Samantha on a scavenger hunt for theirs, with envelopes containing clues.

Jessica had gotten her brothers hunting knives and some rugged work boots, which they both appreciated. Living on the island, both would get used. She also got Jimmy a hunting knife and had the blade engraved with the initials JG. He enjoyed the sentiment and knew his cousin wanted him to know she acknowledged he was family, even though they couldn't publicly.

Samantha had gone for the fun gifts and got everyone a different version of the game, *Cards Against Humanity*. They were all looking forward to playing later that night.

Timothy opened Jessica's present. It blew him away by its thoughtfulness. It contained pictures of him and her and various places they had been together so far in their relationship. He hugged and kissed her and told her how much he loved the gift and her. Then he handed her his gift. It was a custom-made snow globe with a replica of her log cabin inside. It was quickly her favorite gift.

The siblings had bought their mother and grandmother a mother's and grandmother's rings with their birthstones. Then, since both their father and grandfather loved golf, they pitched in and bought them both a membership at the local country club.

By mid-afternoon, they had finished opening gifts, and nobody mentioned the presents that remained unopened in Jessica's bathroom closet, the ones found in each of the family's rooms. Finally, Richard Jr. excused himself to go spend some time with Danielle. Grandma and Grandpa Kennedy headed back home to Connecticut, and Samantha headed to Zach's, spending some time with him and his family.

Jimmy also excused himself to spend some time with his parents. Jessica debated whether she should tell Jimmy about the gifts sitting upstairs. Then, deciding it could wait until he got back from seeing his parents, she kept quiet.

By dinnertime, everyone had gathered back at the house. Danielle had returned with Richard Jr., and Zach had returned with Samantha. After dinner, they gathered to play pool and some *Cards Against Humanity*. Laughter by all filled the evening. It genuinely was a Merry Christmas. After the chaos and heartache the family had endured the past few months, it was calming to have some normalcy.

Once Mira and Richard went to bed, though, Jessica knew she and Timothy had to tell the others about the random gifts left for each of them.

"Guys, I hate to ruin the night. But Timothy and I found presents for the family in our rooms last night. We waited all day because we didn't know who they were from. Since no one has piped up, we assume, our friend left them. They are upstairs in my bathroom closet."

Jimmy went upstairs with Timothy and Jessica to retrieve the presents. His gut was twisting and turning. He thought they had made it through two whole days with no incidents from the unknown predator. The only thing that bothered him was the beer cans no one else knew about.

"Are you sure these gifts aren't by anyone else?"

No one recognized them. Agreeing it would be safer to open them at the security shack, they all bundled up and headed over there.

They followed the directions and opened them all at once. Zach and Danielle opened up the ones addressed to Mira and Richard. It mortified them to find a dead crow in each box, not believing what they saw. Jessica's box was the only one that also had a note. It simply stated: *You should have listened to my first warning, now you all will pay.*

Chills went down her spine. She was the only one who knew what the note meant. The letter left on her porch months ago warned her not to return to the island. The same letter had been the only item taken from her house when it was burglarized. After researching symbolism the other day, she knew what the crows meant.

Death. Whoever left the gifts was the same person who left the note, the same person who left the deer carcasses, the same person who left the deer hearts, the same person who tried to kill her and wanted them all dead. Shaking, the tears fell from her eyes.

As her body still shook and she struggled to breathe, she told the others about the note through her tears.

"I didn't think. Assuming it was just one of my crazy stalkers from my past. I am so sorry everyone. This is all my fault."

Feeling guilty, she had not told them about it before. They all assured her it was not her fault, and they sat there trying to brainstorm who it could be.

None of them could think of anyone who would have a motive to hurt the family. There was no gift for Jimmy, however, that wasn't odd. Seeing that it was not public knowledge, he was part of the family. It was only Jimmy that felt the dread of not receiving one. The nagging feeling that he somehow was responsible for the torture occurring to the family just wouldn't go away.

Before heading to bed, they all agreed to bring the gifts to the police the next day. Since they felt it was a direct threat, in context with everything else that had been occurring, they thought it was time to bring in the authorities.

Tossing and turning in his bed, Jimmy struggled to fall asleep. With his mind racing with thoughts of self-doubt. Exhaustion won out, and his eyes shut. His breathing became steady and even. His eyes started rapid movement beneath his eyelids, and he reached a dream state.

He was riding his ATV in his dream, and he found the deer carcass again. Staring at the corpse, it morphed into Jessica. He turned and ran, finding himself at the second deer carcass. Which then morphed into Richard Jr. Panicking, again he ran stumbling upon the third carcass that morphed into David. Looking at his hands, thick, sticky blood covered them. The smell of rotting flesh was overwhelming. Then, just as he retched, he sat up in bed.

Covered in sweat, Jimmy realized his sheets were soaking wet. Looking at his hands, he realized it was just a dreadful nightmare. Getting out of bed, there were no empty beer cans to be seen. That calmed his mind a bit. Still, he needed to make sure everyone in the family was okay. So, he tiptoed to each door and peeked inside to see all were sound asleep.

It was early, but Jimmy knew he couldn't go back to sleep. He stripped his bed of his sheets. Then took a nice hot shower and got dressed for the day. The kitchen was quiet and dark when he entered it. It was too early for Stella to be up preparing breakfast for the family. Making himself a cup of coffee, he looked out the kitchen window. Seeing the light on in Samuel's window above the garage, he wondered what had him up so early.

Then, as he watched, the door to Samuel's place above the garage opened. Samuel and another person exited. It was dark, so it was hard to tell who the other person was. Samuel opened the passenger side door and helped the person into his truck, taking a moment to kiss them. Jimmy realized it was a female, and as the door shut to the vehicle, he thought he recognized her. He couldn't be sure, though.

If his eyes weren't deceiving him, he had just seen Rita Duvall get into Samuel's truck. That didn't bode well if their mechanic was having an affair with a very affluent woman from the mainland. Not to mention she was the grandmother of Richard Jr.'s girlfriend.

The thought of Danielle finding out about her grandmother and Samuel alarmed him. A discussion would have to be had between him and Samuel. Jimmy didn't care so much about the affair. He just cared about the ramifications of it. Already aware of how these matters can lead to messy, unintended consequences.

His thoughts went to how Melissa said the island had a curse. Was she right? Was the land void of morality that led to the destruction of the lives that lived on it? Maybe he should move away, as Melissa did. But the thought of leaving his home and his parents was too much for him to consider. A tear fell down his cheek.

He hadn't felt so lost in a long time. Jimmy would call his therapist later in the day. He hoped he could get help before he descended into the madness of psychosis again. If he hadn't already.

Chapter Nineteen

The Fury

They had awakened early to listen to the audio recordings from the party. Smiling as they listened intently to all the secrets the party guests spoke. This one speculates about the eldest Gardiner son and his romantic interest with the mainlander, and that one talks about how peculiar the youngest Gardiner son acted in social scenarios. It was good to know what others thought about the Gardiners. It helped in their plans.

The reappearance of Richard was a hot topic of the party-goers. Some speculated he had actually killed the others on board the sailboat to gain complete control of the island. The only reason people felt he hid away was that Alexandria had not gone on the trip. There was no evidence or bodies to prove or disprove his story that he had told, so people felt they were free to make up their own theories.

Laughing at some conversations overheard about themselves and how they cleaned up well. They had turned a few heads that night and even had a few admirers approaching them. It felt good to be looked at with respect instead of disdain. That feeling fueled the fire and desire for more power.

Just imaging the respect and admiration they would receive when their secret was revealed. It would catapult them into a new hierarchy among the inhabitants and mainlanders alike.

Turning off the recordings from the night before and saving the rest to listen to later, they switched to listening to the family live. The family was still eating breakfast. Their chatter was nauseatingly dull. The family recapped the party from the night before, discussed the food they were eating, and other boorish musings. Nothing was mentioned yet of the mysterious gifts left for the family.

The conversation was too joyous for them to believe the family had already opened the gifts. Instead, they assumed they were waiting to open them until after breakfast. So they sat through the ordinary conversations hoping for just a sliver or slight morsel of a secret.

Disappointed, their heart started racing when they heard the family was done with breakfast and headed into the parlor to unwrap gifts. Waiting as patiently as possible, they suffered through the disgusting exchange of gifts between the family.

No mention of the gifts they had left. Even when the family finished unwrapping their contributions from one another. Anger built inside them, and they clenched their fists. Why weren't they opening the gifts they left?

They seethed as they listened to the family disperse to do their own things. The family had not followed the instructions to open the gifts altogether. Why? They hadn't even mentioned them.

Determined to discern what went wrong in their plan, they resumed listening to the tapes from the night before. However, it wasn't until they tuned in to Jessica's room recordings they found their answer.

That Bitch! They thought to themselves. She will pay dearly!

Switching back to the live feed to listen in on the family. They suffered through more boorish conversations. Listening to the laughter emanating from the devices made them physically ill. The love shared between the siblings and their significant others made them hate the lot of them even more. It wasn't until much later in the evening they heard Jessica tell Jimmy about the gifts. When the family members took the packages to the security shack, they got up and paced back and forth.

They didn't have listening devices at the security shack. This would mean they wouldn't get the satisfaction of hearing the family's reaction. The fire of rage building inside them was burning to burst out of them.

Grabbing their hunting knife and drone, they left their place for a nighttime hunt. They had perfected attaching the blade to the drone, so it wasn't off balance and could still fly. Using it had made sneaking up on the deer so much easier. Slitting their throats with one swift fly by. Once the deer had fallen and stopped moving, they could cut it open and remove the heart.

Then, using a branch, they covered the tracks they had made with leaves and debris so that it would look as if no one had been there. The light snow that had fallen the night before had all but melted during the day.

Releasing the pent-up anger helped. They felt more powerful again. Their thoughts were calm, and they could think clearly about what needed to be done.

Showering and getting dressed, they decided to have a late-night drink at the mainland bar. They were feeling a bit more adventurous about bringing potential admirers back to their place after the party.

Morning came early, and they knew they needed to get their guest home before it got light out. So, rousing the guest, they drove them home and made it back to the island before too many of the early risers were up and about.

They noticed the Manor house's kitchen light on. Someone was awake early, and they hoped that the house's occupants did not see their comings and goings.

As they ate their breakfast, they smirked, knowing the family may have won the battle on Christmas. Unfortunately, however, they would lose the war. In every war, there are casualties. This one would be no different.

They would be victorious in the next battle, and the family would suffer. The casualties would be significant, but first, they needed to lull them into a sense of calm. They learned that the family was already too close-knit and protective of each other. So when they felt threatened, they rallied around one another, and their defenses were more significant than expected.

They had to learn to space out their torture. It would be more fun that way. But just when the family was lulled into a false sense of security, they would need to remind them who was boss.

Chapter Twenty

Family Matters

The mood at the breakfast table was more subdued than the previous mornings. The siblings had agreed not to discuss the presents in front of their parents. Instead, Jimmy had eaten and rushed out to work. David and Richard Jr. followed closely behind.

They knew their morning would be busy answering questions from the police when they came. Mira and Richard had made plans to spend the day with Lena and Steven. Those plans worked perfectly for the siblings because the police could arrive and do what they needed to do without their parents knowing.

Jessica and Timothy had decided to do more exploring of the island. They borrowed one radio from the security shack, so they could if they needed to get in touch with anyone. Samantha and Danielle were off to work at the café for the day.

Everything seemed normal on the surface of the island until the state police pulled up to the security shack. Jimmy met the officer and walked with him into his office. He closed the door and showed the officer the pictures of the deer carcasses and the hearts. The officer was dismayed and admitted he had seen nothing like that before. When Jimmy showed him the presents left for the family, the officer had no words.

Taking fingerprints would be fruitless, since it had been a day and a half since someone left the presents at the house. Jimmy knew Betty and Martin kept the house spotless and dusted and polished surfaces daily. The police officer and Jimmy went around the island, asking the inhabitants about the deer carcasses to see if they could rattle anyone's cage.

Everyone seemed genuinely upset about the deer carcasses themselves. No one gave any sign they were the ones that killed the deer. Stella broke down in tears when they were questioning her. She never had in her life known of anyone on the island that would have hurt those poor animals.

When they interviewed Betty at the Manor house, she too broke into tears and likened it to finding Ms. Mary in the tub. Jimmy felt terrible since she seemed so shaken up by it all, and it brought up those horrific memories for her.

Samuel even displayed utter disdain for whoever had killed the deer. The police officer took information from Captain Bill about the guests who attended the party and took the ferry across. When he finished, he told Jimmy he wasn't sure what they could do since they had no evidence pointing to who could be tormenting the family.

As the police officer drove away, Jimmy wondered if he should have said something about the beer cans and his own suspicions. Going back to his office and closing the door again, he made the phone call to his therapist. She was more than happy to fit him into her schedule.

Feeling relief that he could talk about what was going through his mind with her, he left the security shack to do his scheduled island rounds. Then, driving towards the windmill to do a security check there, the crackle of his radio startled him.

It was Timothy, and he sounded out of breath and distraught. Once Jimmy could get Timothy to slow down while talking over the radio and not cut himself off. He realized Timothy and Jessica were over by Bostwick Creek, and they needed him to get there ASAP.

When Jimmy pulled up to where Timothy and Jessica were, his heart sank. Their faces told him everything he needed to know without even seeing what they were pointing at. Seeing Jessica's eyes, he read the fear. Timothy had his arm around Jessica protectively.

Zach, Richard Jr., and David on their ATVs in no time joined them. They realized whoever was doing this would not stop. Jimmy briefed them all about what the police officer had said. They all felt defeated. Like they were sitting ducks waiting for the hunter to shoot at them.

They buried the fourth deer carcass, and then they made plans to check Samantha's room every couple of hours. They would have to take turns and not make it clear, so their parents didn't start asking questions.

It was time to head home for dinner by the time they were done. Danielle and Samantha would be home before Mira and Richard, so they knew they could fill them in on the day's events.

Samantha sat on the couch in the parlor with Zach sitting next to her. Danielle sat next to Richard Jr. Jimmy let the two young women know about the police visit and the new deer carcass. Rattled by the news, Samantha cried. Zach put his arm around her, and she leaned her head on his shoulder.

Just when everyone felt a bit defeated, Martin came into the room with a package that had arrived addressed to David. David opened it excitedly, knowing that the contents inside would help them in their quest to determine who was tormenting them.

It was the security cameras! They all felt a bit of relief, and they worked together to figure out where they should go. In no time, they had most of them up and running. They had several on the outside of the house and a few on the inside. Making sure the cameras were not noticeable, they felt more confident and safer.

When their parents came home, the group was more relaxed playing pool and having fun. Mira and Richard were unaware of the family's dangers and enjoyed watching the young adults having fun.

Jimmy refrained from even having a beer at the advice of his therapist. They had been able to have a session over the phone, and Jimmy felt a little more at ease. She had commended him for recognizing potential signs of an impending break. Assuring him, she didn't think he was having one, but it was good that he reached out for help, just in case.

When the others questioned why he wasn't having a beer, he just shrugged it off as wanting to start the new year on a healthier note. They had all agreed that they could all do with being a bit more healthy and also refrained from drinking that evening.

The following morning Jimmy was happy to awake to no empty beer cans. As the morning progressed and finding no deer's heart anywhere near Samantha's room, everyone seemed to relax a bit more. Finally, Samantha and Danielle headed off to work, as Jimmy, David, and Richard Jr. also did.

They left Timothy and Jessica with her parents, who had taken it upon themselves to set up some appointments to meet with caterers and bakers for the wedding. So naturally, Jessica was a little more than annoyed. Yet, she bit her tongue and went along with the plans.

Her parents started talking about serving caviar and pate at the first caterers. This was when Jessica had had enough. It was her wedding, after all.

"We do not want caviar or pate. Timothy and I like neither of those, and we do not want something that we dislike at our wedding. Sorry to disappoint, but we want simple finger foods. We want a choice of three entrees. A fish dish, a chicken dish, and a beef dish. Nothing too fancy."

Timothy shifted a bit in his seat. This was the first time he had seen Jessica lose her temper. There was no blame on her, and Timothy was glad she spoke up. Bracing for the potential backlash from her parents, he reached for her hand to let her know he supported her.

Both Mira and Richard sat with stunned looks on their faces. Mira was a bit more wounded-looking, and her bottom lip trembled ever so slightly. Richard furrowed his brows and rubbed his hand along his chin.

The caterer sat across from them, frozen mid-turning of a page. Not knowing whether to proceed or step out of the room and let the clients have a moment of privacy.

"I apologize, Jessica. Your mother and I seem to have overstepped our boundaries. Of course, we do not mean to. But Timothy, we owe you both an apology. We are truly sorry."

"Look, Mom and Dad, I appreciate your enthusiasm in helping us plan our wedding and all. But we grew up differently than you did. Our tastes and styles are different. We accept your apology."

"Dear, we had to have a small wedding because of many circumstances. So we have gotten caught up in the idea of throwing you a big glamourous wedding that we never had. We are sorry."

"Mom, I know you mean well. I do. We are just very different from you. I would be perfectly content with a small backyard wedding."

Timothy relaxed. He felt that clearing the air had helped ease the tension felt in the past with Jessica's parents. Jessica also relaxed. She felt better about finally getting her feelings out in the open with her parents. It surprised her they took it so well.

Mira and Richard sat quietly as Jessica and Timothy discussed options with the caterer. When they finished, they had received a detailed quote. The following two caterers went smoothly, with Mira and Richard letting Jessica and Timothy do all the talking.

By the end of the day, they decided which caterer they would go with and the menu that would be served. Jessica and Timothy felt good about getting that settled and out of the way.

When everyone was back at the Manor house for the evening, Jessica set up her photography equipment to take the family photos she had promised to take. First, she took a few of just her and her siblings. Some of her parents, her siblings, and herself. Then she took a couple with Timothy, Jimmy, Zach, and Danielle all in there, too.

It was another fun-filled, relaxing evening, and they all went to bed feeling as if the craziness of the last few days was all over.

Timothy and Jessica were lying in bed. He raised himself up on his elbow and looked at Jessica proudly.

"Babe, I can't believe you finally stood up to your parents! I know it was hard, but I think it was the best thing for all of us."

"Thanks, I just couldn't hold it all in anymore. Especially with all the other stress we are going through. I know they don't know about all that, but I just needed to clear the air."

"I got to admit, though, you were pretty scary. That was my first time seeing you so angry. I never want to see you like that again. Remind me not to piss you off!"

Jessica laughed and pushed him onto his back.

"That's right, Mr. Sullivan, don't get on my bad side. It won't bode well for you!"

Reaching up to pull her to him, Timothy kissed her lips softly.

"I never want to get on your bad side, not because I fear you, but because your good side is just so good!"

Jessica stroked his hair lovingly while looking him squared in the eyes and smirked. Then she kissed him tenderly and lovingly. It wasn't long before they were fast asleep in each other's arms.

Chapter Twenty-One

The Late Gift

After the New Year, everyone had to get back to their respective routines. So Jessica and Timothy said goodbye to her family and headed back to Connecticut. As Jessica sat in the passenger seat, she watched the scenery go past her window. Although things had started off crazy during this visit to the island, things had calmed down, and it had actually turned out pretty good. After the blowout with her parents and the ensuing discussion, she felt better about her relationship. In addition, sharing the experiences with her siblings and cousin solidified her gratefulness for finding her biological family.

Timothy had gotten a call from his editor the day before, asking them to go to Ireland to do a piece on plants that survive the winter there. It would be a quick trip home to unpack from the holiday and pack for their Ireland trip. Jessica had been to Ireland only a few months before and was looking forward to returning. It was one of her favorite countries to visit. However, this time would be unique because Timothy would be with her.

Richard and Mira headed back to their home in Boston. The mood in their car was melancholy. They were both coming to terms with their adult children's choices. Mira quietly contemplated what it would mean to not have her kids at home or even close by. It would be a new chapter in their lives and in their relationship.

She and Richard had been together for so long. They had children quickly in their relationship. So they really hadn't had time as just a couple. Sure, they had the moments they stole behind everyone's backs in the beginning.

That was exciting to both of them. Holding each other as a secret. But keeping the secret of Richard's true identity for so long had given their relationship a constant sense of excitement. Wondering if their secrets would ever be discovered.

Now the entire world knew, and they were just an ordinary couple. Mira didn't know how she felt about that. Looking over at Richard, she still felt those butterflies in her stomach. He had aged well. Grey hairs peppered throughout his dirty blonde hair. His piercing blue eyes still made her weak in the knees, just as they did when she was a schoolgirl. The thought of having more time alone with her husband made her appreciate the new opportunities presented to them by their children's decisions.

Looking in the car's side-view mirror, she saw Samantha and Zach following behind them to pack up Samantha's things to move her into the Manor house.

Driving Samantha's car, Zach followed behind her parents. Samantha looked out the window and then over at Zach. She was so enamored with him. Never in a million years did Samantha ever think finding her soulmate would happen while waitressing.

Sure she had dated other guys before him. None that Samantha had met while working, though. Most had been in high school, and the rest she usually met through friends of friends.

The quiet kindness and respect Zach always gave her was a stark contrast to previous guys from her dating history. However, their relationship had blossomed quickly, and with it, she had a newfound understanding of her sister's relationship with Timothy. Discussing their relationships with each other had strengthened the bond between sisters. Samantha felt blessed that they had found her big sister.

Samantha realized fate had played a significant role in both of their relationships. However, this differed from their brother's current situation. His connection with Danielle had begun as children and grew organically over the years. While the family situation had moved the process along, there was no doubt in Samantha's mind that Richard Jr. and Danielle would have ended up together, anyway. Their kinship was destiny.

David had the day off and had made plans to hang out with Joe, the bartender from the party. It was the first time they could hang out since they had first met. Discovering that they both enjoyed bowling, they went, so they had a chance to talk more.

The closest bowling alley was in Riverhead. Driving together gave the men more opportunity to get to know one another. David was enjoying Joe's companionship. It was easy between them. He had opened up to Joe about his conflicting feelings about his sexuality at the party.

Joe was completely understanding. This made David feel less alone and accepted than he had ever felt. It was a good feeling. For the first time in a long time, David thought it was okay not to be sure of himself. He took Stella's advice, just being who he was and letting life flow freely.

Jimmy had to work. Richard Jr. and Danielle stayed back at the Manor house. They both had the day off. Danielle was secretly hoping that since things had quieted down, she and Richard Jr. could take their relationship to the next level.

Danielle had planned out their afternoon. First, she had asked Stella to make a picnic-style lunch in a basket and all. Then, when it was ready, she sent Richard Jr. down to get it. Hoping Stella would remember her instructions to stall him from immediately coming back upstairs.

The candles she wanted to place around the room hid in a bag under the bed. As she got them out, her heart pounded in her chest. This needed to be perfect. Strategically, she placed a few candles in the fireplace across from the four-poster bed. Then she put a few on the mantel and on the bureau in the room. Each side table had one candle placed on it.

Quickly she went around, lighting the candles. The scent of vanilla promptly permeated the room. She knew she had little time left, so she spread the checkerboard patterned blanket in front of the fireplace and then went into the bathroom to change.

Richard Jr. returned to the room with the basket. Smiling when he saw the candles and the blanket. Taking the cue from how Danielle had set up the room and spreading the basket lunch on the throw. He then poured them each a glass of the Merlot placed in the basket by Stella at Danielle's request.

As Danielle opened the door to the bathroom, Richard Jr.'s breath was taken away at the sight of her. She was wearing a long, flowing red satin dress with spaghetti straps. The satin clung to her body and showed every curve.

"I saved your best Christmas present for last. I hope you don't mind it being late." Danielle walked over and took a seat next to Richard Jr. on the blanket.

Richard Jr.'s heart raced in his chest. He was feeling so conflicted. His desire for Danielle was strong, and he wanted to act on all those impulses. Yet, his brain flooded his mind with the "what ifs" of taking their relationship to the next level. Losing Danielle would rock his world. He realized she was ready for the next level in their relationship, but was he?

He didn't want to disappoint Danielle. She had clearly gone to a lot of trouble to put this all together for them. Would he disappoint her if his heart wasn't fully ready for this step? If he turned down her advances, could it hurt their relationship? Would she feel as though he didn't love her enough?

The pause in Richard Jr.'s response concerned Danielle. Was he ready for this step? He was such an overthinker—the one quality that she had issues with about him. Sometimes, she wished he would just be more spontaneous and not so concerned with what might happen. She wanted him to learn to live in the moment.

"I love you and the present. No, I don't mind it being late."

Richard Jr. handed her a glass of wine.

He followed the wine by offering her a chocolate-covered strawberry. She bit into it while he was still holding it. Then, they took turns feeding each other their lunch. Before they knew it, Richard Jr. tipped the wine bottle to pour more wine into Danielle's glass. The last drop of the wine slowly rolled into Danielle's glass. Finally, they had finished the Merlot bottle and their lunch's last bites.

Richard Jr. Stood up and reached his hand out to Danielle. Pulling her up into his arms, he let go of any thoughts he was having and gave in to his desires. Scooping her up in his arms, he carried her over to the bed and gave her what she craved most of him.

When they were done, they lay quietly in each other's arms. There were no more doubts in Richard Jr.'s mind. This was what he wanted for the rest of his life. He just prayed it was what Danielle wanted as well. Then, the constant overthinker made plans for their future.

Later in the evening, they joined Jimmy for dinner. Jimmy had ridden the ATV all day, making security rounds, and caught up with Richard Jr. on the day's developments. It wasn't much. Things had seemed to quiet down a bit, and the fourth deer's heart had not shown up anywhere. That had been a considerable relief to them all.

They attributed the quiet to the installation of the cameras. While they felt they had placed them in hidden areas, it was the only reason the torture had stopped. But, except in Jimmy's mind, there was another explanation.

He had stopped drinking altogether and had talked to his therapist again regularly. Unfortunately, this information was not shared with his cousins. So they all thought that somehow the person responsible for terrorizing the family had found out about the cameras.

They were all happy the terror had stopped. Being more relaxed was helping them all settle into a routine on the island. After dinner, Jimmy challenged Richard Jr. to a game of pool. Danielle contemplatively watched.

Richard Jr. seemed different, in a good way. He kissed her a few times between turns and called her his good luck charm. The spontaneity of affection publicly was something he had never done in the past. She smiled at her wish coming true. Winning the first game, Richard Jr. then challenged Martin, who had joined them in the parlor.

After winning a few more rounds of pool, Richard Jr. announced he was retiring for the evening. Then, taking Danielle's hand, he led her upstairs to his bedroom. While lying beside her in bed, he propped himself up on one arm, facing her.

"I think you should officially move in with me."

"Don't you have to check with Jessica and Jimmy?"

"Of course, but I need to know if you will or not before I even bother with that step."

And there was the overthinking again. Danielle smiled, knowing he wouldn't change completely, especially in one day.

"Well, I practically live here anyway, so why not? It isn't like I will take up a whole other bedroom. And it will be good for Samantha to have another woman in this house of men."

"Then it's settled! I will talk to Jimmy and Jessica tomorrow, although I do not see them objecting to it."

Leaning over, he gently kissed her lips. Danielle returned the kiss with passion and fire running through her veins. They made love until they were both exhausted and craved sleep.

Chapter Twenty-Two

Ireland Escape

It was 5:00 am when Jessica and Timothy landed in Dublin, Ireland. They claimed their baggage and then headed to the rental car desk. Jessica was excited to show Timothy around this beautiful city. They had never assigned him to write anything in Ireland before, so it was his first time on the Emerald Isle. Jessica had been there multiple times, including a few short months ago.

Excitement filled Jessica, and Timothy loved watching how she hurried to get through all the rental car paperwork. Since Timothy had never driven on the opposite side of the road before, they agreed Jessica should be the one to drive.

Driving to the Crowne Plaza, the hotel they were staying overnight in, they hoped they could check in early. The desk clerk was more than gracious, letting them check into their room. They both felt the need to take a quick nap and then they would explore Dublin for the rest of the day.

When they got up, they both showered and got ready to start the day of exploring. First, they walked to the corner and caught a bus into the heart of the city. From there, they bought tickets for the Do Dublin Hop-on Hop-off bus tour.

Timothy, who was used to New York City, was amazed at the cleanliness of the buildings and streets in Dublin. However, he understood Jessica's love of the old and new blend of architecture. It definitely gave the vibe of stepping back in time with the modern conveniences.

They hopped on the bus at O'Connell street and hopped off for the first stop at Parnell Square North. Jessica figured Timothy would enjoy going to the Dublin Writers Museum. Timothy could appreciate the Irish literary tradition displayed proudly throughout the museum as a writer. Hopping back on the bus where they got off, they looked at the map and planned their next hop.

Choosing to check out the Natural History Museum next, they hopped off at Merrion Street Upper. The walking they needed to do to get to their destinations daunted neither of them. The people they met along the way were friendly, and the crowds were nowhere near what they encountered back home in New York City.

After touring the museum, they found a quaint Irish bar called Foleys. Jessica loved the blue facade surrounding the doors, and as she stepped into the place, she felt transported in time. The colorful bar stools and high-top tables added an air of Irish whimsy. While the fireplace added warmth and ambiance.

They were seated by their server and were given menus to look over. Everything looked delicious. Settling on the fish and chips, they both ordered a beer and waited for their food to arrive.

Timothy noticed a difference in Jessica, although he had a hard time pinpointing exactly what it was. Her eyes seemed to sparkle with a bit of magic that he hadn't seen back in the States. There was a glow around her that radiated from within.

"Let's stay here for a bit after we are done with our assignment."

Timothy didn't know where the idea had come from; he just knew he didn't want to rush away from this place.

"You were reading my mind! I will do you one better. Let's look for a home here in the country. A retreat we can come to whenever we want."

By the end of their lunch, they had booked the rest of the month at various stops in Ireland. They would meet with their tour guide the next day to show them the plants on which they were there to do the article. They didn't expect the assignment to take long at all to complete. Timothy had already done research on the subject. It was only a matter of interviewing people with knowledge of the plants, their uses, and the pictures.

Rounding out their afternoon, they visited St. Patrick's Cathedral, the Teeling Whiskey Distillery, and Guinness Storehouse. The drivers of the Do Dublin bus tour made the trip entertaining, telling stories about the city and the history behind it all, embellishing along the way. When Jessica and Timothy returned to their hotel, they were exhausted.

For the next couple of days, Jessica and Timothy completed their assignment. When they were done, they turned their attention to looking for the perfect place to purchase as their getaway retreat. They drove throughout the country until they came across the small townland of Manorhamilton in the county of Leitrim.

Something about the quaint main street lined with small shops and pubs felt like home for both of them. They stayed in a small bed-and-breakfast and met with a realtor to show them properties in the area. It wasn't long before they found the perfect cottage with several acres and a few outbuildings.

Jessica wanted to share the news with her siblings, especially Samantha. Yet, she desired to keep it a secret. She knew Samantha would adore the cottage and would help her decorate it perfectly.

Samantha had a flair for knowing just what Jessica liked or disliked. It was amazing how the two sisters seemed to meld into one person when they were together. The more they got to know each other, the more they freaked everyone around them out with their uncanny ability to finish each other's sentences and read each other's minds.

By the time Timothy and Jessica got back to Connecticut, it was the beginning of February. Jessica missed her sister immensely, so they made plans for a girls' weekend after Valentine's Day.

Jessica had told Samantha about the Ireland retreat and swore her to secrecy for the time being. Jessica felt the need to keep this bit of news from the rest of the family. She didn't understand her gut feeling that she would need this retreat in the future, but the inkling was there. Until she could discern why, she had the feeling, though, she would keep it under wraps.

Samantha loved having secrets with her sister and gladly agreed to keep it. She didn't need a reason. If her big sister asked her to keep a secret, she would do so no matter what.

Samantha's only other female friend was Danielle, Richard Jr.'s live-in girlfriend. Jimmy and Jessica had agreed that she could move in, and Samantha really appreciated having another female in the Manor house.

Samantha and Zach hadn't committed to living together yet. Samantha was still adjusting to moving from her parents' home into the Manor house with her brothers and cousin Jimmy.

She felt that there was a closer bond with her brothers now than when they were younger. Yet, her bond with her sister was the strongest. She and Jessica had discussed this frequently since they met. Neither could explain the instantaneous connection they had. They both felt it deep in their souls, though, and they knew it was an unbreakable bond.

Because of this bond, Jessica knew her secret Ireland retreat was safe with Samantha. Timothy agreed it was best to keep the new purchase under wraps for now. He also had an unwavering feeling that it might be necessary to hide away there someday. Even though it had been quiet since Christmas day, Timothy still felt Jessica was in danger. He would do everything possible to keep her safe.

Chapter Twenty-Three

Happy and Sad News

Samantha was getting ready for her date with Zach. It was Valentine's Day, and they were going to the mainland for dinner. They had been dating for almost two months now. Choosing her outfit was becoming difficult, and she wished her sister was there to help.

Finally settling on a pair of jeans and a blue v-neck sweater with a white tank top underneath. Again, she felt comfortable, but pretty. Finally, she decided on a pair of brown short-cut boots.

Zach was always punctual, and this time was no different. Martin called up to Samantha to let her know her suitor had arrived. As she walked down the staircase, Zach let out a whistle. She blushed and laughed, remembering how he did most of the blushing in the early stages of their relationship.

Kissing him on the cheek when she reached him at the bottom of the stairs, it was Zach's turn to do the blushing. Zach handed her a bouquet of carnations. They were red, pink, and white with a few sprigs of baby's breath. She thanked him and gave the flowers to Martin to put in a vase.

After helping Samantha with her coat, Zach made sure she was nice and warm before they headed out into the blustery cold. They made it to the mainland and headed to the 1777 Restaurant Tavern.

The hostess seated them at a corner table when they entered the restaurant. It was pretty busy, and Zach was glad he had made reservations. In

January, they had both turned 21, so they started off with some Pino Grigio and some appetizers.

When their entrees came, they were both feeling the effects of the wine. They both ordered another glass. They giggled amongst themselves as they ate, drank, and people watched.

People watching made them realize they knew a lot of the customers in the place. They saw Betty and presumably her date for the evening. Jimmy was there entertaining a young woman. Even Samuel was there, but they could not see who he was with. Much to both of their surprise, Samantha's brothers were there with Danielle and Joe for the evening.

Richard Jr. and Danielle were sitting across the room at another table in a corner. Richard Jr. seemed nervous. However, Danielle didn't notice and was discussing something with him.

As they watched, Richard seemed to drop his fork on the floor, and he got up from his chair to get it. When he moved the chair and got down on one knee, though, Samantha realized what he was about to do.

Patting Zach's arm frantically, Samantha pointed over at Richard Jr. and Danielle's table. Sitting there eagerly watching the scene unfold in front of them, they intertwined their hands together, praying Danielle would say yes.

Watching Danielle's face as it registered what was happening was priceless. She covered her mouth with her hands.

Richard Jr. looked into Danielle's eyes.

"Danielle, you have been my best friend since we were children. I can't imagine my life without you. Will you marry me?"

The entire tavern erupted in cheers and applause when Danielle uncovered her mouth and said yes. It had gone quiet when everyone had noticed what Richard Jr. was about to do.

Samantha and Zach hurriedly went over and congratulated the newly engaged couple. David and Joe also joined in on the congratulations. Betty and her date were just leaving and stopped by the table to congratulate them. They were all surprised when Samuel and Rita approached the table to congratulate the couple.

Rita, Danielle's grandmother, had recently filed for divorce. The fact she was out with Samuel didn't seem appropriate to Danielle. Not wanting to ruin the moment, she kept her opinion to herself. Sensing discomfort, Rita and Samuel didn't linger long at the table of the engaged couple.

Zach and Samantha returned to their table and finished their dinner and their glasses of wine. They ordered a dessert and a cup of coffee to sober up a bit. Both were feeling quite tipsy, and they knew neither was okay to drive.

Even after dessert and coffee, they both felt very disoriented. The only person still there that they knew was Jimmy. Sitting at the bar with his date, they didn't want to interfere.

Samantha and Zach both had difficulty walking to Zach's car. First, they debated whether to get a room at the Inn for the night. Then they figured it was probably already booked full because of Valentine's Day.

Sitting in the car, both felt their eyes were getting heavy. Samantha couldn't form words anymore, and Zach couldn't hear anything but muffled voices. Not recognizing where or who the voices were coming from. He couldn't even tell if one voice was his.

Danielle and Richard Jr. had gone to her parent's house to show them the ring. They had known he would propose because Richard had asked for permission earlier in the week. Lena and Steven were ecstatic, and Danielle's sisters were fawning over her and the ring.

It was a magical night for the happy couple. They couldn't wait to plan the wedding.

David and Joe had left the tavern and went to Joe's apartment after congratulating the newly engaged couple. They had been hanging out for a month now, and tonight was their first official date. To anyone watching them, they looked like two friends hanging out. However, only the two of them were aware they were calling this a date.

David was still unsure of his sexuality, but Joe made him feel comfortable about his uncertainty. They could talk about anything. This was why David had finally agreed to go on an actual date with him. Joe was very sure of his sexuality and had made it very clear to David that there was an attraction.

As they settled on the couch to watch a movie, Joe put his arm around David. He knew David wasn't sure of the physical aspects of their relationship, so he wanted to take things slowly and one step at a time. David didn't flinch or pull away. Instead, he felt content and safe. So he leaned in and put his head on Joe's shoulder.

It was late, and David was too tired to drive home after the movie. Joe got him a pillow and blanket and set him up on the couch. As much as Joe wanted to share his bed with David, he wasn't sure David was prepared for that yet.

Joe cared enough about David to wait until he was ready and confident about what he wanted. Finding yourself was never easy. Realizing you were a homosexual was even harder, only because of society and the negative connotations.

Joe knew it all too well. Caring about David, he wanted to help him through this challenging period in his life. Indeed, he didn't want to add to David's confusion about his autonomy and identity.

Jimmy left the tavern with his date for the evening. As he opened the car door for her and helped her into the passenger side of his car, he recognized Zach's car still in the corner of the parking lot. The windows were pretty fogged up, so he assumed Zach and Samantha were just being bold and having a marathon make-out session in the parking lot.

It wasn't until the following morning that the state police came knocking on the door to the Manor house. That was when he found out he was dead wrong. Martin had let the police sergeant in and then went to get Jimmy.

Jimmy at first thought the police officer was there with a lead who had been terrorizing and threatening the family months ago.

"Mr. Driscoll, does a Samantha Gardiner live here? And does Zach Zimmerman live on the island?"

Remembering the night before and thinking they must have gotten themselves into trouble with indecent exposure or something. Jimmy chuckled.

"Yes, Samantha lives here, and Zach lives down the road. So what trouble did they get themselves into?"

"Well, sir, the kind they can't get themselves out of. We found them in the young man's car this morning. Seems they got themselves mixed up with some dangerous drugs. Overdosed. We found them with needles still sticking in their arms."

Jimmy's head spun. He sat himself down on the stairs in the entranceway.

"Overdosed? Needles? Drugs? They both just turned 21 a few weeks ago. They were just drinking. There must be some mistake."

Jimmy choked out as he cried.

"I am sorry, sir. Preliminary findings are no other fingerprints other than the victims on the needles. Of course, the coroner will do an autopsy. Can you point me toward the young man's home so I can notify his family?"

Jimmy gave the officer the address of Zach's parents. He followed him over to the house. Standing beside the officer as he delivered the devastating news, he could barely watch as he saw Zach's mom fall to her knees on the floor. The wailing that came from the depths of her soul was unbearable to watch. Matt gently kneeled next to his wife and held her as he also sobbed.

Jimmy somberly returned to the Manor house to face the daunting task of telling Samantha's brothers she was dead.

Chapter Twenty-Four

Notifications

David was driving up to the Manor house. The state trooper was leaving, and he could see Jimmy getting off his ATV. The sweat on his palms made it hard to grip the steering wheel. David could tell the trooper's visit wasn't a good one, watching Jimmy's movements. Jimmy looked frazzled, and as he got closer, it looked as if he was crying. They had all been through some pretty harrowing times together. But never had he seen Jimmy in such a state.

The anticipation made David's heart race. What could have his cousin so distraught? Jimmy stopped short of the back kitchen door, noticing David's car pulling up. His shoulders raised and dropped as he breathed a tremendous sigh, preparing himself for what he had to do.

Meeting David at his car, he waited for him to park and get out.

"Man, what's got you in such a tizzy, bro? Another carcass."

"I... wish... Samantha.... and Zach... they both. They're gone, kid. An overdose or something."

Jimmy stammered out the words. Then he grabbed his younger cousin in a big bear hug as he finished.

David could not process what was just said. An aching in his chest worsened with each second that passed. His mind was numb. His cousin's arms around him were the only thing that told him this wasn't a dream.

His eyes welled up. He melted into his cousin as his breathing hurt, and he sobbed.

The two cousins stood there for what seemed like an eternity. They helped each other into the house. Faced with Danielle and Richard Jr. staring at them as they walked into the kitchen.

Danielle's face went from glowing and smiling to concern about why the two men seemed unhinged. Richard Jr.'s expression also went from jovial to one of worry.

David walked up to his big brother and hugged him harder than he ever had. As he did, he broke into another round of sobs. Richard Jr. hugged his little brother back, not knowing why David wouldn't let go.

He had never seen his little brother this way. Not knowing how to react, Richard Jr. squeezed as hard as possible. David reciprocated, pressing him back. The unusual exchange between brothers only added to the eldest brother's confusion.

"Richard, I... don't.. know... how ..."

Jimmy was trying to get the words out between his own tears.

"Jimmy, just tell me what the hell is going on?"

"Samantha and Zach.."

David pulled away from his brother as he gave him the news.

"They are dead! They're gone."

Richard Jr. felt as if he was going to get sick. His baby sister was dead? Too many questions ran through his head. Then he felt Danielle's arms around him and her body shaking with tears of grief.

"They were just fine last night!! What happened? How? Please don't tell me the psychopath got them."

"The police have ruled it an accidental overdose. They found them in Zach's car this morning. No signs of foul play. I know. It makes little sense."

Nothing about this felt right. Richard Jr. felt as if he was in a horrible nightmare. Balling up his fists, he pounded them on the counter. And then came the tears. He couldn't be strong a minute more. Breaking into full sobs, he crumpled to the floor. Danielle sat next to him and just held him, crying with him.

The news spread over the island, and the shock was seen and felt in the inhabitants' faces. Everyone rallied around Zach's parents while Jimmy set out to tell Jessica and Timothy in person. He just couldn't tell them over the phone. Richard Jr., David, and Danielle headed to Boston to inform their parents.

The long trip to Connecticut was torturous for Jimmy. He didn't know how he was going to tell Jessica, and imagining how devastated she would be made his stomach turn.

Only knowing his cousins for a short time, they still had bonded in a flash. Jessica and Samantha had been like two peas in a pod. Instant best friends. He knew this would shake Jessica to her core. It had shaken him to his crux. Samantha was his cousin, and Zach was not just an employee. He had been a friend and like a brother to him. Losing both of them ripped at his soul.

Jimmy wanted to numb the hurt. He hadn't craved alcohol or even drugs for years. Although, right now, Jimmy felt the descent into the depths of hell could occur at any moment. He texted his therapist as he sat on the ferry crossing the Long Island Sound.

The therapist responded in short order, and during the entire ferry ride across the sound, they had a texting session. In the end, Jimmy felt better and not as out of control as before reaching out to her. He was still dreading notifying Jessica of Samantha's death.

The ride to Jessica and Timothy's seemed to take forever, and as he drove up the driveway, his stomach lurched. He needed to keep it together.

Jessica heard the tires coming up the driveway. The hair on the back of her neck stood up. Every fiber of her being sensed impending danger or doom. It was out of the ordinary for them to have unannounced visitors. But, looking at Timothy, she could also see a bit of alarm and concern in him. They both peeked out the window and recognized Jimmy's truck coming to a stop.

This was not a planned visit, so Jessica knew something was wrong off the bat. She and Timothy met Jimmy at the door. He didn't ring the doorbell or knock.

Jessica sized him up. He looked like he had aged five years in the month she hadn't seen him. His eyes were puffy and bloodshot. The disheveled look of his hair was as if he had been running his hands through it. Jessica knew this was a habit he had in stressful situations.

"Hey, Jimmy, what brings you all the way out here?"

She saw him tremble as he stepped inside the house. His hands went through his hair as he walked to the living room and sat down. His thoughts raced, and he couldn't find the words to tell her. He couldn't shatter her heart.

"Jimmy?"

As she watched her cousin's bizarre behavior, dread overcame her. Sitting next to him on the couch, she put her hand on his knee.

Jessica's touch startled him. He looked at her and saw the genuine concern in her green eyes. Yet, the fear was there too, and he knew that deep down, she knew something terrible had happened.

Jimmy drew in a deep breath and looked his cousin in the eyes as he told her what had happened to Samantha and Zach.

Jessica couldn't breathe. She hadn't heard him correctly, had she? Jessica knew what he was saying was true, though feeling it in her soul. Getting up, she ran out the back door and dropped into the snow on her knees. Looking up at the sky, she screamed as her body shook with grief, and she sobbed.

Timothy ran out after her and encircled her in his arms. Soon, he realized the coldness of the snow, and he helped Jessica back into the house.

Jimmy didn't stay long. He headed home to the island, and for the first time in his life, he contemplated not returning. Again, he understood what Melissa had said about the island, feeling as if there was a curse. Melissa would come to the funeral. So he assumed, at least. But, oh, God, how could he face her after the drunken proposal? Would she even step foot on the island, thinking that would send a message of acceptance to him if she did? He had made a mess of things.

As Jimmy returned to the island, Richard, Jr., Danielle, and David were just pulling into their parent's driveway. None of them wanted to get out of the car. They seemed frozen in place. Richard Jr. sighed and opened the car door. The others followed his lead.

It was the first time he had been back at his childhood home since he had moved out. These were not the circumstances he had wanted to return for. But, as he went to knock on the door, it opened in a swift motion.

Mira and Richard had heard the car pull into the driveway. They were excited to congratulate Richard Jr. and Danielle on their engagement. Assuming that was what the surprise visit was for since Richard Jr. had called them to tell them the news the night before.

Richard Jr. stood confused as his mother and father enveloped him in a friendly hug and stated their congratulations to both Richard Jr. and Danielle. It wasn't until his parents registered David was also with them. Along with Danielle and Richard Jr.'s stiff response to the congratulations, Mira sensed another reason for their visit.

"What is wrong?"

Richard Jr., David, and Danielle ushered Mira and Richard back into the house, closing the door behind them. Making sure their parents were sitting before telling them the dreadful news.

It seemed like an eternity that it took for what they said to register with Mira and Richard. The color drained from their mother's face as it sunk in. Richard wrapped his arm around Mira and pulled her to him. As he did, Mira broke and, through her sobs, kept repeating.

"NO, NO, NO!"

Danielle, Richard Jr., and David stayed the night at the house because they couldn't function. In the morning, they would head back to the island to help with the funeral arrangements.

Mira seemed to enter a trance and went through the motions of getting the guest beds ready for her children. Afterward, she retired to her own bedroom, where the others could hear her sobs through the door.

She refused to come down for breakfast and see her children off in the morning. Richard, however, hugged his sons and his daughter-in-law to be extra tight as he said goodbye. Then, as he watched them drive away, he contemplated if he had done the right thing, coming out of hiding and taking control of his share of the inheritance.

Sitting in his living room, he put his head in his hands and cried. The guilt washed over him. Was this karma for the deaths of his cousins so long ago? His beautiful Samantha, named after his beloved cousin Samuel, was taken from him at such a young age. He did not lose the irony.

The thought of giving up his entire inheritance crossed his mind. It wouldn't bring his little girl back from the grave. However, maybe it would stop the karma that seemed to have been set in motion.

Chapter Twenty-Five

Re-evaluating plans

They had heard the news through the grapevine on the island. But, of course, they pretended to be shocked and sad when they were told. Some part of high school had paid off, at least. They had become very good at acting through their years of theatre classes.

The deaths of Samantha and Zach were not a shock to them. They relished the fact that they had been successful again in killing their victims and making it look like something other than murder. The power surged through their veins.

It had all worked out so perfectly. They had heard the family's plans. Knowing they would all be at the same restaurant, even when they all didn't know each other would be there.

The engagement plans fit perfectly since they knew it would provide the perfect distraction to add something to Samantha and Zach's drinks to enhance the effects. The only gamble had been making sure their own date was home safe before they returned with the syringes.

The gamble had paid off. The couple was still there, sitting in the parking lot, when they returned. They laughed, remembering how completely out of it both of their victims had been. When they had offered the syringes as a cure to their hangovers, they both jumped at the chance. Little had the two naïve victims known the syringes contained fatal doses of heroin and fentanyl.

The pair had so willingly shot themselves in the arm. It was almost comical. As they had watched, the pair's lips had turned blue within seconds. Their breathing gurgled, and as their bodies stiffened, they foamed at the mouth and went unresponsive.

They had felt for a pulse on both of them to ensure they indeed had expired. Neither Samantha nor Zach had any sign of life as they left them in the car to be found by whoever might stumble upon them.

The joy they felt in realizing that they were one step closer to their goal was overwhelming. It almost made them giddy. Soon enough, the entire family would be gone, and they could take their rightful place on the island.

They would have it all: the island, the Manor house, the inheritance. Everything would be theirs. The power would be theirs. The control would be theirs.

No one could stop them. No one even suspected them. The police had ruled Samantha and Zach's deaths an accidental overdose. They had been meticulous not to be seen doing anything.

Just knowing they had gotten away with murder again emboldened them. They needed to kill again, sooner rather than later. They craved the surge of energy that came with each kill. It couldn't be an animal either.

That had become mundane and boring. The next kill needed another human, and it needed to be another one of the family members. The question was, which one would they take next?

Would it be the youngest boy, David? They had found he had secrets of his own. Those secrets could definitely come in handy in their master plan.

The oldest boy had just gotten engaged, which posed another threat to their plans. That added another heir to the mix when they got married. Two couples engaged. That made the elimination of them a chief priority.

Then the matter of the parents being so far away. They had hoped that with the children all moving to the island, mommy and daddy would follow suit. They had heard the conversation between Mira and Richard. Mira had no desire to move to the island. Maybe it was time to arrange a need to live on the island. That would make it so much easier for them to accomplish their plans.

Not to mention the possibility of any unplanned pregnancies occurring. The immorality of the family was the reason for so many buried secrets.

It would be the downfall of them all. The Gardiner children were all just as immoral. Could they kill a child if it came down to it? They needed to make contingency plans just in case.

If another life posed a threat to their ultimate plans, that life needed to be eliminated. No matter what.

They felt they were the one chosen to restore balance and morality to the island.

They were feeling more powerful every day.

Chapter Twenty-Six

Preparing to Say Goodbye

Jessica and Timothy prepared to head back to the island to say goodbye to Samantha and Zach. Jessica had not stopped crying for days. Every time she thought she was done, something would remind her of the gut-wrenching sorrow she felt.

When she heard her sister's favorite song on the radio, she tried to sing along like Samantha always had, but she ended up choking back the tears. Then, walking past the fireplace mantel and seeing the picture of her and Samantha taken at Christmas would stop her in her tracks, and the tears would start again.

Repeatedly, she would apologize to Timothy for her constant tears. He would tell her it was okay, and he was there for her forever. Feeling blessed, she had him in her life. However, also feeling guilty, he had to endure her depressive state. Every night she fell asleep in his arms, crying.

The sadness she felt was so deep. She had never felt such a profound loss. Yes, she had mourned the loss of her adoptive parents, and she had been sad. But this, this grief cut deep in her heart. She didn't know if she would ever recover from it. The soul connection she had with her sister was a connection she had never felt with another human being before. The severing of it was unbearable.

She had been in contact with her brothers and her parents, and they all still seemed in disbelief and shock. Talking to her mother, she could barely form coherent sentences and sobbed most of the time they tried to talk. Her father talked crazily, somehow blaming this all on himself and his past actions.

Her eldest brother was angry at the world and himself, somehow thinking it was his job to protect Samantha from all harm. And her youngest brother, who had finally seemed less lost and more sure of himself, had become broken and reclusive. Later in the day would be the first time she would see them since they all received the news. Dread filled her. She didn't want to go.

Going back to the island facing the awful truth. Saying goodbye to Samantha would make it all absolute and final. She wanted to believe this was all a dreadful nightmare. A dream she would wake up from at any moment. Like some of the lucid dreams of her past.

They finally had everything packed and ready to go. Jessica took the picture with her. It made her feel closer to Samantha.

The mood at the Manor house was somber. Arthur helped make all the arrangements for the funeral. Betty hurriedly prepared the house and rooms for the family's arrival. Samuel made sure he plowed the driveway clear and the family cemetery was accessible.

Stella prepared comfort food that hopefully would help the family feel better. As she did, though, she broke down in tears. The thought of losing a child, even an adult child, was something a parent never wanted to endure.

She had been checking on the Zimmermans, Zach's parents, daily and brought them meals too. Melissa was there helping her parents deal with the loss of Zach and helping to make arrangements. The Gardiners had offered to let them bury Zach in the family cemetery. They had accepted.

Stella was worried about Jimmy. He wasn't eating. The look in his eyes was reminiscent of when he had spiraled out of control before. She couldn't talk about her concerns with anyone because the family didn't know about his past. Afraid to even bring it up with Jimmy, she kept her mouth shut.

When the rest of the family got to the Manor house around dinnertime, they hugged and cried. It was quiet. No one knew what to say. When they tried to speak, whoever it was, it would overcome them with tears.

Everyone turned in early for the night. The next day would be hard. First, they would hold the viewing in the ballroom and the memorial service. Then the caskets would go to the family cemetery by horse and carriage. Finally, they would usher mourners back to the ballroom for a late lunch after the internment.

Alone in their room, Jessica and Timothy settled in to get some sleep. Jessica couldn't hold back the tears, and as she had for every night since her sister's death, she cried herself to sleep in Timothy's arms.

Richard Jr. and Danielle were both having a hard time dealing with the loss of Samantha and Zach. They hadn't been able to celebrate in their engagement with the overshadowing of the loss. Danielle felt guilty, feeling a bit slighted. She couldn't even be happy for herself. She also questioned whether their relationship was strong enough to withstand this hardship.

Richard Jr. had become distant the last few days. Often shunning away from her affection. When she tried to talk to him about it, he changed the subject. She wasn't trying to be unsympathetic, but if they were to be married, they would have to learn to navigate hardships together.

David withdrew since the news of his sister's death. He did his shifts, came home, ate, and then went to his room. He hadn't talked to Joe since Valentine's Day. Joe had texted and called, and David just refused to respond. Joe didn't know how to feel about being ghosted. David didn't know how to discern anything or anyone at the moment.

Losing his sister made him question life in general. Was it worth caring about anyone else? Was it worth falling in love? The pain of loss at this moment made him not want to cherish or get close to anyone ever again. He couldn't bear to feel this pain again.

Mira and Richard hated the feeling that shrouded the Manor house. Their living children were not dealing with the loss of their sister well at all. They didn't know how to help any of them, since they struggled with their own grief.

They both felt strongly that they wanted their children to move off the island. However, they didn't know how to even bring up the subject.

Jimmy couldn't sleep. He hadn't slept in days. The fear gripped him. Something seemed off about Samantha and Zach's death. Guilt haunted him. He should have checked on them when he was leaving. Were they still alive when he left? Or were they already dead? Then the realization he had drank that night himself. There had been no beer cans, and he didn't see himself leave on the cameras. But something told him that their deaths were no accident.

Out of pure exhaustion, Jimmy fell asleep. When he awoke to his alarm sounding, it startled him. He needed to get up and oversee the funeral preparations.

Stella was happy to see that Jimmy looked better when he came into the kitchen for some breakfast. She watched him eat, and it eased her mind a bit more that his appetite was returning.

As each family member came down and ate breakfast, the silence became deafening. A few short weeks earlier, the house had laughter and love filling it. Today, silence and sadness were filling its halls and rooms.

Jimmy went into the ballroom to ensure they set everything for the viewing. The funeral director was preparing both caskets for their loved ones to say their goodbyes. From all over, they had delivered flowers. Jimmy helped place the flowers around the coffins.

He couldn't look at Samantha or Zach lying there. At one point, he thought he saw Zach's chest rise and fall out of the corner of his eye. Then, shaking his head, he made himself look and realized it was just his imagination.

Turning around to walk out of the ballroom, he noticed Melissa standing in the doorway and stopped in his tracks. They hadn't seen each other since that night in the bar. He didn't know what to say.

Melissa didn't expect Jimmy to be helping to set up. She had just wanted to spend a few moments alone with her baby brother. But seeing Jimmy there brought back a flood of emotions. She was angry with him for what he had done the last time they saw each other. The anger bubbled up to the surface, and she couldn't hold it back.

Walking up to Jimmy, she slapped him across the face.

"I am here on the island to only say goodbye to my brother. I am not staying, and I am trying to convince my parents to leave here, too. So that is my answer to your proposal."

Pushing past Jimmy to get to her brother's casket, she didn't look back. Instead, tears streamed down her face. Saying goodbye to Zach was the hardest thing she had to do, but telling the man she loved goodbye simultaneously broke her heart into a million pieces. She had no future on the island with Jimmy, and Jimmy would never leave. So she had to let him go. The tears were both for her brother and for Jimmy.

Jimmy looked back at Melissa while rubbing his cheek. The slap hurt. Not as much as her words, though. They cut like a knife right through the center of his heart. Then, turning back to the doorway, he walked out of the room to give the woman he loved the privacy she deserved.

Melissa meant every word she spoke. She was determined for this to be the last time she stepped foot on the island. Her parents were stubborn, though. Since Zach was being buried in the Gardiner family cemetery, it would make it even harder for them to leave. She would have to give them the most heartbreaking ultimatum. Leave with her when she went, or lose her forever as well. Zach was gone. Staying just to be close to his grave was not a healthy decision.

Chapter Twenty-Seven

The Funeral

The weather didn't cooperate for the funeral, and many people could not attend who had wanted to. It was snowing pretty hard, making it impossible for the small ferry to run with the whipping winds.

A few people had got over to the island before the storm hit, and Jimmy informed Betty to make sure she prepared all spare rooms in case their guests could not leave.

Much to Jessica and Timothy's surprise, both Jack and Allison came to pay their respects. It warmed Jessica's heart to see that Jack was there for Timothy, especially since she was such a mess herself. Likewise, Allison being there was heartwarming. Considering they still hadn't figured out if there was a connection between her and Timothy. Jessica assumed she was there because she worked for the family.

Most of the mourners present were the inhabitants of the island. The Zimmerman family was sitting upfront before Zach's casket. The Gardiners sat upfront before Samantha's casket. The minister started the memorial service after everyone present paid their respects.

After his eulogy, he asked people to come up and share stories about each of the deceased's lives. Some stories brought laughter, and others brought more tears. Jessica could not get up to talk. She trembled as the sobs came forth from her body. Her brothers and parents couldn't either. It was too painful for any of them.

Melissa got up to speak of her brother.

"Thank you all for coming to pay your respects to my baby brother, Zach, and the love of his life, Samantha. I never met Samantha, but from what Zach had told me and how happy she had made him. I know she was a beautiful soul. They both were too beautiful for this world and this island. My only consolation is that they are together and free from the darkness surrounding this place."

As she finished the last sentence, she looked straight into Jimmy's eyes. The tears welled up as she sat back down with her parents. It astonished them that no one seemed shocked at her words. It was as if she spoke about what everyone had been feeling for years. The darkness that enshrouded the island was impenetrable.

The service was brief, and the procession to the cemetery was cold. Because of the cold, the mourners didn't stay long at the cemetery as the winds whipped the snow harder against the mourner's faces, freezing the tears as they fell.

They urged everyone to join them back at the ballroom for a nice warm meal, and those who could not leave could stay the night. The weather station upgraded the storm warning to a blizzard warning. Many inhabitants ate and then headed home to hunker down for the storm.

Samuel ate, and then he got to work plowing the roads on the island so everyone could get around. It wasn't long before the power went out. Fires were lit in all the fireplaces, and lanterns were brought out to light the rooms.

The darkness just added to the mourners' overall mood. The Manor house got much creepier with the power out. David first recognized that one of their main security measures would be ineffective without power. It was as if he snapped out of his sadness at realizing they were all at risk. They had attributed the silence from their tormentor to the cameras. With the cameras down, that gave the harasser free rein again.

David found Jimmy and pulled him aside.

"Hey man, I know none of us want to think about what happened before Christmas, especially now. But, the cameras are down. No power, no cameras."

Jimmy heard him loud and clear, which snapped him out of his funk. It was his job to make sure everyone on this island stayed safe. He already felt guilty about Samantha and Zach's deaths. He didn't want to feel any more guilt.

"Shit, David. You are right! Go up to your room. Get your drone. It's charged, right? Please tell me it's charged. Fly it out your window. Keep flying it around the perimeter of the house. We need to keep everyone here safe. We never figured out who did that crazy stuff before."

Jack and Allison had joined at a table, Jessica and Timothy. Jessica had seen David approach Jimmy and could tell by their body language something was up. She didn't want to be rude and leave Jack and Allison, so she sat there, watching her younger brother and her cousin. David left the ballroom, and Jimmy seemed to scan the room.

It was Allison who broke her focus.

"I don't know if this is a good time to discuss this."

"Discuss what?"

"Well, remember how Jack here told me how Timothy is related to him at Christmas? And his Mom took a DNA test to see if she matched with Timothy to determine whether it's Jack's mom's or Jack's dad's side."

"Yeah, we knew all that, Allison."

"The DNA came back that Jack's Mom is a match. So Jack started asking me questions."

Both Jessica and Timothy glared at Jack. They had agreed to tread with Allison and the possibility of her being related to Timothy.

Jack shrugged his shoulders.

"You two went missing in action in Ireland for a month. I couldn't wait to help solve the mystery. Sorry."

"Anyway," said Allison. "Jack asked me if I had ever been pregnant. The answer is yes. I agreed to take a DNA test, too. The results came yesterday. I am a match. I am your mother, Timothy. Please forgive me for putting you up for adoption."

Timothy sat in stunned silence. Sitting across from him was his biological mother, whom he searched for. Now that he had found her, he didn't know what to feel. Jessica was happy for Timothy. She got up and went over to hug Allison. Allison stood up and hugged her back. Then she walked over to Timothy.

"Can I hug you?"

Timothy got up and hugged his biological mother for the first time. He squeezed hard as he felt her arms around him, and she embraced him back. Then the tears flowed, first from her and then from him. He felt unconditional love for the first time in his life. Allison never thought this day would happen. She had never wanted to know the child she gave up for adoption. Now, knowing him and hugging him for the first time, she never wanted to let him go.

As Jessica watched mother and son, they let go and sat back down to get acquainted with one another. She was happy for them both. However, part of her couldn't help but feel a bit of worry after what she had just endured. Finding her biological family, bonding with her sister, and then losing her sister in a matter of months. She didn't want Timothy to experience that. She prayed their reunion would stay happy.

Allison told them she was 15 when she became pregnant. She didn't go into detail. However, she said that the pregnancy was a product of rape. This was a gut punch to Timothy; Jessica could see it on his face. She reached over and squeezed his hand.

Allison explained that even though he was a product of rape, she could not fathom aborting him. To her, it felt as if that would punish him for something he didn't do wrong. So she just prayed the whole time he would be more like her.

She explained how she wound up in a psych ward for the duration of her pregnancy. First, her parents didn't believe her claims of rape, especially when she refused to get an abortion. Then she wound up being committed when she had a full-fledged breakdown.

This wound up being a blessing for her because she could carry him to term and make all the preparations to have him adopted. In addition, it saved her parents the embarrassment of their daughter's pregnancy. Although they weren't too embarrassed to tell their friends, their daughter was in a psych ward.

After giving birth and being released from the psychiatric hospital, she couldn't wait to turn sixteen and pursue emancipation from her parents.

Their lack of support for her through the most challenging time in her life opened her eyes to the toxic relationship she had with them. This had been a driving factor for her to give up her child for adoption. She felt she didn't know how to be a good parent.

Timothy's heart broke for his biological mother hearing her retell her story. However, he felt she was brave and appreciated everything she had gone through to give him life.

Upstairs, David had gotten his drone out. He opened the window to his bedroom, facing the front circular driveway. The snow was still coming down at a blinding pace, and the wind was whipping. He didn't know if the drone would fly in this weather. He was determined to try, though. Controlling the drone proved difficult. He made one complete pass around the house.

As he was going for the second pass, he heard Samuel's plow truck coming up the front driveway. It stopped in front of the house, just under the open window. Samuel left the truck running and carried a thermos into the house.

Within minutes, David heard someone enter his room. By the time he reacted and turned around, he felt himself being shoved out the second-story window. The blizzard raging outside muffled his yell for help.

When Samuel returned to his truck, the gruesome scene met him. It seemed David had fallen out of his window onto the snowplow blade. Samuel ran into the ballroom to get help.

By the time he reached Jimmy, told him what he had found, and had returned to David, he had bled to death. Jimmy was in shock at what he saw. He contacted the Coast Guard to have David's body removed from the island since they could not run the ferry during the storm. He accompanied the body to the mainland. Richard Jr. had been put in charge of investigating the accident.

Richard Jr. taped off David's room and didn't allow anyone in or out. He wanted to make sure everything was as they found it when the police came, so he set up guards inside and outside the house and made sure nothing was touched.

This annoyed Samuel because he couldn't use his truck to plow, and he had to resort to the backhoe to keep the roads on the island clear.

Everyone was in shock. Especially Mira and Richard. They had just buried their youngest daughter, and now they had lost their youngest son to a tragic accident. Richard made Mira a potent drink and brought her to their room to rest. He was worried she was about to have a breakdown.

Jessica and Timothy couldn't fathom what had occurred. They had been so busy getting to know Allison and her story that they hadn't seen or heard anything out of the ordinary until Samuel came in to get Jimmy.

Jessica's stomach lurched, and she told Timothy she needed to go to their room. They showed Allison and Jack to their rooms for the night and then went to theirs. Jessica made it into the bathroom before her stomach let loose.

Mourning her sister's death, her sister's boyfriend's death, and now the death of her youngest brother was too much for her. She had always felt she was a sound person, but this was too much for one person to handle.

Timothy didn't know what to say or do. His emotions were on a rollercoaster. He was happy that he had found his biological mother. Still, it was devastating with the loss of Samantha, Zach, and now David.

That feeling of dread crept back over both of them. It was as if Timothy and Jessica both knew in the pit of their stomachs it was no coincidence that Samantha and Zach overdosed and David fell to his death.

Both of their minds wandered back to the night of Alexandria's fall. She had been pushed. Even though the police closed the case because of Mary's suicide note confession, they still did not know who. They now knew they were dealing with a serial killer targeting their family.

Sleep eluded most of the occupants of the Manor house that evening. The events had made it hard for anyone to feel safe, and the blizzard raging outside didn't help.

In the morning, the blizzard had stopped. It had dumped two feet of snow on the island. Jimmy returned with the state police, and they began their investigation. They questioned everyone present.

The police went over David's room with a fine-tooth comb. There was no evidence of foul play found. Ruling his death by an accident, they left the family to deal with their grief.

Chapter Twenty-Eight

Unexpected Opportunity

They had gotten rid of another one. Their power was growing with each kill. They loved how opportunities just dropped in their laps.

The storm had provided a perfect opportunity for them to size up the family and possibly take out another member.

With the power being out, they knew the cameras would be ineffective. Also, it gave them plenty of work to do and a plausible alibi. They just needed to be observant and find the perfect opportunity.

It didn't take long for the opportunity to arise.

They saw the youngest Gardiner boy next to his open second-story window as they worked. They seized on the opportunity and pushed him out the window. He couldn't have landed more perfectly on the snowplow blade.

No one seemed to suspect them. Even the police in the morning had found no evidence of foul play and ruled it a tragic accident.

They loved when a plan fell into place.

Witnessing the unraveling of the family was sweet revenge. They wanted them all to suffer. To feel misery. They had overheard Richard speaking with Mira.

His guilt over the deaths of his cousins was coming back to haunt him.

Mira was on the verge of a mental breakdown, setting up for possibilities of her demise.

Jimmy, not eating or sleeping, was also playing right into everything.

They needed to keep the family close, though. They needed to prolong their misery.

The only way they could accomplish that was to make sure the family needed to stay on the island.

Now to make sure that goal came to fruition.

Plans needed to be made.

They couldn't be found out.

Chapter Twenty-Nine

Love and Loss

The police finished interviewing Allison and Jack, and they headed off the island and back to the city. As much as they felt for the family and their grief, it thoroughly freaked them out. Melissa's words echoed in their minds, and the eerie silence of the inhabitants after she spoke the words made David's tragic death almost prophetic. It had been a whirlwind of a night between the blizzard and David's death.

Timothy was sad to see his family leave in one respect, and in another, he wanted them off the island, where they could be safe. However, their goodbyes were short, and they promised to stay in touch.

Jessica just wanted to crawl back into her bed. She tried to cover up with the blankets and disappear into the dream world where her sister and brother were still happily alive. Where Samantha visited her, and they shared secrets again. Where David was happy and free. But sleep was eluding her. Making her face the grim reality of her life. When she joined the others in the dining room, she sensed a shift in their world.

There was tension between Danielle and Richard Jr. It was so thick. Their body language showed a divide in their relationship. Danielle sat at the dining room table with her arms folded, deep in thought. Richard Jr. was in a deep discussion across the room with Jimmy about upping security measures, his back to Danielle. They seemed as if they were in two separate worlds.

Jessica observed and felt sad for them both. She wondered what was going on with them and whether they could patch things up. Then, abruptly, Danielle got up from the table and left the room. Richard Jr. didn't even seem to notice. However, he noticed when she returned with two suitcases. Looking at her, confused.

"What are those for?"

"I am going home. I need space from this place. And from you, from us. I will be here for David's funeral, but I can't stay here anymore. This place is filled with evil. Melissa was right."

Finishing her statement, she took the engagement ring off her finger.

She handed it to Richard Jr. She kissed him on the cheek, with tears streaming down her face, and walked out the door to her car. Richard Jr. Stood there in complete shock. His worst fear had just materialized before his eyes. It splintered the rest of his heart into a thousand pieces.

Part of him wanted to run after Danielle and beg her to stay, and the other part of him said even though he was hurting, this was the best thing for both of them. This way, he knew she would be safe forever.

Jessica watched in awe. *Was that a ring she just handed back? When did that happen?* She was confused and heartbroken for her brother.

Jimmy put his hand on Richard Jr.'s shoulder.

"Sorry, man. I know that has to hurt."

"She's gotta do what she's gotta do. And I gotta do what I gotta do. Right now, my focus is catching this psychopath who is killing our family. We all know deep down this was no accident. And we all know deep down that Samantha and Zach didn't overdose. So, how are we going to stop this person from killing us all off?"

Richard Jr. finally verbalized what they were all feeling. He was right. They all knew it. Danielle knew it. She was the smart one. She left.

At that moment, Jessica craved the solitude of her previous life. She may have felt lonely, but at least she was safe. Then she felt guilty for even thinking that. Jessica loved Timothy and her biological family. With love came risk. She knew that. She just never thought it would be her life at risk.

Adding to Jimmy's stress with upping security measures, Matt Zimmerman had notified him he was retiring and moving off the island. Losing Zach was too much for them. He and his wife were moving to upstate New

York to be closer to their only living child, Melissa. That meant security was missing three men, leaving them even more short-staffed.

They spent the next couple of days preparing for David's funeral. It seemed like Déjà vu for them all. They were tired and weary of all the loss.

Mira and Richard stayed up in their room except for meals. Mira had spiraled into a deep depression, and Richard was desperately trying to help her through it. The guilt he felt about everything that had happened to his family increased daily. He fully believed all that was occurring was karma for the sins he had committed in his life.

Contemplating ending it all, he thought maybe Mary had the right idea. Perhaps he could release his karma and spare his family any more heartache. But then Richard knew Mira could not live without him. Losing him would end her beautiful life, and he could not do that to her. He could not put his children through any more loss, either.

The Zimmermans said their goodbyes to the Gardiners the day before David's funeral. They had apologized, but they would not be there to attend. They explained they just couldn't handle another funeral of someone so young. The Gardiners understood.

Before they left, Melissa found Jimmy alone.

"I am sorry for slapping you the other day. I was angry and hurt. But I meant every word I said. I will not be back, ever. I convinced my parents to leave. So now I have no reason to come back. I love you, Jimmy, I always have, But I can't live here. So if you ever leave, look me up."

Melissa gave Jimmy a quick kiss on the cheek.

"I can't leave. My family is here. I love you, Melissa. I always have and always will, but this is my home. Like it or not."

"Take your mother and father with you, Jimmy. Save yourself and them from the evil that surrounds this place."

"They aren't my only family here."

As he let the words tumble out of his mouth. The secret that he had kept for months, he turned and walked away from the love of his life. He didn't want her to see the tears forming in his eyes.

The realization that he had an obligation to the Gardiner family, to his family, weighed heavily on his shoulders. He wished he could take his adoptive parents and run, but he couldn't.

Instead, he had to face the evil and try to bring it to justice. Maybe if he did, Melissa could return, and they could have their happily ever after.

Melissa stood there, stunned. She didn't understand the words he had spoken. Not at first. Later, she thought about his sudden move to the Manor house after the deaths of Alexandria and Mary. Then it clicked. He had to be some long-lost Gardiner relative.

The wheels in her mind turned. The stories about Mary Gardiner's child that she had lost. They explored every inch of Gardiners Island as kids, including the family cemetery. They had seen the infant's grave. But, there were warnings not to ever bring it up to Ms. Mary.

Zach had told her all about Samantha's sister, Jessica, and the scandal surrounding her birth and adoption. But he didn't tell her Jimmy was also a Gardiner. Wouldn't Zach have known? Maybe he didn't. Maybe there was a reason they kept his secret. Could Jimmy be that child?

Melissa thought about the deer carcasses Zach had told her about. Whoever was killing those deer was clearly a psychopath. She had done enough studying of psychology to know that. It hit her like a ton of bricks. She needed answers from Jimmy. When she got home, she would sit down and write him a letter. The drive home was torturous.

David's funeral was small, with mostly family. At least this time, the weather was sunny, even with the snow-covered ground. Joe showed up, and when everyone else had headed back to the ballroom for the luncheon, he quietly placed a bouquet of white roses on David's casket.

Jessica was the only one who witnessed this act of love. As she did, tears streamed down her face. Then she approached Joe and hugged him.

"Thank you for loving my brother when he didn't know how to love himself."

Pawns

The Lyons Garden Book Three

D.M. Foley

REMEMBER MY ROOTS PRESS

Prologue Three

"In life, as in chess, one's own pawns block one's way. A man's very wealth, ease, leisure, children, books, which should help him win, more often checkmate him." CHARLES BUXTON

Chapter One

Surprises

Jessica's heart hurt. Her chest was still tight. She found it hard to catch her breath. The tightness, caused by losing her sister, her best friend, left a gaping hole in her universe, which was unbearable. She only just functioned after the death of her youngest brother, days after her sister's death.

Each week, the calls from Anne, her agent, went unanswered by Jessica. This had Timothy, her fiancé, worried. His editor called with jobs for both of them as well. He declined each time. Jessica was in no shape to work. He could not fathom leaving her in this mental state.

The tightness in her chest had gotten worse.

"I think you should get checked in the emergency room, just to make sure nothing more serious is going on with you."

"It's just grief, Timothy. No one has died of a broken heart."

"I am not so sure of that. Do you want to be the first one? That isn't what I want. We are going to the hospital to get you checked out."

"Okay. But, I am telling you, it will be a waste of time."

The drive to the hospital was short. In the emergency room, when Jessica filled out the form stating she had chest tightness and some breathing issues, they brought her into triage right away. Jessica tried to understate what she was experiencing while the nurse took her blood pressure and other vital signs.

"There is nothing wrong. My fiancé wants me to get checked out. I think it's just grief and stress. Within days of each other, I lost two of my siblings."

"I am sorry for your loss. It could be just the stress of your losses. However, your fiancé is correct in getting you checked out. I am sure he doesn't want to lose you."

The kind nurse made a valid point, and Jessica looked at Timothy. His green eyes watched the nurse with scrutiny and paid close attention to the numbers she was writing. His brow furrowed, and he rubbed his cheek with his hand. She could tell he didn't understand the numbers, which added to his concern.

She reached for his hand, took it, and squeezed it. It was her attempt at reassuring him she would be okay. The nurse showed them to a cubicle with a hospital bed, and another nurse hooked up the leads to an EKG machine to check her heart.

The doctor came in to examine Jessica. After discussing her symptoms and the concerns Timothy had, he ordered a full workup of blood work to rule out anything serious.

The emergency room had a steady flow of patients. The nurses and doctors were working hard to take care of them all. Jessica felt guilty because she didn't feel she needed to be there. Timothy sat with patience by her bedside, praying nothing serious was wrong with her.

The doctor returned to the cubicle two hours later to discuss the test results.

"Ms. Greenhall, your heart is in great shape. You are not at risk of a heart attack. However, you are anemic. Could you be pregnant? Anemia is fairly common in pregnancy. You stated you had your last period eight weeks ago."

"Irregular periods are normal for me. I never considered being pregnant. However, now that you mention it. I've had a queasy stomach. I just attributed it to stress and emotions."

"We can run tests for pregnancy. We will go from there."

Timothy stared at Jessica. The possibility of the woman he loved carrying his child brought up a bunch of emotions. His heart fluttered, and his palms were sweating. He thought of being a dad. He grinned, trying to hide his terror.

Jessica returned from using the bathroom and provided the urine sample to be tested. The nurse drew more blood. She wasn't sure how to feel. Her dream was to be a mom. However, she feared the timing wasn't right. They still didn't know who was trying to kill the family. The thought of their child becoming a target swirled in her mind. She prayed the tests would come back negative.

While waiting for the results, Jessica voiced some of her concerns to Timothy.

"What will we do if I'm pregnant?"

"What do you mean what will we do? We are going to love this child with all our hearts. We want a family and we will make it all work."

"What about the issues on the island?"

"What about them? I won't let anything happen to you or our child, Jessica."

The doctor interrupted their conversation when he returned to the cubicle.

"Ms. Greenhall, the tests revealed you are indeed pregnant. Therefore, I will prescribe you some iron pills and prenatal vitamins. Also, I recommend you get in touch with your ObGyn Doctor as soon as possible."

Jessica's heart sank. Timothy squeezed her hand and looked into her eyes. What she saw was determination. His resolve erased her trepidation.

"Oh, thank you, Doc. I will."

A nurse came in and gave Jessica her discharge papers. As they left the emergency room, Jessica felt a range of emotions. The tightness in her chest eased up. A warmth radiated from her heart as if the pieces were mending together again. Hours earlier, hopelessness filled her, and she struggled to hold on to the will to live. Now, she would do everything to keep this child growing inside her safe. Keeping the secret would be vital until they felt the threats against them were gone.

"Are you okay, Jess? You are extra quiet."

"Yes, I am fine. We can't tell anyone about this. No one. And we must move up the wedding date. Perhaps move the wedding off the island altogether."

"Whatever you want, dear. I want to keep you happy and safe. Both of you."

Timothy was beaming at Jessica, stealing glances at her while driving them home.

"It's just I want to keep our child safe. I still feel like there is a black cloud following us around. And I am scared."

"I understand. We will call Jimmy and tell him we changed the wedding date because of everything. I still think we can have it on the island. If we change that, I think we will raise more suspicions."

"Okay, but how will we keep ourselves safe on the island? Every time we go there, someone dies. I feel like I am the bringer of death."

"Jess, honey, you are not the reason they died. Samantha and David would never want you to feel guilt for their deaths. If we have a girl, we can name her Samantha, and if it's a boy, we can name him David."

The tears trickled down Jessica's cheeks. Timothy always had the answers. The idea of naming their child after either her sister or her brother helped to soothe her broken heart. Whether their baby was a boy or girl, they cherished and loved them already.

They had ordered some food from Village Pizza and picked it up on their way home. Jessica realized hunger ravaged her. The barbeque chicken pizza hit the spot. After dinner, they set about calling Jimmy to let him know they needed to move the wedding date to April second. That would give them four weeks to throw the wedding together. Jessica prayed that their caterer, photographer, and DJ would all be available for the new date.

Jessica dialed Jimmy's number. Her heart raced, and her brows furrowed when it took a couple of rings for him to answer. Usually, he was quick to pick up the phone. She breathed a sigh of relief when he answered.

"Hey Jimmy, how are you doing?"

"Oh hey Jessica, I guess I am doing as well as expected. And how are you doing?"

"Honestly, I am struggling. I'm trying to get back to normal, but it's hard processing everything that happened."

"Understandable. You have suffered a terrible loss."

"About all that. Any leads?"

Jimmy took a deep breath and released it. He wished he could tell his cousin they had something to point them toward who had been terrorizing the family. He sought evidence that her sister and brother's deaths were not accidents, as they suspected. But he couldn't find any.

"None. Rich and I have been working nonstop to figure it all out. I think he is working harder than I am. To keep his mind off the loss of your siblings. Not to mention the breakup."

"I appreciate everything you two are doing. Since you mentioned the breakup. I am thinking of asking Danielle to take Samantha's place as my maid of honor. But I know I need to talk to Rich first."

"I'm not sure he will be okay with that. Keep in mind also that Danielle might not even set foot on the island again."

"I will talk to him and to her. On another note. Concerning the wedding. Tim and I have changed the date to April second. I hope that is okay. I know it is short notice and all. We want to bring some happiness to the family after all that has happened."

"Of course, Jessica, whatever you two want is okay with me. I might hire outside security, though, for that day. To be extra safe. We are still understaffed with the loss of Zach and Matt from the security team."

"I appreciate that, Jimmy. I knew you would understand."

"Of course. Hey, your brother just walked in. You want to talk to him now?"

"I might as well, thanks."

Jimmy handed the phone to Richard Jr.

"Hey Rich, how are you holding up?"

"Eh, I am hanging in there, and you?"

"I am coming out of my fog. However, I need to make some decisions regarding the wedding."

"What does that mean for me? Unless you guys have eloped."

"No eloping here. With Samantha gone, I have no maid of honor."

Richard Jr. winced at the mention of his kid sister's name.

"What do you want me to do? Be your maid of honor and be Timothy's best man? Wear half of a dress and half of a tux?"

"Hilarious. No, I don't have a lot of close girlfriends. But Samantha and Danielle are the closest best friends I have ever had."

Closing his eyes at the mention of Danielle's name. He felt the ache in his heart. The realization hit him that his sister was asking his permission to ask his ex-fiancée to be her maid of honor. He didn't want to hurt his sister any more than she was already hurting. The need to swallow his pride and deal with the pain of losing Danielle to appease his sister was overwhelming.

"Jess, if you need to, ask Danielle, and if she accepts. I will have no problem. Of course, seeing her will hurt. I love her and always will."

"Thank you, Rich. I love you."

"Love you too, Sis."

Jessica hated hurting her brother more than he was already hurting. She hoped that maybe there was some redemption in his and Danielle's relationship. The hope of getting them back together at the wedding was there. Her next phone call was to Danielle.

"Hey Danielle, how are you doing?"

"I am okay, Jess. How are you? I can't imagine what you're going through."

"Thanks. I am doing okay. I am calling to ask you something."

"Jess, I can't go back to Richard Jr. right now. If that is what you are thinking."

"No, of course not. I can understand your concerns, but you know Rich still loves you."

"I'm aware. The love I feel for him is still there, too. That's why I let him go."

"Would you be able to handle seeing him for just one day? For me?"

"I don't know... it's hard. He was my best friend."

"I understand. Samantha was my best friend, and losing her has been the worst thing I have ever dealt with."

"I am so sorry."

"It's okay. You are my next closest girlfriend, Danielle. That's why I want you to be my maid of honor."

"Oh my, Jess. It would be my honor. Yes, I will suck up my feelings for one day. As I am sure, he will too."

"Thank you. Oh, we moved the date to April second, though."

"Okay. Tell me what to do."

Jessica felt a renewed sense of excitement about the wedding as she talked to Danielle about what she needed help with. When they hung up, she had begun to feel some hope that the wedding would be perfect. But she just had one more phone call to make. She needed to have some legal documents done.

Arthur was more than happy to help her and Timothy. Divulging their secret to him, he swore to secrecy. It was an attorney-client privilege, anyway. Together, they made sure their future child would be secure if something happened to them.

Chapter Two

Truths

Jimmy got off the phone with Jessica and stared at the envelope he had been holding. The name on the return address shocked him. Melissa Zimmerman. Just seeing her name on the envelope made his heart beat faster. He never expected to hear from her again after Zach's funeral.

He slid his finger under the flap and opened it up. It was a letter written on pink stationery with her flowing cursive handwriting. The faint smell of her perfume lingered on the paper. His eyes closed and his mind wandered to their younger years. The sweet memories of holding her hand and walking her home after school every day. He unfolded the letter and braced himself for what the letter might contain.

Dear Jimmy,

I hope this letter finds you well. My thoughts have revolved around what you said the last time we saw each other. Something you said made little sense to me. You said your parents are not your only family on the island. This has me thinking. Are you alluding that you are a relation to the Gardiners?

That is the only way your comment makes sense. It would explain why you were living in the Manor house as well. It is hard for me to figure out where your connection to them is. I know the Driscolls adopted you, as does everyone on the island, so I know there is a possibility that your biological parents somehow are part of the Gardiner family. I just don't know exactly who or how.

I know none of this is my business. However, it will help me understand why you won't choose me over the island. I believe you still love me as much as I love you. I see it in the way you look at me and I felt it in the bar when you kissed me. If you don't, and I am reading you all wrong, then I will understand if you do not answer this letter.

Your Friend Always,

Melissa

Jimmy was shell-shocked. Right there in black and white, Melissa had admitted she still loved him. She wanted him to choose her. He hadn't chosen her. Guilt rose in his chest. The desire to choose her was there. It had always been there. He felt so anchored to the island he grew up on, though, and he didn't know why. Up in his room, he found some stationery and started writing a response to Melissa.

Dear Melissa,

With everything that has occurred in the last several months here on the island, I am as well as I can be. I guess I should never have mentioned that in our last encounter, but since I did, I suppose I owe you some sort of explanation.

Yes, I am a Gardiner. My mother was Mary Gardiner. My father was Benjamin Timmons. They were having an affair behind Richard's back. Unknown to both of them, Benjamin was Richard's half-brother. The doctor revealed this information to Alexandria when she forced Mary to have a paternity test through amniocentesis. She had caught Mary and Benjamin in the act one day. It was through that testing that Alexandria found out who Benjamin was, although she did not share that information with them. When she found out Richard was not my father, she forced them to agree to put me up for adoption. They all conspired to tell Richard I died at birth. On Alexandria's deathbed, she revealed these secrets to me and my cousin Jessica. After we had agreed to DNA testing, to verify we were both Gardiner heirs.

While I am spilling my guts, I must confess. I do not believe your brother's death was an overdose. I believe his death was not accidental. A psychopath is targeting the Gardiner family.

I know your brother spoke to you about the deer carcass. He did so, per my request. There have been four. After each one except the last one, we found the hearts in the rooms of my cousins.

We believe we are all in danger, or at least those that are known Gardiners. I don't seem to be a target, since it is not public knowledge that I am a Gardiner. There is more. Jessica and Timothy intercepted Christmas presents that were addressed to each family member, except me. They were dead crows. We have researched the symbolism and have taken them as death threats. I will not sleep until I bring justice to this crazy killer. It is unfortunate we feel Zach was collateral damage because of his relationship with Samantha.

Love Always and Forever,

Jimmy

The letter sat in front of him. He folded it and put it in an envelope. Jimmy tucked it into the inside of his jacket. Since it was his day off, he could go to the mainland and put it into the mail. Melissa deserved some answers. He didn't know if it would help her or hurt her.

"Where are you headed to, my son?"

Stella was working in the kitchen as Jimmy walked through and headed towards the door.

"I have some errands to run. I will be home in time for dinner if Rich asks where I am."

Jimmy and Richard Jr. had become closer through all the craziness and he had called him Rich to distinguish his cousin from his uncle. They had become more adamant about sharing information as well. It helped them both to feel less anxious about the serial killer stalking the family.

"Okay, Jimmy. I will let him know. Be safe. I love you."

"I love you too, Ma."

Stella was very aware of the danger her son was in. She wished she could protect him. There was no way she could, though.

Jimmy took the ferry to the mainland. When he dropped the letter off at the post office, his heart raced. There was no taking back the information he shared. He hoped the information was enough to placate Melissa's curiosity. As much as he loved her, he prayed she stayed away. He could not stand the thought of anything happening to her.

While on the mainland, he stopped at the police station. He had asked for copies of all the police reports pertaining to the Gardiner family tragedies. The hope was that he could find something, anything, to lead him to clues about who was tormenting the family.

"Hey Jimmy, here are those reports you wanted."

Sergeant Rollins handed Jimmy the reports. They were friends from their high school days. Jimmy appreciated the professional courtesy he was being afforded.

"Thanks, Rolly. I appreciate the help. If I come across anything, I will let you know."

"You are welcome, Jimmy. I want answers too. If there is a serial killer in the area, that affects everyone."

"Rolly, as I explained before, I don't think this killer has aspirations to kill anyone other than the Gardiners. But if I have any inclination that things have changed, I will let you know."

Jimmy had some time before he was due back for dinner. He headed to his office and started going through the reports. When Richard Jr. came into the security shack from patrolling, he just shook his head.

"Man, you are such a workaholic."

"I know I am. I can't rest right now, though. The bodies are piling up. And now with Jessica and Timothy pushing up their wedding date. I am eager to keep them safe."

"Yeah, I understand the anxiety. Did she tell you who she replaced as maid of honor?"

"Yeah, bud. I am sorry. That's gotta be rough."

"I will be fine. I just hope we can keep everyone safe."

"Yeah, me too."

Jimmy went back to poring through the reports. He smiled when he realized his buddy had also added the coroner's reports. Good old Rolly. Even though they came from different backgrounds, he had been the one true mainlander friend he had made back in high school.

Alexandria's accident/ homicide report was first. As he read through it, nothing new jumped out at him. He read through the pages of statements from those who had been in the house. Arthur, Stella, Martin, Betty, Mary, Jessica, and Timothy. Everyone seemed to have a reliable alibi, except Mary. Therefore, when Mary committed suicide and left a note stating she had pushed Alexandria, they closed the case. He reread Alexandria's statement made from her hospital bed.

It stated, "Victim states the perpetrator pushed her down the stairs. When asked by whom she mumbled something, got the sound b, out, and then went unconscious again. I assume she was attempting to say by. When asked the next time she awoke, she could not remember."

She knew. Alexandria had known who had pushed her. The injuries to her brain must have affected her memory. This knowledge only frustrated Jimmy even more.

As he read the statements, he pictured in his mind where everyone in the house was at the time of the incident. Stella had been in the kitchen, still cleaning up after dinner. Martin was cleaning the dining room. Betty was upstairs making sure all the guests had what they needed and checking on Mary. She stated Mary had not responded to her knock on her bedroom door. Mary had gone to her room earlier in the evening. Betty had assumed she had passed out. According to her statement, Mary said she only recalled she had drunk wine in her room. Timothy had been in Jessica's room with her. Arthur was taking a shower in his room. *Maybe Mary had been the one to push Alexandria?*

There was a knock on his office door. It was Samuel.

"Hey, Jimmy. I was wondering if I could have a few days off. I want to go away for the weekend with my lady friend."

"Sure, Samuel. Have a good time."

"Thanks. We will."

Jimmy rubbed his temples with his fingers. The answers had to be right in front of him. He closed Alexandria's file and opened Mary's.

This was going to be difficult. The scene etched in his mind of his biological mother's death. Reading through everything, nothing seemed out of the ordinary. Open and shut case of suicide. The toxicology report confirmed lethal doses of Xanax and alcohol. The tears welled up in his eyes. It seemed as if Mary's suicide was legit. The only thing that still didn't fit was the fact she could not have tried drowning Jessica. So why would she confess to that? Is there someone she could have been covering for?

Who was Mary close to? Then it hit him. Samuel. The one beneficiary of her estate. The one who seemed to care for her in a more intimate way by leaving flowers at her grave. Jimmy put his jacket on and headed to the garage. He needed answers. It was time to be blunt.

Samuel was under the tractor tinkering when Jimmy walked into the garage.

"Hey Samuel, you got a moment?"

"Sure."

Samuel rolled out from under the tractor.

"Look, I need answers. I am not explaining why I need to know them. All I am going to say is they are security-related."

"Okay. What do you need to know?"

"What was the relationship between Mary Gardiner and you?"

Samuel winced at the question. He shoved his hands into the pockets of his pants. It had been a while since he thought about Mary and their relationship. That was a part of his past he was eager to forget.

"I am going to answer only because you are in charge of security, otherwise I would tell you it's none of your damn business. Ms. Mary hired me. We met in town one day. I was having a hard time finding a job because of my injuries from an accident. I told her I had grown up on Gardiners Island, however, I had moved away for a while. She asked me what my skill set was. I told her I was a mechanic. She hired me. We became friends. I wanted more than friendship. She couldn't see herself with a lowly mechanic. When she had too much to drink, however, she came to visit me. She shared my bed frequently."

"You were lovers."

The revelation shocked Jimmy. It made him reflect. Could Mary have been protecting Samuel? He knew he had to be careful with his next questions.

"I guess you could have called us that, yes. Not in public, though. Except for once, she had me escort her to her cousin's wedding."

"Did you ever go to her in the Manor house?"

"Yes, occasionally, when she would call me to come to her."

"How did you avoid anyone else seeing you go to her?"

"She showed me the passageways."

Samuel knew about the passageways, and so did Mary.

"Did Mary tell you why she had tried drowning Jessica?"

"No, she didn't tell me anything about Jessica. It shocked me she confessed to that. She had come out to the garage the day I showed Jessica and

Timothy the osprey nests on the ATVs. I didn't see her touch any of the ATVs, though."

Jimmy believed him. There was no reason for him to lie. Everything Samuel had said was unverifiable and Samuel knew it. It would have been easier for him to lie and say there was no relationship. Jimmy was back to square one.

Chapter Three

Connecting Dots

Melissa opened her mailbox. The pile of bills was not new. No surprises, as she shuffled through them. Until she reached the letter. Her jaw dropped. It had been only a couple of days since she sent the letter to Jimmy and here there was already a response. Her hands shook. The urge to rip open the letter was great. However, she could wait until she entered the house.

She didn't want her father to see her open the letter and ask questions, so she went up to her bedroom. There were flutters of nerves in her belly. The bed gave her some stability as she sat and read the words he wrote. The words on the page swirled in her mind. Psychopath. Murderer. He was a Gardiner. Zach's death might not have been an accident. As she read those words, her blood boiled. Questions started flooding her mind. Did her father know this information? She needed answers. Now.

When she stormed into the living room and assessed her mother was still out with friends, she knew she could unleash on her father.

"What exactly do you know about Zach's death?"

Her father looked up at her, puzzled. The anger in her voice was accusatory. The small pang of guilt stabbed at her heart.

"What do you mean, Melissa? Zach and Samantha died of an overdose. Nothing less and nothing more. Why are you bringing up such a painful subject?"

"What about the deer carcasses, Dad? On the island. What else are you keeping from me? What about Jimmy?"

"Woah, how do you know there was more than one carcass? I am not keeping anything from you. The deer deaths on the island have no connection to Zach and Samantha's death. Yes, there is a psychopath killing the deer and tormenting the family with their hearts. What are you getting at asking about Jimmy?"

Melissa realized her father didn't seem to know anything about what Jimmy had told her in the letter.

"You really don't know, do you? Jimmy is a Gardiner, Dad. He was Mary's child. She had an affair with Richard's half-brother. She put the child up for adoption and lied about his death. Jimmy seems to think Zach's death was no accident."

"Hold on a second. What?"

Matt shook his head and couldn't understand the information his daughter was sharing with him. His heart hurt. The realization of what she was saying, and the implications, was just too much for him. He got up out of his chair and went to the kitchen. The beer he cracked open and took a swig of, choked back the tears welling up in his throat.

Melissa's demeanor shifted. Her stance softened as she followed her father into the kitchen and grabbed a beer for herself.

"You really didn't know. I am sorry. He loves me, Daddy, but he can't leave the island because of the family obligation. They are all in danger, except for him for now. That is only because it isn't public knowledge he is a Gardiner."

Matt looked at his daughter. She was a beautiful soul and deserved to find the right guy. Years ago, he felt that guy had been Jimmy. Guilt flooded him. How could he have missed all those connections? He had worked security for so many years side by side with Jimmy's dad and then Jimmy. He was a good kid. Now, knowing details he hadn't known before, he could understand the added stress Jimmy seemed to be under.

The guilt of leaving weighed heavily on his heart and mind. As he looked at his daughter, though, he knew he couldn't go back. He would do what he could to help Jimmy and the Gardiner family find the truth. So he went into the den and picked up the phone.

Jimmy sat in his office, poring over the reports for the fiftieth time. Nothing jumped out at him to point him in any direction. Each report led to more questions than answers. He jumped when the phone on his desk rang. Looking at the caller id, his brows furrowed when he saw Matt Zimmerman. Did he want to have this conversation right at this moment? Reluctantly, he answered.

"Hey Matt, how is retirement treating you? I hope all is well with you and the family."

"We are all doing as best as we can, Jimmy. I need answers, though. Melissa thinks I am holding back information. She filled me in on what you wrote. A lot makes sense to me now. I even understand why you kept it all secretive."

"I am sorry, Matt. It must be hard knowing I kept information from you. The premise was to keep everyone safe, but I failed."

"You didn't fail. We failed. It's a team effort. Even though I am no longer employed there and part of the team, I will do what I can from here."

"I appreciate the help. Can I send you copies of the reports I received from Rolly? Or would that be too much to ask? I don't want to open the wounds any wider than they already are."

"Send them, Jimmy. I will deal with the wounds. If it helps prevent more deaths and helps us get justice, I will gladly suffer."

"Thank you. I will make copies and put them in the mail. Yes, you can share it with Melissa. She might give us some valuable insight. The more eyes, the better at this point. Timothy and Jessica have moved up their wedding, and it is still here on the island. I need to keep them safe."

"I will do what I can."

"Thank you, Matt. And I am sorry I didn't trust you earlier."

"It's all good, kid."

Matt hung up the phone and went to get another beer. Melissa was sitting at the table brooding over the letter Jimmy had sent. She was deep in thought, almost in a trance. Then she looked up at her father with a look of complete understanding, as if a light bulb had turned on in her head. She pushed away from the table, stood up, and left the room.

"It all makes sense now."

The words trailed behind her as she ran upstairs. Matt just shook his head. When Melissa got to her room, she grabbed a pen and stationery and wrote a letter back to Jimmy.

Dear Jimmy,

Thank you for your honest response to my last letter. We are committing to helping you figure this all out. In doing so. I need to be completely honest with you.

It all makes sense now. Everything. Leaving the island was not a choice I wanted to make. I had to. Someone knows. Someone knew all those years ago that you are a Gardiner.

They didn't want us to be together. They warned me many times in numerous ways to leave you be. To leave the island. I was young and scared.

I found notes written to me to leave the island. To leave you. Warning me you were evil. Warning me that if I stayed, the evil would overcome me. I found dead crows at my window all the time. I wish you would leave the island too. I fear for your safety. Please be careful. I love you.

Love Always and Forever,

Melissa

Jimmy had followed through with his promise. He copied every report and overnighted it to Matt. The first report Matt started with was Alexandria's. Nothing jumped out at him. He understood Jimmy's frustration. Knowing Alexandria seemed to have known her attacker at first, but then couldn't remember. When he got to Zach's and Samantha's report, he choked back the tears. Reading the details didn't help him forget his loss. The toxicology report killed him to read. The list of drugs found in their system, alcohol, fentanyl, heroin, and trace amounts of GBH. Nothing they didn't already know. He still couldn't believe his son willingly injected himself, or Samantha. Neither of them were the type to do drugs. However, Matt was not naïve to the fact addiction could hit anyone at any time.

When Jimmy received Melissa's second letter, he smiled. At least they were communicating. It brought a sense of peace to his broken heart. The realization of what she implied in the letter, though, left him speechless. This psychopath had started a long game years ago. Sabotaging his relationship with Melissa. That much forethought took patience. A psychopath with patience was scary. It showed that this person had waited in the wings for a long time to execute their plans. What caused them to speed them up, though? Then it hit him. If this person knew about him, why wasn't he being targeted? What was his role in this?

He had lived on the island his entire life. Oblivious to the fact he was a Gardiner by birth. No threats were directed towards him, ever. They still weren't. This still bothered him. And now, knowing they had threatened Melissa to stay clear of him all those years prior, he wondered why. The nagging in the back of his mind still drove him crazy. The beer cans had stopped, but he had stopped drinking completely as well.

In the meantime, Melissa read over the reports and the pictures Jimmy sent of the deer carcasses, hearts, and crows. The crows hit Melissa the hardest. She knew without a doubt the wheels of thought in this psychopath had been turning for quite a long time. Now they just needed to figure out who it was, and how to stop them.

Chapter Four

Weekend Plans

So, the family thought they could outsmart them? Jessica and Timothy changing their wedding date didn't change their plans one bit. Everything would still happen the way they wanted it to. They already had plans for the weekend that would help eliminate some obstacles.

Their plans were being executed flawlessly, with no fingers pointing at them. This made them so happy. The thought of one day soon having everything they ever wanted. No, everything they deserved. Everything that was rightfully theirs would come to fruition.

They would eliminate everyone that stood in their way. Everyone. No matter who it was. The power inside them grew. As it grew, their attraction to holding even more power grew. Others must have been able to feel their power because they were already attracting potential lovers. They had been seeing one regularly.

The thought of sharing their newfound life with a potential love interest was exciting to them. But they couldn't divulge their secrets to anyone. The Gardiners would pay for every misdeed and every transgression they ever endured because of their secrets. They would have the last laugh and the last of everything. Literally.

As they packed for their weekend getaway, they felt a sense of pride. A feeling they admittedly had never felt before. They certainly never felt pride or praise from their mother.

The thought of their birth vessel, as they had become accustomed to thinking of their mother, brought back anger, disgust, and hatred. They remembered the day they had found their birth certificate among their mother's possessions. They were seventeen. The questions their mother refused to answer.

Yet, the truth revealing in her demeanor. The look of fear in her eyes. Disgust consumed her when they looked at them. The reminder of who they were and what she was on the island.

That was the day their mother died. It was the day they had hatched the plan. The one that would eventually give them what was theirs by birthright.

It amazed them that no one found similarities between their mother's death and Mary's death. Although their mother had committed suicide decades before Mary. And, of course, their mother was just a lowly inhabitant of the island. No one of importance, replaceable. In fact, they replaced her position within days of her passing.

That had been their first human kill. The first boost in energy. They had left the island for a period afterward and came back. No one had missed them when they were gone. That was the blessing of obscurity.

The blessing of no one caring who they were or what they did. They had always blended into the crowd. Seen and unseen all at once. No prestige or position of power in life. Yet. It would come.

They would be sure to manifest their destiny and bring about the changes necessary for them to become who they were. With no regard for who they hurt in the process. No one had cared about them all these years. Why should they care about snuffing out the very essence of those who never cared?

Their lunch break was over, and their packing was complete. After their shift today, they would leave the island and take a trip to set in motion the next aspect of their grand plan.

Chapter Five

More Tragedy

Grief still engrossed Mira over losing Samantha and David. Her manicured nails had a chipped and rugged look to them. The curls in her red hair matted together to her head. Richard had to coax her to shower or bathe every other day. Eating had become almost nonexistent to her. Richard was content if he could get her to eat bites of toast and jelly along with sips of herbal tea. Her cheeks had become hollow and her eyes had as well. The sadness consumed her.

Richard's concern for Mira absorbed him and took over his grief. He mourned the loss of his children, but he was terrified of losing Mira. She had been his whole life and world for so long. He had given up everything for her and now he felt on the brink of losing her, too.

When their house phone rang, they were both surprised. Very few people had their home phone number, let alone called it. They had almost forgotten they still had it. Both had been ignoring texts and calls on their cell phones by well-meaning family and friends checking on them. It was Mira that answered the annoying ring of the phone.

"Hello?"

"Hi Mira, it's Lena. I have been trying to reach you every day on your cell. I know nothing I say or do will take away your pain. You are my oldest and best friend, though, and you and Richard should not have to go through all this alone. Steven and I are coming up for a visit this weekend."

"Lena, I appreciate the concern, but we aren't up for company."

"We aren't taking no for an answer. We won't stay at your house. But we are coming and we are going to throw you a small dinner party. Just the four of us. We will do all the work. Let us spoil and take care of you."

"Lena. We aren't up for it."

"Mira, you will never be up for it. Take small steps. Samantha and David would want you to keep living."

Mira closed her eyes at the mention of her children's names. Deep down, she knew her best friend was right. They would not want her wallowing in her self-pity and grief. They would want her to live her life to the fullest.

"Okay. Okay, you can visit. I am a mess. My house is a mess. I don't even know what food we have in the house."

"No worries. In the morning, we'll be over. We will pick up groceries. We will clean the house. You and Richard, clean yourselves up. Take care of yourself. Take a long soaking bath."

The tears streamed down Mira's face.

"Oh Lena, thank you for always knowing what to do or say. You are the best friend anyone could have. Thank you."

"No, thanks needed. That's what friends do. I love you. See you tomorrow!"

"Love you too."

As she hung up, Mira felt overwhelmed by the kind gesture from her oldest friend in the world. She followed her friend's suggestion and took a long soaking bath. Shampooing and conditioning her hair. It took a couple of comb-throughs to get all the tangles and mats out.

Richard was waiting downstairs with the Chinese takeout. Mira smiled. Her hunger had not returned. However, the gesture reminded her of the tender, caring nature of her husband. She couldn't refuse to eat. As the rice and vegetables hit her taste buds, she savored the flavors she hadn't had in some time. To her amazement, she finished the entire meal. There was a renewed sense of energy in her. Richard sensed the shift in mood and he relaxed his guard a bit. He smiled and took her hand in his.

Leading the way upstairs, he took her to their bedroom and loved her the way they had at the start of their relationship. It was the first tenderness they had shared in weeks. The moment brought peacefulness to them both. As they lay together in their bed, Mira shared the discussion with Lena through tears of grief, comfort, and peace.

They fell asleep in each other's arms, content for the first time since the tragic loss of their two youngest children.

True to Lena's form, she and Steven showed up bright and early the next morning. Mira gave Lena a long gripping hug, conveying her gratitude towards her lifelong friend. The four of them got to work cleaning the house, stocking the cabinets with food, and all the little things Mira and Richard had put off doing over the last few weeks.

At dinner time, the four friends sat and shared memories of their children growing up together. They laughed and cried while they ate the meal Lena had prepared for them all. When they finished, they all retired to the living room to finish drinking wine and visiting.

A knock at the door disturbed their conversation. Richard got up to answer the door. Much to his surprise, he found Samuel and Rita standing on the threshold of his doorway.

"Richard! Samuel and I are spending the weekend here in Boston and I couldn't be here and not swing by to see my daughter's best friend and the love of her life!"

Stunned by the surprise visit, Richard ushered them both in.

"Rita, Samuel, come in. How nice of you both to surprise us like this. Your daughter- and son-in-law are here visiting as well."

"I thought I recognized the car in the driveway! I knew it wasn't yours with the New York license plates."

As they joined the others in the living room, they exchanged hugs with all.

"Mother, what are you doing here?"

"Lena, I am visiting a dear friend, just as you are. Is that not allowed?"

They could cut the tension between mother and daughter with a knife. It was clear Lena did not approve of Rita's new beau.

"You can visit whomever you choose to. I am just surprised, that's all. You have been scarce with visiting anyone."

Mira felt the tension and wanted to help her friend.

"Rita, I am thrilled you and Samuel stopped by for a visit. The more the merrier, right Lena? Isn't that what you were trying to do, anyway? Let's go get more wine."

Steven, Richard, and Samuel started discussing fishing while Rita, Lena, and Mira went into the kitchen to gather more wine and wine glasses. When they returned, the men were in the middle of discussing a fishing trip.

"I hope this trip won't involve a boat?"

Mira couldn't help having flashbacks to the past and the sailboat accident Richard had survived.

"Oh, hell no! My feet will stay planted on shore, my dear."

"I concur. I am not a fan of boats myself."

Samuel shuddered as he stated his affirmation against a boating trip, too.

The friends finished several bottles of wine before the guests headed back to their respected hotel rooms. Richard and Mira were both feeling pretty drunk and hugged their friends, thanking them all for the great visit.

Mira stumbled up the stairs, fumbling with her clothes as she got ready for bed. Followed by Richard, who was also stumbling up the stairs. They both quickly passed out from the amount of alcohol they had consumed.

Smoke burned Richard's nostrils and woke him from his slumber. Frozen in his bed, he choked on the smoke filling the room. He tried to yell to wake up Mira. The terrifying truth was he could not speak or move. As the flames engulfed him and his lovely wife, he realized they were going to perish in the fire.

The heat of the flames woke Mira and she tried to move. Terror gripped her when she realized she could not speak or move. The blackness consumed her as she lost consciousness from the smoke and flames.

The sirens of the firetrucks wailed as they pulled up to the house. Flames, brightly flickering illuminating the pre-dawn sky, were engulfing the two-story home pushing out every window on arrival. Neighbors ran to the firefighters with terror-filled voices, telling them they believed the residents were still inside. When the rescue team assembled to go inside to search for the inhabitants, the command stopped them at the front door and told them it was too dangerous. The fire had grown too big to go inside without risking more lives. It became a surround and drown attack.

It took hours for the overhaul to become complete and for the remains of Mira and Richard to be found. When Lena and Steven pulled up to the scene, her heart was racing. A police officer stopped her from approaching too close. They watched in horror as officials carried two black body bags out of the house and put them in the coroner's van.

Lena felt faint, covering her face with her hands while dropping to her knees. Steven enfolded his wife in his arms as he tried to lift her and escort her to their car. Her best friend, they had been through so much together. The fear that Mira was gone forever gripped her with grief.

She had no siblings, and neither had Mira, so they were more like sisters. After getting Lena back to their car, Steven tried to get information from some officers on the scene. They couldn't confirm the identities of the two bodies found. The police would release the information when confirmation occurred and after the family notification was done.

The thought of Jessica and Richard Jr. learning of their parent's death snapped them back to reality. They needed to get home so they could be there for their friend's children. Too much tragedy had befallen the family already, and this was just another dreadful blow.

As they headed home, Lena knew she needed to call her mother. Rita was in Boston too, so she would certainly hear about the fire on the news. The cell phone rang several times before her mother picked up, and Lena rolled her eyes, thinking of what delayed her mother from answering.

"Hello, Lena. What may I owe this phone call from you for?"

"Mother, there has been a fire. A horrible fire! Mira and Richard might be dead. Their house is gone. They found two bodies. Identities not yet known."

Sobbing, Lena choked out the words. Not believing what she was saying could even be true, but knowing it was.

"Oh, my god! Please tell me this isn't true."

"I wish it wasn't, Mom. Steven and I are on our way home. The kids are going to need all of us to be there for them. "

"We will be on our way as well. Lena, I am so sorry. I know she was more than just a friend."

"Thank you, Mom."

It was a long trip home and Lena kept replaying the memories of her and Mira in her head. That first summer together, while she and Steven were off spending time with one another, Mira and Richard had started their secret affair. She recalled how she had found her friend clutching a breakup letter, and how she had rubbed her back and held her hair as she got sick. Neither of them realized at that moment Mira had been pregnant with Jessica.

As the memories poured through her mind, the tears freely streamed down her cheeks.

Chapter Six

More Bad News

Jimmy sat in his office. Things had been quiet on the island. The roar of an engine and tires on gravel pulling up to the security shack interrupted the stillness of his thoughts. When he realized it was Samuel, his concern peaked. Samuel was supposed to be out of town until Monday, and he rarely stopped at the security shack.

When Samuel came into the shack and came directly to Jimmy's office, the hair on the back of Jimmy's neck stood up.

"Is Richard Jr. around?"

Samuel reached up to the back of his neck and nervously rubbed at it.

"No, he is out doing rounds right now. Do you need to speak to him? I can radio to him to come back to the shack."

"No. No, I need to talk to you. Alone."

Samuel closed the office door behind him and sat down. The creases on his forehead were deep. Adding to the anticipation and anxiety, Jimmy was feeling about what he needed to talk about.

"Is everything okay, Samuel?"

"Honestly, I don't know, boy. As you know, I went away with Rita for the weekend. We went to Boston. She insisted we stop and visit Mira and Richard. They are old friends of hers. Lena and Steven were there visiting. The visit went well. Until this morning. Lena and Steven went to stop by again, but the house had burned. Two bodies found, not identified yet."

"Oh, my god. Are you telling me Mira and Richard are dead?"

"They could be. Don't know who else the bodies could be. I figured I would come home to the island early and give you a head up. I am sure someone will notify you as soon as they identify the bodies."

"Thanks, Samuel. Sorry, your weekend got cut short."

"It's okay. I just am getting creeped out by all these tragedies."

"Me too, man. Me too."

Samuel left the office and the shack. Jimmy sat in stunned silence. He had been in Boston himself, following up on investigating Samantha's death. He had talked to several of her past co-workers. Asked if she ever did drugs or any kind of illegal substances. They had all said no. She had been a straight-laced hard worker. Which they all said was commendable since in the restaurant industry substance abuse is prevalent.

Jimmy had even driven past Mira and Richard's house and had seen they had company, so he hadn't stopped. The nagging in the back of his mind came back, but he shook his head and dismissed the thoughts.

It wasn't until Jimmy and Richard Jr. were sitting down to dinner that the knock at the door Jimmy had been expecting disturbed them. Martin had led the state trooper into the dining room. Jimmy braced himself for the news and the reaction from Richard Jr.

"Good evening, sirs. Sorry to bother you at dinnertime and all. Unfortunately, I have some information to relay."

Jimmy and Rich both stood and motioned for the trooper to sit down. He stood, so they both stayed standing.

"We received word from the Massachusetts state police that there has been a fatal fire at your parent's residence, Richard. I am sorry. The coroner has confirmed this through dental records. Both your mother and father have perished. Your sister Jessica is being notified by the Connecticut state police as we speak. I am sorry for your loss."

Richard Jr. grabbed the back of his chair to steady himself. His thoughts raced as fast as his heart did. The pounding of his heart became deafening in his ears and his breathing quickened. His mom and dad were both dead. How could that be? He looked at his plate of food sitting on the table and immediately wanted to hurl.

Jimmy shook the trooper's hand and showed him to the door. When he returned to the dining room, Richard Jr. had sat down at the table with his head in his hands, sobbing.

"I am sorry, cuz. What can I do?"

Richard Jr. looked at Jimmy.

"Let's catch the son of a bitch that is killing our family. You know, and I know this was no accident."

"I know. There is nothing tying any of the deaths together, though. No commonality. How the hell do we figure out who is doing this?"

"I have to call my sister. This is going to devastate her even more. Maybe she should call off the wedding? At least move it off the island."

"Call her. Don't let her move the wedding off the island, though. That will give whoever it is control. We need to take back dominance. We will protect them."

"Okay. But how?"

"I have some ideas."

Richard Jr. composed himself and called Jessica. When she answered the phone in uncontrolled gasps, he knew they had notified her.

"Hey Jessica, I am calling to see how you are doing?"

"Rich, I can't. This can't be happening. It's like a bad dream. No nightmare. How could I find my biological family and lose all but two members in six months?"

"I know. It doesn't seem possible. We need to figure out who is killing us off before it's too late."

"But, how? We can't even connect any of the deaths to each other. They made them all seem like accidents. And occurred in various places."

"Wait, that's it!"

Richard Jr. looked at Jimmy while he was on the phone with Jessica

"What's it, Rich?"

"The commonality. They all seem like accidents! Now to pinpoint who had access to all the crime scenes and the family."

"You might be on to something. We need to plan to lay Mom and Dad to rest, though, first. Then focus on investigating the so-called accidents."

They made plans for Jimmy and Richard Jr. to go to her house the next day to discuss funeral arrangements for their parents. Then Richard Jr. made the call to Arthur to tell him the devastating news.

"Hi Arthur, sorry to bother you this evening. I have some bad news."

"Hello, Richard. I hope it's not another death. I can't handle anymore."

"Unfortunately, that is exactly what it is. Mom and Dad's house burned with them inside it. They did not survive. I know this might bring up your own terrible memories of how your family passed away. I am sorry."

"Oh, Richard. I am so sorry for your loss. Your Dad was a good man, despite some of his past decisions. Your Mom was smart and gracious. Do you need help with anything?"

"Actually, yes. Can you meet us tomorrow at Jessica's house to go over arrangements?"

"Absolutely, I will be there."

Richard Jr. and Jimmy played pool and brainstormed ideas on how to figure out who was targeting the family. Jimmy was careful not to have a beer when Richard Jr. grabbed one for himself. He was also careful not to mention the thoughts running through his head.

He was the last person to see Samantha and Zach. Granted, he didn't know if they were dead or alive at that moment, but he couldn't shake the guilt of not going to the car. Then he was the last person to see David alive. He was the one that told David to go upstairs and fly his drone out the window. Now, knowing he was also in Boston at the time of the fire that killed Mira and Richard, he couldn't help thinking the psychosis was back, and he was the one targeting the family.

Jimmy decided he would call his therapist the next day. He needed to get all of his concerns off his chest. He would tell her everything and let the chips fall where they may. The cost of keeping his thoughts secret was too much. Losing more of his family was too high of a price.

Richard had several beers. When he finally felt numb, he stumbled upstairs to his room. As he lay in his bed, his mind wandered to Danielle. It was late, and he was drunk, but he didn't care. He needed to talk to her. So he dialed her number.

"Hello, Richard? It's so late. Why are you calling me?"

"My parents are dead. I love you, Danielle. I need you. Please come see me tonight."

"What? Are you drunk? How are your parents dead? What happened? I love you too, Richard, but I can't go there."

"There was a fire at their house. They didn't survive. Yes, I am drunk. Please come, I need you."

"Oh, Richard, I am so sorry. My heart is breaking for you, but I can't. You know that place is dangerous. Please tell me when the funeral will be, and I will be there, but I can not come to you. I am sorry."

"Please, I love you."

"I love you too, but I can't. You know that."

"Then I will come to you."

"You are drunk! You can't drive!"

"I need to see you."

"Okay, okay. I will be there shortly. This one time, only because I don't want you getting in a car and driving."

"Thank you, I love you."

"I love you too."

It was annoying how she let him manipulate her this way, but Danielle loved him and wanted to be with him. She had been missing her best friend. The way they had always shared every detail of their lives. From the mundane, routine, daily tasks to the more complex questions that arose in their brains. She knew he was hurting. He had lost so much in such a short amount of time.

Captain Bill was grumbling at the late-night passage across the bay on the ferry. Danielle was very apologetic. Thankfully, she still had a key to the Manor house and she let herself in and found herself in Richard's waiting arms.

He buried his head in her shoulder and released the tears he had been fighting to keep inside. She didn't realize how much she missed being in his arms until they wrapped around her waist, pulling her closer. Her hands reached up to his face, lifting it off her shoulder.

Danielle kissed the tears on his cheeks and then made her way to his lips. Oh, how she had missed his soft, warm lips. The heat rose in her cheeks and traveled through her body. Richard Jr. broke the embrace, picked her up, and carried her to his bed.

In the morning, she awoke to him kissing the nape of her neck as he cradled her. The feeling of contentment overshadowed her concern for her safety. She stayed longer than she had expected. When she finally rose to leave, he tried to coax her back to bed.

"I have to go, Richard. There is work that I have. I love you. I will call you later to make sure you are alright."

"Alright. I love you too. I have to get up anyway and head to Jessica's. We have a lot to go over. I will fill you in later"

Chapter Seven

Last Plans

Getting off the island was easier than they thought it would be. Others were gone too, which made it easier for them not to be missed. When they realized Jimmy would be in Boston also for the weekend, they laughed at how easily the kid made things for them.

Plans were falling into place, and no one suspected them. Their companion for the weekend was so oblivious to the purpose of the trip. Keeping them drunk kept them from suspecting anything nefarious.

Watching Richard and Mira's house was a bit frustrating when they realized that Lena and Steven were there. They had to wait for the right time to execute their plans. It had been late when the guests stumbled out of the house.

The lights went out in the downstairs rooms, and the ones upstairs went on. When they went back off, they knew it was time to go into the house.

Assuming both occupants were just as drunk as their guests made things simpler. They found the key under the mat and chuckled that they had learned that through listening to the routine conversations in the Manor house.

They were careful not to make too much noise. Even though they knew the occupants were more than likely passed out cold, they didn't want to chance them waking up. That would make things messy. The gloves they wore to prevent leaving fingerprints as a precaution were cumbersome.

The stairs creaked slightly with each step they took in the darkness leading up to the master bedroom. Both occupants were where they suspected they would be. A smile crept over their face. Pulling the syringes out of the bag they brought with them. One for each of them. Neither flinched as they administered the paralyzing drug.

Next, they set the candles around the room. They needed to set the stage to make it look like a horrible accident. After they strategically placed the candles around the room and lit them, they threw the discarded clothes of the occupants on top of some of the lit candles, closed the bedroom door, and took the batteries out of the smoke detectors, replacing them with dead ones.

When they locked and shut the front door, they could already smell the clothes burning. They sat in the car with their companion passed out in the passenger seat, watching as the house became fully engulfed.

The neighbor must have woken up to the glow from the flames and alerted the fire department. As they drove away from the fire, the fire trucks screamed past them.

When they got back to the hotel they were staying at, they roused their companion just enough to get them back to the room. It annoyed them when they realized their companion was more awake than they had expected. The companion wanted to do more than just sleep.

The rush of adrenaline still pumping in their blood enhanced the experience. They noted this feeling. They would keep it in mind for after the next kill.

The next kill would be the grand finale. If all went as planned, they would get all the prestige they had always wanted. They would receive what birth rite entitled them to.

When they found out Jessica had moved the wedding date, it made them speed up their plans. They had four weeks to complete their grand scheme. Getting rid of Richard and Mira was the first step.

Three more deaths needed to happen, then it would be all theirs.

Chapter Eight

Realizations

Jimmy woke up early and called his therapist. Thankfully, she had time to talk to him. He got everything, every little piece of self-doubt and guilt out. What he told her was shocking. However, she assured him that everything he had said would remain confidential between them as patient/therapist protected. He felt better after talking to her.

When he was done, he met up with Richard Jr., and they headed to Jessica's house. Pulling up the driveway a few hours later, Jimmy's stomach churned. He hadn't been here since informing his cousin of her sister's death. Now here he was again visiting because of tragic circumstances.

Knocking on the door, a sense of déjà vu overcame him. Timothy opened it and the men entered the living room exchanging hugs, along with tears. Arthur joined them a short time after their arrival.

"I am so sorry for your losses."

Richard Jr. took the role of head of the family now, so he spoke first.

"Thank you, Arthur. We need your help. None of these deaths have been accidents. Proving it, though, is the hard part. There are no leads who could do this."

"How can I help?"

"We want to transfer ownership of the island and the business to you and Allison. Secretly. The only motive for wanting the family dead is what we own."

"Wouldn't that just put a target on my head, and Allison's, if something happened to you all?"

Arthur was nervous about this plan. He didn't understand Richard Jr.'s thought process.

"That's why I say secretly. If something happens to us, whoever is doing this will seize the opportunity to take control. Think about it. Dad hid in plain sight for years when everyone thought he was dead. Could someone else have survived that accident? If so, everyone on that boat was an heir to the estate. Even Benjamin, even though he supposedly didn't know."

Jimmy looked at Richard Jr., stunned. Why didn't he think of that? The thought of his biological father potentially surviving the boat accident oddly excited him and terrified him all at once.

"Wait, that makes sense! But who has access to the island, and us, that we wouldn't recognize as our relatives? I have seen pictures of David, David Jr., Samuel, and Dorothy. Your Dad knew them all very well, even Benjamin. How could any of them pass through our radar of recognition?"

It was Timothy who had a memory surface that he thought was insignificant at the time but now might mean something.

"Samuel was on the ferryboat with me the first time I came to Connecticut to visit you, Jessica. The day I got a flat tire, and the threatening note appeared. He has scars on his hands and face and walks with a limp. Possibly injuries from the boat accident?"

Jessica shuddered, remembering that day.

"He was leading us the day I had the ATV accident, and he was less than sympathetic."

Jimmy recalled the conversations he had recently with Samuel.

"Samuel admitted to me he knew about the passageways and that he had an affair with Mary. He is about the right age to be Benjamin. But we still have no proof to link him to any of the deaths."

Arthur sat in complete shock. Could the theory be correct?

"Okay, let's get the legalities all in order. However, it will only transfer to us if all of you die. Which I hope does not happen soon. I still don't know how that will help catch whoever is killing the family."

Richard Jr. had it all thought out.

"After Jessica and Timothy's wedding, we will set a trap. We will fake our deaths. If our theory is correct, Samuel, or should I say, Benjamin, will come out of hiding to claim his fortune. Jimmy and I just need to keep us all alive until we fake our deaths. That will be the hard part."

They spent the rest of the day making the funeral arrangements for Richard and Mira. Their emotions ran up and down like a rollercoaster. They all felt hopeful the nightmare they had been living would soon be over. And then, the reality of the danger they faced would hit them like a punch to the gut.

It was late afternoon when Arthur, Richard Jr., and Jimmy left Jessica's house to head home. Jimmy was glad he wasn't driving because he couldn't focus on the road. All he could think about was the possibility of Samuel being Benjamin. His fingers tapped on the passenger side door, as he was deep in thought.

Richard Jr. could tell his cousin was brooding over something and broke the silence.

"Hey, what's got you all knotted up? You are tapping louder than a busted piston in an engine and your knees are bouncing like rubber bouncy balls."

"Dude, if Samuel is our guy, he is a master liar and deceiver. And he is my father. It's all a bit unsettling, to say the least."

"I understand. When my dad came clean with all of his deceptions, it threw me for a loop. I was so angry at him. But now, with everything that has happened, I understand. He just wanted to be with my Mom, have a family, and be safe and happy."

"But my father is the bad guy. I can't see a redeeming quality or reason for him killing everyone. His only reason is greed. If it were to keep everyone he loved safe from harm, self-defense would be one thing. It's not though. This is cold-blooded murder."

"We need to make sure we don't tip him off that we suspect him, though. So you need to rein in your feelings on all this. We can't let him get away with it."

"Thanks for the reminder. This is just a lot to take in. I will keep my cool in front of him. Thankfully, he is a sort of reclusive, so we have minimal interaction."

The men got home right around supper time. Jimmy entered the kitchen and sat down at the island counter. Stella was busy preparing dinner as she normally did. She stopped when she noticed Jimmy staring into nothingness with his brows furrowed.

"What's got you all stressed out, son?"

"I have a lot on my mind, Mom. All these deaths. They just make you thankful for every breath you breathe."

"Yes, a lot of loss and a lot of grief. Way too much for one family to handle. I am scared for your life. I don't want to lose you."

Jimmy got up and walked over to his mother. He wrapped her in a big bear hug and kissed her forehead.

"Don't worry, Mom, we got this and nothing is going to happen to me. I promise you that. I love you."

After dinner, Jimmy and Richard Jr. retired to the parlor to play some pool. Richard Jr. cracked open a beer and offered an unopened one to Jimmy. Jimmy frowned and refused.

"I can't. There is something you don't know about me, cuz. I should have told you before, but I was afraid and ashamed. I had issues seven years ago with alcohol and drug addiction. It got worse. I went to rehab and everything. With what is going on right now, I need to be really careful not to consume anything and get back into that cycle."

"Oh man, I wish you told me sooner. We are getting all the alcohol out of here. I don't want to be a reason for you to relapse. I got your back."

Jimmy let out a sigh of relief. It felt good to get that off his chest. True to his word, Richard Jr. poured out his beer and removed all the alcohol from the house.

Then both men went up to their rooms to go to bed. Richard Jr. called Danielle.

"Hello, Rich."

"Hi Danielle, I wanted to let you know when the funeral will be for my parents. It will be Thursday. Here on the island. Can you please let your parents know?"

"Thanks, Rich. I will let them know. I will be there."

"Thanks, Danielle. For everything."

"You are welcome. See you, Thursday Rich."

All Richard Jr. wanted at that moment was to catch the serial killer targeting his family. Then he could marry Danielle and live the rest of his life happy and content. Thinking of living happily and content, his mind wandered to his sister and his brother. They both would never get to live the rest of their lives. Thankfully, his parents had lived happily for many years.

His eyes welled up with tears. The ache in his chest hurt so much. He wished he hadn't removed the beer from the house. This was when he realized he had been using the alcohol himself to numb the pain of his emotions.

The realization brought a deeper understanding of what his cousin must have gone through with his battle with addiction. There must have been a deep pain that he had been trying to numb. Richard Jr. resolved to talk to Jimmy more about it in the morning.

Jimmy lay awake contemplating the theory of Samuel actually being Benjamin, his biological father. He wanted to confront him in the worst way. That would jeopardize everything, though. How was he going to keep his cool? The thirst for a beer grew.

He was so grateful that Richard Jr. had removed the alcohol from the house. It made it easier to resist the urge. The night dragged on and sleep eluded him. He wished Melissa were with him. Remembering the weekend and that she had met him up in Boston to do some digging on Samantha's past.

They had gone to dinner at the restaurant Samantha had worked in and questioned her co-workers. The co-workers had remembered Samantha fondly and had even remembered Zach, as he was a regular there until Samantha moved to the island. Even though they both paid for their own meals since it wasn't a date but instead information gathering, Jimmy had felt the undercurrent of feelings between them bubbling up to the surface more than once.

They shared a hotel room just out of convenience and cost. With each of them sleeping in their own double bed. That had been so hard for him. He had wanted to crawl into bed with her and hold her close, as he had as a lovesick teenager in the past, but he had restrained. That made him proud that he had learned self-restraint.

As he thought of Melissa and how much he loved her and wanted to end the killer's reign on the island so she could come back, he fell asleep. In his dreams, he faced off with his father, and his father confessed to killing everyone, including his mother. Then Jimmy took a pistol out of a drawer and shot his father.

Jimmy bolted awake, shaking with terror at what he had just dreamed. It was going to be a long day.

Chapter Nine

Going Back Again

Jessica woke up early in the morning. Sleep had become something of an enigma in her life. The last six months had brought more chaos than she could ever imagine. Finding her biological family, then losing most of them tragically to a series of tragic circumstances that a serial killer orchestrated.

Then, she was also adjusting to the knowledge of being pregnant and was trying hard to take care of herself. Which meant she needed to try to sleep and ease stress. The death of her biological parents made that difficult at the moment.

Her thoughts went to the discussion they had the previous day about who they thought might be killing off their family members. The revelation that it might be Samuel all along made her tremble. It all made sense, and the puzzle pieces seemed to fit perfectly.

Samuel had admitted to Jimmy he knew about the passageways in the Manor house. That gave him a way of almost drowning her without being caught. They knew it could not have been Mary because she was not wet, and Jimmy had investigated and found there was no way she could have done it, even though she confessed in her suicide note.

He was the one who showed Timothy and her which ATVs to take for their assignment and led the way along the trails. Did he purposely take them down that particular trail, knowing the throttle would stick? Also, knowing there were steep declines to the narrow edges of those trails.

He also could have easily used the passageways to gain access to Alexandria and push her down the stairs. Then using the passageways to escape without being noticed.

Timothy and Jessica had passed Samuel in the hallway on the way to their room on Christmas Eve. The night they found the gifts for the family members.

Jimmy and Richard had explained how Samuel had been out with Rita on valentine's night. The night Richard Jr. had proposed to Danielle. The same night, Samantha and Zach died.

He was the one who found David's body. And to top it all off, he had been in Boston when her parents died in the fire. He had access to every single crime scene.

He had a motive, if he was really Benjamin. The question was, did he kill Mary or did she actually commit suicide? Samuel had admitted that he had an affair with Mary in conversation with Jimmy. If he loved her, why would he kill her? Although she left him an inheritance. Did he know? Could that have motivated him to kill her? Samuel had also said how Mary only used him and didn't want an outward relationship with him because he was just a mechanic. Was that truth or a lie? Did Mary know Samuel was potentially Benjamin? Mary and Benjamin had been lovers prior to the boating accident. If Samuel was Benjamin and Mary was intimate with him, wouldn't she have known it was him? The fact that Mary confessed to things they knew she couldn't have done led them to believe she did not commit suicide.

Thinking about it all overwhelmed her. The rage she felt bubbling under the surface of her emotions from overlooking him in the past made her palms sweat and heart race. Then the sadness at the fact they hadn't told their parents of the dangers they faced added to the guilt she already felt for surviving while her brother and sister had died. All of this filled her heart with such pain. Then her heart raced faster with the possibility of catching Samuel and being able to raise her unborn child in peace and safety.

The tears welled up and spilled out of her eyes, down her cheeks, and onto her pillow. Timothy awoke to the sound of her crying. He rolled over and cradled her in his arms.

"What's the matter, my love?"

"This nightmare could be over soon. We might get our happily ever after. And Rich and Danielle might, too."

"That would be nice. Then why are you crying, though?"

"Guilt. Samantha, Zach, and David will never have their happily ever after."

"Ah, my dear, they wouldn't want you to feel guilty. Let's get up and eat breakfast. We need to make sure you and our little one stay healthy."

Jessica took a shower while Timothy went downstairs to make them both breakfast. The smell of bacon and eggs wafted up to their bedroom, and her stomach growled. That motivated her to get dressed a little more quickly.

When she made it downstairs, Timothy had her plate made and a glass of orange juice waiting for her.

"Ah, this all looks so delicious. Thank you!"

"Anything for you and our little one. Make sure you drink that OJ. It's filled with folic acid, and that's important for the baby."

Jessica chuckled. It didn't surprise her that Timothy had done research on pregnancy and the things she should eat and not eat. With him being a writer, research was his middle name.

"Yes, sir. Have I told you lately how lucky I feel to have you?"

"No, you haven't, but we can go upstairs after breakfast and you can show me your gratitude."

Timothy just smiled a flirtatious grin at Jessica and wiggled his eyebrows.

"Hmm, that's a possibility."

"Ooh, is that a promise?"

"Yes, if you promise to make this kind of delicious breakfast for the rest of my pregnancy."

"Deal."

Jessica and Timothy ate breakfast and then went upstairs, where Jessica fulfilled her promise to Timothy. Afterward, while Timothy showered, Jessica worked on their wedding plans.

She was revamping the seating chart. She wanted eyes on Samuel at all times. He would be Rita's plus one. Poor Rita. Jessica wondered how she was going to deal with the news that she was dating a serial killer.

Jimmy had already assured Jessica he was upping security for her wedding. He told her and Timothy that he was hiring his friend Rolly to be an undercover detective to follow Samuel the entire time. This made her feel they would all be safe during the wedding.

The catering was all set; the cake was all set, the photographer, the DJ, and even the bartender. She had hired Joe. Since David's funeral, she had kept in contact with him. She wanted to make sure he was okay. He appreciated her checking on him. David's death had more of an impact on him than he had expected, considering they hadn't known each other for long.

When Timothy came downstairs, he joined her in her office where she was working.

"Whatcha doing, my dear?"

"Rearranging the seating chart for the wedding. I want to see Samuel at all times. I know Jimmy is going to have a detective on him, too. The more eyes on him, the better."

"Good idea. Did I ever tell you how incredibly smart you are?"

"Nope."

"Well, you are. That is just another one of the million reasons I love you so much. How about we go for a walk and take some pictures? It is a beautiful day and I feel spring is in the air."

"Sure, let me just finish this up."

When she finished Jessica grabbed her camera, and Timothy grabbed his notebook. He loved writing little snippets of descriptions of the things Jessica took photographs of. This had become a favorite pastime for them both. He loved watching her capture nature in her pictures. She conversely loved reading his descriptive words about the same things she was taking pictures of.

They had told his editor and her agent they were taking a sabbatical until after the wedding and their honeymoon. They planned on spending a month at their cottage in Ireland for their honeymoon. Jessica could not wait to get to Ireland. She felt safe there and relaxed. The relaxation and safety would be welcome after the craziness of the last few months.

When they returned home from their walk, Jessica packed for their trip to the island for her parent's funeral. She didn't want to go. The thought of saying a last goodbye to her biological parents filled her with an overwhelming sadness.

From the moment she found out about being adopted, she had wanted to know her birth parents. It took her years to find them. Now they were gone, along with her adoptive parents. At least she wasn't alone.

She had her brother Richard Jr. and her cousin Jimmy. Also, she had the love of her life with Timothy. What she would do right now, without him, she didn't know.

Timothy helped Jessica pack and then they headed on their way back to the island. He could not wait until they could stop going to that place. It creeped him out. The only good thing that had come from him going to the island in the first place was meeting Jessica. He had been a big fan of her photography. When Alexandria had mentioned to Arthur that she wanted Jessica to do the pictures for Timothy's article, he was more than happy to request that his editor contact her agent. Now his focus was on keeping her and their unborn baby alive.

The trip to the island seemed to take such little time. The more they went, the quicker the route seemed to be. Captain Bill was solemn and offered his condolences as they boarded the rickety ferry to cross to the island. The new ferry would not be there in time for the wedding since they upped the date.

As they drove up to the Manor house, they passed Samuel working on the tractor. He always seemed to be working on that thing. He looked up from what he was doing and gave them a solemn nod as they went by. Jessica shuddered. She couldn't wait until they could prove he was behind everything and put him behind bars.

When they entered the kitchen, Stella stopped what she was doing and wrapped Jessica in a big hug. Jessica could not contain her tears and melted into Stella's motherly arms. Stella let Jessica stay in her arms until Jessica felt the need to break the connection.

"Thanks, Stella, I needed that."

"You are welcome, child. I am here anytime you need a hug."

Stella wiped the tears from Jessica's cheeks with her apron and then got back to fixing food for the funeral. Jessica and Timothy headed upstairs to their usual room. They bumped into Betty in the hallway.

"Ma'am, sorry for your losses. If you need anything, just let me know."

"Thank you, Betty. I appreciate the condolences and the hospitality."

By dinnertime, Jessica's grandparents had arrived. Her mother's parents were just fragments of the people they were before their two grandchildren and only daughter died. Jessica noticed the frailty. They looked as if they had aged twenty or more years in the last two months.

For the first time, she felt her grandparents were just like her. They seemed lost without their loved ones, too. Their eyes were red from crying and they hunched their bodies with fatigue and stress. It shocked them when she approached them both and gave them each a big, long hug. They weren't usually the affectionate type, however; they were receptive to Jessica's gesture.

Dinner was solemn. They discussed minor details about the funeral the next day. Jessica, Timothy, Jimmy, and Richard Jr. were careful not to discuss their theory about the deaths with the grandparents. When they were all done eating, they all retired early to bed. They knew all too well the next day would be emotionally draining on them all.

Jessica lay in Timothy's arms and tried to drift off to sleep. She was tired in every way possible, yet her eyes did not want to close. Then she was thirsty, so she went down to the kitchen. When she looked out the window, she saw Rita ascending the stairs to Samuel's apartment above the garage. She felt bad for Rita.

Rita had divorced her husband to be with Samuel. Unlike her cousin Mary, Rita wasn't ashamed to be seen with him. She found Samuel exciting, which kept her interested in every way. Jessica shook her head. She couldn't worry about Rita's feelings. The woman would get over it, she would have to. Their lives were more important than her feelings. When Jessica went back upstairs, she lay in bed with her hands on her belly and fell asleep thinking of her unborn child.

Chapter Ten

Goodbye Again

It was ironic that Jessica got the best night's sleep she had had in a long time the night before her parent's funeral. Her body must have sensed she would need the strength to get through the day. The smells of breakfast made her open her eyes as her stomach growled. Timothy was already up and getting dressed.

"I didn't wake you, did I? You were sleeping so peacefully, I was trying to be extra careful not to wake you up."

"No, I think my hunger is what woke me up. The little one wants breakfast."

She rubbed her belly.

"Okay. do you want me to go downstairs and get a plate from Stella and bring it up to you? Or do you want to eat downstairs in the dining room?"

"I will get up and go downstairs. We have to start this day at some point."

As they descended the staircase, a bustle of activity was occurring at the bottom. People were preparing for the funeral. The bodies of her parents were burnt beyond recognition. They had opted to have them cremated and their ashes put in decorative boxes.

The boxes were to be buried in the family cemetery alongside the rest of their ancestors. Arthur was in charge of everything. He stood tall, calm, and dignified as he directed everyone with the setup.

"Good Morning Jessica and Timothy. Your grandparents are already in the dining room for breakfast."

"Thank you, Arthur, for everything."

"You are more than welcome."

They entered the dining room and served themselves breakfast from the chaffing dishes filled with various foods Stella had prepared. Arthur was correct when he mentioned her grandparents were already there. Neither seemed to have a voracious appetite. Instead, they both looked at their plate of food and pushed the food around.

Jessica felt a little self-conscious about the amount of food she had on her plate and the speed at which she could devour it all. She hoped nobody noticed. Her grandmother was always overly critical of the amount of food she ate. This time she didn't seem to notice, lost in her own world of grief. It was a relief to Jessica.

She and Timothy were not ready to share their news about expecting the baby yet. With the deaths of her parents, she knew she was not safe, and neither was her unborn child. Part of her though wanted to tell her grandparents just to give them some sense of hope and happiness, despite the loss of her parents, but she knew it was not a good idea.

After breakfast, they all filed into the garden where the decorative boxes sat on pedestals, the flowers sent from people to show their condolences arranged around each one. The chairs in the garden filled up quickly, and they soon filled the garden with mourners who came to pay their final respects.

Richard Jr. joined Jessica and Timothy, sitting in the front row sitting with their grandparents. Jessica couldn't help but think about the day she had met her biological parents and her siblings. It had been a day not unlike today. A day of sorrow and of saying goodbye.

Yet that day had turned into the beginning of her family's reunion and its demise. There were secrets revealed that day. After moving forward to be a family, an unknown entity started to tear them apart.

They thought now that every tragedy, including Alexandria's death, was being orchestrated by the same sadistic serial killer. Samuel was their suspect. As her mind went to him, she looked over her shoulder and saw him sitting a few rows back from them, holding Rita's hand.

As Jessica watched him, she tried to see the cold-hearted killer inside of him. At that moment, though she couldn't, he was gently consoling Rita, squeezing her one hand with his and wiping her tears with his other.

This image of Samuel didn't fit with their summarization of the crimes they felt he committed. She reminded herself that most serial killers seemed normal and fit in with society.

Lena and Steven were there with their daughters, including Danielle, sitting beside Rita. Jessica's gaze scanned them all. The pain and sorrow were so visible on each of their faces. It was at this moment she realized that, although she had an emptiness inside her, their loss seemed so much deeper than her own. They had known her parents for a lifetime; she had known them for a few short months. This made her feel as though she should not be sitting in front and they should be.

The minister startled her out of her thoughts as he started his sermon. The words seemed to float in the surrounding air. They passed through her mind without registering. The familiarity of the funeral service had become so routine that she actually felt numb.

When the minister asked for family and friends to come forward to share stories with the mourners of her parents, it again reminded her of the first time she had met them. The dramatic way in which her father had revealed his true identity.

Jessica hadn't planned on getting up and saying anything, but she found herself getting up and walking to the podium. As she stood there looking out at the mourners, she saw so many now-familiar faces looking at her with sympathy.

"As you all know by now, my name is Jessica Greenhall. I am the daughter of Richard and Mira Gardiner. We all learned that only a few short months ago. After that moment, my family had been trying to mend from years of separation and secrets. Yet tragedy has constantly barraged us. One loss after another."

Jessica paused, looking straight at Samuel.

"Without the love and support of all of you, our friends and family, we could not continue to go on. We thank you all for your support. The senseless loss of our parents so soon after the tragic loss of our brother and sister has rocked my brother Richard and me to our core."

As Jessica continued to lock her gaze on Samuel, he didn't flinch. Either he didn't notice she was looking directly at him, or he didn't care. He showed no reaction to any words she spoke.

"In a couple of short weeks, my fiancé and I will wed in the gardens of the Manor house. That will be the last time I set foot on this cursed island."

Jessica finished and looked at the other remaining two members of the Gardiner family. Jimmy showed such deep sadness. She knew her words hurt him, cut him like a knife. The island was his home. He had given up the love of his life to stay. He didn't know about the child she was carrying, though. Her baby needed her to protect it from the evil on the island. Jessica knew eventually he would forgive her.

Richard Jr. registered a look of understanding. Timothy extended his hand as she sat down next to him. He cradled her in his arms as they sat and listened to more mourners share memories.

The rest of the service seemed to happen in a fog and a blur. When the service finished, they all filled the gardens for a luncheon. Jessica sat and picked at a plate of food absentmindedly.

Rita sat down beside her, placing her hand on Jessica's arm.

"I am so sorry for your loss. Mira was like another daughter to me. I hope you know you will always be welcome to come to visit."

"Thank you, Rita. My mom thought fondly of you as well. I will keep your offer in mind."

Samuel stood behind Rita. Jessica looked up at him. For the first time, she thought she saw a touch of sorrow. It was on the edge of his eyes. *Could he be feeling remorse? Did he not realize the emotional damage the loss of her mother would be to the woman he proclaimed to love?* The thoughts raced through her mind. He broke her thoughts.

"Jessica, I know you and I haven't had a close relationship. I know I haven't always been friendly to you. Please know I am truly sorry for your loss. Your father and mother were gracious and kind people. They didn't deserve the fate dealt them."

As Samuel spoke, almost choked with emotion, Jessica couldn't process the words he was saying with what she knew. She couldn't tip their hand. The rage she felt toward him bubbled up inside of her. It was hard to swallow, but she had to.

"Thank you, Samuel. I hope someday the tides of fate will turn in the Gardiner family's favor."

With those words spoken, she got up and walked away. She was exhausted and just wanted to go take a nap. When she found Timothy, they said goodbye to her grandparents, who were heading home, and then they retreated to their bedroom.

They both fell asleep with their dress clothes on, holding each other tight. It had been an emotional day. Jessica dreamed of their wedding day.

It was beautiful. The weather was sunny with wisps of clouds in the sky. She faced Timothy to exchange their vows, and to her horror, realized blood covered his face. She awakened covered in sweat and shaking. Timothy stirred next to her and woke up with a start when he heard Jessica crying while covering her face with her hands.

Timothy held her close as she recounted the nightmare.

"It's okay. It was just a horrible nightmare. Soon we will be married and we will be free of this place."

"Will we ever really be free of here, though?"

"Yes, remember our plans. We will be free and safe."

There was a knock on the bedroom door, and Timothy got up to see who it was. To his surprise, it was Betty.

"Sorry to bother you both. Ms. Stella has sent me up to tell you dinner will be ready shortly."

"No bother, Betty. Thank you. We will be down momentarily."

"You are welcome. Oh, and I am sorry for your loss, Ms. Jessica."

"Thank you, Betty."

Jessica was still groggy from her nightmare. She didn't know if it was the grogginess or her emotional exhaustion, but she sensed something different about Betty and she couldn't figure out what it was.

Timothy and Jessica changed and got washed up. Then they went down and joined Richard Jr. and Jimmy for dinner. Arthur had already left, and Jessica felt a pang of guilt for not saying goodbye.

As the four of them sat and ate, they kept the conversation light. Jimmy and Richard Jr. had kept their pact not to drink, which helped Jessica not feel obliged to make excuses why she wasn't having any alcohol herself.

Jessica kept staring off and contemplating the events of the day. The interactions she had with people. The oddities of how Samuel's actions and words didn't fit what they thought he did. And that's when it hit her. The difference she noticed in Betty was in her words. Specifically, how she spoke. Her diction was more proper than backwoods, as she had always spoken.

She needed to find Betty and talk to her. Jessica didn't know why this change bothered her so much, but it did. When she got up and left the room, the men were all looking at each other, a bit confused. Especially Timothy. He didn't go after her though because he didn't want the others to suspect anything was wrong with Jessica. He imagined she was having a bout of pregnancy sickness. It did hit her at odd times.

Betty was upstairs cleaning out the guest rooms used the previous night.

"Hi Betty, I hope I am not bothering you or interrupting your work?"

"Hello, Ms. Jessica. No, you are not bothering me. Is there something you need? I can get it for you when I am finished in this room."

"No, no. I don't need anything. I just wanted to ask you something."

Betty froze. She looked at Jessica quizzically.

"What do you need to ask me?"

Jessica didn't know how to ask what she wanted without sounding offensive, but she did anyway.

"I couldn't help but notice a difference in you. You are speaking a bit different from how you usually do."

Betty gave Jessica a smile and shrugged.

"I have been taking speaking lessons. I met a new guy, and I didn't want to seem uneducated."

Jessica paused and felt stupid for having broached the subject at all.

"Oh, that's nice. I am glad you have a boyfriend. I am sorry again for bothering you."

"It's okay, Ms. Jessica. You aren't bothering me one bit."

Jessica went back downstairs and met the men who had moved to the parlor after dinner. She felt ashamed that she had pointed out the change in Betty's speaking. Why shouldn't Betty better herself? Good for her.

Chapter Eleven

Preparations

They filled the weeks leading up to the wedding with the hustle and bustle of final preparations and plans. Everyone welcomed the chaos, as it filled their minds with happy thoughts and took their minds off of the intense grief they had all been feeling for months.

Jimmy was working on making sure security was the tightest it could be. He wanted his cousin's wedding to go off without a hitch. He had weekly meetings with Rolly to discuss the best strategic placement of their manpower. They knew their threat was Samuel, so they were concentrating on keeping their eyes on him at all times.

Melissa had refused Jimmy's invitation to be his date. As much as it bothered him knowing the woman he loved wouldn't step foot on the island, it made him even more determined to catch Samuel and lock him up for good. Then they would be free to live their lives together and pursue their relationship.

Timothy and Jessica had gone back to Connecticut the day after Jessica's parent's funeral. However, they were back on the island helping with the preparations for the wedding, which was coming up on Saturday.

Danielle wanted to take Jessica out for a bachelorette party. Jessica was trying to come up with every excuse in the book not to go out. She didn't want to tell Danielle about the baby. Thankfully, her tiny baby bump really wasn't showing.

"Come on Jess, it's a tradition. We have to take you out. I will drive and not drink, and I will make sure you get home safely."

"Danielle, I appreciate all that you are doing as my maid of honor. I just don't feel up to going out and drinking. I am afraid if I drink, I won't stop."

"Okay, how about we just take you out to dinner, then? No drinking."

Jessica resigned herself to going out just for dinner. At least, then she wouldn't feel obligated to explain why she wasn't drinking.

When Danielle showed up to pick up Jessica, Richard Jr. had answered the door. The awkwardness between the two was palpable in the air. Jessica wished they would just talk and work things out. You could tell they were both miserable without each other. But she also knew the danger they all faced and they couldn't be happy until the danger was gone. Jessica met them in the foyer and gave Timothy a kiss and a hug.

"I won't be out late. See you when I get home. Love you."

"Love you too. Have fun."

As the women drove away, Danielle looked over at Jessica. She envied Jessica's resiliency. If she had gone through everything Jessica had been through in the last six months, she wouldn't be able to keep her composure as Jessica always seemed to.

"How do you do it?"

The odd question startled Jessica.

"Do what?"

"How do you seem so together? So confident of yourself when your entire world is seemingly crumbling around you?"

"What is the alternative? Curl up in a ball and stop living? How would that honor those we have lost?"

"I suppose you are right. You just amaze me. I didn't even have the strength to stay with Richard Jr. through it all."

"He still loves you. You know that, right?"

"Yeah. I still love him too, but I can't. I just can't risk having to watch him die. It would kill me. That's why after your wedding I am moving away. I can't stick around and watch what happens next."

Jessica couldn't believe what Danielle was saying. She understood all too well, though. The need and desire to get away and never come back. She and Timothy had discussed it many times. The urge to tell Danielle all about the cottage in Ireland and how they were going to go live there was strong. However, she resolved to keep that to herself.

After they picked up Danielle's sisters, mother, and grandmother, the conversation turned lighter and focused on the upcoming nuptials. The restaurant they went to was fancy, with crystal chandeliers and silk table clothes. Jessica felt a little underdressed. Then Danielle pulled out a bride-to-be sash and a tiara and made her put it on. At least the tiara made her feel more at ease in the restaurant.

Dinner was delicious and the women all enjoyed the festive night out. Jessica abruptly excused herself and hurriedly walked to the ladies restroom. She barely made it into the stall when her entire dinner came back up. There was a quiet tap on the stall door.

"Jess, are you okay?"

It was Danielle.

"Yeah, I am fine. Something I ate didn't sit well, I guess."

As Jessica came out of the stall, Danielle eyed her carefully.

"Are you pregnant?"

"What? No, what gave you that idea?"

"Um, I don't know. A ravenous appetite, not wanting to drink, and now getting sick for no reason."

"I told you it must be something I ate."

Jessica said it with a little more annoyance than she really wanted to. She felt sorry after she did because the look on Danielle's face changed from concern to hurt.

"Okay. I am sorry I mentioned it. I just remember my mom telling me stories about when your mom was pregnant with you and your mom was awfully sick."

The mention of her mom made her close her eyes. She contemplated telling Danielle the truth and then, without warning, Danielle pushed past her and closed the stall door behind her just in time. As she lost all content of her stomach into the toilet.

"Are you okay, Danielle?"

"Yeah, I am fine. As you said, it must be the food."

Both women splashed water on their faces and rinsed out their mouths by cupping the water into their hands and drinking it. They gave each other a smile in the mirror.

When they got back to the table, the others were talking about ordering dessert. Neither of them really wanted to eat another bite after being sick, but they didn't tell the others. They ordered a small slice of carrot cake each, hoping it would stay down.

It wasn't until after Danielle had dropped off her family she mentioned what happened in the bathroom again.

"You know, if you were pregnant, I would understand why you want to keep it a secret. I won't discuss what happened back in the bathroom with anyone else."

Jessica looked at Danielle as she was driving. There was something different about her lately, but she couldn't figure out what it was. She hadn't changed her hair or the style of clothes she wore. It wasn't like Betty, who talked differently. But she was different.

"Well, thank you, but I am not pregnant. I won't tell anyone about what happened in the bathroom either, though. So that you know."

When Jessica got dropped off, Danielle didn't come inside. The guys were hanging out in the parlor playing pool when Jessica entered. Timothy came over and gave her a hug.

"How was your evening?"

Pressing against his chest, her breasts hurt. Another aspect of pregnancy she was becoming accustomed to.

"It was nice. I am tired though, so I am going to bed."

"Do you want me to join you?"

"Nah, you are having fun. Don't stop because of me."

"Okay, if you say so. Love you. Goodnight."

"Love you too."

Timothy kissed Jessica, and she headed upstairs. She couldn't wait to get in bed and go to sleep. She was so tired. That was another aspect of the pregnancy she was getting used to. Being tired all the time. After getting into her pajamas, she quickly fell asleep when her head hit the pillow.

In her dream, she was in the Manor's garden. She was holding a baby, her baby. Happiness filled her heart. When she looked up, Danielle was walking toward her, smiling. She had something in her arms. The realization hit Jessica that Danielle had a baby in her arms. Jessica jolted awake just as Timothy was climbing into bed.

"Are you okay? Another bad dream?"

"Not really a bad dream. Not at all. I was holding our baby."

"Oh, was it that ugly? You startled awake."

"NO. Not at all. It was just we were here in the garden, with the baby."

She didn't want to tell Timothy everything about her dream. About Danielle. She hated lying to him, but she knew if her gut was telling her that Danielle was pregnant also, it was best nobody knew.

"I can see why that would startle you. We have no plans on bringing the baby here, ever."

"Exactly!"

Timothy climbed into bed and cradled her. They were both soon fast asleep.

Chapter Twelve

Boats and Bad Luck

Timothy woke up, still holding Jessica. He didn't want to disturb her; he knew she needed the sleep. Carefully, he extracted himself from their bed. The guys were going fishing instead of having a bachelor party. After getting dressed, he went downstairs to meet the guys for breakfast.

Jimmy and Richard Jr. were engaged in a conversation at the dining room table. They both looked up and paused when Timothy entered the room.

"Are you ready to catch some fish today, Timothy?"

"I already caught the best fish out there, but sure, it's going to be a fun, relaxing day."

"Jessica isn't here right now. No need to suck up, bro."

"I'm not. She is truly the catch of a lifetime for me. Sorry if you guys can't understand that."

Jimmy looked at Richard Jr. They both understood, in more ways than one. Both of them had felt the same about the women they loved.

The men joked around while finishing their breakfast. Just as they were getting up from the table, Jessica entered to have her breakfast.

"Good morning, boys. I am glad I caught you all before you headed out. Enjoy the day. Have fun. And be safe."

Timothy hugged Jessica and gave her a quick peck on the cheek.

"Good morning. We will have fun, but as I told the guys already. I caught the fish of a lifetime."

Jessica smiled and laughed as she watched the guys head out of the Manor house. At that moment, she didn't have a care in the world. All she thought about was in three short days she would marry the love of her life and then leave this island forever.

The guys went to the garage to get some ATVs to ride to the dock. Samuel was in there working on something that had broken. Jimmy was the first to acknowledge him.

"Hey Samuel, you sure you don't want to go fishing with us to celebrate Timothy getting hitched?"

"I don't enjoy fishing out on boats. I used to, but no more."

"Okay, man, but I have a feeling you are going to miss out on some good fun. If you change your mind, just meet us down at the docks. My friend will pick us up there in a half-hour."

"Thanks, but I am good. Besides, I have a lot of work to do around here."

Jimmy had purposefully asked Samuel if he wanted to go for three reasons. First, the guys could monitor him, so they knew Jessica would be safe while they were gone. The second reason was to get more information on Samuel. If Samuel really was Benjamin, it would fit that he used to enjoy fishing on boats, but since the accident no longer enjoyed it. The third reason was if Samuel was Benjamin, then that meant he was Jimmy's biological father and it would be nice to know more about him. Other than he was a complete psychopath.

Richard Jr. led the way with the ATVs down to the docks. As they boarded the boat, they noticed Betty coming out from the galley entrance.

"Good morning fellas, Ms. Stella sent me down here to stock your galley with plenty of food. Thank goodness she did. All that was down there was beer!"

The guys laughed, helped Betty off the boat, thanking her, and got ready to launch on their trip. To all of their amazement, Samuel rode up to the docks at the last minute. As he climbed off the ATV, there was a look of trepidation on his face.

"Is that invitation still open?"

Jimmy, Timothy, and Richard Jr. all looked at each other, still awestruck that he had actually shown up. It was Richard Jr. that spoke up.

"Sure, climb on board. There is plenty of room for one more."

They watched him shakily board the vessel with beads of sweat on his bald head. He wobbled as some small waves rocked the boat gently from side to side. Putting his hands on the rail, he steadied himself and went and had a seat with the others.

Jimmy's friend Robert, who owned the boat, untied from the dock and steered the boat out into Gardiners Bay, heading towards Long Island Sound.

Getting into the Sound, they started casting their lines. Samuel eased into the fishing with the others. His face was pale, and the others could see the visible shake in his hands as he tried to maneuver the rod and reel.

Jimmy observed Samuel. It really seemed that something petrified him about being on the boat. He felt sorry for him and almost forgot that he was the prime suspect in their investigation.

The boat rolled back and forth more when the waves grew bigger. Samuel clumsily put down the fishing gear and went into the galley area of the boat. Jimmy followed him. The door to the head shut behind Samuel and Jimmy heard the retching noises from within. He shook his head, thinking *poor guy* to himself. He grabbed a water and headed back up to the deck, leaving Samuel behind.

It was about a half-hour before Samuel showed his face on the deck again. The paleness of his face was quite obvious to his fellow passengers. He sat down, taking deep breaths of the salty sea air. Slowly, the color returned to his cheeks.

As Jimmy watched though, Samuel's eyes widened as if he was seeing a ghost. Following his gaze, Jimmy saw what he was looking at. There were wisps of smoke coming from the galley area.

"Robert, I think we might have a problem!"

The men jumped into action as the smoke got worse. Samuel froze in his place.

It turned out to be a small electrical fire, but the incident rattled them all enough to call it quits for the day. When they docked the boat, they all sat there eating the food Stella had packed, so it didn't go to waste, except Samuel. He couldn't get off the boat fast enough.

As Jimmy cracked open the first cold beer in weeks, he reflected on what had transpired out on the Sound. He had witnessed a vulnerable side of Samuel. If he had been acting, he should get an academy award.

When the men made it back up to the Manor house, Jessica was sitting in the parlor reading. She placed her bookmark inside the book and set it down as Timothy bent down to give her a kiss.

"How was the fishing trip?"

"Well, it was going well until we had a minor problem."

"What slight problem?"

"A small electrical fire in the galley."

"OMG, are you guys all right?"

"We are all fine. As for Samuel, he looked like he saw a ghost."

"Wait, Samuel went with you all?"

Jimmy and Richard Jr. jumped in to help fill in the details of what happened. Timothy sat down next to Jessica and she wrapped her arms around him, leaning her head on his chest.

"Do you guys think Samuel is responsible for the fire?"

Jimmy shook his head.

"I don't know. It shook him up just as much as it did us. Robert is going to look more closely at the wiring and see if he can determine what happened. At this moment, though, it looks like a freak accident."

"I am just glad you are all okay and safe."

They spent the rest of the night playing pool and just hanging out. Jessica thought about how much she was going to miss this. She loved hanging out with her brother and cousin. Maybe once Samuel was behind bars, she could feel safe coming back. But until then, there was nothing else they could do except plan on staying far away from the island.

Timothy watched his bride-to-be. He could almost read her thoughts just by watching her eyes. They would sparkle when she laughed with her brother and cousin. Then they would dim as her gaze stared off into the distance. He knew she was contemplating their plans. Leaving the only family she had. It was what they needed to do to stay safe, but it would not be easy at all.

Even Timothy felt the pangs of guilt and sorrow creeping over him about the decision they had made. Jimmy and Richard Jr. had become the closest thing to brothers he ever had.

Soon they all were too tired to stay up any later, and they knew the next day would be a busy one. Out-of-town family and friends would come in for the wedding and stay at the Manor house. Jimmy would have last-minute meetings with Rolly and the security crew. Rehearsal would take place and the rehearsal dinner.

As Jessica climbed the stairs, it hit her that was the last time they would sit in the parlor, just the four of them, and a tear rolled down her cheek.

"Are you okay?"

"Yeah, I am fine. Just thinking about everything and everyone. And as much as I hate this place, how much I am going to miss the people here."

"I know Jess, I am too. I am too."

Timothy wrapped his arm around Jessica's shoulder as they walked to their bedroom. It would be the last night they slept together before their wedding. Danielle insisted that the night before the wedding, she and Jessica would have a sleepover. Timothy would take another of the guest rooms.

Jimmy stumbled up the stairs to his bedroom. He was kicking himself for having a few beers. The anxiety rose in his chest. He swept the room and made sure there were no beer cans anywhere. Then he locked his bedroom door and stripped down to his boxers. The bed was comfortable, and he relaxed as he fell asleep.

Richard Jr. hadn't drank as much as Jimmy had. He was monitoring his cousin. The fact he had entrusted him with his past secrets made him feel responsible for looking out for him. After getting into some pajama bottoms, he went out into the hallway and sat across from his cousin's door, keeping watch.

In the morning, Jimmy awakened with a bit of dread. He didn't want to look and see if there were beer cans strewn around, but he did. To his astonishment, there were none. He carefully unlocked his door and opened it to find Richard Jr. fast asleep in the hallway, blocking his bedroom door.

Jimmy smiled, closed the door, and went to take a shower. As the door closed, Richard woke up. His back was sore from lying on the floor all night and his neck was stiff. He heard Jimmy inside his bedroom and the door to the bathroom shut, so he took that as his cue to go get ready for the day as well.

The sun shone into the bedroom where Jessica and Timothy were still sleeping. She rolled over into his arms that were encircling her. Her eyes were still closed, and she nuzzled her face into his chest.

Timothy pulled her tighter against him and slowly opened his eyes. He knew they needed to get up and start their day, but he just wanted a few minutes more of just this. Softly, he kissed her forehead. Her eyes fluttered open, and she looked up at him.

"Are you ready to get this show on the road?"

He looked back at her.

"As ready as I will ever be. How about you?"

Jessica smiled at him.

"Let's do this."

Chapter Thirteen

Judgement Day

They were giddy with excitement. Soon, all their years of planning would pay off. The island would be theirs to have forever and no one would be any the wiser about their hand in it all. It almost seemed too simple.

Everything had fallen into place beautifully in the last six months. They had reserved themselves for the long game years ago and had eventually changed it to a quick game with the turn of events that had occurred at Alexandria's funeral. Now the time had come to finish the job.

They had heard whispers of Jessica and Timothy about a pregnancy. It was the only tidbit of information that was interesting that they had heard in weeks. The family had started discussing more important issues outside the walls of the Manor house. This had become annoying.

Not being able to hear the secrets of the family was infuriating and fueled their anger further. Soon, all the secrets would reveal themselves.

Nobody paid any attention to them, so as the hustle and bustle around the island for the wedding preparations happened, they set up the final grand finale of their plan. The piece de la resistance.

They weren't worried about the cameras since they had invested in a Wi-Fi jammer. By using it, the cameras were inoperable. They could move about The Manor house freely when needed. It had taken them weeks to put everything they needed in place, but it was all there, ready to go.

Tomorrow, their life would change forever. Tomorrow, they would finally have everything they ever desired. It was judgment day for the Gardiner family.

They would have it all, everything they ever wanted and deserved.

Chapter Fourteen

Sharing Secrets

Jessica and Timothy entered the dining room and were pleased to see that her grandparents were already there. She had been afraid that they would not attend after the deaths of her parents. Alison, Timothy's mother, was also there, and she was chatting with Mr. and Mrs. Kennedy.

Alison beamed as she looked at Timothy. She placed her hand on Mrs. Kennedy's arm and excused herself from the conversation. Sliding out of her chair, she walked up to Jessica and Timothy and hugged them both.

"Ah, there are the bride and groom. We have been waiting for you both to emerge from your bedroom. Stella has prepared a feast for breakfast. Grab some before your cousin Jack gets here. His appetite is monstrous!"

Timothy laughed and followed Jessica over to the sideboard filled with chaffing dishes. He filled his plate, even though his stomach was feeling queasy. The nerves were rattling him the closer they got to the wedding.

He was sure he wanted to marry Jessica. The fact was, he was never so sure about anything in his life. The nerves were not cold feet. It was more about executing their plan after the wedding and catching the serial killer. He prayed they were successful so they could all resume living a normal life. Timothy pushed those thoughts back into his mind and focused his attention on his bride-to-be.

Jessica filled her plate, which garnered a look of repugnance from her grandmother. Her grandmother never appreciated her appetite and how much food she ate. While she never actually called her fat. There had been several instances where her grandmother noted women should watch what they ate and remain slender in build. Jessica loved food and while she wasn't exactly overweight, she wasn't slender either. She had her curves, and she was comfortable with her body that she didn't really care what anyone else thought.

At the moment, she was thankful for the curves that hid her pregnancy. She started to worry less about hiding her growing appetite since everyone knew she loved food as well.

Jimmy, Richard Jr., and Arthur joined the others in the dining room. They kept the conversation light and focused on the wedding. There were too many people who were not aware of the danger the family was in to discuss all of that.

Martin escorted Danielle into the dining room. Jessica watched her brother's facial expression. The love he still felt for Danielle was apparent in the way his eyes glistened when he looked at her. She could see the muscles in his shoulders tense as he held himself from going over and pulling her in his arms. The pain her brother was in made Jessica feel guilty about asking Danielle to be her maid of honor.

Danielle's face was soft, but when she looked at Richard Jr., a hint of sadness filled her eyes and her jaw tightened into a set of blank expressions. The tension between the two was still as thick as a dense fog.

"Hey Jess, are you ready to go get our manicures and pedicures?"

"Sure, Danielle. I am just finished eating, anyway. Let me go get my sandals from upstairs."

Jessica had never had a manicure or pedicure in her life, but Danielle had insisted they get them for the wedding. She caved and let her schedule an appointment for them both. As they were leaving, she felt bad about not inviting her grandmother or Timothy's mom, but she noticed the two women chatting it up nicely in the parlor, which gave her a little comfort. She kissed Timothy goodbye and left with Danielle.

The ride to the mainland was short. However, it was just enough time for the two women to talk. Jessica opened up first.

"Danielle, the other day. When we were in the bathroom, and we both got sick. You asked me if I was pregnant. Is that because you are pregnant?"

Danielle looking out the corner of her eye while driving opened her mouth, then closed it. She seemed flustered. Jessica felt bad about asking her. The thought had been nagging at the corner of her mind since she had the dream the other day. Danielle finally responded.

"I am. No one knows. I mean it, no one. I don't want anyone to know, especially Richard. When the wedding is over, I am moving away on Sunday. My parents don't even know. I will call them when I get to where I am going. That, though, will remain a secret. So, what about you? Are you ready to come clean and tell me the truth?"

Jessica took a deep breath in and exhaled. Danielle had confided in her. Should she keep her secret or should she tell her the truth?

"Okay. I am sure you understand why I am keeping it a secret. I promise to keep your secret. Please keep mine. Yes, I am pregnant."

Jessica felt as if it lifted an immense weight off her shoulders, sharing her and Timothy's secret. The rest of the afternoon, the two women giggled and just thoroughly relaxed while being pampered. When they returned to The Manor house, their jubilation continued and carried over to the others.

There was an air of happiness that hung over the island and it gave Jessica hope that their future would not comprise any more tragedy or dark clouds. Timothy's cousin Jack had arrived while they were gone. A mean game of pool consumed the guys in the parlor.

The tension between Danielle and Richard Jr. seemed to ease a little and more than once, Jessica caught the two of them laughing in conversation with one another. She thought about Danielle's secret and wished her brother could know he was going to be a father. He would be a great dad. Unfortunately, she could not tell him and she knew Danielle had no intentions of sharing the information with him.

Jessica glanced outside the window and daydreamed about a time in the future when they could all be together again. Safe. Where her child and her brother's child could grow up knowing each other. Timothy sat down next to Jessica and whispered in her ear.

"Penny for your thoughts."

"Just daydreaming about the future, my dear."

"Ah, that's why you have such a huge smile on your face."

"Definitely, I am feeling very hopeful that all of our futures will be brighter than the last six months."

Jimmy was the only one that seemed tense. He excused himself from the parlor and took a long walk to the security shack. His mind was stuck on making sure all the security measures they put in place would be enough to keep the family and all their guests safe during the wedding festivities. He just couldn't fathom losing anyone else. If there were any more deaths on his watch, he would feel as though he failed. He couldn't live with that.

He wished Melissa were with him at the moment. Taking out his cell phone, he dialed her number.

"Hey Jimmy, is everything okay? I figured I wouldn't be hearing from you until the wedding was over."

"Yeah, everything is okay. I am just feeling a lot of anxiety about tomorrow. I needed someone I could trust to talk to about it."

"It's normal for you to feel anxious, Jimmy. You have a big job. Sometimes I don't know how you do it. I am sure everything is going to go fine. The wedding will be beautiful and everyone will stay safe."

"I wish I was as confident as you are about this. I don't know why I am so unsure. We have done everything to make sure we keep everyone safe. However, my gut just tells me we can't."

"Jimmy, you got this. When the wedding is over, and everyone leaves the island, you should take a vacation. Come and visit me. You deserve some downtime."

"I will think about it. Thanks for having confidence in me, and for the invite."

After finishing up the conversation with Melissa, Jimmy felt a little more relaxed. The thought of going to see her cheered him up. She wanted to be with him, just not on the island. He understood. The thought of leaving the island for good was starting to be enticing. Maybe Jessica and Timothy had the right idea. Leaving the island for good.

They were planning on leaving the island and not coming back, at least not until they caught Samuel. Jimmy didn't know if he could leave his adoptive parents behind. He would have to sit down with them and discuss the possibility of them all moving off the island, as Melissa had with her parents.

Then there was Richard Jr. How could he leave him with the sole responsibility of the island? Everyone he loved was dead or leaving. He couldn't add to that burden on his cousin. They had become close in the last few months. Almost like brothers.

As Jimmy walked back to The Manor house, he noticed Rita's car parked next to Samuel's truck. Seeing it made Jimmy relax a little. Samuel would be busy entertaining Rita, hopefully too busy to kill any of them. Although she had been with him the weekend of the fatal fire.

Everyone was still in the parlor having a fun time. Richard Jr. walked up to Jimmy and put his hand on his shoulder.

"Come, let me beat you in a game of pool. It might take your mind off your worrying."

"What makes you think I am worried?"

"The lines on your forehead, man. They are deeper than the grand canyon."

Jimmy laughed and grabbed a pool stick while Richard Jr. racked the balls.

"I guess beating you would be fun and would clear my mind."

Jessica and Danielle said goodnight to the rest of them and headed upstairs to bed. They were both exhausted, and they knew the next day would be full of a barrage of emotions.

Tomorrow, she and Timothy would become husband and wife. Their lives together would start. Tomorrow, their future would be hopeful.

Chapter Fifteen

The Wedding

It was the morning. The sunshine was bright through the windows. As the dust danced in the sunbeam, Jessica opened her eyes. Danielle was awake already and was busying herself organizing the girl's dresses. They knew they needed to go downstairs and get their breakfast. The hairdresser and the make-up artist would be at the Manor house in a short period.

Both of them gathered themselves in their robes labeled Bride and Maid of Honor and went down to the dining room. None of the guys were awake, yet it seemed. They didn't know what time they had eventually gone to bed.

They filled their plates and then took trays of their food up to the bedroom to eat. When they were done, they called down to the kitchen to have Stella send Betty up to get the trays.

Betty knocked on the door. Jessica opened it.

"Ms. Stella sent me up to grab the trays."

"Of course. Here they are. Thank you, Betty."

"You are going to be a beautiful bride, Ms. Jessica."

"Thank you, Betty. Maybe someday soon your new guy will make you his beautiful bride."

"Maybe. That would be nice."

Betty smiled as she left Jessica and Danielle to get ready.

Martin escorted the photographer, the hairdresser, and the make-up artist up to Jessica's room. A flurry of activity began as they prepared the girls for the wedding.

The men were congregating and preparing in Timothy's room. They had brought a photographer up to take pictures of them preparing.

When Jessica's hair and make-up were complete, the photographer wanted to take some photos of her looking at her dress. Looking at it, emotions washed over Jessica. She struggled to blink back the tears as she remembered Samantha picking it out and both of them falling in love with it.

The photographer caught a single tear escaping from Jessica's eye. It made a beautiful picture. The make-up artist, though, was fraught with anxiety.

"No, no. Do not cry! You will mess up your beautiful make-up."

Danielle caught the make-up artist's hand and calmly explained the situation.

"Ma'am. Her sister, who passed away a few months ago, picked out that dress. There are bound to be some tears. I am sure the job you did can weather the potential storm."

"Oh, I am so sorry, ma'am. I didn't know. My deepest condolences."

"Thank you. It's okay, you didn't know. I will try not to shed any more tears."

When Danielle's hair and make-up were complete, it was time for the women to have some more before pictures taken together. The photographer posed the two girls for various shots and they all laughed as Jessica made silly faces. She was used to being on the other end of the lens and she was feeling self-conscious.

Then it was time to slip into their dresses. It dismayed Jessica that her dress was slightly tighter than it had been at her last fitting, although it still fit. Danielle had the same issue.

Neither of them mentioned it, even though they both knew why the dresses had become snug. They smiled a knowing smile at each other and left it at that. The photographer took more pictures and then ushered both women down into the gardens to take some more pictures before the guests arrived.

Jessica and Timothy had opted not to have a first-look picture taken before the wedding. They both wanted to have their first look at each other as Jessica walked up the aisle. The photographers had made sure they would position themselves in the right place to catch both of their faces.

Soon, it was time for the ceremony to begin. Jessica's palms were sweating as she picked up her bouquet to hold while walking down the aisle. She gently slid her hand over the charm bracelet fastened to her bouquet that held pictures of her mother, father, sister, and brother. They were with her in spirit and she choked back the tears, remembering the promise she had made upstairs.

The music started and Danielle walked through the gardens in front of Jessica, to the gazebo where the minister stood waiting in the center. Timothy was standing to the right and next to him was Richard Jr. Her heart ached. She wished she could tell Richard she was carrying his child. The thought of them being able to marry each other someday flashed through her mind. She knew it could not happen until the serial killer was found and caught.

When she got to the gazebo, she took her place and turned to watch Jessica walk down the aisle. Arthur and Jimmy escorted her. The smile that spread across Jessica's face as she saw Timothy waiting for her melted Danielle's heart. That was true love. Love that wasn't afraid to face danger in the eye. She wished she had that courage.

Timothy's breath hitched as he got his first glimpse of Jessica. He wiped his eyes as a few tears slipped out. She was stunningly beautiful. He already knew this, but seeing her with her hair pulled up on the top of her head with a ring of baby's breath and little ringlets of her red hair framing her face, just emphasized it. Now he knew why she and Samantha had fallen in love with this dress. It was perfect for Jessica.

When Jessica reached Timothy, they faced each other as the minister began the ceremony. It all seemed like a dream, except in this one everything went as planned and there was no blood. Jessica was relieved when they exchanged their vows and they were pronounced husband and wife. Her nightmares had not come to fruition, thankfully.

They both seemed to relax more when the afternoon festivities began. While they sat at the head table, they could see Samuel with his date, Rita.

Rolly was sitting at the same table, conversing and acting as though he was just another wedding guest.

The wedding guest list was small and many of the guests were coming up to the head table and congratulating the newlyweds. Lena and Steven made their way up as well.

"Oh Jessica, you look as beautiful as your mom did on her wedding day. I know she is smiling down at you."

"Thank you, Lena. I feel her presence today too. Thank you for coming."

As the evening went on with no incident, Jessica and Timothy loosened up. They danced to their hearts' content and felt truly happy.

Just as the evening was coming to a close, the DJ made an announcement.

"The bride and groom would like to thank all of you for being a part of their special day. Now, if everyone could bring their chairs to the open area of the Gardens, we will conclude the festivities with a fireworks display."

Jessica and Timothy sat side by side with Richard Jr. and Danielle flanking each of them. With a sideways glance, Jessica saw that Rita and Samuel were sitting to the side of Danielle and slightly behind, while Rolly was sitting directly behind them.

Jessica was relieved to see Rolly still closely monitoring Samuel. It made her feel the safest she had felt in months. She clasped Timothy's hand in hers and leaned her head on his shoulder as they prepared to watch the display.

Jimmy had excused himself from the festivities under the tent to go supervise the fireworks display to be set off. He was feeling lighter than he had in a long time. The stress of the last few months seemed to wash away as the day progressed without a single incident.

Maybe they had been wrong, maybe their grief had turned to paranoia and there really was no serial killer. All the deaths might have been accidents. Maybe their grief had led them all on a wild goose chase. The pyrotechnicians started the display and Jimmy watched wistfully.

Back at the gardens, the lights went out as the fireworks display started. The guests oohed, aahed, and clapped their hands. The bursts of red, green, blue, and purple lit up the night sky.

Timothy squeezed Jessica's hand and as she looked over at him with her eyes sparkling with happiness, the grand finale started. The booms were loud and startled Jessica.

Timothy dropped Jessica's hand and in the flash of the bursts, Jessica saw him clutch his chest. His white suit turned red. He looked down and then looked at her. She went to scream and as she did; she felt the searing pain in her own back. Jessica looked down and realized she was also bleeding. She turned and grabbed Danielle's arm as her vision went dark.

Danielle was enjoying the light display as she felt a firm hand on her arm. To her horror, realizing it was Jessica who was bleeding from a wound on her back through to her front. The hand let go just as Jessica collapsed to the ground. Danielle looked over at Timothy, slumped in his chair, bleeding as well. And then her eyes went to Richard Jr. lying on the ground with a wound to the head. She screamed as the grand finale finished and everyone went silent.

Chaos ensued as the security team and Rolly called for medical help to the island and herded the guests into the grand room in the Manor house. Rolly was determined not to let anyone leave.

As the grand finale finished, Jimmy felt content that the evening had gone as planned. It surprised him when one of his security team members came riding up on his ATV, looking distraught.

"Boss, we have been trying to reach you on your radio."

Jimmy went to reach for his radio and realized he had left it on his ATV parked fifty feet away. His gut wrenched.

"What happened? Why are you trying to reach me?"

"There has been a shooting."

"Oh, my God. Who was shot?"

"Jessica, Timothy, and Richard Jr."

Jimmy's heart sank as he ran toward his ATV. He heard the crackle of the radio and the frantic voices on the other end. He slipped his radio on his belt. As he started up the machine, something rattled off the front of it he hadn't seen before. It was a drone controller. He did not know what it was doing there. He picked it up and secured it, then headed back to the Manor house and the gardens.

Rolly met Jimmy in the gardens.

"It wasn't Samuel. I had my eyes on him the entire night. Especially during the fireworks display."

"Where are Jessica, Timothy, and Richard?"

"We have transported them to the open field, awaiting life flights. It's bad Jimmy, I doubt if they are going to make it."

Jimmy crumpled to the ground, holding his head in his hands. Rolly was trying to help him up and console him when one of his detectives approached.

"Serg, We think we found something inside the house."

Jimmy jumped up and tried to compose himself. They followed the detective back to the house. Jimmy's stomach tightened as the detective led them upstairs and then down the hallway. They stopped at Jimmy's bedroom. Confusion spread over Jimmy's face.

The detective opened the door. Rolly looked inside and then looked at Jimmy.

"Whose bedroom is this?"

Jimmy stood there looking at his room. It was his room, but the stuff in it he had never seen before. There was a birdcage with crows. A jar on his dresser had something floating inside that he recognized as a deer's heart. And sitting on his bed was a drone with a gun strapped to it. His window was wide open with a slight breeze blowing the curtains.

"Mine. But I swear I have never seen this stuff before."

Rolly looked at his friend. He was just as perplexed. Then he looked at his detective.

"Is the drone controller in here also? Anyone could have done this."

It was Jimmy that answered, not Rolly's detective.

"I have it. Or I think I do. It was on my ATV when I was coming back. I swear, bro, I didn't do this!"

Rolly looked at Jimmy with a pained expression on his face.

"You know what I have to do, right? I can't just ignore all this evidence because we are friends."

"I know."

Jimmy stuck out his hands and let Rolly handcuff him.

The gasps and murmurs of the guests being allowed to leave after being interviewed echoed in Jimmy's ears as Rolly escorted him into a waiting police cruiser.

Chapter Sixteen

Chaos

Jessica slipped in and out of consciousness, never opening her eyes. She could hear sirens and voices. She felt the pressure of hands on her. All she could think of was Timothy and their unborn child. Would any of them survive?

Timothy heard voices, and felt hands on him, but also could not open his eyes. He thought about how the most perfect day in his life had now turned into the worst.

"This one is DOA. Let's call the coroner's office. The other two are critical. We need those birds ASAP."

Jessica's mind raced. DOA, she struggled to remember what that stood for. Then it hit her, dead on arrival. Someone was dead. God NO. She knew it wasn't her, although she knew she was clinging to life by a thread. Please don't let it be Timothy. Then she felt guilty for thinking of her husband first. Please do not let it be Richard Jr. or OH God, please not Danielle and her baby!

Timothy heard the words DOA, and he panicked, thinking he had lost the love of his life and their unborn child. He hadn't kept them safe. The promise he made to keep them safe, was broken.

Danielle was in the grand hall of the Manor house with the other guests being looked over by medical personnel that had been called to the island. They were watching her for shock. Her parents hovered over her.

"I am fine. I just want to know if Richard Jr. and the others are okay."

Lena held onto her daughter's hand and looked imploringly at the medical personnel. They wouldn't look her in the eye.

"I am sure they are going to be okay."

"Mom, there was so much blood. How can they be okay? Especially Richard? It was coming from his head."

Danielle burst into tears and started shaking. The medical personnel convinced her to go to the hospital for observation.

Allison sat holding Jack's hands as the police interviewed them both. She was trembling. The thought of losing her only son after finding him was overwhelming. When they were told they could leave, her first thought was to go to where they brought Timothy. But she did not know where that was.

"What hospital were Timothy and Jessica brought to?"

The officer told her, and then Jack and Allison headed straight to the hospital.

Jessica vaguely remembered being placed in the helicopter and transported to the hospital. She would hear voices and then things would go dark and silent again.

This time, she recognized two of the voices as Arthur and Allison. There were beeps and other sounds that she recognized as hospital-related. She tried to move, but couldn't. Her eyes would not open either.

"They are keeping her sedated. A medically induced coma. They have stabilized her. But they can't do anything more until she gets stronger."

"What about Timothy? What about my son?"

"Let's go out in the hall. They say there is a possibility she can hear us. It's best we discuss other things out of earshot."

NO! Jessica shouted in her mind. She wanted to hear about Timothy. Was he alive or dead? A tiny tear trickled out of the corner of her eye and ran down her cheek onto the pillow.

Jimmy sat in the cell at the police station. Rolly had put him in his own cell instead of the general holding cell. They would arraign him on one count of murder and two counts of attempted murder in the morning. More than likely, with the severity of the charges and the rest of the case that might build against him with the evidence found in his room, it was likely that they would set no bail. If that occurred, he would wind up being transferred to an actual prison. He was terrified.

Despite all of his previous doubts about himself, he knew he didn't do this. There was no way. He had not touched a drop of alcohol all day. His memory of the day's events was crystal clear.

Arthur awoke the next day dreading what needed to be done. He had to gather all the inhabitants of the island and give them the news. There would be a lot of questions. What would happen to them and the island?

He picked up Allison, and they drove to the island together. The inhabitants all gathered inside the Manor house and waited for Arthur to start speaking.

"Good morning everyone, thank you for gathering here. I wish I had good news to share, but unfortunately, I don't. Richard Jr. was pronounced dead on the scene last night. While Jessica and Timothy both succumbed to their injuries in the early morning hours."

Gasps went through the inhabitants, and they could hear sobs throughout the room. Someone asked the first question.

"What does that mean for us?"

"Good question. I will try to answer it. As you know, they have arrested our own Jimmy Driscoll for the murders. What you all do not know is he is the last living heir to the Gardiner estate."

Everyone's eyes went wide. Hands flew up over mouths and rumbles of, *"But how?"* went through the crowd.

"He is the son of the late Mary Gardiner and her lover, Benjamin Timmons. Benjamin was Richard Sr.'s half-brother. He was a Gardiner by birthright."

As Arthur stated this, he looked squarely at Samuel. Samuel's reaction was one of absolute shock. Arthur thought he saw a shimmer of tears in his eyes. Samuel left the room and Arthur continued.

"This is the motive the police think propelled Jimmy to commit these crimes. He was aware he was a Gardiner, and he wanted it all for himself."

"My boy didn't do this!"

It was Stella, and she was looking furious.

"Stella, I understand your feelings. We are all in shock, too. The police have overwhelming circumstantial evidence pointing to Jimmy. I wish it wasn't so. We are going to get him the best defense attorney around. Allison and I will take over operations of the island and the business until we sort things out with Jimmy. For now, you all remain employed."

A collective sigh went through the room. Many of the inhabitants left the room mumbling to themselves and shaking their heads.

Arthur left the island and headed to the courthouse where Jimmy was awaiting his arraignment. He could get a few minutes to talk to him.

"Hey Jimmy, how are you holding up?"

"Not good Arthur. I did not do this. Swear to God. I know it looks bad and all. Samuel must be framing me."

"I don't think it was Samuel. When I gave the news to everyone who you really were, he seemed convincingly shocked and upset."

"Then who could it be, Arthur? Who wants me to go down for this?"

"I don't know, kid. That is the biggest question. I have to tell you, though, what you are being charged with."

"Lay it on me."

"You are being charged with 3 counts of murder in the first degree. They are also investigating whether you could have done the other deaths."

"Jessica, Timothy, and Rich are dead? They are pinning me for everything?"

"Yes, I am sorry. They are trying to. I have a colleague though. He is the best defense attorney around. He will be here shortly to talk to you. We are going to fight this."

"Okay Arthur, thanks."

Arthur left the room and Jimmy waited for the guard to bring him back to the courthouse holding cell. Instead, the guard came in and said he had another visitor. Jimmy assumed it was the defense attorney that Arthur had told him about.

When Samuel walked into the room, Jimmy froze, looking at him. Was he here to finish him knowing he was a Gardiner now, too? Jimmy thought of yelling to the guards. Samuel sat down in the chair across the table from Jimmy and rested his head in his hands.

"My boy."

The tears spilled from Samuel's eyes freely as he continued speaking to Jimmy.

"I always hoped I would get to know you. To know how you grew up and who you became. I didn't know I watched you grow up on the island. And I didn't know it was you. Did your mother know? Did she know I was a Gardiner because I sure as hell didn't know?"

"Ms. Mary, my mother didn't know until the day she died. As I had not known either until Ms. Alexandria told us on her deathbed. So we were right. You are Benjamin, my father."

"Yes, I am. I barely survived the boating accident with my life. When I saw Mary afterward, I tried to tell her who I was so many times, but I couldn't come clean with her and she never realized it was me. Too much of my outward appearance had changed."

"Does anyone else know who you really are?"

"No. Why?"

"I am being framed. I thought it was by you. We suspected that you might be the only other unknown heir to the Gardiner estate. It made sense it would be you picking the family members off one by one."

"You mean to tell me the other deaths weren't accidents?"

"No, we do not believe so. And now I am being pegged for them all. I didn't do this. You need to keep it a secret that you are a Gardiner and you are alive. Can you do that?"

"I will do what needs to be done to help clear your name, kid."

"Thanks, Dad, it's okay for me to call you that, right?"

"Sure, Kid."

Before Samuel left, he gave Jimmy a quick hug. His mind was still spinning at the revelation that all this time he was a Gardiner. If he had known that so many years ago, so much would have been different.

Jimmy resolved to not tell anyone about his conversation with Samuel. He didn't know who he could trust. He felt, though, in every fiber of his being, that Samuel had not known that he was his son or that he was a Gardiner.

Jimmy met with the defense attorney, Mr. Devine. He would enter a not-guilty plea. The attorney assured him they would do everything in their power to get him out on bail, but considering the charges, it was unlikely.

The arraignment went as expected. They charged him with three counts of first-degree murder and had no bail set. They ordered him to be detained while awaiting trial. His attorney attempted to get him to be released to attend the funeral of his cousins, but the judge would not allow it. This was a devastating blow to Jimmy. He could not say goodbye to Jessica, Richard, or Timothy.

Arthur, who had been sitting in the courtroom, left to go back to his office. There was so much to do. He had the funerals to arrange. Out of loyalty and devotion to Alexandria, he would continue to help the family and see Jimmy through his trial. However, he was thinking retirement was sounding pretty good.

When he sat at his desk and opened his mail, there was an envelope with no return address and no stamp. He brought it to his secretary's attention.

"Where did this envelope come from?"

"A courier dropped it off, sir."

Sitting back down at his desk, he opened it and found a birth certificate. The names of the father and mother surprised him, along with the name of the child. This opened up a whole new headache. He knew he had to tread lightly with this information. It had to be authenticated, and he had to have a DNA test done.

He didn't want to place another person in danger. Another previously unknown heir. He had phone calls to make and appointments to set up if the person was willing. This changed a lot of things. And in the back of his mind, he questioned if this person had been behind everything. It seemed unlikely. He couldn't imagine them being a serial killer. Just another pawn in the never-ending game of chess being played with the family.

Chapter Seventeen

Perfect Timing

Excitement pumped through their veins! They had executed their plan flawlessly. Jimmy was sitting in jail, rotting for the crimes they committed. No one suspected them. It had been so easy to get everything into place. They had stored all the evidence pointing to Jimmy in the attic and, while everyone was busy at the wedding, they moved it into his room. The fact the family had been so focused on Samuel as the one targeting them made it easier to set up Jimmy, too.

The old buffoon was grumpy and was in the same spots as them and Jimmy during the crimes. It was great that the family focused on him.

Using the gun attached to the drone to kill the remaining family members worked so effortlessly. Placing the remote on Jimmy's ATV while they used their smartphone to control it worked perfectly.

Now all they had to do was wait for Arthur to get his mail and come find them. Of course, they will act shocked. The years of the drama club and high school theatre really paid off. It was all part of their master plan.

One more funeral, then they would claim their stake in the family estate. When the courts proclaimed Jimmy guilty and then sentenced him to death. They will become the sole living heir. They will have it all. It was perfect.

As they sat there, their phone rang. Looking at the caller ID, they saw it was Arthur. Right on cue.

Chapter Eighteen

Big Revelations

Arthur sat with the DNA test results in front of him. They confirmed indeed there was another Gardiner. He shared the information with the police and Jimmy's defense attorney even though he doubted this person had committed any of the crimes they accused Jimmy of committing. He would discuss the results later that day with the person after the funeral.

He was sad that Jimmy could not say goodbye to his cousins properly. He visited Jimmy the day before to let him know what the results were. Jimmy had been just as astonished and also could not fathom that person committing any crimes.

Arthur showed up early on the island to make sure they set up everything for the funerals. Jessica and Richard's grandparents had arrived. They had refused to stay at the Manor house and were determined to leave as soon as their grandchildren were in the ground.

They lay Richard out in a tan coffin with white satin inlaid. They cremated Jessica and Timothy per their wishes. Their remains were inside two beautiful decorative boxes. Flowers adorned the casket and arrangements surrounded the boxes from loving friends and family mourning the losses of the three young adults.

Danielle was early. She went up to Richard's casket to have a private moment with the body of the man she loved. As she said her goodbyes to him, the tears slid down her cheeks and landed on his. In her mind, she vowed to keep their child safe. Unbeknownst to her family, she had packed up many of her belongings that morning and placed them in her car. She planned on leaving right after the funeral.

It was a beautiful funeral service, and it went by quickly. As Danielle left, she headed for the open road off Long Island and to her new beginning. She would call her family when she stopped for the night. There was no definitive plan on where she would end up. She just planned on driving as far away as possible.

Samuel lingered a bit at the graves. He looked at all the past ancestor's headstones. Realizing they were mostly family he never knew he had was overwhelming to him. He hadn't shared with Rita the information that Jimmy and he had discussed. She just assumed he was as shocked and devastated as the rest of them still were.

Everyone seemed like they were in a fog and few stayed long afterward for the luncheon. Arthur sought the person he needed to speak to.

When he found them, he ushered them into another room where they could speak privately.

"Good Afternoon. Do you want me to call you Beatrice or Betty?"

"Either is fine with me. However, I believe Beatrice is a more dignified name. If you are speaking to me privately, this must mean you have the DNA results."

"Yes, Beatrice. I do have the results. It seems you are, in fact, a Gardiner. But, I must warn you. Even though the police have arrested Jimmy. I am not convinced he is the one responsible for the murders. I am worried about your safety."

"Oh my. That is a lot to swallow. I know when you called me the other day and told me of the birth certificate, I assumed it was some sick joke."

"It is no joke. It seems you are Alexandria's half-sister. You had no clue you were a Gardiner?"

"No sir, I had no clue who my daddy was. My Momma, God bless her soul, was very promiscuous. She told me she didn't know who my daddy was."

"Well, with Jimmy in jail and his fate unknown, you are the only surviving heir. You may live in the Manor house. You also will sit in on the business board meetings. We will help mentor you, Allison and I."

"So I can live in the Manor house? Am I expected to still do my housekeeping duties like Jimmy continued to do his security duties?"

"Yes, you can live in the house. No, they will not expect you to do the housekeeping duties. We will hire a new housekeeper. The only reason Jimmy continued to work security was to keep up appearances he was not a Gardiner. Do you want to keep your heritage a secret?"

"That is a lot to think about. I suppose if I move into the house I will need to tell that I am a Gardiner. I guess I am okay with that. That means I will take my chances, but I am sure the security team will keep me safe."

"Well, I guess that is settled, then. I will call a meeting of everyone on the island once all the mourners have left. We will tell them your news and then you can move into the house."

"Thank you, Arthur."

Beatrice left the room. When she was in the foyer, she ran her hands over the furniture and the pictures on the walls. It was all hers. It was hard to contain her happiness. She finally had everything she had always wanted. What she had worked so hard for. Poor Arthur was worried about her safety. How sweet.

Little did he know she was the safest Gardiner ever. She was the mastermind behind it all. The best part was no one suspected her. Poor little Jimmy, taking the fall for everything she did. That was the icing on the cake.

Her hand trailed along the banister as she slowly went upstairs. Now to choose her bedroom. Which room suited her best? She opened the door to Ms. Mary's room, and she remembered her performance screaming as she found Ms. Mary. The memory made her laugh. She should get an academy award for that performance.

This room would be perfect. She would claim it as her own and have all of Ms. Mary's things removed. She would also restore the parlor to its previous glory. No pool table belonged in an elite manor house.

After all the mourners left the island, Arthur wrangled the inhabitants for a meeting. The room was abuzz, not knowing why they were being called together.

"Good evening everybody, thank you for coming on such short notice. I know we are all tired. It's been a long and emotional day for us all. I have some developing news though to share with all of you. It came to my attention anonymously that there was another potential living Gardiner heir besides Jimmy."

Samuel stiffened. He trusted Jimmy not to tell anyone. Jimmy asked him not to say anything, either. He looked on in fear that his secret was about to be revealed.

"Beatrice Adeline Smith, better known as Betty to us all. She apparently did not know who her father was. According to her original birth certificate that she never saw, her father was Alexandria's father as well. I have confirmed this with DNA testing. We have discussed her role as a Gardiner. She will learn the family business and she wants to live in the Manor house. We will look for a new housekeeper to take her previous position."

Samuel relaxed. It wasn't him. His secret was safe. But, Betty. Betty was a Gardiner as well. That was something he could not believe.

Murmurs and whispers ran around the room. Stella eyed Betty suspiciously. Everyone was completely in disbelief at what they were just told. Betty heard someone whisper, "The Gardiner men surely didn't know how to keep it in their pants."

Betty ignored the comment but thought to herself. If they only knew how true that statement was.

Samuel eyed Betty. She appeared as if all of this was news to her. He needed to see Jimmy and tell him what had happened. Maybe this could open up leads into the case. Who knew how many other Gardiner heirs were out there? Others may actually live on the island too, just like Betty. They may need to test every single person on the island to determine their lineage and see if there are any more unknown Gardiners. However, that would mean revealing his secret.

That was something he would have to think about. He knew the accusations against him implicating him in the murders of Alexandria's family. Was he willing to give up his present life to atone for the sins of his past?

Betty was reveling in the astonishment of her fellow inhabitants at her good fortune. There were a few snide comments, of course, especially about her mother. Nevertheless, she took it all in stride, knowing full well she had all the control in the world now.

"Congratulations Betty, Let me know what your favorite meals are since I will be cooking for you regularly."

Stella had approached Betty. She didn't trust what was going on, maybe because her only child was sitting behind bars for a crime he didn't commit.

"Oh, thank you, Stella. Please call me Beatrice from now on, though. This is such a whirlwind surprise. When Mr. Arthur called me up, I did not know what he was talking about. I will let you know tomorrow about my favorite dishes. I eat breakfast early. By five o'clock in the morning, if that's okay with you."

"That is fine. I will have a variety of breakfast foods ready for you in the morning. Do you need help to move your things into the Manor house? I am sure my husband can get some of the men to help."

"Sure, that would be helpful. We can do that tomorrow, though. I think today has been tiring enough for all."

"That's for sure. Just be careful and watch your back. You don't want to end up like my Jimmy or the other Gardiners."

Betty narrowed her eyes at Stella.

"Is that some sort of threat?"

"Why no! I am just worried about your safety with everything that has happened."

"I am sure I will be fine."

The next morning, Samuel set off to visit Jimmy. Stella was up early cooking Betty breakfast and Betty was already making plans for changes at the Manor house. Arthur had given her a charge card connected to the business until they could get one of her own.

When the guards came to get Jimmy for visitation, he had been staring up at the ceiling, wondering how he had gotten himself into this mess. If he had left the island when Melissa asked him to, he wouldn't be sitting in jail. He was the convenient scapegoat.

He wasn't expecting a visitor today, so it surprised him to see Samuel on the other end of the glass holding onto the telephone.

"So what brings you to see me? Should I call you Samuel, Benjamin, or Dad?"

"You can call me whatever you want, son. I am here because there was a big revelation after the funeral yesterday. It turns out there is another Gardiner heir besides me. It's Betty. Betty is Ms. Alexandria's half-sister."

"What? That's crazy!"

"Yeah, it got me thinking. How many other secret Gardiners are out there, especially living on the island? It seems the Gardiner men weren't very faithful, and they were prolific at multiplying."

"You have a valid question. How do you suppose we find that answer?"

"We could have your defense attorney subpoena everyone on the island to submit to a DNA test. If there are more heirs, then there could be enough reasonable doubt to get you set free."

"But that would mean revealing who you are, Dad. I can't ask you to do that. I know what that means."

"If it means clearing you, I would do it. I did what I did years ago because I wanted revenge. Revenge for having to give you up and pretend you died. Ms. Alexandria had no right to force us to give you up. However, your mother wanted the Gardiner fortune, and I loved her so much, I would do anything for her."

"I will talk to my attorney about it. Your name won't be mentioned. I will just say I thought that there could be other heirs and see what he thinks."

"At least you are safe inside these walls."

"Yeah, I guess. You don't think Betty is behind all this, do you? I can't see her being a serial killer."

"I don't know. Time will tell."

Chapter Nineteen

Disappearing

Danielle's eyes were getting heavy. She had been driving for nearly eight hours, with a few bathroom breaks. Her intentions were to get as far away as possible before she stopped for the night. The motel parking lot she pulled into was semi-full.

As she walked up to the front desk, the frumpy woman with spectacles hanging off the tip of her nose looked her up and down.

"What can I do for you, dear?"

"I would like to rent a room for a couple of days."

"It is sixty-nine dollars a night, dear. So how many nights will you be staying?"

"At least two. Can I let you know tomorrow if it will be longer?"

"Sure, dear."

The woman took the cash Danielle handed her and gave her the change and the key to her room. When Danielle opened the door to the room, the smell of stale air, mustiness, and cigarette smoke filled her nostrils. She opened the windows and left the door open as she unpacked her things from her car.

It was a small room with one double bed, a desk with a chair, a bureau that served double duty as a TV stand, and a small refrigerator. She lifted the sheets and checked for bedbugs. Peering into the bathroom, it was cleaner than she expected, which impressed her. This would have to do.

For now, she was too tired to go any further. She had made it to somewhere in Pennsylvania.

It was late, almost midnight by the time she settled in. She needed to call her parents. They had called and texted her multiple times. Guilt crept over her. She didn't want to worry them, but she needed to get as far away as possible before she contacted them. Taking a deep breath, she dialed her mom's cell phone. Her mom picked it up after the first ring.

"Danielle, where are you? We have been worried sick."

"I am okay, mom. I need space, though, and time."

"Honey, I know losing Richard Jr. and the others is hard on you, but you don't need to deal with it all on your own."

"Yes, I do, Mom. In time, you will understand why I left."

"Where are you, though?"

"I am safe, and that is all that you need to know right now. I am sorry."

"Danielle, I don't understand. Why can't you tell us where you are?"

"I am sorry, Mom, truly I am. This is just as hard for me, but this is the only way to ensure you all stay safe and I stay safe."

"You are scaring me, Danielle. Please tell me what is going on."

"I don't mean to scare you. In time, I will let you know what is going on and why I had to leave but now is not the time. Love you, Mom."

"We love you too, Danielle."

She hung up as she heard her mom choke back the tears. Danielle knew this was crushing her. The guilt kept creeping over her. She pushed it out of her mind as she placed her hands on her belly.

Danielle needed sleep. She pulled back the covers to the bed and put her head on the lumpy pillow. Closing her eyes, she saw Richard's lifeless body in the casket. The tears came, and she cried herself to sleep.

In the morning, she showered and then went to find some breakfast. The little diner she found a mile down the road seemed to be the only place she could find. When she stepped through the doors, she felt transported back in time. It reminded her of the old diners she saw in the movies of the fifties and sixties. It had black and white tiled floors and round red covered seats at the chrome-colored counter. There were a few booths, and some tables scattered throughout.

There was a petite waitress taking a customer's order behind the counter and another, more plump waitress taking orders from a table. Danielle chose a table in the corner. She felt out of place here. There was a difference in what the customers were wearing compared to what she was used to. More rugged. Yet, the people all seemed happy and friendly.

She watched as the plump waitress came over to her table.

"Hey there honey, my name is Selma. I will be your waitress this morning. What can I get you to drink while you are looking over the menu?"

"I will have a glass of water and a large orange juice, please."

"Sure thing."

Selma seemed nice. She was back in a flash with the water and orange juice. Danielle placed her breakfast order and watched as more customers filed in. The two waitresses seemed to work well together, taking everyone's orders. They were busy. This gave her a brilliant idea. She thought maybe they could use an extra hand.

When Selma brought her plate and set it down, Danielle thought it was a perfect opportunity to ask.

"Are you looking for any waitresses?"

"Actually, yes. We are down two. They got up and quit yesterday. You got any experience?"

"As a matter of fact, I do! I am looking for a job. I just pulled into town last night."

Selma tilted her head and eyed Danielle.

"Why'd you pick here?"

"I just stopped for the night, but I think I like it here and want to stay awhile."

"Where are you coming from?"

"Long Island, NY."

"What brings you all the way out here?"

"My best friend died, and I needed a change of scenery. Too many memories back home."

Selma's eyes softened, and she put her hand on Danielle's arm.

"I am sorry for your loss. I will bring you an application and I am sure Wendy and Bruce will look it over and want to interview you."

"Who are Wendy and Bruce?"

"Wendy is the waitress at the counter and Bruce is the cook. They own the place."

"Oh okay. Thank you."

As she ate her breakfast, she filled out the application. When Selma brought it over to Wendy, she looked it over and handed it to Bruce. Danielle watched as the three of them had some discussion and looked over at her a few times. Wendy walked over to Danielle's table.

"So, you want a job here?"

"Yes ma'am. If you will give me one."

"When can you start?"

"Immediately."

"Here then."

Wendy handed her an apron and an order pad.

"Thank you."

Danielle quickly adapted to her new job. She put in a full 8-hrs shift and returned exhausted to the motel room. Before she turned in for the night, she asked the desk clerk for extended stay rates and she paid for the next month.

She didn't know how long after that she would stay, but for now, she was content to stay and save up more money. It was a small town, and she felt safe. That was all that mattered to her at the moment.

Lena and Steven were frantic about Danielle's disappearance. They were relieved when she had finally called them, but her mysteriousness of not telling them where she was worried them. First thing in the morning, they paid a visit to Sergeant Rollins.

"There is nothing we can do. She has left of her own free will and she is an adult. We can't force her to tell you where she is."

This was not what Lena and Steven wanted to hear. They were determined to find their daughter, even if she didn't want to be found. It would be up to them to do what they could to get their daughter back home safely where they felt she belonged. After a few phone calls, they set up an appointment with a prominent private investigator who specialized in tracking down missing persons.

It didn't take them long to get to Mr. Davis's office.

"Mr. and Mrs. Weston, come in and have a seat. I know this must be a difficult time for all of you."

"Thank you, Mr. Davis. Please call me Steven. We just want to find our daughter and get her the help she obviously needs. She has been through so much."

"Yes, of course. First of all, is her cell phone, car, car insurance, any of that in your name?"

"No, none of it is in our name. We tried to foster responsibility and self-sufficiency, so once she was eighteen, we had her get a job and put those things in her own name."

"Okay, so that makes things a bit harder. Not impossible, but harder. If any of those things were in your name, we would have a few options."

"Like what?"

"We could have reported the car stolen if it was in your name. That would have enabled us to put an all-points bulletin out on the car."

"Oh."

"Do you have any of the tracking apps on her phone?"

"She turned off the location sharing."

"Hmm, she definitely does not want you to know where she is. Do you know what prompted this disappearance? Has she done this in the past?"

Lena broke down as she wrung her hands.

"She has never done this before. If something was bothering her in the past, she would come to me or her father to talk through it. The last six months have been crazy, though. I am sure you have seen the news about the Gardiner family. She was best friends with Richard Jr., and was engaged to marry him until she called off the engagement after his siblings died."

"Oh wow. Yes, I am familiar with the saga of the Gardiner family. Tragic. All of it. I imagine she is suffering from a lot of emotional trauma herself. You said she had a job. Where was that?"

"She worked at the café in East Hampton. We didn't know she quit the day after Richard died. She didn't tell us. We went there first when she didn't come home after the funeral. We figured she had picked up a shift to take her mind off everything. That was when they told us she had quit days prior."

"Okay. So she knew she was leaving. I will do what I can to track her down, but there isn't much to go on so far. I will keep you updated as I find anything."

"Thank you."

When they left the private investigator's office, they felt defeated. They had very little hope they would find Danielle. They had to try, though. She was their firstborn, and they didn't want to lose her. They had already endured so much loss recently.

They went home and explained everything to their other two daughters. Neither of them had any idea where their sister had gone and were just as worried and confused as their parents.

Chapter Twenty

Lady Beatrice

The attention from everyone on the island sent thrilling jolts of excitement through Betty. What she had imagined she would feel didn't even compare to the actual emotions running rampant in her. She had got to her old bungalow before the men of the island came to help her move her stuff. It was imperative that she hide the listening devices and equipment she had used to spy on the family. So she carefully placed it all in the root cellar portion of the basement. Moving an antique armoire in front of the narrow doorway to block anyone from noticing the door. With minutes to spare before the men showed up she finished the task at hand.

Since she was leaving all of her old furniture, it wasn't suspicious that the piece of furniture was being left in the basement either. By late afternoon, all of her personal possessions were moved into Ms. Mary's old room. Looking in the full-length mirror, she pulled her shoulders back and lifted her chin, an air of power radiated from her reflection. The new lady of the manor wanted to throw herself a party to introduce herself to the Hamptons social scene. She went down to the kitchen.

"Stella, I am planning a big soiree. I am going to need to go over the menu with you."

"Sure thing, Betty. When are you planning on having this party?"

"I already asked you once to call me Beatrice. Actually, I prefer Lady Beatrice. I am your employer now, Stella. You must address me accordingly."

Betty had always been a mild-mannered woman. Quietly going about her job. This change in Betty's demeanor took Stella aback. She hadn't expected the change in her status to go so quickly to her head and bring out so much ego. However, it was apparent it already had.

"Yes, ma'am. I apologize for offending you. It won't happen again."

"Make sure it doesn't or I may need to re-evaluate your employment here. I am already skeptical of having you here, considering your son is awaiting trial for murdering my kin."

"Lady Beatrice, surely you are not threatening to fire me because of the allegations against my son? He is innocent until proven guilty in a court of law. And I fully believe in his innocence. I would think you would too, considering you have watched him grow up here."

"I am not the threatening type Stella, I am just telling you how it is. If I feel anyone is a danger to my safety in any way, I will take the necessary precautions. And I am planning the party to occur in two weeks. You will be able to accomplish that, correct?"

"Yes, ma'am."

Stella stood in utter dismay. It was as if this was a different person than the Betty she had worked alongside for many years. Someone she once considered a friend. How could she have changed so drastically in such a short amount of time?

That night when she walked in the door of her home, for the first time in her life, she thought about moving. Her husband John saw the look of frustration and confusion in the worry lines on his wife's face as he took the meals she had prepared for them out of her hands.

"Stella, what has gotten you so worried?"

"Betty, or should I say, Lady Beatrice, as she wants to be called. I had a very uncomfortable interaction with her today. She believes Jimmy is guilty, and she basically threatened to fire me because he is my son."

"Ah, yes, I too had an interesting interaction with her while helping her move. She insisted that we also all call her Lady Beatrice. The security guys told me she has also ordered all the security cameras to be removed from the manor house."

"That makes little sense. Why would she downgrade the security? Jimmy is innocent. He isn't the killer. She is just putting herself in danger."

"We all tried telling her the same thing. Something has her convinced of Jimmy's guilt. And she wants to throw a big party introducing herself to the Hampton socialites as Lady Beatrice in two weeks! It is a logistical nightmare considering we are down four security members. I may have to come out of retirement. There has been an influx of trespassers since the news of the killings broke."

"Do what you have to, John, but if I start feeling we are not welcome here, I may want to consider leaving the island. For good."

"Dear, if you want to leave, we will. I am going to visit Jimmy tomorrow. I will discuss it with him, too."

"John, do you think Betty could have killed everyone and framed Jimmy?"

"You know, before today, I would have said no way. Now, after seeing such a change in her personality, I am not so sure. No one knows how her birth certificate appeared. The more I think about it all, the more suspicious it is."

"Maybe you should discuss all this with Matt? I know he doesn't live on the island anymore, but I am sure he could help sort some of this out."

"You have a point there. I am gonna go call him."

As John left the room, he stopped to hug his wife and give her a peck on the cheek. Her husband's arms wrapped around her gave her comfort in what seemed like a never-ending nightmare.

In his den, John sat in his recliner and dialed his friend Matt.

"Hey there John, how are things going? Sorry to hear about Jimmy's troubles. Just so you know, we don't believe he is the killer. Melissa and I are still doing our own investigating from here."

"Hey Matt, that is so good to hear. We can't seem to make sense of it all. And now, with Betty being named a Gardiner heir and the changes in her personality, it's got Stella and me wondering if she could be the actual killer."

"What did you just say? Betty is a Gardiner?"

"Yup, someone anonymously mailed her birth certificate to Arthur. She seemed just as shocked as everyone else at first, but now she has really slid right into the role of Lady of the Manor House. She is even insisting on being called Lady Beatrice."

"Holy crap! That's crazy. How is she a Gardiner, though?"

"Well, apparently, Alexandria's father had an affair of sorts with her mother, but since she was always so promiscuous, it was an easy secret to keep."

"Oh wow, I remember her mother. I remember our mothers telling us to stay away from her."

"Yeah, I remember that warning, too. Whatever happened to her mother?"

"Didn't she die of a drug or alcohol overdose?"

"Wait, I believe you are correct. In the bungalow, they found her in the bathtub! We should still have those records on file. I am going to pull that file tomorrow."

"She overdosed in the bathtub? I didn't remember that. That is interesting though. I would love to compare the scene of her death with that of Ms. Mary's."

"I will send you a copy of the report by fax tomorrow if I find it. If we find similarities, it might just cast enough doubt on the killer being Jimmy to get him set free. And if there are enough commonalities, it just might shed light on whether Betty could be the actual killer."

"Sounds like a plan. I know Melissa is planning on visiting Jimmy. She wants him to know we are on his side still and we believe in him."

"I am sure he will appreciate that, Matt. Thank you both for all your help."

"No problem. We want to know who the killer is, too. We want justice for Zach and all the others."

"We will get it."

The two friends hung up. John couldn't wait until morning to head to the security shack. He knew he wouldn't get any sleep until he had that file in his hands. So he headed on down to check things out. It took a couple of hours to go through several file cabinets to find the file on Betty's mom's death.

At the time, it was an open and shut case. Everyone knew that she drank and did drugs, so there was no question of her overdosing in the bathtub. He pulled Ms. Mary's report as well. As he read through the reports, glaring similarities jumped out at him. The chair with the bottle of wine and the wineglass. The bottle of pills. All very theatrical. Obviously, the bathrooms were different, but it was eerily ironic. The pictures of the chair with the wine bottle, glass, and pills appeared they could have been from the same crime scene.

As he was sitting at Jimmy's desk going over the files, Samuel walked in, looking concerned.

"Hey, John. I didn't know who to go to, but I saw the lights on in here, so I figured I would come to see who it was. I am glad it's you. At Betty's bungalow, I found something."

"What did you find?"

"Well, I was in the basement, shutting off the water and prepping it to be closed up. Putting sheets over furniture and such. There is an armoire in the basement. I went to put a sheet over and noticed someone had moved it. There were scuff marks on the dirt floor as if they dragged it over several feet. It got me wondering why Betty would have done that by herself. It's a sizeable piece of furniture. So I moved it back."

"And?"

"I found a door to a root cellar behind it."

"What is so mysterious about that?"

"I found many electronic listening devices and boxes of recordings. I listened to some. She had recordings of every conversation that was had in the Manor House. She must have had the whole place bugged."

"Why would Betty be listening in on the family?"

"I don't know, but she would know when and where they were coming and going."

"Where are all the equipment and the recordings now?"

"They are in the back of my truck. I pushed the armoire back to cover the door to make it look as though no one had been in there. But I put everything in my truck and brought it here."

"Great job. Let's put it in here until I can turn it over to the police in the morning. Thank you, Samuel. I appreciate your help in trying to clear Jimmy's name."

"No problem. He is a good kid, and he didn't do all this. He shouldn't pay for crimes he didn't commit."

"I agree. We need to be careful, though. If Betty is the killer, she is dangerous. She has been doing this for years."

"What do you mean, years?"

"Her mother died similarly as Ms. Mary did."

"You don't think she killed her own mother, do you?"

"I don't know what to think right now. All I know is my son is in jail for crimes he didn't commit and now Lady Beatrice is showing us all a different side of herself."

"Yeah, I can't get used to calling her Lady Beatrice. She will always be Betty to me."

"Same here. She threatened to fire Stella today."

"You are kidding me? Stella is the kindest, most hardworking employee on this island. Why would she fire her?"

"Because she is Jimmy's mother, and she called her Betty."

"Unbelievable."

"Watch your back, Samuel. We do not know what she is capable of."

"I will, and you watch yours and Stella's. If I see or hear anything else, I will let you know."

"Thank you."

Chapter Twenty-One

Visitors

Jimmy had gotten a new cellmate the day before. The guy snored on the bed beneath him. He was a big burly guy covered in tattoos. He was glad the guy was on the bottom bunk just because of the sheer size of him. Sleep eluded Jimmy already he couldn't imagine trying to sleep on the lower bunk underneath his cellmate. In an effort to lull his mind to sleep he started counting the holes in the ceiling tiles.

His counting was interrupted constantly. The noise of the other inmates yelling at the correction officers, who made their rounds every fifteen minutes. Or by the catcalls made to the female medical personnel who made their rounds twice a day. The amount of respect given to the members of the clergy when they toured always surprised him, though. It got a little quieter during those moments.

Most of the inmates acted like caged animals, pacing in their cells. There had been a fight in the yard the day before, and the prison had been on lockdown for the rest of the day. With the lockdown lifted, Jimmy could feel the tension in the air, as if chaos could ensue at any moment.

Fear caused him to perspire more than usual, with beads of sweat forming on his forehead. He had never been scared for his life before, not even with the serial killer on the island, but now he did not know how to survive in this environment. His stomach tensed and tightened.

His job was security on the island, but he never dealt with hardened criminals before. The inmates were hardcore. Not petty trespassers or vandals. They were murderers and rapists. Being out of his element did not sit well with him.

The realization hit him: he might wind up living in prison for the rest of his life. His stomach churned at the thought. He swallowed hard to hold back from letting his stomach win the battle. Jimmy knew he couldn't survive living here. He missed the island and everything about it. His mother and father, the security crew, everything. The thoughts ran through his head about his cousins and how much he missed them already. How could he let this happen? They were dead because he couldn't protect them. Maybe he was guilty in that sense. But he didn't pull the trigger.

"Jimmy Driscoll, you have a visitor."

The guard's announcement roused Jimmy out of his thoughts. He didn't have a meeting scheduled with his attorney until the next day. Could it be Samuel, again? As the guard led him to the visitor area, it shocked him to see Melissa sitting on the other side of the plexiglass this time.

She was a sight for very sore eyes. Her smile made his heart beat a little faster. The compassion and empathy he saw in her eyes calmed his spirit.

He picked up the phone as she picked up the other one.

"What are you doing here?"

"Checking on you? I wanted to make sure you are okay."

"I am doing as well as expected."

"You look like hell Jimmy."

"I'm not getting sleep. It is noisy as hell in here, never mind the intense fear I have, Melissa. I can't survive in here."

"We are going to get you out of here. Please don't worry."

"How? There is so much circumstantial evidence against me I even sometimes question if I really am guilty."

"Don't say that Jimmy. You know, and I know you didn't kill anyone."

"Okay, but the longer I stay in here, the harder it is for me to have any hope."

"Just hang on, please. Your dad called my dad last night. There might be evidence to clear you."

"What? Samuel called your dad. What evidence?"

"Wait, Samuel? Why do you think Samuel called my dad? I said your dad called my dad. You know, John Driscoll. This place is really getting to you, isn't it? Your dad and my dad were talking because now that Betty is living in the Manor house, she has changed drastically. She is demanding to be called Lady Beatrice. She even threatened to fire your mom. Then they both remembered her mother dying very much like Ms. Mary."

"Okay. Things are getting really confusing. So I need to tell you a secret. Samuel is really Benjamin, who is my biological father. He had no clue he was a Gardiner. He came and visited me when he found out I was a Gardiner and, subsequently, he is too. I am the only one who knows his secret. We suspected him to be the killer originally, but we had eyes on him the entire time of the wedding. So he couldn't have planted the evidence in my bedroom or flown the drone. And he wants to help get me out of here. So now why did Betty threaten to fire my mom? And what is this about Betty's mom dying like Ms. Mary?"

"WOW, that's a lot to unpack! Betty threatened to fire your mom because she called her Betty instead of Lady Beatrice and because she believes you are the killer. Our dads are comparing the files of Betty's mom's death and Ms. Mary's. Apparently, they are eerily alike. And Samuel found tapes of recordings Betty had made of conversations in the Manor house. She had many types of recording equipment and listening devices hidden in a root cellar of her bungalow."

"That's great, but it's all circumstantial evidence. None of it can link her to any of the murders. We need strong direct evidence to clear me and convict her. Right now, there is more circumstantial evidence pointing to me than her."

"Well, they turned everything over to Rolly and your lawyer. Everyone is doing everything they can."

"I appreciate it. It really is great seeing you, Melissa. And it helps to know you are still in my corner."

"Of course, Jimmy, I will always be in your corner. I love you, and when all this is done and over with, maybe we can give ourselves another chance."

"I would love that."

The guard escorted Jimmy back to his cell. His cellmate was awake and grunted at him, so Jimmy just went back to lying on his bed and counting holes again. He finally dozed off, thinking of freedom and his potential future with Melissa. It was late afternoon when the guard awakened him again, telling him he had another visitor. His cellmate piped up.

"Look at you, such a social butterfly. Two visitors in one day, most of us in here barely get a visit a week. You must be the big man on campus."

Jimmy just looked at him and shrugged. It was the guard that responded.

"I would be careful Maddog, this guy is in here for several counts of murder. He is a serial killer. You are in here for attempted murder."

Jimmy watched as his cellmate's eyes widened at the words the guard was saying. He nodded his head toward Jimmy.

"Is that true?"

Jimmy shrugged again.

"That's what they say."

The guard guided Jimmy back to the visitor area. This time, it was his adoptive dad. It was so good to see him. Although Jimmy could see the worry in his eyes. The creases in his forehead were deeper, and the crow's feet around his eyes seemed more prominent.

They both picked up their phones to talk to each other. Jimmy's dad broke down in tears.

"I am sorry son, we are doing everything to get you out of here."

"I know, Dad. It's okay. Melissa stopped by. She filled me in."

"She did? That's great. I am glad to see she is coming back around. I hope when all this mess is clear, you two can start to have a normal relationship again."

"Me too, Dad. Me too. How is Mom? I am worried about her working for Betty. It seems Betty isn't fond of Mom."

"She will be fine, son. If things get too bad, we have already decided we will leave the island."

"You promise me?"

"I promise. We are going to do everything possible to stay safe and get you free so we can all be happy again."

"Okay, give Mom a hug and kiss for me."

"I will."

Their visit was brief, but it was another morale boost for Jimmy. As he got back to his cell, he was feeling more hopeful than he had felt earlier.

Until the guard closed the door behind him and walked away. Then his cellmate grabbed him by the collar and jacked him up against the wall.

"You think you are some badass because you murdered a few people?"

"No sir."

"Good, because I can and will kill you if you so much as look at me the wrong way."

"Okay, just put me down and I will give you your space and you can give me mine."

Maddog lowered him back down and Jimmy climbed back into his bunk and resumed counting the holes in the ceiling tiles. It was another restless night. There was banging on the bars and yelling again, and Maddog snoring. He tried to drown out the noise with his pillow as he closed his eyes and thought about Melissa again.

Jimmy imagined it was early in the morning when things finally quieted down and he could fall asleep. It felt good to get some sleep. He woke up choking on smoke and panicked. Jumping from his bed, he yelled for the guards. His heart was beating fast as he realized the fire was in his cell, and his cellmate just sat and laughed.

The guards got there to the cell and put out the small fire with an extinguisher. Maddog blamed Jimmy for starting the fire and they moved Jimmy to segregation housing.

For the rest of the day, Jimmy tried to just sleep. His cellmate in segregation housing was quieter, which was a plus. He knew he didn't start the fire, and he remembered Maddog's threats. Why would this guy start a fire and get him moved? What beef does this guy have? He must have looked at him the wrong way.

Prison life was already wearing thin on Jimmy's nerves. He just wanted out, but couldn't figure out how he was going to get out of this mess.

Chapter Twenty-Two

New Boss

Lady Beatrice was accompanying Arthur into the city for her first board meeting. She was determined to make sure everyone knew she was in charge. Her appearance was much different now. She had burned the old grey maid uniform she wore in the past the first day she moved into the Manor house. The power suit, skirt, and blouse she wore now with three-inch heels exuded confidence and power.

As they rode the train, she took in the eyes, watching her. They only made her sit up straighter, with her shoulders back and her chin up slightly higher. She wanted everyone to know she was important.

When they reached the office building that she was now in charge of, excitement ran through her veins. Power. This was everything she had worked so hard for.

People shook her hand and welcomed her as they made their way through the building and up to the boardroom. She shook hands back, although looked down upon everyone she came in contact with. When anyone called her Betty, she sharply corrected them to call her Lady Beatrice.

She took her position at the head of the conference table as Arthur introduced her to the board members.

"This is Lady Beatrice. She is now the new co-owner of Cromwell Realtor Corporation and Gardiners Island. Please make her feel welcome."

After each board member went around the room and welcomed her and introduced themselves, Lady Beatrice addressed them all.

"Thank you for the warm welcome. As Arthur has mentioned, I am in charge now. I will finalize all decisions. I will listen to everyone's input and weigh opinions, but in the end, the only opinion that really matters is mine. Does everyone understand?"

Arthur's mouth dropped open and everyone else's around the room did, too. Allison looked at Arthur as Arthur responded.

"Lady Beatrice, with all due respect. All of us have been running this business for years. I would hope that you rethink your position and your statement."

"Arthur, I am in charge here. Not you. I can fire and replace all of you if you don't agree with what I stated."

They exchanged looks among all the board members. Eyebrows raised and heads bowed with pursed lips. Bodies shifted awkwardly in chairs and tension filled the room. No one felt comfortable with how this meeting was starting off, except Lady Beatrice herself. Allison broke the silence.

"Well then, I guess we should all bring you up to speed on what is happening within the company then, so you can make informed decisions."

"Thank you, Allison. That is appreciated. Oh, and I am sorry for the loss of your son- and daughter-in-law. Such a tragedy."

"Thank you, Lady Beatrice. And yes, it was a tragedy. It was a deep blow to all of us personally and to the business. Jessica was a tremendous asset to this company. She is missed dearly."

Allison's words cut through Lady Beatrice. The smug smile that had been on Lady Beatrice's face since entering the boardroom thinned into a neutral, resting scowl. Allison knew the shot she fired across the bow had hit its mark, and she smiled sweetly back at Lady Beatrice. She didn't care if she got fired. Arthur already knew her plans.

Allison had control of the property in Ireland that Jessica and Timothy had purchased. She was planning on moving there in six months. So if she got fired by Lady Beatrice, she really didn't care. She hadn't worked her entire life at this company to let some power-hungry control freak tell her what to do.

Lady Beatrice kept her composure, however, she was fuming inside. She did not like the idolization of Jessica. It made her blood boil. She regretted not taking Allison out of the equation when she had the chance at the wedding.

Each board member gave a detailed report on the various projects they were in charge of. Lady Beatrice gave her unsolicited and uninformed opinions about each. Many times over making poor business decisions that would cost the company money. She overrode any votes and claimed she had the final say in all matters.

When the meeting was over, Arthur accompanied Lady Beatrice back to the Manor house, where they would be interviewing candidates for several new security positions and the new housekeeper. Martin had been pulling double duty since Lady Beatrice had moved into the Manor house. He ushered each potential candidate into the parlor when it was time for them to be interviewed.

They filled the security positions first, and Arthur felt confident about each one Lady Beatrice had hired. He was thankful he had pre-screened the applicants beforehand without her knowledge, so that those without the proper qualities needed for the job were weeded out.

When it came time to interview the housekeeper candidates, it was between three potential employees. Arthur knew which one he wanted to hire, but ultimately, the decision would be Lady Beatrice's. He hoped to come up with a way to persuade her to pick the one he favored without her catching on that he favored her.

The first potential employee was a young woman named Mindi. She was just 18 and had no prior work experience. Lady Beatrice eyed her up and down as she walked into the room and sat down across from her.

"So, why do you want to work for me?"

The straightforward question and the briskness in the tone in which Lady Beatrice asked it threw off Mindi.

"Um, well. Ma'am, everybody who is anybody around here is curious about this place. You know, so I need a job and figured why not? At least it wouldn't be boring, right?"

Lady Beatrice frowned. She didn't like this one. This one seemed a bit too eager and curious. What she didn't need was a snooping employee.

"I see. You do know curiosity killed the cat, don't you?"

Mindi's eyes widened at Lady Beatrice's reply. There were a few more questions and answers between the two, and then she was dismissed without getting the position.

The next one was a little older. She was 22 and her name was Lorraine. She had previously worked as a nanny and a housekeeper for one of the prominent families of East Hampton.

"I see you worked for the Hammervilles. Why did you leave their employment?"

"Well, to be completely honest. Mr. Hammerville was a bit inappropriate towards me, and it felt extremely uncomfortable. So I quit. I have been waitressing until I can find something better."

Lady Beatrice took pleasure in the revealed secret of the prominent family. She loved collecting secrets about people. They could always be used to her advantage. It is a shame this girl didn't share her passion for power. The poor girl didn't even realize the missed opportunity she had.

"Oh, what a shame. That must have been such a horrible experience for you."

After more questions and answers back and forth and again, Lady Beatrice dismissed Lorraine without hiring her.

The last candidate was a 32-year-old with over twelve years of experience as a housekeeper for one of the elderly gentlemen in East Hampton who had just passed away, leaving her jobless. Her name was Verna.

"Well, Verna, you are our last hope. I see you have experience and you present yourself maturely, unlike the other candidates for this position. Tell me, why should I hire you?"

"Lady Beatrice, as you know, I have worked for a very prominent family in the past. I know how to keep confidential information and I know how to do my job while staying out of family matters. You will barely notice I am here unless I am performing a task that you require to be done in the presence of others."

Lady Beatrice smiled and nodded at Arthur. Arthur was relieved she picked the candidate he wanted her to.

"Arthur, I believe we have found our new housekeeper. Please have Martin show her to her new home and have him show her the duties she is responsible for performing."

Arthur ushered Verna out of the parlor and introduced her to Martin. Martin took over in showing Verna the Manor house and her responsibilities. When he was done, he showed her to the bungalow Betty had once lived in, which would now be her home. Samuel came by to make sure he turned all the utilities back on and that they were in working order.

Verna unpacked her things, changed into her crisp new uniform, and headed back to the Manor house to get to work. It was after dinner and she knew she had to draw a bath for Lady Beatrice and turn down her bedspread.

When she reached the door of Lady Beatrice, she knocked on the door.

"Come on in."

Lady Beatrice was sitting at her desk writing in what looked like a diary or journal of some sort. When she saw Verna, she closed the book, slid it into the desk drawer, and locked it closed. She held onto the key and slipped it into her bathrobe pocket. Verna watched all of this carefully.

"I am here to run your bath water and turn down your bedspread."

"Then get to it, please. At least you are punctual. You don't have to tell me why you are here, though. I already know. Please, just do your work."

Verna went into the bathroom and started the bath water. She wondered how she would get access to the desk drawer. It would be imperative that she read what Lady Beatrice wrote in the diary. When the bath was full, she went back into the bedroom and turned down the bedspread as Lady Beatrice entered the bathroom and shut the door behind her.

With a slim glimmer of hope that the lock on the desk drawer didn't actually work, Verna tried opening it. It disappointed her when it didn't budge. She needed to figure out how to get that diary, but tonight would not be the time.

She finished the rest of her nightly tasks that were required of her and then headed back to the bungalow. As she looked around at the dingy and dusty place, it boggled her mind that the former housekeeper lived there. It definitely wasn't the definition of clean, but then again, she had known carpenters who had unfinished projects at their own houses. She spent the rest of the evening scrubbing and cleaning the small bungalow.

In the bedroom's closet, it surprised Verna to find an old high school yearbook. She thumbed through it. Finding that it had belonged to Lady Beatrice. There was no one who had signed it. No teachers. No friends. Nobody. There were faces crossed out. Devil horns added to some. There weren't many pictures of the young Betty. However, she was interestingly in drama club. This was an excellent find. Verna would keep it. It would be an early morning the next day, so she turned in to get some sleep.

Lady Beatrice finished her bath and then sat down at her desk. She unlocked the drawer and took out the diary. She completed her daily entry. Since she was a child, she had been writing in it. The desk drawer held several journals already filled with her daily life. It was imperative that nobody get ahold of them, which is why she guarded them under lock and key. The key went with her everywhere she went. It was never out of her possession.

She knew the secrets revealed between those pages could be her demise. So she would do everything she could to keep that from happening. If she burned them, it would ensure that no one would use them against her. However, she wanted them to be read, eventually. When she died, she wanted people to know how powerful she had been. They were her last legacy.

Chapter Twenty-Three

Starting Over

Danielle had been living out of the motel room for two weeks now. She went to work daily at the diner. They loved her there. The customers loved her charm and her attention to detail when serving them. She was efficient. It was her first day off since she had started.

The first order of business was she needed to find a more permanent place to live. She had decided to settle down in this small town. An efficiency apartment would be perfect if she could find one. She opened up the classified page of the local newspaper and started her search. Going through the columns, she found three that looked promising, so she circled them.

She set up appointments for the afternoon to check them out. Her phone rang, and she looked at the screen. It was her mom, again. She called daily, leaving her a message begging her to come home. This time, she picked up.

"Hi, mom."

"Oh Danielle, it's so good to hear your voice. Your texts are always so short and monotonous."

"Well, mom. Like I keep saying in my texts, I am fine. I am safe."

"That's good honey. But we miss you. Why can't you tell us where you are? Why can't we come to see you?"

"It's better for everyone if I don't tell you where I am or why you can't see me. Tell me what you have been up to?"

"I am worried about you. That's what I am up to. Your father misses you. Your sisters miss you. You have turned our lives upside down."

"I am sorry mom, You will understand eventually. Any fresh news there? Anything on Jimmy?"

"Jimmy is still in jail, thank god. I can't believe he killed his own family members. But I guess greed does that to people. The joke is on him, though. He isn't the only heir to the Gardiner fortune."

"What? First of all, if you believe Jimmy killed them, you obviously do not know him. He considered his cousins more like siblings he never had. And who is this heir you are talking about?"

"Well, it appears Betty the housekeeper was a product of an affair. She is Ms. Alexandria's half-sister. Although, she calls herself Lady Beatrice now. She is having a big party tomorrow night at the Manor house, introducing herself to society. They have invited all the elite socialites. Anyone who is anyone is going."

"Oh, my god. You are kidding me. Betty? A Gardiner? Are you and Dad going to this party?"

"Of course we are going!"

"Mom, please be careful."

"Why? The killer is behind bars. I know you don't believe Jimmy did it, but the police arrested him. They don't arrest innocent people."

"Mom, it happens all the time. Please just be careful, that's all I ask."

"Danielle, all I ask is that you tell us where you are."

"That's not possible, mom. I love you. I gotta go."

"Love you too."

The news that Betty was a Gardiner and was now living the high life in the Manor house as Lady Beatrice left Danielle more than just a little unsettled. It solidified her belief she did the right thing in getting away and not telling anyone where she was going or why. It also strengthened her conviction that Jimmy was innocent.

She wished her parents would stay far away from the island and the Manor house. Unfortunately, though, she knew her parents and grandmother were so entrenched in the Hampton social scene. She prayed they all stayed safe.

Danielle took a shower and then headed out to look at the three apartments. The first one was really a small one-bedroom house on the property of a bigger house. It was cute, with an eat-in kitchen and a small living room. The bathroom was a decent size. The bedroom was too small, though. Danielle had to think about when the baby was born. She needed room for a crib.

The second apartment was a loft above a garage converted into a one-bedroom apartment. The size was substantial, but the stairs concerned Danielle with the thought of carrying the baby up and down them constantly.

The third one was the one that captured her heart. It was a cottage with a small stream bordering the yard. It had two small bedrooms, a bathroom, an eat-in kitchen, and a living room. The owner was an older woman, named Ms. Ditters, who lived next door in an old Victorian-type house. She explained the cottage had once served as the servant's quarters.

Danielle felt at home.

"What is the rent again?"

"I usually ask $1000 a month, but I have a good feeling about you. I want to give you a deal. $800 a month. First and last month up front."

"I will take it! Thank you! Can I move in, in two weeks? I have already paid for the motel ahead of time that I am staying in."

"Absolutely! You can move in when you want to."

"Thank you! Oh, I think I should tell you since you are my new landlord. I will be having a baby in about six months. I hope it's still okay if I rent from you?"

"I already knew, dear."

The old woman smiled at Danielle. It startled her. She didn't think her baby bump was showing yet.

"How did you know?"

"You are glowing, us old timers can tell."

Danielle smiled and thanked the woman again. She felt like this was going to be the perfect place for her and her child to start their new life. Then she realized she needed to find herself an obstetrician. That was the next item on her agenda for the day. She called around and finally got in for an appointment in the next week.

She was tired by the end of the day. When her head hit the pillow and she closed her eyes instead of seeing Richard lying in a pool of his own blood or in his casket, she saw the cottage and her holding her child, cradling them in her arms.

For the first time in weeks, she didn't cry herself to sleep. She peacefully drifted into a restful slumber. She woke up the next morning more refreshed than she had felt in a long time. When she got to work, even Wendy quipped at how chipper she looked.

"Good morning, Danielle. You look like a ray of sunshine this morning. That day off did wonders for you. I am sorry we have been working you so hard. We hired another waitress to lighten the load, too."

"Thanks, Wendy. I guess I didn't realize how much a good night's sleep can do for the soul until I finally got one."

"Well, those dark circles are fading. Hopefully, a couple more good nights and they will be gone for you."

"I didn't realize my fatigue showed so much."

"Dear, people round here notice more than most folks. Oh, and your new landlord stopped in last night. Old Doc Ditters. I am glad you found a permanent home. I was worried you would leave us when your time was up at the motel."

"Doc Ditters?"

"Yeah, Old Doc Ditters, she is the oldest obstetrician in the area still practicing. She runs the Family Obstetrics practice on Hollow Road."

Danielle laughed to herself.

"That all makes sense now."

"What makes sense?"

"How she knew before I told her."

"How she knew what before you told her what?"

"Oh, I am sorry Wendy. I should have told you sooner, too. I hope it doesn't affect my work here. The baby is due in six months. I am pregnant. On my next day off, I will have an appointment with Doc Ditters."

"Not much gets past Doc Ditters. And yes, it's okay you didn't tell me. You are telling me now. You are one of the best waitresses we have ever had. We aren't going to lose you."

Danielle got to work filling the salt and pepper shakers and the sugar containers on all the tables as the morning regulars started filing in. Wendy came out with an old mayonnaise jar cleaned out and a piece of paper stuck to it. She placed it next to the cash register. Danielle was curious about what it was for. It wasn't uncommon for restaurants to raise funds for various charities. She wanted to know what one they were raising money for.

"Hey Wendy, what is that for?"

"You, my dear! It's the Danielle maternity leave fund! We have six months to fill this jar to help you out!"

"Are you serious? Thank you so much!"

"Who's having a baby?"

Pete, the regular who had just sat down, piped up.

"I am."

Danielle answered as she filled his coffee cup and plated a blueberry muffin without him even asking.

"Who is the lucky father?"

Pete broke a piece of muffin off and popped it into his mouth.

Danielle swallowed the lump in her throat and fought back the tears.

"He is dead, unfortunately."

"I am so sorry."

Pete reached across the counter and squeezed Danielle's hand.

"Thanks."

Danielle became occupied with other customers and settled into her day. She didn't notice the hundred-dollar bill Pete had slipped into her maternity leave fund. Wendy did, and she smiled to herself.

Chapter Twenty-Four

The Big Soiree

It was the night of Lady Beatrice's big soiree. Stella had been cooking all day since Lady Beatrice refused to have it catered. Verna did what she could do to help, however, her workload had been doubled as well. John was in the kitchen dressed as a server, as most of the inhabitants of the island were as well. Lady Beatrice invited none of them to the big party as guests.

Verna had tried every chance she could to get into the locked desk drawer. On one or two occasions, Lady Beatrice almost caught her in the act. Not knowing what she wrote in the diary consumed Verna's thoughts, day and night. She was certain whatever was written in it was very important since Lady Beatrice kept it so guarded.

As guests filed into the Manor house, Lady Beatrice stood inside the entrance and welcomed them personally. Her attire was regal in her mind. She had chosen a purple spaghetti strap dress with a scoop neckline. It gave the appearance of curves where she had none. The hairdresser she had hired pinned her hair in an updo, and she had a small tiara placed strategically on her hair. Arthur did the introductions since this was the first time most of the socialites were being introduced to Lady Beatrice.

When her introductions to Mr. and Mrs. Hammerville occurred, she noted how good-looking Mr. Hammerville was. It was good to have secret knowledge of him. She would definitely use that to her advantage. Rita showed up on the arm of Samuel and Lady Beatrice bristled.

"I did not invite employees as guests to this party, Samuel."

"My invitation included a plus one, and he is my escort."

"Ms. Duvall, I understand that you have different standards than I do, but how would that reflect on all my other employees? If I let him into the party and not the others, that would be me showing favoritism."

"There is a simple solution, Lady Beatrice. I quit as your employee, and now I am just my lovely date's escort. I will remove my things from my quarters tonight."

Samuel escorted Rita right past Lady Beatrice, who clenched and unclenched her fists at her sides. They were the last of the guests to show up, so Lady Beatrice went to the bar to get herself a drink. It pleasantly surprised her to see Mr. Hammerville bellying up to the bar himself.

"I do hope you are enjoying yourself, Mr. Hammerville."

Lady Beatrice slid her hand down his arm as she sidled up next to him at the bar. He downed his shot of whiskey and ordered another.

"You can call me Mike."

"Ah, I like that name. Mike. It's strong. Are you powerful, Mike?"

"Depends on who you ask, I guess."

"I am asking you."

He swallowed the second shot and asked for a third.

"Well, yes, I am powerful. Is that what you like, Lady Beatrice?"

"Yes. Powerful is exactly my type. And you can call me just Beatrice."

Lady Beatrice picked up her drink with one hand, turned while trailing the other down his arm again, and walked away to mingle with the crowd. She was certain she had just planted the right seed. He would seek her out, eventually.

Oh, the gossip that these people spread was tantalizing. She would have so much to write in her diary. Hearing these secrets straight from the people themselves gave her a whole new rush. As she looked over at the bar, she saw Mike and his wife. His wife looked mad, her face was flushed red, and she was grabbing for his drink. He, of course, kept it from her and downed it in one swift gulp. This didn't sit well with his wife. She turned and stormed off. Lady Beatrice thought to herself, *Hmm, trouble in paradise. No wonder he was looking for love with the nanny.*

Lady Beatrice felt on top of the world. By the end of the night, exhaustion set in from talking to everyone. As the last of the guests left, she realized there was one still standing at the bar. It was Mike.

"Mike, where is your lovely wife?"

"She left hours ago."

"Oh, she did. Do I need to call you a cab?"

"No, I was thinking I could just spend the night with you."

"Did you, really? And what made you think I would want you to spend the night?"

"Beatrice, we both know you do."

As he finished his sentence, he finished his last drink, took Lady Beatrice's hand, and led her upstairs. At the top of the stairs, he stopped.

"I do not know which room is yours, so you are going to have to lead the way."

Lady Beatrice smiled and led him the rest of the way to her room. As she opened the door, she pulled Mike along with her. She let go of his hand and slipped out of her dress, letting it fall to the floor. Mike looked her up and down. The smile on his face and the lust in his eyes told her he liked what he saw.

"You are a very mysterious woman, Lady Beatrice. Where have you been hiding away all these years?"

"I have been here all along, waiting in the wings for just the right time."

Lady Beatrice wrapped her arms around Mike's neck and pulled him closer. She brushed her lips against his. He couldn't resist any longer. Lifting her up, he carried her over to the bed. She helped remove his clothes in a flurry of heated passion. This was power. She had craved this her entire life. She had finally fulfilled her destiny.

In the morning, she awoke to an empty bed and a note on the pillow.

Dear Beatrice,

Thank you for a wonderful evening. I look forward to many more.

Love Mike.

She smiled. This was everything she had always wanted. Power, prestige, love interests. Nobody could stop her now. She called down to the kitchen through the new intercom system.

"Stella, could you have Verna bring my breakfast up to me this morning? I feel like having breakfast in bed."

"Yes, ma'am. She will bring it up momentarily."

Verna was upstairs within fifteen minutes, carrying a breakfast tray. She knocked on the door.

"Come in."

She walked in and Lady Beatrice was still in bed.

"Bring it here and put it over my lap."

Verna did as she was told. She watched as Lady Beatrice took a bottle of eye drops and put them in her eyes right over her food tray.

"Lady Beatrice, you know you should be careful with those eye drops. You could poison yourself if it gets in your food and you ingest it."

"Don't be ridiculous Verna, I know how to put eye drops in my eyes. I have been doing it for years. None is going into my food."

As Lady Beatrice ranted with the bottle in her hand, she hadn't noticed several drops had in fact fallen into her breakfast.

"Don't say I didn't warn you."

"You are dismissed. Don't you have work to do?"

"Yes, ma'am."

Verna left the room to finish her morning routine. The woman was batshit crazy. She was going to poison herself if she continued to do that.

Lady Beatrice ate her breakfast and then got out her diary to write in. It wasn't long before she felt sick to her stomach and dizzy. She attempted to call Stella through the intercom to have Verna bring her something to settle her stomach, but Stella wasn't answering. She did not know where in the house Verna or Martin were, so she decided she would attempt to go to the kitchen herself.

She hugged the wall as she made her way to the stairs. The pain in her stomach was getting worse. Her vision was blurring as well. Making it to the stairs, she gripped the railing with both hands to steady herself. Her breathing was becoming laborious. The outer edges of her vision closed in until darkness consumed them. She lost her footing and tumbled down the stairs, coming to an abrupt stop at the bottom, and crashing into a small table holding a vase of flowers.

The noise of Lady Beatrice falling down the stairs and crashing into the table echoed throughout the house. Martin, Verna, and Stella all came running. The sight of Lady Beatrice at the bottom of the stairs caught them all by surprise. Verna was the first to come out of the shock and went to render first aid.

"Stella, call the ambulance! Martin, get me some towels or anything to stop the bleeding!"

Soon, emergency personnel and chaos filled the house. Hours after they had transported her to the hospital, Sergeant Rollins returned with the news that Lady Beatrice had succumbed to her injuries. Stella was the first to break the silence.

"What happened?"

"I was going to ask you three the same question. You were the only ones in the house with her, right?"

It was Verna who spoke up next.

"Serg, we were all outside. I was just coming in from hanging sheets on the line to dry. Stella here was in the kitchen garden cutting herbs, and Martin was bringing the runners in from shaking them out. We all came inside together and heard the crash. We found her at the bottom of the stairs. I have a theory, though."

"What's your theory, Verna?"

"She accidentally poisoned herself with her eye drops."

"How the heck did she do that?"

Verna relayed what had happened earlier when she brought Lady Beatrice her breakfast.

"Thanks, I am going to call the hospital and let them know to test for that. I am also going to have my investigative team come and look over her room and take pictures and prints. To rule out foul play, considering everything that has happened here in the recent past."

"Oh, Serg. You may want your investigators to check out her desk drawer. It's locked, but she keeps her diary in there. I couldn't get in."

"Thanks, Verna."

Stella just watched as Verna and Sergeant Rollins conversed. It filled her with confusion.

"Verna, why do you keep calling Sergeant Rollins, Serg?"

Verna looked at Sergeant Rollins. He nodded his head.

"Stella, I am an undercover detective. We were investigating Lady Beatrice to clear Jimmy. After Samuel found the listening devices in her bungalow, our suspicions grew. We needed more direct evidence, though. They put me here to try to find some."

Stella burst into tears. Martin put his arm around her.

"I am going to bring her home to John unless you two need anything more from us."

"We are good. I will have an officer come and get your official statements as to where you all were at the time of her fall. Seeing as you all were together, I don't see any issues."

The investigative team dusted for prints, took pictures, and picked the lock of the desk drawer. When they started reading through the many journals tucked away in it, they immediately called Sergeant Rollins back to the Manor house.

"Serg, you need to get these to the state prosecutor's office and Jimmy's attorney ASAP. They clear him of any wrongdoing. It's all here, in gruesome detail. She was the serial killer, not Jimmy."

"Good work team. I think it's safe to say this case is closed. Unless you found any evidence of foul play with today's events, I think we can chalk this up to accidental poisoning."

"We found only one set of prints on the bottle of eye drops, Serg. We assume they are hers."

"Okay, follow up on that and make sure the prints match, so we don't get caught up on any loopholes."

"Roger that, Serg,"

Sergeant Rollins left the Manor house and called the prosecutor's office and Jimmy's attorney with the news. When he was done, he sat back in his chair and smiled. It was a great feeling when justice was served. He was happy that his friend would be out of jail soon and back home, where he belonged.

Chapter Twenty-Five

Sweet Freedom

A guard woke Jimmy up.

"Hey, Jimmy Driscoll, it's your lucky day. Grab your belongings. You are being released."

"Are you serious? Or am I dreaming?"

"You're not dreaming. Come on, your lawyer is waiting for you."

Jimmy was dazed and confused as he followed the guard to where his lawyer was waiting for him with his release paperwork.

"Hey, Jimmy, sign right here and you are a free man."

"Okay, what changed? How is all this happening?"

"Well, there have been some startling developments in the serial murders of the Gardiner family. First, Betty, or Lady Beatrice as she liked to be called, is dead. Seems she accidentally poisoned herself with her eye drops. Then, when they were investigating her death, they found countless journals detailing the crimes that she committed. There, in her own writing, she confessed to the murders and framing you."

Jimmy's eyes welled up with the realization he was a free man again. He hugged his lawyer and then they walked out of the correctional facility. As they got in his lawyer's car, Jimmy stopped for a moment and took in a breath of fresh air.

"I wasn't sure this moment was ever going to happen. Not that I didn't have faith in you or the others working to get me out, but while I was in there, I couldn't see a way out."

"Well, Jimmy, you had many people in your corner. We were determined to get you out. I hope you are ready for a party because everyone is waiting for you back at the Manor house."

"I am absolutely ready to party!"

It took them several hours to make it back to the island and walk in the doors of the Manor house. When Jimmy did, the first person he saw was his mom, Stella. He wrapped her in the biggest hug and squeezed her as if he never wanted to let her go again. She reciprocated just as fiercely as the tears flowed down her cheeks freely.

It took several minutes for all the hugs to be exchanged between everyone. Melissa and her parents were there. Allison and Jack were happy to see Jimmy free and were there to celebrate along with Arthur. Even Rolly was there to celebrate.

It overwhelmed Jimmy with happiness that he was free. However, the sadness of the loss of his cousins overshadowed the joy. Melissa could see the anguish of the battling emotions on his face.

"Hey, you want to go for a walk and get a little fresh air?"

"I would love that, thanks."

Jimmy took her hand, and they excused themselves from the party. They wound up walking over to the family cemetery. The feelings of guilt washed over him. He hadn't been able to protect his cousins, especially on their special day. Dropping to his knees in front of their graves, he openly wept. Melissa knelt down beside him and put her arms around his shoulders.

"I am so sorry. I couldn't protect you all."

"Hey, you did your best, and that's all we could ask."

Jimmy's head snapped up as he looked at Melissa and it registered she had heard the voice, too. They both stood up to see Timothy smiling behind them.

"What the hell? We thought you were dead. They had a funeral and all. I couldn't attend, but they had it. They charged me with your murder! Is Jessica alive too? And Richard? Please tell me they are alive, too."

"I am so sorry we had to lie to you. Jessica is alive. Well, she is in a medically induced coma. She is stable. There is a bullet fragment lodged very close to her spine. They can't operate yet. It's too risky for her and the baby. Richard, unfortunately, his wounds were fatal."

"Oh my God! Jessica is pregnant but alive!"

Jimmy ran his fingers through his hair in disbelief.

"Again, we are sorry we had to lie. It was the only way to keep Jessica and the baby safe. To tell everyone we were dead. We knew you weren't the killer. We had to draw the actual killer out. The decision was made between me and Arthur to go ahead with the plan we had discussed before. We knew you were being framed. It was the only way."

Jimmy pulled Timothy into a big bear hug.

"I get it and I forgive you. When can I see Jessica and visit her?"

"Tomorrow we will go see her, but today we celebrate your freedom."

"Do they all know inside?"

"Arthur, Allison, and Rolly know. No one else could know. We had to limit who knew to pull it off."

"Okay, well, let's let everyone else in on the secret then!"

"After you."

Timothy followed Jimmy and Melissa as they headed back into the Manor house.

"Hey everyone, I got another big surprise. Look what the cat dragged in."

Jimmy stepped aside and showed Timothy standing behind him. There were gasps and looks of confusion on the faces of those not in on the secret. Jimmy filled them all in. They were all excited to hear that Jessica was alive too, even though she had a tough battle ahead of her.

The celebration went on until everyone was just too tired to party anymore. Timothy left to go back and stay at the hospital with Jessica, where he had been by her side for weeks. Allison, Arthur, and Jack left to go home. The only person who stayed was Melissa.

"Are you okay staying on the island now?"

"Yes, now that the evil is gone, I will stay on the island with you. If the offer still stands?"

"Of course, it still stands. I have always wanted to marry you, Melissa. I love you."

"I love you too, Jimmy."

The next morning, Stella was in the kitchen making her son breakfast like she normally did. The killer had gotten what she deserved, and she was content that her son was free. She opened the cabinet to get some salt and pepper to season the scrambled eggs she was making. She knew that's how Jimmy liked them. Pausing when she saw the bottle of eye drops.

Who would have guessed the crazy Lady Beatrice would accidentally add more eye drops to her breakfast that morning? Stella had resigned to poison her slowly. She took the bottle and threw it in the trash, covering it with the broken eggshells. No one would know what she had done to save her baby boy from going to prison for the rest of his life.

She washed her hands and finished making breakfast. Jimmy and Melissa came down together, grabbed some plates with eggs and coffee, and sat at the island in the kitchen to eat.

"Thanks for the breakfast, mom. You don't know how much I missed your home cooking."

"You are welcome. You don't know how much I missed cooking for someone who appreciates my cooking."

"Hey, mom, where was Samuel yesterday?"

"Oh, he quit the night of Lady Beatrice's party. I think he moved in with Rita. Why are you so concerned about him, son?"

"I feel like I owe him an apology. We thought he was the killer."

Jimmy hated lying to his mother, but he had promised Samuel he would keep his secret. He would go to Rita's to see him in person and offer him his job back.

"I am going to stop by Rita's and talk to him on my way to go visit Jessica in the hospital."

"Okay, send our love and prayers to Jessica and the baby."

"I will, mom."

Jimmy and Melissa drove to Rita's house and rang the bell. When Rita answered the door, the look on her face was one of puzzlement.

"Hi Rita, is Samuel here?"

"Yes, he is. Why are you out of jail?"

"Oh, I guess the news hasn't hit the papers yet. Lady Beatrice accidentally poisoned herself and during her death investigation, they found journals she had written detailing her crimes, including framing me for all the murders."

"WOW. Nope, hadn't heard that news, but that's wonderful you have been cleared. Come on in and I will get Samuel for you."

Rita ushered them inside her living room and went to tell Samuel they were there to see him. As he came downstairs with Rita, he was smiling.

"Is it true? Did Lady Beatrice confess to the killings and poison herself?"

"Yup, it's all true. I am here to offer you your job back on the island if you want it."

"Can I commute to work?"

"Absolutely! Nothing says you have to live on the island. That's just a perk most people choose to take."

"Then yes, I would love to have my job back. Can I speak to you privately, though, out on the back deck?"

"Sure."

Jimmy followed Samuel onto the back deck.

"You haven't told anyone I am your biological father, have you?"

"Well, I told Melissa. She won't tell anyone. I promise."

"Okay. I trust you both. You know my past, son. I am sorry for my sins and I know someday I will atone for them fully, but I am happy with Rita and my life now. There is no reason for any of it to be brought out. I don't care about the Gardiner fortune. I care about having a relationship with you, though, even if we have to pass it off as a friendship."

"I would also like to have that relationship. Your secret is safe with me. Oh, by the way. Timothy and Jessica are both alive. Well, Jessica is in a medically induced coma and pregnant, but she is alive. We are going to visit her now."

"Well, tell her she is one tough cookie and she can make it through this."

"I will. Thanks for all your help and support."

"Anytime kid, Anytime."

Jimmy and Melissa left Rita's house and headed to the hospital to visit with Jessica. Jimmy was nervous. He didn't know what to expect. They walked into her hospital room and saw Timothy sitting beside her, holding her hand. There were machines beeping, and many things hooked up to her.

"Hey guys, I told Jessica the news. The doctors say she can hear us. She responds by squeezing your hand too."

Jimmy went over and held Jessica's hand.

"Hey cuz. We did it, we found out who the killer was. She's dead. I guess that's justice. It's kind of poetic that she poisoned herself and fell down the stairs."

Jessica squeezed Jimmy's hand, and a tear slid down his cheek.

"Oh, yeah. Samuel said you are one tough cookie, and he knows you are going to get through this."

Jessica squeezed his hand again. Jimmy and Melissa stayed a short time and then headed back to the island and the start of their life together. They had a wedding to plan and some rearranging of furniture again because Jimmy was bringing back the pool table.

Jimmy's phone rang, and it perplexed him that it was Rolly on the other end.

"Hey Jimmy, I hate to bother you. I know you are probably still celebrating your freedom and all. I just have some questions and figured you are the one to ask."

"Sure, Rolly. No problem. What do you need?"

"Well, first, we don't know what to do with Betty's body. Who to turn her over to for burial? Technically, since she has family, we have to ask you all."

"Wow, that isn't something we were even thinking about ourselves. Can I talk to the others about it and get back to you?"

"Sure thing. Then there is another dilemma. Her journals Jimmy. They contain a lot of dirt. On the family and others in the community. Nothing necessarily criminal, but the information in the wrong hands could be used against these people. We photocopied the pages detailing her crimes and her framing you for our records. I am thinking we should turn the journals back over to you and let you guys destroy them."

"Yeah, let me discuss that with the others, too. I will get back to you."

"Okay, Jimmy. Just let me know as soon as possible. By the way, it's great to have you back."

"Thanks, Rolly, for everything."

"No problem."

Chapter Twenty-Six

New Friendship

Danielle had moved into the cottage early even though she couldn't get a refund of the money she had paid upfront to the motel. The cottage was just homey, and she loved living there on her own. Her first appointment with Doc Ditters went well, and she was told the baby was growing according to schedule.

Pete had become more than just a regular customer. He offered to help her move and get items for the baby coming. They even went out to dinner a couple of times. He knew she was still mourning the loss of Richard, so he was willing to just be a supportive friend for now.

She had ignored several of her mother's calls, but one particular morning, her mother would not stop calling. She answered it.

"Yes Mother, I am still okay. I am still safe and no, I will not tell you where I am. Please stop calling me repeatedly."

"Danielle, I am trying to call you because I have important news."

Guilt crept over Danielle. She prayed her father and sisters were okay.

"I am sorry, Mom. What's going on? Is Dad okay? Are Erica and Stephanie okay?"

"Yes, they are all fine. It's Jimmy. They have released him from prison. It appears you were correct, and he was not the killer. It was Betty or Lady Beatrice, whatever you want to call her."

"Wait, what? How did this all come about?"

"It appears Betty journaled about everything, including framing Jimmy. And get this, she accidentally poisoned herself with eye drops, of all things. Made herself so sick that she passed out and fell down the stairs. Ironically, she died. When they investigated her death, they found the journals."

"Holy cow! That's amazing! I am happy for Jimmy. And now the others can all rest in peace."

"Oh honey, that's the other thing. Timothy and Jessica are alive! They lied to draw the actual killer out. And Jessica is pregnant. She isn't out of the woods yet. She is stable in a medical coma until they can take the baby safely and get a bullet fragment out."

"What about Richard? Is he really dead, or is he alive?"

Danielle's heart pounded in her chest, and her mind swirled. There was no way he survived those wounds, but her heart hoped.

"No, baby. He is dead. I am sorry. I know how much you loved him. Please come home. We will help you through whatever you are going through."

The tears flowed freely down her cheeks. She couldn't go back. This was her home now. Going back would be too painful. Too many ghosts and memories.

"Mom, I'm not coming back. I started a new life here in a small town in Pennsylvania. I have a good job. A nice little place of my own. I have made new friends. Now that the killer is dead, I can tell you why I left. I am pregnant with Richard's baby. It wasn't safe for me to tell before. I hope you understand, Mom."

"Danielle, thank you for finally being honest with me. I understand, honey. Can we come to visit?"

"I would love for you to come to visit. Please tell Jimmy, I am happy for him. And send my love to Timothy and Jessica. I gotta get ready for work, Mom. I love you."

"I love you too."

Danielle got ready for her shift at work. Pete was picking her up because she had heard a noise coming from her car the day before. He had said he would bring her to work and bring her car into his shop. It was convenient that he was an auto repair mechanic. It wasn't long before he knocked on her door. When she opened it up, she found him standing with a bag of groceries.

"What is all this?"

"It's dinner for later. I figured I would cook you dinner tonight after I pick you up."

"Pete, you are already doing so much for me. I can't keep letting you do all this."

"Why not? I am not asking for anything in return. Not even a relationship. You are a hard-working woman in a tough spot. You shouldn't have to do all this alone."

"I do have family, Pete. Just because I haven't talked about them doesn't mean they don't care about me. I have kept them in the dark since I left. They didn't even know I was pregnant till this morning."

"Okay, so why did you run away if they are a loving family? I don't get it."

"It's really complicated, Pete. I will fill you in on our way to my work."

On the short ride to the diner, Danielle filled Pete in on why she left everyone and everything she had known in life to raise her child on her own. When he parked the car, he turned in his seat and stared at her with compassion in his eyes. He ran his hand through his hair and then scratched the scruff of his beard.

"So you are telling me your ex-fiancée was a member of some big wealthy family that became the target of a serial killer? Which turned out to be another member of the family nobody knew about?"

"Yup. Sounds crazy and something completely out of some movie plot, but that was my life for the last six months."

"No wonder you took off and wanted no one from your past to know where you were. But, I don't understand why you don't want to go back. You have a family to help you out."

"It's hard to explain. At first, I had no proper plan. I just knew I needed to leave and not go back. There was no doubt in my mind that I was in danger if anyone found out about my baby. Then I wound up here in this town, and it felt like home so quickly. Like I have always belonged. Now I have put roots down, and I don't want to leave. I want to raise my child here, not in East Hampton."

"I can understand all of that. Thank you for trusting me with your story and your past, Danielle. It means the world to me."

"It is the least I can do for you, Pete. You deserve to know my story with all the help you have been giving me."

She quickly gave him a peck on the cheek and exited the car. He watched her enter the diner and then drove to his shop to work on her car. The fact she came from money had been a shock. She didn't seem like the typical rich girl stereotype. He was glad he hadn't known beforehand. It helped him to get to know her better with no preconceived notions.

Danielle's shift flew by and when it was time for her to go home, Pete was patiently waiting for her outside. He was leaning on the hood of her car with a bouquet of wildflowers. She smiled as he opened the car door for her and helped her in while handing her the flowers. She appreciated the chivalry he had, but she also didn't want him to think she was some damsel in distress who needed a knight in shining armor to rescue her.

"Hey Pete, did you figure out what was wrong with my car?"

"Absolutely, it was the right front tie rod. It's all fixed now."

"Thanks. What do I owe you?"

"Nothing."

"Pete, you can't just fix my car for free. I have money to pay you. Your time and energy are worth something. Not to mention the parts."

"I want to fix your car for free. Let me take care of you, Danielle. Why can't you do that?"

"I don't need you to take care of me. There is no reason for you to. I am not some damsel in distress. I appreciate everything you have done, but I never want to feel I owe you anything or that I am taking advantage of your kindness. So please tell me what I owe you."

"Okay, Okay. I get it. Six hundred dollars is what you owe me for fixing your car."

There was a little grit to his voice like he was trying not to clench his teeth. She couldn't understand why he felt so compelled to do everything for her. The rest of the drive to her cottage was awkwardly silent. Pete's brows furrowed as he stared at the road ahead of them, and his hands were tightly gripping the steering wheel. This was a different side of him.

When they got to her cottage, Pete parked the car and exited it, leaving the keys dangling in the ignition. He said nothing and just walked to his pickup truck. Danielle sat in the passenger side of her car, watching him with confusion. She grabbed her keys and left the vehicle.

Standing in front of her cottage door, she turned and watched as he pulled out of the driveway. He looked her way out of his side window and stopped as she gestured with both her hands out, questioning what was happening. The window slid down.

"What?"

Danielle didn't know how to feel. She didn't want him treating her like a damsel in distress like she needed him, but she was realizing deep down she wanted him in her life.

"Your money is inside. I have to go get it for you. And I thought you were making me dinner tonight?"

"You can drop the money off to me at my shop tomorrow. As for dinner, you just told me you don't need me to do anything for you. You don't want to feel obligated to me, so I guess you are making your own dinner tonight. By the way, add thirty dollars to that bill for the groceries."

Her heart sank. She had hurt him without realizing what she had done. After all of his kindness, she had stuck a knife in his heart. The window went up and he drove away. As he did, the tears welled up in her eyes. She whispered to the night sky.

"I don't need you, but I do want you in my life."

She couldn't believe she had messed things up so badly with Pete. Whether she wanted a romantic relationship with him, she honestly didn't know, but he had been a good friend since day one. How was she going to fix this?

The first thing the next morning, Danielle headed over to Pete's garage. She had to apologize, and she had to figure out how to fix their friendship. When she pulled up, the garage door was open, and she saw Pete standing next to a convertible and a tall, curvy blonde. The blonde was animated as she spoke with Pete, presumably trying to explain what was wrong with her car. Occasionally, she flipped her hair with her hand and tilted her head. She was flirting with him, and it surprised Danielle to find out that didn't sit well with her.

She never considered herself a jealous person. This feeling that was bubbling inside her wasn't quite a rage, but it was unsettling nevertheless. As she got out of her car and closed the door behind her, she startled herself when the car door slammed shut. Pete and the blonde both looked in her direction.

The blonde ignored Danielle and went on with her flirtatious behavior while Pete took off his ball cap and wiped his forehead nervously. Danielle leaned back against her car, crossed her legs and her arms, and waited.

When the blonde's ride showed up for her and she left, Danielle watched as Pete took a deep breath and started walking over to her.

"Good morning, Danielle. Look, I owe you an apology."

"No, Pete. You don't. I owe you an apology. You have been nothing but kind and compassionate to me this entire time. I hurt you with my words last night and that was wrong."

"Okay. I accept your apology, but I still owe you an apology. I should not have just shut down and left last night. You aren't the only one with a past that haunts them."

Pete shoved his hands in his pockets and rocked back and forth on his heels. Danielle was even more confused than before.

"Okay, so tell me, Pete. You don't have to carry your past alone. Share the burden with me. That is what friends do."

"It is a long story. Have you eaten breakfast yet?"

"I have all day. It's my day off. No, I couldn't eat this morning."

"Let's go up to my apartment and I will cook us some breakfast while I tell you everything."

"Okay."

After Pete closed the garage door, he led Danielle up the stairs to his apartment above his shop. It was small, but surprisingly clean for a bachelor pad. She had a seat at the small kitchen table as he set to work making them breakfast.

"I wasn't always a nice guy. Actually, I was quite the opposite. I was an egotistical ass."

"That is really hard for me to believe."

"It's true. I was the hometown hero, the captain of the football team. My girlfriend was the captain of the cheer team."

"No way!"

"Yup, I thought I was god's gift to this entire town and made sure everyone knew it too."

"Pete, I can't see it. What made you change so drastically?"

Pete dashed into his bedroom and came out with a high school yearbook. Danielle flipped through it. There he was in all his glory on pretty much every page of the candids.

"I didn't care about the prom, honestly I didn't even want to go. The party was all I cared about. My girlfriend, though, wanted to be prom king and queen. It had been her childhood dream. I didn't understand. She had spent a lot of money on her dress and hair. She bought the tickets. The pictures she paid for. I rented a used tuxedo."

"Okay, so you made your girlfriend pay for prom. That doesn't mean you were a jerk."

"Well, we were there less than a half hour and I wanted to leave. Before the king and queen were announced. She begrudgingly left with me. We fought on the way to the party. At one point, she yelled at me to let her out of the car. I obliged. She started walking back to the prom. I watched in the rearview mirror as a car came speeding around the corner and hit her."

"Oh my god, Pete. That's awful. It still wasn't your fault, though."

"But it was. I was too concerned with what I wanted, what I felt I needed, that I didn't care about her happiness. If we had stayed at prom, she would have lived. If I had put her first, she would still be here."

Pete sat across from Danielle and put his head down on his arms. He sobbed.

"I get it now. You put everything you have into helping others because you feel your selfishness killed your girlfriend. You need to know, though, that you didn't kill her. She could have stayed in the car and just gone to the party. She was a little selfish, too. But you were both young, just kids. Don't punish yourself forever."

Lifting his head and wiping his tears, he looked at Danielle.

"I never looked at it like that."

"There needs to be balance and understanding in every relationship. Give and take. Too much, either way, is unhealthy."

"Now I understand what you were trying to say yesterday about not needing my help with everything."

"Yeah, about that. I may not need you to do everything, but that doesn't mean I don't want you in my life."

Pete smiled and tilted his head.

"What I am hearing is you want me?"

He wiggled his eyebrows and made Danielle laugh.

"Honestly, I don't know what I want. All I know is I was sad thinking you were out of my life. Just as sad as missing Richard. And when I saw that blonde flirting with you this morning, I felt something I have never felt before."

"Really? What did you feel?"

"Jealous."

"I kind of got that impression when you slammed your car door."

Danielle laughed.

"Would you believe me if I told you that was an accident?"

Pete stood up and took Danielle by the hand. He guided her out of her chair and into his arms, then kissed her gently on the lips.

"No more than you would believe me if I said kissing you just now was an accident."

Danielle leaned her head onto Pete's chest and just hugged him.

"I don't know if I am ready for all this yet. But I am willing to see where it goes."

Chapter Twenty-Seven

Goodbye Betty

Jimmy had contacted Arthur about Betty's remains and journals. They agreed to have a small private burial in the family cemetery. It was just the two of them as they placed the journals inside the casket with her. They felt it was important that no one would know where the journals were. They were sure they would safely bury the journals along with Betty. When they were finished and closed the casket, they let the workers know it was time to bury her.

They had no big send-off. No flowers. There were no mourners. Nobody was going to miss Betty. Her death hadn't really made big headlines other than it led to the revelation she had been a serial killer. Most people in the Hamptons had gone about their daily lives. It was just more fodder for the gossip mill until the next affair occurred or the next movie star bought a piece of property in the area.

There was only one person who even seemed to notice her obituary. Mike sat on his back deck overlooking the Atlantic ocean swirling his glass of whiskey as he read the small blurb about Betty and her death. Such a shame. Their one night together had left an impression on him. One he would not soon forget.

He watched the new nanny his wife had hired interacting with their kids on the beach. This time, his wife had gone out of her way to find the most unattractive woman she could find. He would have to find some other way to fulfill his needs. He scanned the beach for any beach bunnies, but had no luck. Betty would be hard to forget. He swigged the whiskey and poured himself another glass.

When Timothy was told that Betty had been buried. He felt the weight of the world lifted off his shoulders. She was gone for good. Now all that needed to happen was for Jessica to heal and their baby to be born safely.

Stella watched from a distance Betty's coffin being lowered into the ground. She took a deep breath and let it out slowly. She was glad to have closure on the entire ordeal, finally.

Arthur left the island to head home. He had contemplated telling Jimmy earlier about his plans to retire. However, he felt it wasn't the time or place. In the next coming days, he would set up meetings with a new attorney who he felt could help represent the family in the future. He felt the younger Gardiners needed a clean slate with someone new.

The new ferry had finally arrived, and Captain Bill was grumpily adjusting to running it. Things seemed to be slowly getting back to normal. The security crew was busy catching teenagers trespassing on the beaches and running off the tabloid reporters itching for their latest scoop.

Jimmy and Melissa spent the rest of the day riding the ATVs around the island. Just spending quality time with each other that didn't include investigating a serial killer. When they stopped on the southern beach, Jimmy pulled out a picnic blanket and basket. Melissa smiled as she watched him set everything up.

After he completed the setup, he grabbed her hand and walked her over to the blanket. Then he got down on one knee and produced a ring from his pocket.

"I figured I better ask you properly and make it official. Melissa, will you marry me?"

"Yes, Jimmy. Absolutely, yes!"

He stood up and picked her up in his arms and swung her around.

"I feel like the luckiest man alive right now."

"Well, I feel like the luckiest woman."

Her lips brushed against his, and their bodies melted together onto the blanket. After several hours, they lay entwined in each other's arms, wrapped in the blanket, listening to the waves crash against the shore.

Jimmy wanted to stay like that forever, but he was afraid Melissa would get cold.

"I guess we better head back up to the Manor house."

"Why Jimmy? I am content to stay here in your arms for eternity, or at least for tonight."

"Aren't you afraid you will get cold?"

"Not when I have you to keep me warm."

"And what if I get cold?"

"Hmm, I guess I will just have to heat you up."

Jimmy kissed her passionately. They spent the night under the stars, knowing they had the rest of their lives together.

Chapter Twenty-Eight

New Beginnings

It was mid-July when the team of doctors assembled to perform the cesarean section on Jessica and to remove the bullet fragment. They felt the baby was developed enough to survive outside her womb. The longer they kept her in the medically induced coma, the more she was at risk for long-term damage. After several discussions, they decided with Timothy to perform the surgery.

Timothy paced back and forth in the waiting room. Allison, Jack, Jimmy, and Melissa were all there with him. A doctor came out and Timothy stopped pacing.

"I am here to give you an update. The baby is out. They have brought her to the NICU. You will be able to visit her shortly. As for your wife, the surgery to remove the bullet fragment is underway. So far, everything looks good. We will let you know when the surgery is complete, and they move her into recovery."

"Thanks, Doc. It's a girl, that's awesome!"

Everyone gathered around Timothy and started congratulating him.

***

Back in Pennsylvania, Danielle was working when she had contractions. At first, she thought they were just Braxton Hicks, but then they got more intense and started coming more regularly. When her water broke, Wendy called an ambulance, and then she called Pete.

Danielle had never experienced such intense pain. As she rode in the ambulance, fear crept into her mind. She was only just seven months pregnant. Would the baby be big enough and developed to survive outside the protection of her womb? The Paramedics did their best to keep her calm. They arrived at the hospital in no time and they wheeled her quickly into a labor and delivery room. Pete arrived just in time to help her through the pushing. He held her hand as she squeezed it with each contraction. A few pushes and the baby was born.

"It's a boy. Congratulations Mom and Dad. Since he is premature, we need to bring him over to the NICU."

The nurses showed Danielle her baby right before they whisked him away into the NICU.

"He's beautiful."

"Just like his Momma."

Pete kissed Danielle's forehead.

"I think we should name him Pete. Pete Gardiner. After the two men I have ever loved and who have loved me unconditionally."

"Danielle, are you sure?"

"Absolutely!"

"Well, I guess if you are going to name your son after me, I better do the proper thing. Danielle, will you marry me?"

"Yes, Pete. I will marry you. Not because it's the proper thing to do, but because I love you with all my heart."

"I love you too, Danielle. I have since the first day I met you."

"I know. Thank you for being patient with me."

***

A few hours later, the doctors came back out to Timothy to give him an update on Jessica.

"Timothy, we have great news. The surgery was a success. Your wife is in recovery. As soon as she is fully awake, you can visit with her. She still has a lot of physical therapy and occupational therapy to go through for a full recovery, but she is strong and young. We have faith that she will be fine. She may have difficulty with speech too at first, so give her time."

"Thank you, Doc. I appreciate everything you have done for our family."

"Go see your daughter and I will have the nurses come to get you when your wife is awake in recovery."

Timothy hugged Allison, Jack, Jimmy, and Melissa goodbye and thanked them for sitting with him, and then he went to meet his daughter.

***

A year flew by, and Timothy shuffled through the mail he had just come back from retrieving. He smiled as he saw the return address of the first letter. It was from Jimmy and Melissa. By the look and feel of the envelope, he assumed it was their wedding invitation. The second took him by surprise. The return address was from Pennsylvania and it was from Danielle. He brought the letters out to the patio, where Jessica was sipping her morning tea.

"Looks like we have mail from the States. I think one is Jimmy and Melissa's wedding invite. The other is from Danielle."

They had moved to their cottage in Ireland as soon as Jessica had recovered enough and baby Samantha could travel. She opened the one from Jimmy first. It indeed was the wedding invitation. The date was in September. She was relieved to see they were not holding the wedding on the island. Jimmy and Melissa were very respectful of Timothy and Jessica and their powerful feelings about never setting foot on the island again.

Then Jessica opened the letter from Danielle. It was an invitation to her wedding the weekend after Jimmy's. She hadn't heard from Danielle other than some get-well cards and flowers sent to the hospital since her own wedding. She understood the distance that had formed between them with everything they both had gone through. Jessica was happy for Danielle, and it thrilled her to be invited to witness her new beginning.

"Well, it looks like we need to plan a trip to the States in September! We have two weddings to attend!"

"That's great! It will be nice to see everyone again. Samantha can get to know her extended family. I will go start making travel plans."

***

Jimmy and Melissa spent the year planning their wedding. They had just sent out all the invitations when things got busy on the island. Jimmy wasn't too concerned about the uptick in trespassers. However, it was unsettling after the relatively quiet year they had when they found a few of the graves at the family cemetery disturbed. Although he chalked it up to teenagers looking for pirate treasure. Nothing further transpired afterward, which validated his belief.

***

Danielle and Pete bought a house together and planned their own wedding. Danielle's family visited her frequently. However, she still refused to go back to visit her hometown. The ghosts of her past were just too much for her to face. They were looking forward to their nuptials within the next few months.

***

Allison remained the CEO of Cromwell Real Estate Corporation, yet she did most of her work from the home office Jessica and Timothy had built for her at the cottage. She had moved with them to help Timothy care for Samantha and Jessica.

***

Jack moved into Jessica's home in Preston and opened up his own restaurant.

***

Arthur had retired, leaving his colleague, Mr. Whitty, in charge of helping the Gardiner family with their legal issues and helping them run their business.

***

Life had become all that they had envisioned, happy and free of a serial killer stalking them or their loved ones. Jessica finally knew who she was. She was a wife and mother.

CHAPTER TWENTY-NINE

The End

The End.... or is it just the Beginning?

Acknowledgements

A big thank you to my family and friends who have supported this journey of mine into authorship. There are way too many of you to single out individually! I appreciate you all!

Thank you to my ARC team, who have been tremendously helpful in catching any missed mistakes that occur throughout the writing and editing process.

R.K., Mr. Kaplan would be proud!

L.C., thank you for utilizing your editing expertise!

My deepest gratitude to all the administrators of the various Facebook groups that provide a platform for independent authors like me to promote our books. Your support is truly invaluable and has helped my books gain visibility. Thank you!

Thank you, M.B., my badass corrections nurse friend, who gave me much insight into prison life.

About Author

A paraeducator, novice genealogist, turned author D.M. Foley is an award-winning writer. Her first book, The Lyons Garden Book One Family Ties, received The New York Best Sellers Gold Award in December 2021. She lives in Southeastern, Ct, with her husband, three sons, and her mom. You can follow her on her social media accounts at:

   D.M. Foley - Author Page on Facebook
   @d.m._foley on Instagram and TikTok
   @DMFoleyauthor on Twitter
   dmfoleyauthor.com
   Contact Information:
   d.m.foleyauthor@gmail.com
   D.M. Foley
   P.O. Box 735
   54 Main Street
   Jewett City, CT 06351

Books By This Author

Family Ties The Lyons Garden Book One
Erasing Secrets The Lyons Garden Book Two
Pawns The Lyons Garden Book Three

Deric Dream Changer Book 1 Of The Dream Walkers Series

The Killer Trip